THE WHISPERING HOUSE

Elizabeth Brooks

BLACK SWAN

TRANSWORLD PUBLISHERS

Penguin Random House, One Embassy Gardens,
8 Viaduct Gardens, London SW11 7BW
www.penguin.co.uk

Transworld is part of the Penguin Random House group of companies
whose addresses can be found at global.penguinrandomhouse.com

First published in Great Britain in 2020 by Doubleday
an imprint of Transworld Publishers
Black Swan edition published 2021

A CIP catalogue record for this book
is available from the British Library.

ISBN
9781784163501

Typeset in 10.5/14.8pt Sabon Next LT Pro by Jouve (UK), Milton Keynes.
Printed and bound in Great Britain by Clays Ltd, Elcograf S.p.A.

The authorized representative in the EEA is Penguin Random House Ireland,
Morrison Chambers, 32 Nassau Street, Dublin D02 YH68.

Penguin Random House is committed to a sustainable
future for our business, our readers and our planet. This book
is made from Forest Stewardship Council® certified paper.

With love for my husband, Chris

THE WHISPERING HOUSE

PART ONE

Freya

August–September 2014

1

I'D NEVER HAVE SET EYES on the place if my cousin hadn't held his wedding reception in the grounds. His fiancée had grown up locally, and once she'd discovered it was possible to hire a marquee in the gardens at Byrne Hall, nothing else would do. You can't blame her. Objectively speaking, it was an idyllic spot for a wedding reception: all those lush, towering trees, and the garden in full-scented flower, and the sea spread out below the cliffs like a sheet of hammered gold. If I were the kind of woman who fantasised about getting married, I'd want a wedding like that.

'You look lovely,' my father said, studying our reflections in the pond. 'A real picture.'

'A picture of what, though?' I was doing my best to make light of the whole thing. 'A picture of misery?'

But Dad wasn't going to fall in with my tone. 'You look very nice,' he insisted gravely.

One of the bride's hearty uncles had told me off for having a long face – that was all. It wasn't a big deal. 'Cheer up, love,' he'd said, as we were queuing for drinks. 'You're meant to be a bridesmaid, not an undertaker's mute.'

I don't think he was trying to be horrible. He clapped me on the shoulder as he said it, and handed me a glass of prosecco, but Dad had overheard and steered me away, and we'd ended up here, by the pond. It wasn't the nicest part of the garden, which is probably why it was deserted. The water flickered with midges and smelled of mud, and there was a stone fountain in the middle – a fat boy blowing on a conch shell – that had gone all black and mossy, and looked as if it hadn't functioned in years.

'Bastard,' said my father, and I laughed despite everything, because he wasn't one for profanities, not even mild ones. He was too scholarly sounding and well-spoken to carry it off. I took his arm and gave it a squeeze, but he still wouldn't smile, so I decided to stop trying and accept that this day was a write-off as far as we two were concerned. I watched our silhouettes waver over the water, brownish-green against the glaring sky. My dress, an 'A-line, scoop-neck, floor-length, chiffon bridesmaid's gown in Pale Sage', had looked so airy in the bridal catalogue, but I wasn't keen on the real thing. Not on me, anyway. It seemed heavier now than it had this morning, and the skirt was damp and wilting round my legs.

'This ought to be a nice day,' I said. 'It's good to be out of London for a while.'

I didn't mean to sound irritable, but how often did Dad and I get the chance to step out of our ordinary lives? Here we were in a garden by the sea, tipsy on wine and sunshine and flowers in bloom, and all we could think about was my dead sister. It wouldn't have been so bad if we'd been able to discuss her in a gentle way – *I miss her; she'd have loved it here; imagine if she'd been a bridesmaid too, wouldn't we have looked a pair?* – but it wasn't possible to think, let alone talk, about my sister in that way.

I pressed Dad's arm. 'Stop worrying,' I said, addressing our watery shadows. 'That Uncle Whatever-His-Name-Is: he probably doesn't have a clue who we are. I bet he's never even heard of Stella.'

There. I'd said her name out loud. It dropped through the space between us, with a whistle and a thunk, and we both flinched. I hated how that always happened. Sometimes I'd say her name accidentally-on-purpose, in the middle of a conversation, just to make us both hear it. One day, I thought, we'd get used to it, and be able to talk about her in a free and easy way, and she would belong to us again. I would be able to say 'Stella' and move lightly on, instead of feeling like I'd drawn a curtain across the sun.

Dad poked me with his elbow as he patted his jacket pockets in search of cigarettes and lighter. He was usually furtive about his smoking habit because he knew I'd tell him off, but he didn't even pretend today, and I didn't say a word. I wouldn't have minded one myself. I was still holding that glass of prosecco, and I took a gulp while he was lighting up.

'Byrne Hall,' he said meditatively, after he'd taken his first puff.

We looked up the tiered lawns to the pale, pillared house. Wedding guests weren't allowed inside – we were under strict instruction not to stray beyond the gardens – but it made a beautiful backdrop, especially on a hot summer's day like today. It was rather austere, with its three identical rows of windows and the severe symmetry of its columns and chimneys, but the framing trees and sunlight served to soften the effect. I couldn't have told you what style or era it belonged to, except that it put me in mind of Jane Austen TV adaptations, but I did my research later on and discovered it was three hundred years old and built in the Queen Anne style. I thought about the person I'd be if this was my home – the expansive way in which I'd live, and move and think; the poetry I'd write; the light and freshness that would saturate my soul.

'I remember that house,' said Dad. 'I remember seeing it in the distance, when they took me to the cliffs in the coastguard boat, and one of the policemen said, *That's Byrne Hall, that is; our local stately home*, and I said, *Oh yes? Nice place!*'

I smiled guardedly and Dad took a vigorous pull on the cigarette, as if it quenched a thirst.

'Funny, isn't it?' he went on. 'Having such an ordinary conversation at a moment like that?'

I shook my head and drained the prosecco to the last drop. It wasn't my first drink of the afternoon, which was probably why the ripples of reflected light in the pond were starting to look psychedelic. I took hold of my father's arm again, as much to keep my balance as to make him stop talking.

'You'd think they would have hesitated, wouldn't you,' he went on, 'before they booked it as a wedding venue? You'd think they'd have had the odd scruple. Or did they just forget?' A cigarette usually mellowed him, but he sounded bitter now.

'I'm sure they didn't mean anything by it. They're only second cousins, after all; they've probably forgotten it happened here – if they even knew in the first place. Anyway, it's not the house's fault that Stella died nearby, and it's a good few miles from – where they found her.'

'It's barely a mile.' Dad flicked his cigarette end away. It landed on the surface of the pond with a hiss and floated motionless, like a dead creature. I watched the last grains of smoke dissolve in the hot air, and tried to concentrate on not falling over.

'Litter-bug,' I said with a nudge, still trying for a light-hearted tone. He made no answer, so I turned away.

One of the guests was emerging into the garden from the cliff path, his hair plastered to his head. He must have been swimming in the sea, and the whiff of salt-water on his clothes made me sit on the low stone wall.

'The sea,' I muttered into my empty glass, feeling hot and sick. I shut my eyes and imagined ice-cold waves lapping my stomach, darkening my vision, roaring in my ears. There'd been some talk on the coach about skinny-dipping, but I assumed they'd be doing it later, in the drunken darkness, once the formalities were over.

When I opened my eyes, the man was standing at the top of the path, looking back the way he'd come. Nobody else appeared. Perhaps he didn't belong to the wedding party? He seemed hesitant when one of the waiters approached with a tray of prosecco, and although he took a glass, he just held on to it unhappily and didn't drink. I wondered whether he'd lost something down on the sand. His feet were bare, so perhaps he'd mislaid his shoes.

The man turned and caught me looking, so I pretended to fiddle with the clasp on my bracelet. He stared at me for a long time before draining his glass and walking away.

'Who was that?' Dad appeared at my elbow and I shrugged. The best man came to the top of the steps and waved his arms at us: the wedding breakfast was about to be served, and would we please make our way to the marquee? I waved back. Dad thrust his hands in his pockets and made a little moaning noise, like a child on the verge of tears. He began rustling through the packet for a second cigarette. If I didn't drag him off he'd stand by the pond all evening, hollowing out his lungs and experimenting with swear words.

'Come on,' I sighed. 'Brave face.'

We skirted the pond and joined the stream of people meandering towards the marquee. I looked up at the house. The frontage had been cream coloured when we arrived from the church around three o'clock, but it was yellow now, in the early evening sun. The blinds were lowered in all the windows and there was no sign of life, unless you counted the fact that the front door was slightly ajar. It must have been cool and quiet in those high-ceilinged rooms, with just a few slivers of light reaching in round the blinds. I wondered if Stella had gone past it too, on her way to the cliffs, and if so whether she'd had room in her head for incongruous thoughts like, *Nice house*. Probably not. I wondered whether her last thoughts had touched on me – but I was always wondering that.

'Hey, watch it!' The woman I'd bumped into ran a worried hand over the back of her dress.

'Sorry.'

Everyone was walking slowly, lingeringly. Sometimes people stopped and took in the view.

'I wonder who owns this place?' someone said.

'A couple, I believe,' another replied. 'Mr and Mrs Byrne? Or it may even be Lord and Lady . . .'

'I'd heard it was a widow, living on her own.'

'Really? Oh well, you may be right. Blue bloods, anyway.'

There was a notice in front of the porch, which read STRICTLY PRIVATE. The letters were black on a white background, large and unmissable.

'Whoever they are, they obviously don't want the riff-raff in.'

Most people laughed at this remark, though some of the effortfully dressed did not.

A tray of filled flutes stood untouched on a trestle-table, so I swapped my empty glass for one as we went past. The wine was flat and warm, and even before I'd lifted it to my mouth I knew I didn't want it, but I drank it anyway.

Dad and I had already studied the seating plan, before the incident with the hearty uncle. I was with the other bridesmaids on the top table, and Dad was miles away, on table five. He didn't exactly complain as we parted inside the marquee, he just tightened his jaw and loosened his tie, as if he were psyching himself up for a confrontation.

The heat felt much heavier under canvas, and it seemed to absorb and intensify all the sweaty, fumy, floral scents that a wedding party gives off. People were complaining, under their breaths, that the marquee was too small, and the long tables packed too closely – and they had a point, though they might have kept their voices down within earshot of the bride. When I'd managed to squeeze myself into my chair I was effectively trapped, with the tabletop digging into my ribs and my elbows pinned to my sides.

The starters were already in place, but once we were seated there was no room for the caterers to move between the tables, so everything – dirty plates and new plates, wine bottles and water jugs – had to be passed along from hand to hand. I could have done with a drink of water, but the jug disappeared to the other end of the table before I could get to it, and when it came back it was empty, except for a curl of lemon peel. A hand kept snaking round my shoulders with a bottle of red and topping up my wine glass, so I drank that instead.

I didn't know the people sitting either side of me, because they were both from the bride's family. The one on my left remained with her back to me, busily chatting to someone else. The one on my right kept up a constant, cryptic murmuring, which may have been addressed to me, and to which I responded with the occasional 'Hmm' and a few vague nods. I kept thinking I heard voices behind me – *Stella Lyell . . . suicide . . . that's her younger sister over there* – but when I glanced round, the people at the next table appeared easy and unconstrained. I couldn't see Dad at all.

Here we go again, I remember thinking. *Elbows in, eyes down, do what everyone else is doing. Don't think too hard or wish too hard. Don't listen to their gossip.*

'Lamb Provençal,' said one of the other bridesmaids with relish, reading off the menu card, as the main course began to arrive. A plate was set in front of me, and the heat and noise seemed to swell up inside the tent, and the stench of close-packed bodies was indistinguishable from the smell of garlicky meat. I gripped the edge of the table and felt myself sway. There was still no sign of a replenished water jug, but at least the flaps of the marquee had been tied back on one side, and I could drink in the green shadows of the garden with my eyes if I leaned forwards and pressed against my neighbour's arm. My gaze meandered upwards, through a veil of trees, to Byrne Hall. The front door was still open, and a cold darkness seemed to seep out of it, like water from a stone jar.

'Beans?' said my neighbour shortly, shifting her chair as best she could so that our arms were no longer touching. I helped myself to French beans, before handing the dish on and feeling

10

for my knife and fork. The lamb cutlet was covered in gritty pepper, and when I pressed it with the flat of my knife it bled like a grazed knee. On the other side of the table the two littlest bridesmaids were getting red-faced and wriggly. One of them threw her fork on to the floor and the other one started to wail, and nobody tried to stop them when they slid under the table and crawled over our feet. I turned to my plate again, and the air around me staled and thickened. Outside, a breath of wind touched the lime trees, and their leaves flashed in the sun, like tumbling emeralds.

'Could you possibly cut up my lamb for me?' asked the woman on my right, with a wave of her bandaged wrist. 'I've only got one hand here.' From the testy way she said it, I guessed this wasn't the first time she'd asked.

'Yes,' I said. 'Sorry. Of course.'

I pulled her plate towards me and began to saw, yanking the chunk of meat from its bow-shaped bone. Blood pooled over the plate and my stomach seemed to rise and fall in time with my breathing. The woman said something, but I couldn't hear her properly over the buzzing in my ears. I set the cutlery down carefully.

'Are you all right?' she was saying from a long way off, and someone further down the table, I think it was my cousin, the groom, said, 'What's up with Freya?'

I tried to shove my chair back, but it was wedged into place, and there was no escape to left or right. With a slippery twist and an apology I sank under the table, into the dim forest of shins and shoes. The two little girls were crouched in conference over a hoard of crumpled napkins, their satin dresses gleaming in the half-light, but they fell silent as I pushed past. White spots were floating in front of my eyes, and the racket inside my head was getting louder and louder. I crawled the length of the table, feeling for the strip of matting where the marquee ended and the lawn began, and as soon as I had grass underneath my fingers I staggered to my feet, picked up my skirts and ran. I made it as far as the rose garden before my insides flung me forwards and doubled me up.

Once I'd finished being sick, I knelt with my head bent over the fizzing soil and hoped the other guests hadn't seen. I moaned and shut my eyes and wiped my hand across my dripping lips.

The front door was still standing open. It was the first thing I noticed over the tousled heads of the roses, when I was well enough to look up.

I sat back on my heels and stared at it. There was something so absolute about the blackness of that interior; it made me want something I couldn't put a name to – not quite sleep, or water, or coolness, but something larger that encompassed all those things. It was like the blackness of space, without any stars. It was also, of course, off-limits to wedding guests: not only was there the sign across the porch, but there'd been a reminder in bold italics at the bottom of the wedding invitation, and the best man had reiterated the message on the coach, as we were leaving the church. 'The family' were in residence at present, he'd said, and we were asked to be respectful of their magnificent gardens, and to remember, if we remembered nothing else, that the house itself was out of bounds.

I kicked my shoes off and left them lying in the grass. A piece of china smashed far away, in the marquee, and there was a whooping cry, followed by a burst of group laughter. I glanced over my shoulder as I walked, in case I could spot Dad, but the sea was so painfully bright that I had to look away again.

I hoisted my skirts to my knees and scrambled up the bank that separated my tier of lawn from the sweep of gravel in front of Byrne Hall. The little stones at the top were sharp against my feet, and I picked my way slowly to the door.

It was a big, sturdy edifice – much bigger and sturdier than it had seemed from down below. The white columns of the porch were spindly when I saw them from the marquee, but they'd taken on a temple-like grandeur by the time I arrived beneath them. Beyond the STRICTLY PRIVATE sign there was a rope, slung museum-style between two metal posts.

I'd never have done it if I'd been sober. Even tipsy I faltered for a moment or two, but the sun kept pushing like a hot hand against my back.

The hall was as black as I'd desired it to be. I opened the door wide and took a few cautious steps.

Shapes and tones materialised slowly: the curling hulk of a staircase; closed doors to my left and right; a tiled floor like a chess-board, with alternating squares of black and white. I was glad I'd taken my shoes off, because it meant I could walk across the cold floor without making much noise. The chiffon made the merest swishing sound against my legs as I stepped from black tile to black tile, avoiding the white ones in case my feet left grubby marks. I felt like a ghost, empty and silent in my long, pale dress, at ease with the darkness.

Daylight began picking things out here and there and making them gleam: the moulded leaves and apples on a gold picture frame; the brass studs on an armchair; the ribs of a plastic water bottle. I picked up the bottle and sat down on the chair, tipsy enough to feel that I wasn't trespassing; that I was expected; that these things had been put out ready for me. The armchair creaked as I settled, and the upholstery prickled through my dress and all along the backs of my thighs. I unscrewed the bottle, tipping my head right back and filling my mouth, till the water brimmed over and trickled down my neck.

The picture with the gold frame was directly in front of me, and I leaned forwards to look at it, but the light from outside was wrong – too yellow, too lush – and all I could make out was a flat surface covered by a network of shiny lines, like a tray of brittle toffee that's been tapped with a hammer. I tilted my head woozily and wondered what sort of picture it was. Not that I was vastly curious. If the chair had been comfier I might not have bothered getting up, but the backs of my legs were starting to itch.

It must, I decided, be some kind of collage, with hundreds of tiny bits of paper fitted together and stuck down on a board. When I ran my fingers over the surface I realised that the shiny lines I'd noticed from the chair were made of dried glue. Whether it was an abstract arrangement, or whether the fragments came together as a coherent image, it was too dark to tell, but there was a spotlight on the wall above the frame and I could just about reach the switch.

An electric hum, a quiver of light, then everything steadied and I found myself standing in front of a three-quarter-length portrait. I didn't gasp or cover my mouth with my hands. It wasn't like that. Recognition crept up on me doubtfully, bit by bit, and even before the bulb popped and the picture flashed back into darkness, I couldn't make up my mind whether this was a portrait of my dead sister or just a picture of a girl with red hair whom I was naturally inclined – given the circumstances, and at least four glasses of wine – to identify as her.

It wasn't a particularly good portrait, whoever the subject

might be. I mean, it was *all right*. Seven out of ten, B plus, averagely competent. In terms of symmetry and proportion it was fine, but as a whole it lacked vitality. The eyes were large, lustreless almonds, the nose was minimal, the lips were over-ripe and over-pink. It was an adolescent picture. An unimaginative man's idea of what a pretty woman amounted to: no greater than the sum of her parts, and perhaps a little less. I looked for the hands – Stella used to have long, tapering fingers with blunt, square nails – but there was a gap, a glaring absence on her lap, where they ought to be.

The light went out with a waspish buzz and I was left in the dark, recollecting the picture as best I could; poring over the after-image on my retinas. There wasn't a single feature that proved it was her, yet I reached out and touched the surface, running my fingers over its uneven scraps and torn edges. I liked the ripped-up effect; I liked the way those fissures and the seeping of glue caught the light in odd ways and gave the picture a mystery it otherwise lacked. It supplied the dull-eyed girl with something like a soul; distancing her from the world, as if she were observing us all through a coarse-grained veil.

'Stella,' I said aloud, into the darkness, and the house responded to my appeal with a stir and a creak. I spun round and peered upwards, in search of the sound. There was a gallery leading off from the staircase, but all I could make out were clustering shadows and a rough sketch of bannisters. I hooked a stray lock of hair over my ear and smiled faintly, although it was difficult to come across as nonchalant when you weren't quite sure which way to face. The sensible thing would be to shout 'Hello?', but that was impossible. I couldn't bear to hear my own voice reaching out into this big, black space, and echoing back again, all husky and small.

I moved out of the block of sunlight and sat down on the floor beside the staircase. This was much better. I was disembodied again – a wraith in a dress of green shadows. Nobody would notice me here. I hiccupped as I squinted towards the open door, my breath tasting of alcohol and sourness. The sun was sinking into the sea now, and the view made my head hurt; it looked less like a garden and more like a heap of gold that had been set on fire. I didn't want to go back to the party and pretend to be amused by risqué speeches. I much preferred to lie down here, with a cold tile against my ear.

I dreamed I was a fish, gutted and laid out on ice. When I woke up, the arm I'd been lying on felt stiff and my neck hurt as I tried to raise my head. I didn't know how long I'd been asleep, but the sun had disappeared, the sea had lost its sheen, and the garden was a gathering of lilacs and blues. Far away, at the bottom of the lawn, there were loops of fairy lights glimmering in the trees, and I could hear little whines and crackles from the loudspeakers as the jazz band began playing 'Dream a Little Dream of Me'. I noticed that the door was half closed, although I'd left it wide open.

It was that, and the thought of Dad, that got me to my feet, despite my pins and needles. I never left him for long – not unless he knew exactly where I was, and when I'd be back – and it baffled me that I'd had the heart to do so here, of all places, when he was in such a jangly mood. I recalled my four glasses of wine and closed my eyes. What an idiot. What a day. I made for the door, and with every step my brain seemed to bounce like a loose rock against the insides of my skull.

I forgot about the picture until I reached the front door and took a bleary look back, just to make sure I'd been wrong.

16

Now that the daylight had lost its glare I'd be able to tell for certain that she wasn't Stella; that the whole thing was a drunken illusion based on hair colour, and a slight similarity in the line of the jaw.

There was no picture. I squeezed my eyes shut and opened them wide again, but there was nothing there anymore – nothing at all. All right, there was a faint rectangular patch on the wall, like the memory of something that used to be there, and a light fitting above it – but there was no gold frame and no red-headed woman. I didn't need to go closer to make sure, but I went anyway. Perhaps she had fallen off her hook, and was lying face down in the shadows? No. The floor was bare. I went right to the back of the hall and spread my palms on the space where Stella's lookalike had hung. The wall was cold and clammy, and there was a ropy cobweb, thick with dust, which clung to my fingers as I pulled away.

The eating and speechifying had finished by the time I got back to the party, and the band was in full swing. Everyone was standing about on the grass, talking and drinking, and I dodged from group to group in search of Dad. The chatter was more raucous than it had been at dinner, and the air felt sticky with the smell of booze. A few people grabbed my arm and asked if I was feeling better, or tried to buy me a drink, but I thanked them and shook them off.

I checked inside the marquee – the chaos of wine-stains and moulting bouquets – but everyone had left, so I wandered back towards the rose garden, pausing at the top of the steps to look at Byrne Hall. There were no lights on in any of the front windows. The house would blend into the night soon, and we'd hardly know it was there.

'Hello stranger.' My father was sitting on a bench beside a couple of empty beer glasses and an ashtray full of stubs.

'Dad, I'm so sorry.' I moved the ashtray out of the way and dropped down beside him. 'I was feeling sick, so I lay down. I didn't mean to disappear off.'

'It's fine.' He touched my hand. 'Honestly. As long as you're all right.'

The last of the outdoor lights came on in the trees, yellowing the undersides of the leaves. A few people cried, 'Ooh!' and someone nearby said, 'How lovely.' It was funny how the noise of the crowd seemed to come and go. Occasionally a quietness fell over everyone, all at the same time, and you could hear the swash of the sea on the rocks below the garden.

The saxophonist threw out a sinuous thread of tune, and the bride and groom laughed their way through a few awkward moves on the dance floor. After a while, the music got livelier, and others began to join them in dribs and drabs. I wondered if anyone had ventured down to the beach, and I looked round for the wet-haired man, but all I could remember was his stare and the salty smell of his clothes. I couldn't have told you what colour his hair was, or whether he was tall, or broad, or anything like that. His eyes were either grey or green – unless I was confusing them with the eyes in the painting.

'You should dance too,' said Dad, but I shook my head, and we sat side by side as the night gathered around us, and the couples held each other close, and the fairy lights swayed in the breeze from the sea.

I stopped noticing the music after a while, but the following day, when the wedding was over, I could still feel the pulse of it thrumming through me like a coded message without a key.

2

IF THE WEATHER HAD BEEN oppressive on the coast, it was a hundred times worse once we got home. Work was manic that week, and unusually tedious. Every evening, as soon as I could escape the office, I made my way to the lido down the road and swam a lazy backstroke up and down until dusk. The pool was hot and soupy and crowded, but it became the highlight of my day, and I was – briefly – a free person, leading a free life, rather than a prisoner serving a life sentence. Sometimes I came close to happiness when I was gazing up at the sky with the burble of water in my ears, thinking about green leaves and chequered floors, and a strange man with bare feet.

I regretted not swimming in the sea at Byrne Hall, and I developed a fantasy in which I left the wedding party and escaped down to the beach with the bare-footed man. Perhaps that sounds strange, given it was the place where my sister had died. But the sea was the element that brought me closest to Stella – as close as I could ever hope to get – and it still made me happy, because it had once made us both happy. In my dream the man and I slipped our clothes off in the darkness, walked into the sea and swam for miles, until there were no sounds except for our own hard breathing and the lap of water on skin. When we looked back, the garden had become a dusting of fairy lights on the horizon and the house itself a ghostly bride, hovering in the night sky.

*

On Friday evening I was forced to break my routine, because I'd arranged to meet Dad after work and walk with him to the Wingate Gallery for the opening of the Renaissance drawings exhibition. Heatwave or no heatwave, there was no getting out of it – not with Tom in charge of the curation. Tom would have seen right through my excuses, if I'd been tactless enough to make them, and anyway, Dad had to go, because he was doing a review for his column in the *London Globe*.

So there I stood in the expensive cool of Room Two, a week on from my cousin's wedding, pretending to appreciate a Madonna and Child in red chalk and trying not to look aloof. I used to love exhibition openings like this; it used to be fun when Stella was alive. Trays of white wine and smoked salmon tartlets were doing the rounds, so I took a glass.

I was conscious of my father hard at work on the other side of the gallery, going from picture to picture and scrawling notes all over his catalogue. I can't say I was conscious of much else. The creak of polished floorboards, the burble of cultured conversation, the tinkling trays of glasses – it was all just background to my thoughts, and I might as well have been loitering outside on the street, or lying in bed with my music on, or back-stroking up and down the lido. I couldn't even focus on the pictures, drifting against the dark red walls in their own orbs of light. It was as if there was a pane of glass between me and the world, which grew foggier with every outward breath. In and among the chatterers, there were people to whom the drawings meant something – you could tell by the way they stood and stared – and I wished I was one of them.

I opened the catalogue again and flipped through, searching for Tom's essay. The Wingate always produced quality catalogues for their exhibitions, but even in my distracted state

I recognised this one as a beauty, with its thick cover and glossy white pages, its razor-sharp reproductions of every picture, and its copious notes. I found Tom's piece at the front. 'Raphael and the Art of Pity', it was titled, in large, brick-red italics. 'An introduction by Assistant Curator Thomas Gardiner'. At the end of the article there was a little mug-shot of him looking faintly startled in his broken glasses.

This was a big deal for Tom and I tried faithfully to read it, but my thoughts kept getting jumbled up with the print and nothing made sense. I shut it again, and wandered to the next drawing and the next: more young women – Venuses and Madonnas and Florentine aristocrats – gazing down from the walls in silent appeal. They looked like living beings that had been turned into chalk and trapped inside sheets of paper, and it made my heart sink to look at them.

Tom came and stood beside me. I wouldn't have noticed, except that he stayed still for so long in the same spot and kept shooting glances in my direction. If it had been anyone else it would have got on my nerves, but even in my current mood I couldn't object to him.

'Shouldn't you be circulating?' I said.

'I am,' he replied. 'I'm just taking my time about it.'

I retreated to one of the benches in the middle of the room and I was happy enough when he followed. Tom was good company. For one thing, he never made me feel I should talk for the sake of talking. For another – and I know this sounds odd – he had a nice smell: sort of biscuity, with overtones of coffee and pencil shavings. It always made me feel nostalgic, as if by breathing it in I was recovering something soothing from the past. People rolled their eyes at Tom; even Dad did. 'Oh, Tom's too nice for his own good' was the general verdict, as though that made him ridiculous. I never found him ridiculous, and there were times I was on the brink of telling him so – but it's not the kind of thing you can say in so many words.

'Congratulations on your essay,' I said, patting the cover of the catalogue, and Tom nodded.

The picture in front of us was a charcoal study of hands: gnarled hands, baby hands, clasped hands, pointing hands, hands in fists, hands lying on a tabletop with their fingers loosely curled.

'Do you think your dad's enjoying himself?' said Tom. 'He's looking very – what's the word? *Avian.*'

I smiled faintly. There was something bird-like about the way my father darted from picture to picture, his sharp nose thrust forwards, his lips pinched, his spectacles opaque where they caught the light. Whenever a thought occurred he'd stop dead and make a note in the catalogue for his forthcoming review.

'It's going all right, isn't it?' I said vaguely. 'I'm sure it'll be fine.'

I had no idea whether it would be fine or not. There was a time when I'd have given my eyeteeth for the chance to sit next to Tom like this, and say reassuring things to him. If it was bleak to admit that Raphael bored me, it was a thousand times worse to admit that Tom did.

Tom drew his fingertips slowly over his chin, as if trying to remember when he'd last shaved.

'Are you all right?' he said after a while. 'Only you seem, I don't know . . .'

'What?'

'Glassy eyed.'

I snorted. A waiter approached with a tray of canapés, and Tom filled his cupped hand with pesto palmiers and tequila-prawn skewers.

'How was that wedding, last weekend?' he said, when I made no further response. 'Down in the West Country, wasn't it?'

I nodded. 'Byrne Hall. It's a stately home overlooking the sea.'

'Oh yes.' He glanced at me anxiously. 'Sorry, of course. I'd forgotten. Near where . . .'

'Mmm.'

There was a long pause while he chewed a palmier and dusted the crumbs off his trousers.

'It's funny you should mention Stella,' I said, in response to his faint allusion, 'because I came across a portrait of her inside the house.'

Tom turned and stared at me, and I wondered how long it had been since we last mentioned her name. Months? Possibly years. I wasn't surprised that he blushed.

'What do you mean? What house?'

'I snuck inside Byrne Hall itself – we weren't supposed to, we were meant to keep to the garden – and there was a portrait of Stella on the wall near the stairs.'

I'd been trying to forget about the portrait that may or may not have existed, but perhaps I'd been trying too hard, because it – she – wouldn't fade. Whatever I did or said or thought she was there, getting in the way, staring me out in my waking hours and striving to speak to me at night. She was like a television picture without any sound, and it bothered me that I couldn't understand a word she said.

'Actually, I was thinking of taking a few days off work,'

I added. 'I want to go back to Byrne Hall and take a proper look; talk to the people who live there; find out if perhaps they knew her . . .'

I picked at the pastry flakes he'd scattered on my lap, pressing them on to my thumb-pad one by one.

'Right.' Tom looked confused, as if I'd been talking quickly in a foreign language. I was relieved to see Dad approaching our bench.

'Don't say anything,' I warned under my breath.

'No, OK.'

Dad was peering at us over the rim of his glasses.

'I'm sorry to interrupt,' he said, 'but I was hoping to have a word with Tom.'

My father could look fierce to the point of terrifying when he was happy, and he was happy tonight. I loved it when he was like this, with his hair standing up round his ears, and his tie askew, and a pencil twitching in his fingers, and no room in his head for anything except art.

It didn't last, of course. The evening drew to a close, we said our goodbyes, and my father's joy glugged away like wine from a toppled bottle. It was difficult to talk on the crowded tube train. All I could do was stand there in the heat, my face pressed up against a stranger's armpit, and watch his euphoria fade.

My bravado was wilting too. *A few days off work?* Had I said that? *A trip away, all on my own, without Dad?* It felt like an impossibility, but now I'd voiced it out loud, I couldn't stop turning it over in my mind. It struck me how narrow I had become over the last five years; how little I thought about anything novel in the course of an average day. I worried about Dad a lot and brooded over my dead sister, and of course there were the mundane practicalities of life – but that was all. My job as a very small cog in a very large machine called K&G Financial Services barely occupied my mind when I was doing it, never mind out of hours.

I used to be known as a reader. 'Freya's the bookworm of the family,' Dad was still in the habit of saying to anyone who might be interested, but even that was becoming a false reputation. I'd barely read a word since Stella's death. I knew a bit about art, but only because Dad was such an expert. I'd lost sight of whether it actually interested me or not.

There was always Tom, of course, to absorb my thoughts – or there always used to be Tom. When I was lying awake at night, wishing I had a life worth the name, I tended to picture myself with him. It was a guilty habit I still clung to, although the guilt and the pleasure weren't as piquant as they used to be. Maybe I'd begun to doubt whether Stella, being dead, minded what Tom and I got up to in my imagination.

I prattled desperately during the walk home from the station, my questions echoing round the silent streets. 'Which was your favourite room?' I wanted to know. 'Which was your favourite picture?' 'Did you read Tom's essay?' 'Do you like the sketches best, or the finished drawings?'

'Not sure,' Dad would answer, or 'Hmm,' or 'It depends.'

When we got in he dropped the catalogue on the hall table and stood like a statue while I locked up; he didn't even move when the cat appeared and wound itself about his legs. At least he let me shuffle his jacket off – shifting his shoulders and unbending his elbows to help – but when I returned from the cupboard under the stairs I found him standing in the same place, absorbed and sad, with an old man's sagging posture.

'Cup of tea?' I stooped to rub the cat's cheek. My phone pinged, but when I opened it to look there were only work emails.

'Uh?'

'*Tea?*'

He pondered my question for a while. 'If you're making one.'

I flicked a lamp on in the sitting room and Dad sat down on the sofa. If only we could have filled our terraced house with Raphaels and Leonardos. Our home was cluttered with things that meant little to either of us; things which had drained themselves of sentimental value over time, instead of accruing it. There were antique maps of counties we'd never lived in; china ornaments whose provenance we'd forgotten; black-and-white photos of ancestors whose deaths had faded to mere dates, or minor biographical details. There used to be framed photos of my mother and sister on the mantelpiece, but these had been deemed too painful to look at – eighteen years ago and five years ago, respectively – so they'd been wrapped in felt cloths and removed to a dresser drawer. Every so often, when I knew Dad wasn't around, I'd creep downstairs and get them out. I know he sometimes looked at them too, because the way he folded the cloths was different.

Otherwise, nothing ever changed in our house. I'd noticed it before, but I noticed it especially that evening, when I was standing at the kitchen sink, emptying cold dregs from a teapot, which we seemed to have been using – in all its brown, chipped ugliness – since the year dot. I stood it next to the kettle and tried not to feel panicked as I scanned the room in search of anything that might be described as new, or newish. Everything seemed so inevitable. The enamel bread-bin, the threadbare ironing board, the poky table with the Formica

26

top. The fridge magnets Stella and I had collected with tokens from a Shreddies box. The Kings and Queens of England poster still stuck to the wall, by some miracle, on flinty shards of Blu-Tack. Even the Christmas cactus on the windowsill. Everything the same as ever and ever, only a little more dust-caked, or ropy, or dried up. I pressed my hands against my cheeks, testing them for deterioration. What would it mean, I wondered, to throw everything out and start again? Would it feel like a joyful rebirth? Or would it be like pulling the skin away from our flesh – Dad's and mine – strip by agonising strip?

A tentative knock on the back door made me jump, but the blurry figure in the frosted glass was unmistakably Tom. I glanced at the clock. It was gone eleven and our house was not, by any stretch of the imagination, en route to his flat.

'Tom?' I opened the door a couple of inches. 'What are you doing?'

He must have stumbled along the back lane, where everyone kept their bins, and made his way into our garden. I was conscious of a younger, sweeter Freya for whom this scenario would have been unbearably thrilling. Rather as she would have done, I crossed the kitchen and closed the door into the hall, so that Dad couldn't hear us.

'Sorry.' Tom lingered outside. 'It's just, I need to speak to you. I tried to catch you as you were leaving the gallery, but I got waylaid.'

The kettle was rumbling to a boil.

'I'm just making Dad some tea . . .'

He pushed the door open and held out his hand, inviting me into the night.

'I won't keep you a minute,' he said. 'I don't want to start nattering with your dad right now . . . It's you . . .'

Our back garden was a sparse strip of grass and uneven paving, ending in a fence. It was too dark to see anything except a few sketchy shapes and a handful of lighted windows in the houses opposite, but in my mind's eye I saw the row of identikit terraces beyond them, and the next and the next and the next, all the way up the hill to the main road. Tom and I walked side by side to the end of the path, and halfway back again, to the edge of the square of light that fell from the kitchen window.

'Are you all right?' Tom said eventually. 'I'm worried about you. You seem . . . I don't know . . . not your usual self.'

'What's my usual self?'

'Oh, well . . .' He hesitated. 'Warm-hearted. Interested in things. Level-headed.'

'*Level-headed?*' I would hate him for that, if it were possible to hate Tom.

'It's not meant as a criticism.'

'You'd never have saddled Stella with *level-headed*.'

There she was again. Tom wasn't having it – 'Oh, for heaven's sake, Stella has *nothing to do with this*' – and I didn't argue, but we both knew he was wrong. Stella always had everything to do with everything. Stella – with all the guilt and love and resentment that attached to her memory – was the distorting lens through which Tom looked at me, and I looked back at him.

We waited – suspended on a long-held breath – and he put his arm round my shoulders, as he'd done countless times in my imagination, and I leaned into him, as I'd always known I would, but my heart didn't skip a single beat. I might as well have been leaning against the garden fence for all the joy I felt. He kissed my head, moving his mouth across my hair – once, twice, three times – and I could tell by the breathless way he did it, and the tension along his arm, that his nerves were wound to the point where mine ought to have been.

'I wish you'd done this before,' I said into his shirt, and he froze.

'Before what?'

I shook my head and pulled away.

'I don't know. A long time ago. Before I grew so old and jaded.'

'Old and jaded? At twenty-three?'

He let me go, and as he moved I caught that nostalgic Tom scent: the coffee and the pencil shavings and the biscuits. I reached for him, but fell short of touching him, and it was too dark for him to notice.

'You even *smell* of ordinariness,' I said.

'*Smell . . . ?*'

We laughed together, ever so slightly, right in the middle of our misery. Pipes gurgled inside our house, and my dad moved in a blur across the bathroom window.

The people next door were watching TV and there was a constant plink-plonk of comedy music, punctuated by bursts of audience laughter. I rubbed my arms, despite the heat, and inhaled the stale breath of the night: tarmac and traffic and the kebab shop and the remains of Dad's furtive fags. The sky over the city was a dirty orange, as if there were a great fire creeping towards us, and it was impossible to tell whether the night was clear or cloudy. I felt the same yearning I'd had at Byrne Hall: a thirst for something I'd never tasted before, and didn't know, and couldn't name.

'What's wrong with ordinariness?' Tom asked, though he seemed to know the question was hopeless.

I closed my eyes and shook my head.

'Everything's wrong with it,' Tom suggested, doing his best to answer on my behalf. 'And everything's wrong with me.'

'There's nothing wrong with you.'

That's what I said, but somehow I failed to show it. My shoulders remained angled against his cautious touch and my arms were folded across my chest. In the kitchen, a thin ribbon of steam was rising from the kettle, and I thought of Dad waiting for his cup of tea.

'I think I need to get away from here,' I said. 'Just for a while. Perhaps that's all it is.'

Tom stood still, staring at his feet. I could hardly bear to look at him.

'I'm sorry,' I said – addressing my long-lost self as much as Tom – but he shook his head as if to say *no need*.

I was going to deal with work emails that night when I got to bed, but I ended up typing a few disjointed lines instead:

Windows with half-closed blinds, like sultry eyes
We swim into the night, our legs (pale legs?) like flickering (?) fish
Our legs flashing like fish in/through the dark water
A girl in pieces on a chess-board floor

I threw myself back on the bed and closed my eyes. I was in love with an ungraspable idea, a woozy dream, a place, an afternoon, a house. I sat up again and wrote:

Let me lie on the thick/green/lush grass
The white-fringed (white-crested?) sea beneath me
The white-pillared house above

I know that sounds effete but I don't mean 'love' in estate-agent speak. I wasn't pondering Byrne Hall's potential as a family home, or admiring it as a good example of Queen Anne architecture, or any of that. My feelings were darker and stranger. They were more like the feelings I used to have for Tom.

3

THE NIGHT BEFORE I TRAVELLED to Byrne Hall – a week after my conversation with Tom – it occurred to me to write about Stella. It was only an idea, but it came to mind so suddenly and unexpectedly that I flicked my lamp on and sat up in bed with my heart hammering, as if I'd heard a strange noise, or seen a dark figure enter my room.

My notebooks were gathering dust at the back of the wardrobe. When she died I'd parcelled them up with string – the spiral-bound jotters, and the exercise books, and the fancy ones people had bought me as birthday presents – expecting to chuck them away, unread, during the clear-out that never happened.

I brought them back to bed with me now and undid the string. Some creaked along their spines as I opened them, some unfurled of their own accord, their pages soft and clammy. I re-read my poems through splayed fingers, cringing at my immature earnestness. There was space left in one of the jotters, so I turned to a fresh page and wrote the date in pencil.

That was it, though I sat and waited for a good hour. Nothing else occurred to me. After a while I tied my old ambitions up, slid them into my case and switched the light off. It was stupid to have got them out again, like picking at a half-healed scab.

I woke properly at dawn and lay with my eyes open, while the light brightened round the edges of my curtains and an unfamiliar block of shadow beside the door became my suit-case, packed and ready to go. When I heard the newspaper drop through the letterbox, about half past six, I went downstairs in my dressing gown.

I'd forgotten that Dad's review would be published today. I noticed it as I was glancing down the Contents column and waiting for the kettle to boil: *Arts & Books, page 13. Robert Lyell reviews the Wingate Gallery's 'Art of Pity' exhibition.*

I spread the newspaper on the table and bit the corner off my toast.

What a Pity!

That was Dad's choice of headline.

What a Pity! in fat, black letters above a sixteenth-century pen-and-ink sketch of The Good Samaritan. It was weird how my mouth dried up completely: one moment I was chewing on multi-seed bread and apricot jam, the next my tongue was like dust. I put the rest of the toast on the sideboard and sat down. I could see Tom in his book-strewn flat, fumbling for the same page with his heart in his mouth.

Arts Editor Robert Lyell is moved by an exquisite selection of High Renaissance drawings, but clever-clever curation and waffling catalogue notes spoil the show.

Oh, Tom! Lovely Tom. I don't know what he saw in us Lyells, or why he stuck around, unless it was for old times' sake. I ironed the pages out with my hands and as soon as I'd managed to swallow, I began to read.

Dad and I didn't talk on the way to the station. I kept waiting for him to ask me what was up, but he never did. Sometimes I think he's so comfortable with silences that he doesn't realise how much their quality can vary. As far as I could see this counted as a difficult silence, and I didn't understand why he was so carefree.

He took my suitcase for me as we left the tube and said, 'Having second thoughts?' but I just shouldered my smaller bag and shook my head, without smiling or meeting his eye, and he seemed to think that was enough. I stood behind him on the escalator. The same posters recurred all the way up – *Seen Anything Suspicious? . . . An Evening with the Stars! . . . Seen Anything Suspicious? . . . Your Chance to Dance! . . . Seen Anything Suspicious? . . . The Royal Ballet Presents . . .* – and by the time we got to the top I felt as if I'd read them all a million times without making sense of a single one.

'I read the review,' I told him, finally, as we made our way on to the concourse. He looked ridiculous – a tall, grey-haired man wheeling a small, plastic suitcase with a purple daisy motif – so I wrested it from his hand.

'The review?' he echoed. 'Oh, my review.'

A faint hardness came over his face; an all-but-invisible rigidity. He didn't ask what I'd made of it; he never asked anyone what they made of his writing. The articles he wrote for the *London Globe* – and various other publications – were their own justification.

'Your train's on time.' He paused under the departures board and glanced at his watch. 'We're early though, if you fancy a quick coffee?'

Dad had a long stride – or he did when he wanted to – and I could only keep up at a lopsided trot, which made me sound breathless and shouty, when I meant to be severe.

'You said Tom's essay was "over-thought and over-wrought".'

'Two Americanos, please.' Dad nodded at the man behind the counter, and then at me. 'Well, I think that was fair

34

enough. That's the way Tom writes, I'm afraid: never uses one word when ten will do.'

'It's not fair at all,' I said. 'And even if it were, I don't understand how you can be so cold about it. The whole exhibition, that was Tom's big moment – he's been worrying about it for ages. And you know how much he takes things to heart, even if he doesn't let on.'

Poor Tom. It was like this when he got married at the age of twenty-one: all raised eyebrows and *what does he think he's doing?* At least, on that occasion, Dad had only thought he was clueless; Stella was the one who'd actually said so, to his face. We never got to know Natalie, but she was marked down as glamorous and urbane – which Tom wasn't and isn't – so when she upped and left, it felt inevitable. Nobody ever seemed able to see matters through Tom's eyes, by which I mean with romance at first, and sadness later on.

I had so much to say in his defence, but no eloquence to match. Not that it mattered: I doubted Dad could hear me over the hiss of the coffee machines and the station hubbub.

Mind you, I managed to hear him, and he didn't even raise his voice.

'I am an art critic,' he said, pocketing his change and handing me my cardboard cup, 'and I don't do special favours. Not for Tom, not for anyone. And that, as you well know, is that.'

There wasn't as much time as we'd thought, and I ended up taking my coffee on to the train. We said a brief goodbye, and I flinched when Dad kissed me, banging my nose against his cheek bone. I didn't kiss him back, although when I was putting my suitcase on the overhead rack and sliding into my seat, I wished I had.

Dad waited on the platform until the train set off, waving uncertainly at the wrong carriage because he couldn't see me through the tinted glass. I leaned forward belatedly and raised my hand, but the train was already moving and he was too far away to notice.

Strange, how we'd parted so brusquely, when mutual reassurance had been the tone of the last few days – 'You're sure you don't mind me going?' 'I'm absolutely sure.' 'Because if you want me to stay . . . ?' 'I just want you to have a wonderful time,' etc. I wished we could make our goodbyes all over again, in that kindlier spirit.

I don't know what Dad thought of my trip. I'd told him a fraction of the story, so it can't be said I lied. He knew I was staying in a guest house near Byrne Hall, and that I had my reasons. The reasons – in his view – were entirely to do with Stella. 'Making peace with the past,' I'd called it at one point, and he'd seemed satisfied with that, although it made me feel oddly guilty, as if I were presenting the whole enterprise as simpler and purer than it was. What would a truer explanation sound like, though? How was I supposed to make him understand, when he was pottering about the kitchen the day before my departure, with one ear on me and one on the cricket commentary?

Northanger Abbey was at the top of my bag. I took it out and laid it on the table without opening it. I'd packed the exhibition catalogue as well, meaning to read Tom's essay during the journey, but I didn't want to anymore. My notebooks were right at the bottom, and I thought about digging them out too, but there was no point trying to write on a train. It was too public. The woman opposite was turning the pages of the *London Globe*, and I could see the Contents column down the right-hand side of the front page, with Dad's name squished up inside her pudgy fingers. *Page 13. Robert Lyell.* I looked out of the window, and wondered if Tom had read it yet. Perhaps I should text him. I reached into my pocket and fingered my phone, before laying my empty hands on the table and watching the warehouses flit past, and the apartment blocks, and the banks of scrub and willow-herb.

I picked up my phone again. Perhaps I should text Dad and say a proper goodbye? Or perhaps I should just stop making so much of this trip to Byrne Hall. After all, there was no reason to think it would lead to anything. It wasn't a *quest*, for heaven's sake. If I were to accept, like Dad, that my main – or most concrete, or sane, or explicable – motive was Stella, it boiled down to a polite enquiry for the people at the big house. 'Did you happen to know my sister?' I'd ask, and they'd give me some banal reply, and the whole thing would be over in two minutes flat. I might be on my way home again by this time tomorrow.

The train slowed, though we were nowhere near our first stop. We trundled past a vast cemetery, which put me in mind of the churchyard on the other side of the city where my mother and sister were buried side by side.

There was a bird carved on to Stella's headstone – a swallow in flight – and her epitaph read, 'Stella Maria Lyell, 1988–2009. *Dance, then, wherever you may be.*' I'd had my doubts about the wording – weren't we allowed to assume she'd gone to heaven? – but Dad thought it was perfect, so I hadn't argued.

I drummed my fingers on the coffee cup lid and wondered what inscription I might earn, when my time came. How about they carve a little picture of a ship? And underneath it they could write: *Freya Claire Lyell: She never rocked the boat.*

Except, of course, I did rock it – once, only once, five years ago – and the next thing I knew, my sister was dead.

The woman with the newspaper frowned, so I stopped drumming my fingers and opened my book. I did my best to read, but it was hard to keep my mind on anyone's story other than my own.

December 1997

In my memory I'm six years old and the Christmas market is teeming. I want to go home, but we're here to have fun, so I cling to Dad's hand instead. Stella is nine and she doesn't want to hold anyone's hand. She glowers and wriggles, and every time Dad relaxes his grasp she slips from her woolly mitten.

Tom is with us. He's often with us after school on a Thursday; I think it's because his parents work late that day. Tom is eleven and sullen – or perhaps he's just shy. When Dad dashes after Stella for the umpteenth time, shouting over his shoulder, 'Tom! Look after Freya!', he snaps to attention. His gloom softens into seriousness and he takes hold of my hand.

Stella is hopping from stall to stall – from handmade soaps to charcuterie, to cuckoo clocks, to artisan gin – and she wants to buy a bit of everything. I want to be ecstatic too, but I don't know how. Mum is Gone, and I think we'd be better off at home, even though Mum won't be there either.

Mum Gone is not what it sounds like; not simply a gap where Mum used to be. Mum Gone is a thing. It's a black, silent snake that slithers everywhere and squeezes thickly

38

around my heart. Everywhere I go the snake goes too, and I can't shake it off. It turns nice things scary – even the brass band playing carols, and the reindeer lights on the town hall, and the gingerbread stall. Even the teddies with Santa hats. They're only pretending to be cheerful and friendly.

We've all been given a ten-pound note, and Stella spends hers within the first few minutes. She buys a hairband with reindeer antlers, which go Ho Ho Ho when you press them, and a jar of shiny red things.

'What on earth . . . ?' Dad says, indicating the jar.

'They're pretty!' Stella cries, but Dad laughs and shakes his head.

'They're sweets,' she adds dubiously.

Dad is still shaking his head, so Stella reads the label out loud, her voice sinking as she goes along. 'Spicy stuffed peppers . . . with feta cheese . . . in an olive oil and herb marinade.'

I glance up at Tom, because I'm not sure whether this is funny, and he is bound to know. Tom tightens his grip on my hand, which isn't much to go on, but I decide not to laugh. Dad wants to usher us all along because we're blocking the pavement, but Stella won't budge. Her eyes are brimming and glinting.

'Come on,' says Dad, who has finished being amused.

The black snake knots itself around my chest as Stella starts to cry. People push past us and give us looks, and if it wasn't for Tom holding my hand I think I would cry as well. Stella says she needs extra pocket money and Dad says No. Stella says that's not fair because she thought they were sweets, and Dad says No very quickly and quietly. Is Stella deaf to the warning in his tone, or doesn't she care? Now she's claiming that she bought the jar of red things for Dad's Christmas present, and anyway . . . anyway . . . she's as shrill as she can go, and she's yanking on his sleeve like she wants to rip it off, and it's only a matter of time before she kicks him on the shins . . . anyway, Mum was generous. If Mum was here she'd have given Stella loads more than ten shitty little pounds. A gasp from one of the stallholders. Someone tuts and says, 'She only looks about ten!'

'I wish you were dead, instead of Mum. Mum loved us way, way, _way_ more than you do.'

Dad is gripping Stella by the arms and readying himself for the shin-kick, but he doesn't look angry. I sort of wish he did. Instead, he looks tired – so tired – as if he might lie down next to the mulled wine stall and never get up again.

Tom and I watch from the sidelines. It's all we can do. Stella's hat is flying off, and she's smashed the jar of peppers, and her hair is everywhere, and she's actually ripped a hole in Dad's sleeve. She's awful, and frightening, and beautiful. She fragments like a firework.

4

THE CHURCH WHERE MY COUSIN had married was in the seaside town of Bligh, so at least I knew which bus to catch from the railway station, even if I didn't have a clue what to do once it got there. I thought Byrne Hall would be unavoidable, dominating the landscape like a fairy-tale castle, but it wasn't.

The bus was full to bursting with end-of-season holiday-makers, so I stood with my suitcase jammed between my feet and clung to the rail. A baby watched me fixedly over her mother's shoulder and I smiled at her, but she didn't smile back. The heat was denser and darker than it had been this morning when I left London, and the passengers swayed listlessly as the bus rounded corners and jounced over speed bumps. Every time the driver braked, my shoulder bag banged against my hip and my forehead knocked on the rail, and it took a lot of calf-strain and concentration not to fall over or plump down on someone's knee.

I peered anxiously through the windows on either side, trying to get my bearings, but nothing looked familiar. There was an old church with a square tower, but I didn't think it was the one where the wedding had been held. We drove beside a harbour, where boats floated motionless on silky water, and I had a brief glimpse of trees on the other side. I blew my fringe out of my eyes, which made the baby laugh unexpectedly, and the bus swerved on to the sea-front.

The windows of the bus were dusty, which lent the view a

mystical quality, even though it was the middle of the day. The sea and sky seemed to form a flat, painted backdrop, and the people who walked in front of it – the joggers and dog-walkers and holidaymakers – were like shadow puppets. Someone had drawn a sad face in the dirt, and that was the only bit of glass I could see through clearly.

As we slowed, I glimpsed a man trudging towards us along the prom with supermarket bags dangling from either hand. The bus braked at a pedestrian crossing and I craned my neck sideways so that I could see him through the cleared parts of the window. It was him, wasn't it? The man at the wedding? He had shoes on this time, his hair was dry and he looked ordinary: not the sea-god I'd constructed in my lido fantasies, but a bloke weighed down by grocery shopping and thought. From time to time he glanced vaguely at the sky, which was blackening rapidly over the sea, and I wondered whether he had far to walk. The plastic bags were bulging with bottles and tins, and the handles must have been digging into his skin. I elbowed my way towards the window to get a better view, but the bus bumped forwards and left him behind.

The baby was sucking her fists and staring at me, so I jutted out my lower lip and puffed at my fringe, but it didn't amuse her anymore. The bus braked to avoid a speeding cyclist, and the baby belched a mouthful of stringy liquid, which slid between her fingers and trailed down her mother's back. I got off at the next stop. Despite the stillness and the heat, there was a sting coming from the sea – an electricity – which you never felt in London. On impulse I crossed the road and walked back the way I'd come. I could see the man ahead of me, walking slowly along the promenade with his shoulders bowed and the bags dragging on his arms.

A girl sat busking with her back against the railings. She was playing a folky tune on her guitar – 'Scarborough Fair', I think – and the notes sounded strange and small in the thundery air.

I drew close to the man without having fathomed my own intentions. Would it seem odd if I tapped him on the shoulder and said hello? It would, wouldn't it? But he was clearly a local, and I could ask for directions to Byrne Hall . . .

The handle snapped on one of his bags, but he managed to catch it before the shopping tumbled out. He lugged everything to one of the benches that stood at intervals along the prom, and sat down.

I stopped and leaned over the railings. My phone pinged but I ignored it and looked out to sea instead. There was no play of light on the water today; the surface was as flat and opaque as a slate, and it was difficult to believe in the complexities that lurked under its surface: the seething depths and the rough tug of tides; the bony shipwrecks and ropes of bladder-wrack.

Grocery bags rustled behind me as the man rearranged his shopping. Further down the prom, the guitar music petered out and the girl began a new tune. She was quite good. Occasionally she'd throw in a lyric, then she'd pause and hum.

The bags stopped rustling. I waited for some other sound to betray his presence – a clearing of the throat, a sniff – but there was nothing. Had he gone? But I would have noticed the clip of his shoes on the pavement. I turned my head a fraction.

43

The man was sitting with his legs crossed and leaning on his knee to write or draw with a biro. His face had altered: there was something intensely childlike about the way he glowered and worked his jaw whilst skimming the blue biro over the paper. I'd had him down as older than me when I spotted him from the bus window, but now he seemed younger. I wondered what he was sketching – the sea? – until he raised his head and narrowed his eyes at me. My cheeks went hot and I frowned. His stare was keenly observant, but distant; sensitive to the lines, shapes and structures of my posture, but unaware of me as me. When he noticed I was watching, it took him a while to register the shift in perception, and his smile, when it came, was shy.

'Sorry!' Reluctantly he stuck the pen behind his ear and began to fold the drawing.

'No, it's OK . . .' I wasn't entirely sure that it was, but he looked at me long and hard and decided to take me at my word. He spread the paper on his knee again. It was one of those bags you get from a bakery, spotted with grease and crumbs.

'Are you sure you don't mind?'

'I suppose . . .'

'And . . . would you mind facing out to sea again, and staying very still?'

I did as he asked, but this time I hardly noticed the sea itself. I itched to watch him watching me, but I kept my back turned and listened to the paper bag crinkling under the strokes of his pen. My phone rang – it was Dad's ringtone – but I didn't dare move. I could call him back later.

'OK, finished,' said the man.

'Can I see?'

'Oh God, please no.' He shook his head and dropped the paper into one of his shopping bags. 'It's only the beginnings of a sketch. It's nothing.'

He stood up and gathered his shopping, pausing when he was ready and turning towards me, as if there was something else he wanted to say. My phone rang again. *Go away, Dad!*

'So, are you an artist?' I said stupidly. One of us had to fill the silence as we began walking down the prom. The shopping bags kept twisting on their handles and banging into his legs, so our pace was necessarily slow.

'Oh, no!' he protested. 'Well, not really. I tried to be, once, but it went wrong and I gave up. It was just a pipe dream; one of those childish things . . .'

The beach had almost emptied by now, and the few people left on the prom – apart from us – were walking quickly to avoid the imminent rain. I wanted to look at him – after all, he had studied me for five solid minutes, and gained an intimate knowledge of the back of my head – but it was difficult when we were ambling side by side like this. I tried to build a picture from the fragments in my head: world-weary shoulders; a frown of concentration; an uncertain smile. Messy hair and brown eyes – or were the eyes grey? It wasn't much to go on. He was taller than me, but slighter than Tom.

'I write poems in my spare time,' I confided. 'In another life, I'd be a real, full-time poet.'

I don't know what made me say that: for one thing, even Dad didn't know about my poems; for another, I hadn't written properly in years. The man tilted his head, as if assessing my chances of success.

'What's to stop you being a real, full-time poet in this life?'

I shrugged. The softest murmur of thunder came rolling over the sea, and the air seemed to catch its breath. 'Life. Work. Being a real, full-time grown-up.'

'Oh yes.' He glanced at me with feeling. 'I know.'

My phone pinged again.

'It's my dad,' I explained. 'We were very close.'

It was the weirdest slip of the tongue. I meant *are*, not *were*, but before I could correct myself the man said, 'I was very close to my mother too.'

'Sorry,' I said. 'I meant *are*. We *are* close. My dad's still alive. Obviously. Given that he's just texted me.'

We stared at one another in confusion and I noted, once and for all, that the man's eyes were grey. My phone rang – Dad again – and the man said, 'Go ahead and answer; don't mind me.'

I sighed. Trust Dad to start worrying because I hadn't messaged him the second I stepped off the train. On the other hand, what if he was phoning for a reason? What if he'd hurt himself? Or if something had happened to Tom . . . ?

'Dad?'

'Oh, thank goodness, there you are. I was getting worried.'

'You didn't need to. Is everything all right?'

The man said, 'Do you think I might sketch you again sometime?' but bashfully, almost soundlessly. I didn't get it at first, not with Dad gabbling away in my ear about fish pie – 'So it says on the box to cook it from frozen, but I've gone and defrosted it' – and by the time I'd registered his question, and the need to answer, he'd turned away with a smile and a self-deprecating, bag-laden wave. I didn't call after him, because my attention had snagged on the uneven, white criss-cross of scars along his soft inner arm.

'Freya? Are you there? I'm sorry to go on about this fish pie.'

I talked competently about fish pie while I watched the man cross the road and disappear into a side street. The clouds muttered over the town and I shivered in the thunderous light. I hadn't asked for directions to Byrne Hall. I wasn't even sure he'd recognised me from the wedding. I wondered what he'd done to his arm, and when, and why.

'Was that thunder?' Dad said. 'Are you far from your B&B?'

'Not far.'

I turned in the direction of the harbour, where it seemed safe to assume I'd find the Harbour View Guest House, but my eye was drawn upwards, over the clustered masts, across the swing-bridge, into the wooded hills. There it was; there was Byrne Hall. Impossible to mistake the graceful white house with its pillared porch, and the tiered garden tumbling down through the trees like a wide, green river.

'I'll love you and leave you,' Dad was saying. 'Drop me a quick text once you've settled in.'

I nearly missed the entrance to the drive. It was only because I stopped to shake a stone from my shoe that I noticed the two mossy gate-posts, half hidden in the undergrowth. On top of each post there was a stone raven – one headless; both badly pocked and weather-stained – and to one side, underneath a fringe of ivy, a shabby sign that read BYRNE HALL. NO TRESPASSING.

Ravens on the gate-posts and an encroaching thunderstorm: Stella would have laughed. I would have laughed too, if I hadn't been alone.

The thunder sounded strange as I set off into the woods, like a bass note coming up out of the earth, and nothing to do with the sky at all. The trees that arched over the driveway met in the middle, so I was protected from the rain when it began spotting the leaves with fat, heavy drops. The faster the rain fell, the darker and cooler it got under all that greenery, but my jacket was in my suitcase, and I'd left my suitcase by the gate.

It seemed silly to turn back, when the snaking lane kept luring me around another corner, and another, until the house began to appear through the trees in flashes of white, and the woods began to thin, giving way to shrubberies and lawns. I kept imagining I was being followed, and with every little noise – the snap of a twig, the chuck-chuck of a pheasant, the clatter of wings in a beech tree – I would turn and wait a moment, half hopeful, half afraid, just to be sure.

What of the family that occupied Byrne Hall? What would they make of me and my questions? I hadn't given enough thought to that; I'd spent too much time fantasising that the house would be vacant. It was a long shot – I knew it was a long shot – but what if the owners were away? What if they only lived at Byrne Hall now and then? It was August, after all – holiday season – and it had *looked* pretty empty, the other weekend, despite all the fuss about privacy. It hadn't felt like a home. What if I could sneak inside and have the emptiness to myself for one night – maybe two? I could picture myself so clearly in a high-ceilinged bedroom facing the garden, my notebooks spread out on the floor. There would be dust dancing in a shaft of sunlight, and the sound of the sea outside my window, and words would find me in the stillness, the way they always used to do.

I emerged on to the edge of the gravel, pumps muddy, clothes wet. My eyes strayed from window to window and round the pillars of the porch, and I noticed that all the blinds were lowered, as they had been at the wedding, except for one on the ground floor which was half raised. The pale smudge of someone's face was visible for a moment, pressed up against the glass, and I swore under my breath.

There was no doorbell, as far as I could see. The rope and the STRICTLY PRIVATE sign had gone, but the double doors were firmly shut. I knocked, but the sound didn't resonate.

'Hello?' The doors changed the timbre of my voice, making me sound faint and frightened.

I pushed the wet hair out of my eyes and looked back across the lawn. The wedding marquee was stark white against the black sky, its ropes and canvas panels flapping in the wind. Some of the fairy lights had come unhooked from the trees and swung in drunken loops a few inches from the ground.

I knocked again, but nobody came.

The rain stung my head as I made my way round the side of the house. Unlike the snow-white frontage, these walls hadn't been painted in a long, long time. Blocked drainpipes dripped rust-coloured water, and there were green stains on the flaky render. Many of the windows were cracked and a few were smashed, though only one was patched with a half-hearted square of cardboard. There were dandelions and chickweeds in the gutters, and roof-tiles half buried in the jungly grass.

I ploughed on and managed to make a circuit of the house. It wasn't easy, what with the broken plant pots underfoot, and elbow-high nettles, and a trailing bramble that ripped a line all the way along my knuckles – and I didn't even find another entrance. There was a kitchen door, but the hinges were thick with cobwebs and ivy, and there didn't seem much point in knocking.

By the time I'd fought my way round to the final side of the house, my clothes were plastered to my skin and my hand was bleeding. I could hear the wind buffeting the trees and I wanted to hide. I was six years old again, and the storm was a bounding, flashing-fanged monster with a taste for human flesh.

'Idiot,' I muttered, stooping to unpick a bramble from the hem of my jeans, and a voice seemed to answer me from the front of the house. I froze. There it was again: a voice that rang and dwindled and spun in the wind, fragile as a feather.

'Who's there?' it called. 'Who is it? Who's there?'

Diana stands at a ground-floor window awaiting the return of her son. It might ease her mind if she could hobble from room to room, window to window, but it hurts too much to walk. The illness she suffers is a greedy one, eating her up from the inside, and she is confident it will kill her before the year is out.

Cory has only gone to town for groceries, but she misses him as if he's gone to boarding school again, or college. As if he's dead. Oh, how she misses him! She presses her nose against the rain-speckled glass and murmurs prayers for his safe return. If it weren't for her illness she would do all the household chores. Cory shouldn't be wheeling a trolley up and down supermarket aisles; he has better, brighter things to be getting on with. Diana conceives of these 'better, brighter things' in the vaguest possible way. She doesn't mean the wedding venue business, even if it is their only source of income at present.

She clutches at the handle of her walking stick and knocks her forehead against the glass. The moment she spots him coming up the drive she will turn away from this window, with its unkind reflections, and pretend she's been relaxing on the sofa.

Diana avoids mirrors as much as possible. It's horrible, seeing herself so changed – especially the hair. The hair breaks her heart. She touches a streak of naked scalp: first in the glass, then on her actual head. When Cory was little he'd wait for his father to leave the house in the morning, before padding along to her room in pyjamas and slippers. He'd sit on her knee at the dressing table – sleepy eyed and milky skinned – stroking her hair with the silver-backed brush, twisting it round his fingers, patting it down, wrapping it round his own neck, like a silky scarf.

She often remembers those mornings – the slamming of the front door; the starting of the car and its fading down the drive; Cory's slippered feet along the corridor. The two of them would place kisses – tiny, bird-like pecks – on one another's bruises, as if that were an amusing thing to do. As if it were a funny game they wouldn't have missed for the world.

Diana squeezes her eyes shut against the pain and breathes through clenched teeth. Come home, Cory. *Never mind bread and tinned soup and wine – or whatever it is he thinks they need. Never mind tablets from the chemist, which make no odds anyway.* Come home, my dove, my darling.

When Diana opens her eyes, there's someone on the edge of the woods, but the 'Thank you, God' dies on her lips. She backs away from the window; opens her dry mouth; tries to call out; remembers she's alone in the house.

The red-haired girl shoulders her bag and starts walking across the gravel.

It's good that I'm alone, *Diana thinks.* It's for the best. We can deal with this invasion together, the house and I. We can sort it out before Cory gets back.

51

A moment later the girl is banging on the door and shouting, 'Hello?'

'Hello.' Diana's reply mists the window. She thought she was perfectly at home with fear, but this is different.

The pain roars when she moves, but move she must. The house laughs in its lugubrious fashion – like wind tumbling down a chimney – as Diana grunts her way across the hall to the front door. 'I hear you,' she mutters, because after all these years it doesn't seem strange to talk to Byrne Hall. 'Don't you laugh at me.'

She wrestles the door open and squints into the rain. The girl is nowhere to be seen, but it's too much to hope she's gone.

'Who's there?' Diana calls. 'Who is it? Who's there?'

5

THE WOMAN TIGHTENED HER GRIP on her walking stick, and the knuckles gleamed like inlaid pearls on the backs of her hands. She was sheltering under the porch with the double doors ajar at her back, and I suppose I must have been quite a sight, materialising round the side of the house without warning, my hair hanging over my face in wet ropes. She opened her mouth to speak, but no sound came out.

'Oh . . .' I said, raking my hand through my hair, unsure if she could hear me over the pelting of the rain. 'Hello.'

She was small and frail, but there was something grand about her too. Everything about her – from her blood-red shoes and coffee-coloured blouse to her ebony walking stick and ruby ring – looked expensive and well made, if a little faded and uncomfortable. The same could be said for her face and hands. Her dyed hair had been scraped back in a ballerina's bun, and her scalp was visible between the thin, reddish strands.

'Go away,' she said, and when I took another step forwards her face contorted. 'Go away! *Go away!*'

'It's all right!' I smiled awkwardly and made as if to touch her arm. It was the most tentative of gestures, but she crumpled as if I'd punched her. I had to seize her by the elbows to keep her from falling, and my wet fingers made dark, spreading marks on her silk sleeves.

'It's *all right*!'

I shouldn't have shouted, but I was frightened by her fear. I think she might have fainted for a second, but I managed to keep her on her feet, and when she came round she seemed calmer. Perhaps she was simply ill; perhaps that explained everything. She was certainly fragile – alarmingly so – a tissue-paper cut-out of a human being. When she leaned on me and held on to my arm, I felt as if my slightest movement might make her crease, or tear, or whirl off on the wind.

'Please go away,' she whispered, her fingers convulsing like a cat's claws. A spasm shuddered through her body and echoed in my own bones, and there wasn't much I could do except stand there and let her lean on me till it passed. She didn't make a sound, unless you count the quick, whistling breaths she drew through her nose.

'Tell me what to do,' I said. 'Is there someone I can call?'

She closed her eyes and shook her head.

I placed a nervous hand around her waist and turned her so that she was facing the house.

'At least let me help you inside.'

She shook her head slowly, sadly, from side to side. I thought she was going to put up a fight, but she gave in with a feather-weight shrug and not another word.

It was dark in the entrance hall; however much I widened my eyes and peered I could barely see the chequered floor at my feet.

'Over there,' she breathed, indicating another door, and we hobbled towards it, my wet pumps squeaking and squelching on the tiles. She hung off my arm, fluttering like a chrysalis on the cusp of disintegration.

'Here,' she said. 'In here.'

The blinds were half drawn in one window and fully drawn in the other, but I could see well enough to help her to the sofa. She eased her shoes off and lay down with a graceful stiffness, like an aged cat. Not that she was old. Sixty? Sixty-five? Perhaps less. It was pain, not age, that defined her face and body, and not just fleetingly, on the surface, but deep down in the sharpness of her bones, and the hang of her flesh, and the heaviness of her eyelids.

'Water,' she said, closing her eyes, and I rummaged for the bottle in my handbag.

I know I'd been fantasising about large, empty spaces, but I was shocked by the bareness of this room. There was none of the usual stately home stuff that you see in museums – no family portraits, no matching sets of leather-bound books, no pianoforte. Aside from the sofa there was nothing at all; although you could see where things used to be. It was as if the place had been plundered. There were bleached patches on the peeling, pink walls where paintings used to hang, and grubby marks where the backs of armchairs used to press, and unvarnished floorboards where there used to be carpets. Cobwebs dangled from the light fittings and swung in the draught from the door. I shivered as the blinds darkened, and the rain came on more heavily than before.

The woman squeezed a pill from a foil strip and gulped it down, before fishing a tissue out of her sleeve and scrunching it against the moist corners of her mouth. She pressed hard, but it didn't stop her hand from shaking.

'Shall I get you some more water?'

She shook her head, angling her body away from me as if my presence oppressed her. I moved back into the shadows at the corner of the room.

'Go home now,' she said, fixing her eyes on the tissue as she stroked it flat across her lap. 'I don't care who you are, or why you think you ought to be here, or any of that. I don't care if you think I'm being rude, there isn't time—'

A bang made us both jump. I knew it was the front door flying open, because the draught made our own door drift ajar, and the sitting room was suddenly alive with the chilly scents and sounds of the outside. The woman stopped speaking abruptly, and forgot to close her mouth.

'Darling!' she said as the man came in, dropping his bags in the doorway. Her tone was difficult to interpret: it may have implied relief, or enthusiasm, or fear, or an uneasy fusion of all three. She tried to rise from the sofa, but he placed his hand on her shoulder so that she wouldn't get up.

I must have been surprised to see him again so soon – here, inside Byrne Hall of all places – but I don't remember being bowled over by astonishment. He fitted the place so well – as did the woman, in her own way – although it's hard to explain what I mean by that. Perhaps it was the way in which he moved through the imposing spaces of the house, without affording them a second glance. Or perhaps it was his appearance: the way he managed, like the house, to be self-possessed and scruffy at the same time. Either way, I felt pretty sure that I was not dealing with a pair of fellow would-be squatters. This was The Family – or part of it.

It wasn't my place to feel annoyed with them, for being at home in their own house, but at least I was entitled to feel annoyed with the man for finding my suitcase behind the gate and wheeling it up the hill. No doubt he'd wondered what it was doing hidden inside his driveway, and it had obviously come in handy as a trolley for his broken shopping bag, but still. I'd have to lug it all the way down again now.

'Give me a kiss,' said the woman, twisting the tissue in her restless hands. The man wavered for a moment before stooping over her head and giving it a peck. She glanced across at me while his head was bowed, and he must have sensed it, because he looked right at me as he straightened up.

'Darling.' This time her tone was one of patient warning. She sounded as though she were about to embark upon a long explanation, but of course she didn't have one, and she was forced to trail off.

'Hello,' said the man.

'Hello,' I said. 'Again.'

I couldn't read anything into his expression, for which I blamed the poor light. All I know is that he rested his clasped hands on the back of the sofa and looked at me keenly.

The awkwardness of the situation hit us both at the same time, and we masked the silence as best we could with introductions – he was Cory Byrne, she was Diana Byrne, they were mother and son.

'I left my suitcase by the gate,' I said.

We both looked at my suitcase. It seemed childish, standing there in the doorway with its pinks and purples, and its cartoon flowers.

'Yes. I brought it up . . .'

We lapsed into silence again, although it was hardly an adequate exchange of information on either side. Tissue shreds drifted on to Diana's lap, like a miniature fall of snow.

'You've met already?' she asked.

'Yes,' he said. 'In town.'

'I'd no idea you lived here!' I said. Cory ran his hand

through his rain-wet hair and smiled politely. Diana made no response at all.

The two of them seemed to flutter between me and the door, as pale and awkward as resident ghosts, their beautiful grey eyes fixed on me. I had to get away. I couldn't remember what I was doing here, except that I'd wanted to look at a picture that bore some, or little, or no resemblance at all to my sister. That was my most tangible reason for coming. All the less tangible ones were dissolving as rapidly as dreams in the light of day.

'Let me tell you why I came,' I said, 'and then I'll be out of your hair. You see, the thing is, my older sister—'

'Stella Lyell?' The name seemed to drop of its own accord from Cory's mouth, and Diana's fidgety hands fell still.

'I knew you reminded me of someone!' Cory threw me one of his almost-smiles, which fell again when he added, 'She went missing, didn't she? And they found her under the cliffs, just along from here. It was a big story in the local press.'

'Yes,' I said. 'It will be five years ago, in October.'

'Five years,' he echoed.

I thought he was going to apologise for speaking out of turn – people often apologised when they referred to Stella – but he didn't, and I was glad of it. There was too much whispery circumspection around Stella's name. She *had* gone missing round here, and she *had* died, and she *had* looked like me. They were facts; why should he be shy of stating them?

'Mum?' Cory moved his hand to his mother's shoulder. 'Do you remember Stella Lyell?'

Diana nodded, although she didn't seem entirely sure.

'But you only knew about her from the news?' I said. 'You didn't meet her in real life?'

The muscles squirmed along Diana's jaw-line. I wanted to look at him – not her – but my eyes kept straying. She was like a barrier stretched out between us. Her legs reminded me of boiled chicken bones, with the flesh all fallen away.

The room was getting darker by the second. It was different from the darkness that comes with night: harsher, somehow, and metallic. There was no birdsong, as there is at twilight, and the seething sound of the rain seemed to deepen, rather than disrupt, the electric silence.

'I didn't *know* her,' said Cory, 'but I did meet her once. She sat for a quick sketch, which I may have made into a painting . . . In fact, I'm almost sure I did.'

'She was very beautiful.'

I meant it as a bald statement of fact, but Cory said, 'Was she?' and I was struck by that. Everyone who met Stella in the flesh came away – one way or another – overwhelmed. Nobody, in my experience, was non-committal with regard to my sister.

'Did you talk to her?'

'Not much. Or if we did, I'm afraid I can't remember what we said. I just took a quick sketch and we parted, and a week or so later her photo was all over the local rag.'

'Oh.'

'Sorry.'

'No, no. I just . . .'

I thanked him, and went to the door to pick up my suitcase. I expressed my hope that Diana would be better soon – she made no reply – and suggested I'd better get going. Neither of them tried to stop me. One last look round the shadowy room, a quick glance at Cory's grey eyes, and I was on my way, trundling my suitcase across the chequer-board floor. I thought about calling him into the hall and showing him the space where the portrait had hung – but what was the point? Suddenly I wasn't especially keen to see it again, anyway.

The front door was wide open, and the rain was coming on wilder than ever, hissing into the gravel and sputtering over the edges of the gutters. I heard footsteps follow me out of the sitting room, and turned to look at him. The hall had been insubstantial before – all stillness and shadow – but it came alive as soon as Cory entered. He seemed larger and freer out here, touched by the stormy daylight, and I noticed how the rain had made his hair frizz and his skin gleam. I felt weedy and chilled in comparison.

'I'm sorry,' he repeated. I wasn't clear what he was apologising for, but I let it pass.

We stood looking out at the rain. I was going to be soaked through before I even reached the trees.

'If you don't mind waiting,' he said, 'I can try and find the picture I made of your sister?'

'It's OK.'

I should have said yes. Having failed to say yes I ought, in all politeness, to have made my final thank yous and goodbyes and gone away. Instead of which I stood and stared at the impossible fall of rain, as if I were waiting for someone to do something about it.

'You could stay here for the night?' Cory suggested. 'We're not exactly short of rooms.'

My hands shook, like they do when I drink too much strong coffee, so I stuck them in the back pockets of my jeans. There were so many sensible, Freya-ish answers ready and waiting on the tip of my tongue:

Thank you, but I'm booked into a guest house and I've already paid my deposit.

That's so kind, but I suspect your mother will have other ideas.

Many thanks, but I was not brought up to accept overnight invitations from strange men.

'I don't know,' I said, after a decent pause. 'Are you sure?'

They think they're whispering discreetly; they think the rain will disguise what they're saying out there in the hall. Well, they're wrong. The house is listening and Diana herself can hear – if not individual words then the tenor of them; the subterranean meanings of which her son and his flame-haired friend are themselves only half aware.

The sofa creaks beneath her as the pain takes another savage bite, but Cory doesn't sense it the way he normally would. He doesn't pop his head round the door and say, 'Mum?' He is too busy urging the girl to stay. It's almost – almost – funny.

Once upon a time, Diana herself stood on the chequered floor of the hall, and a man bent over her saying, 'Stay.'

The house was beautiful in those days, brimming with richness and light. It is beautiful now, but only on the outside, like a rosy-faced apple with a maggot inside. The man knew it would sway her, if anything would; he knew it was his only hope.

'This house will belong to you, if you marry me,' said Mr Byrne. 'Just think about that.'

'God, it's like being in a Jane Austen novel,' she quipped, but he looked blank and she remembered that he never read fiction.

Back in Kensington, amongst her friends, it was common knowledge how things stood. 'Look at him,' Diana would say, slit-eyed, through a cloud of cigarette smoke, and they would all turn dutifully to look him up and down. 'He's got no sense of humour and no culture, and he always wears a tie, and he manages to be good-looking without having any sex appeal whatsoever. Do you know what I mean?' She would grimace and shudder, and all her friends would laugh and say yes, they knew exactly what she meant. He never said anything in his own defence, and it was hard to tell whether he minded her jibes or not. If he minded, why did he always show up to the next party, and the next, his tie more carefully knotted than ever?

Mr Byrne – her friends went by their Christian names, but he was always Mr Byrne – kept inviting her to stay at his ancestral home in Devon, and she kept saying no, until one day she felt especially rootless and bored and said yes.

He showed her every room, from attic to cellar, in his efforts to persuade her. She longed to say something cutting, but it wasn't so easy without her friends there to egg her on, and anyway, Byrne Hall had rendered her speechless. The Georgians and Victorians on the walls, the antique books, the furniture, the gardens, the woods, the views, the sheer scale of the place. They meandered from room to room – she in her gypsy dress and sandals, he with his jacket and tie and his hand on the small of her back – and as she took it all in she made rapid calculations in her head.

On the one hand, she disliked Mr Byrne.

On the other hand, she didn't like anyone much. Or rather, she liked people en masse, at parties, and she liked the way she saw herself through their eyes, but she didn't like anyone in particular. There was a general idea, amongst her friends and the world at large, that Love was the be-all and end-all of life, but she took this to be a cliché.

'What you've never known, you'll never miss,' as one of her nannies used to say – she forgets which; there were several.

'All right!' Diana said it with a little shrug. 'I'll marry you.'

She tried to move past him into the garden – she wanted to see those roses again – but Mr Byrne blocked her way and kissed her. Her mouth hurt afterwards, and she could feel the imprint of his fingers on her arms long after he'd let go, but she made a decision not to mind. She owed him something in return, she supposed.

Cory and the girl are still talking in the hall. He has asked her to stay overnight, and she has hummed and hawed and said yes, and now they are both wondering what exactly she's said yes to, whilst pretending that they're not wondering anything of the sort. Diana listens, grey-faced, struck by the accommodating softness of their voices.

6

Hi Dad, all well but slight change of plan – I'm staying at
Byrne Hall!! Long story but I'll give you a ring tomorrow.
Hope the fish pie worked out OK. Lots of love F xxxxx

Mine was a first-floor bedroom at the front of the house, large
and sparsely furnished, with two sash windows that overlooked the sea. There was a four-poster bed without any
curtains, and a wooden chair where I'd draped my wet things.
That was all. It was eerily close to the room I'd created in
my imagination, albeit without the dusty shafts of sunlight.
At first I sat politely on the edge of the mattress, waiting
for Cory to return with sheets and blankets – but he didn't
come.

My stomach rumbled as I paced the room, the floorboards
wobbling and yielding against my bare feet. It must have
been over an hour since he'd gone. I'd changed into a dry
sundress, but I could still smell the rain in my hair and on
my arms.

Hi Tom, hope you're OK. I read Dad's article before I left
and spent most of the morning feeling cross with him
and worrying about you.

I clicked my tongue impatiently and pressed delete. I
couldn't think what to say to Tom – how to act and sound – a

problem I'd never experienced before. It hurt to think of him being hurt, and why should I put up with that? There ought to be a way of deleting awkward conversations from your mind. There ought to be a way of erasing the memory of particular people, and starting life all over again without them.

If my life were to begin right here, right now, I would make it a thing of such simplicity and promise. Such coherence.

I opened the blinds and wished Cory would come. The ragged edges of the sky had merged darkly with the sea and it looked later than it was. I sat on the chair for a while, leafing through my notebooks, but my old poems were as exhausted as my thoughts. I wished my breath didn't smell stale. I got my sponge-bag out and smeared a blob of toothpaste round the inside of my mouth, though I wasn't convinced it would help.

The corridor was entirely dark. I hesitated, but Cory had been gone for ages and there was nothing wrong with going to find him. I wasn't being nosey. He might need a hand, carrying pillows and things.

I felt my way along the landing in what I thought was the direction of the stairs, but I wasn't sure. I turned back after a moment, but couldn't remember which was my room, so I changed my mind again and carried on.

Their whispered argument blended so well with the house that I almost missed it. I stopped just in time, clamping my hands over my mouth to muffle the sound of my own breathing. Diana was doing most of the talking. I couldn't catch much, but I knew she was upset by the way her voice kept rising in high-pitched spikes.

'Shh,' Cory kept saying. 'Shh.'

'Darling, you of all people should see—'

'Oh, don't give me that!' Cory's voice was heated. 'Since when have you been superstitious?'

'Cory, I'm begging you, I'm ordering you—'

'No. You don't get to order me anymore.' He struggled to soften his voice. 'You're ill. Stop fretting.'

In shrinking back against the wall, I banged my shoulder against a switch, and a dull light washed along the landing. Diana's mouth slackened when she saw me, and Cory jumped. His arms were full of blankets and pillows.

'I'm sorry,' I said. 'I wasn't eavesdropping, I was just . . . I couldn't find the light switch.'

One of the pillows fell to the floor, so I picked it up, and Cory deposited the rest of the bedding in my arms.

'My mother's tired,' he said. 'She's not well. Give me two minutes to get her settled.'

I nodded.

Diana shrank when Cory touched her arm. He glanced at me over her head, his smile a little clownish, as if he were trying to make light of a sad situation. I couldn't help liking that look, and the tentative way it made an 'us' out of him and me.

'Come on,' he said – addressing her but watching me.

I stood with the bundle of bed-clothes in my arms as Cory steered his mother away. The further they got from the landing light, the more they seemed to merge with one another, so that by the time they started up the stairs to the second floor they'd become a single creature, hunched and improbable, with four ill-matched legs and two heads.

'Goodnight!' I called as an afterthought, but neither of them seemed to hear me.

*

'So, your father,' Cory said. 'Would that be Robert Lyell? The art critic?'

I'd switched the light on, and my bedroom had become a harsh patchwork of yellow light and black shadow, with no in-between shades. I was unfolding a blanket and Cory was shrugging a pillowcase over a pillow.

'The art critic,' I echoed, struggling to throw the blanket over the bed. 'Yes, that's right, he writes for the *London Globe*. How did you know?'

Cory shoved awkwardly at the pillow. 'I just remember, from when your sister was all over the news.'

'Oh yes, of course.'

I'd been getting on all right with the bed-making until Cory came in and I lost the knack. I couldn't get the blanket straight, and even when I did I kept fidgeting with it – tucking in corners that were already tucked and smoothing out non-existent wrinkles. I'd started hating my dress as well, the same way I hated my childish suitcase. The dress was cheap and shabby, with its crumples and its ditsy flowers, and every time I bent down it rode up and showed the backs of my knees.

Cory tossed the pillow on to the bed and picked up one of my notebooks from the chair – the orange exercise book I'd been leafing through before I went to find him. I made a faint gesture of protest as he smoothed his hand over the cover, but when he apologised and offered to hand it over, I didn't take it away.

'They're just poems,' I said. 'I wrote them ages ago, years ago, before Stella died. I thought if I re-read them it might get me going again, but I don't know. They all seem so thin and corny.'

'I understand,' he said. 'It's the same with me and my paintings. It's like they were done by a different person.'

His thumb rifled the page corners and I itched to take the book back.

'Will you let me look inside?' he said. 'Please? I'll let you laugh at my old paintings.'

No, I thought. But if I said no, a veil would fall between us – he would be suitably courteous and contrite, and I'd never get to know what I'd lost.

'OK.'

I turned away and finished making the bed, while Cory turned the pages.

'I was very much into abstract nouns at one point,' I said, in the hope that he couldn't listen to me prattle and read at the same time. *'Lone Despair weeps on her sunless isle*, and stuff like that . . .'

I hoped he had found 'Lone Despair', or similar, because although it was a terrible poem, it was also fairly impersonal. *Please God, let there not be any Tom poems in the orange exercise book.*

'Who's Tom?' he said.

I gave up on the bed and leapt across the room, so that I could read over his shoulder.

'Oh no, no, no!' I reached round and prised the book out of his hands. 'Tom's just a family friend,' I said. 'My parents were friends with his parents. He's a curator at the Wingate Gallery.'

'A family friend? Really?'

I suppose I looked surprised, or uncomprehending, because Cory added in an undertone, 'I'm only teasing you.'

Teasing is such a light word, and so lightly meant, but it was the word I took, and turned over, and thought about most that evening. I'd forgotten what it was like to tease or be teased, but from the moment Cory said it I wanted to remember.

I was glad we didn't eat in the kitchen: it was a big, cold, loveless barn of a room. 'We don't cook much,' Cory explained, when he saw my shiver. 'Mum doesn't have any appetite, and when it's only me . . .' The plastic shopping bags were by the door waiting to be unloaded, so Cory emptied everything on to the kitchen table and we cobbled together a picnic from sliced bread, peanut butter, tortilla chips, KitKats, under-ripe bananas and a bottle of white wine.

'All right?' said Cory, as he heaped everything on to a tray and added a couple of glasses.

'Very all right.'

'We'll take it to my room. It's nicer in there.'

'Your room, as in your *studio*?' I wanted him to remember his promise to show me some of his artwork.

'Yeah, well.' Cory laughed, a little sadly. '*Former* studio.'

When I first saw Cory's room, I thought of those Arabian Nights tales where genies whisk palaces from one corner of the globe and set them down in another. I suppose you might call it a cheap effect if you were being detached about it. Light two dozen candles and place them in clusters around a large, untidy room – which is what we did, with a box of matches each, once Cory had set the tray down on the floor – and of course the shadows will come to life, and the dirt will turn to gold dust, and the bare plaster will look as if it's been gilded. I didn't want to be detached, though. I fell for it willingly.

'Look at this place!' I said. 'It's *waiting*. It's waiting for you to take up art again, and bring it back to life.'

'Do you think?'

'I do!'

Aside from a few oddments of furniture, every single object in the room was art-related: leggy easels, rolls of canvas, jars of brushes, boxes overflowing with masking tape and mannequins, bulldog clips and string; even the floorboards were streaked and freckled with paint. I wondered how long it had been since he touched them; beneath the flattering glow of the candlelight the place felt sad and neglected. It didn't smell of inspiration – by which I mean it didn't smell of oily rags, or paint, or turpentine, or coffee, or glue. There was a fuzz of dust along the top of every canvas, and here and there the candle flames picked out a spider's web, stretching like a mesh of copper wire from one picture frame to the next.

We spread a rug on the floor and threw cushions on top. There was a midnight enchantment in the air, though it can't have been late, and it reminded me of when Stella and I were little, and we made dens out of our duvets when we were supposed to be asleep. Cory sat cross-legged in the middle of the rug and I knelt opposite, pulling my dress as low as it would go over my knees.

'Here,' he said, 'have something to eat while I open the wine.' His voice had gone quiet, as if we were doing something illicit; risking discovery at any moment.

'So,' he whispered, passing me a full glass. 'You were telling me about your dad, and poetry-writing, and Tom.'

'Was I?'

Oh Lord, what exactly had he gleaned from that orange exercise book? I couldn't see his expression. The nearest candle was guttering, and the shadows round his mouth and eyes flickered so rapidly that his face altered half a dozen times a second. One moment his smile was light and jokey, the next it was tender, or serious, or searching.

'Honestly, Cory . . .' I wanted to be cross, but I found myself laughing instead. 'Don't take those poems seriously. I know they sound febrile, but I wrote them a long time ago. Tom isn't – wasn't . . .'

Cory was watching me, waiting; I wasn't used to such interest and encouragement when I talked. I twisted my glass by the stem, mesmerised by the way the candlelight glanced off the liquid: now flashing, now glowing, now fading to nothing.

'I was a *little bit* in love with Tom, once,' I confessed. 'Stella and I both had a thing for him when we were in our teens. He's about five years older than me, and we'd known him since we were small, but he got married and his wife left him after only a few months, and it made him seem so, I don't know . . .'

I petered out. The whole thing was dark and complicated all those years ago when Dad let Tom sleep on our sofa, and we lay awake listening to the murmur of voices downstairs. Tom on the phone, Tom talking to Dad, Tom talking to himself. More than once, we heard him cry. It seemed silly now to have desired him so much, just because someone else had made him suffer. It was adolescent.

'Anyway, let's not talk about it.' I sat up straight and pushed my hair off my face. 'It seems so long ago. He's just Tom again now.'

Cory rose to his feet, and my imagination quailed for a moment. He looked overly tall when he was standing up – his

71

shadow heightened the effect by quivering up the walls and looming over the ceiling – but he was only crossing the room to raise the blind and open the window. The sash rattled up and the night breathed in on us, damp, cool and earthy. Some of the candles shivered and went out. The storm had passed, but the dripping in the woods sounded like fresh rainfall, and water was spattering from the gutters and smacking on to the gravel down below. The hairs stood up on my arms with a pleasurable chill, and Cory stretched his arms as if he'd just woken up.

'Can I draw you?'

Before I'd even answered, he was upturning piles of papers and boards, flipping through sketch-books and folders, rummaging for pencils.

'Only if you show me some of your old pictures.'

He froze.

'You did promise. You said if I showed you my poems—'

'Yes. So I did.'

He dusted his hands uneasily down his shirt and glanced round the room. There were dozens of canvases on every side – some in frames, all with their faces turned coyly to the wall – but he paid them no attention.

'Wait a moment,' he said, 'let me think . . .'

I got to my feet as he turned a few, reluctant pages in one of the smaller sketch-books, and approached one of the large canvases. I only touched the edge of it with my fingertips – I wasn't going to turn it round without his say-so – but he grabbed my wrist.

'Not that one!'

For a split-second I was scared, and he was scared, but it was over too quickly to be real.

'Here, look at these,' he said, and I thought he hadn't *grabbed* me by the wrist, as such. He'd only touched me to draw my attention to the sketch-book.

I took it from his hands and tried not to glance in the direction of the canvas.

'Oh, yes.' I turned the pages shakily and nodded. 'Very nice.'

They were drawings of Byrne Hall as viewed from the garden, and he must have done them in winter because the trees and shrubs were all bare and twisted. It was a different house from the one in my head, but it was also the same.

'So, *can* I draw you?' he said, when I'd finished looking.

'Yes, if you like.'

I sat down again on the rug, while Cory went round the room gathering pencils and sticks of charcoal.

'Did you study art at college?'

'No. Well, once, but I chucked it in after a couple of terms. Waste of time.' He touched his chest with the flat of his hand. 'It's all in here, isn't it, if it's anywhere? Same as you and your poetry.'

I nodded uncertainly and picked a flake of old paint off one of the floorboards.

'Which art college was it?' I wondered. 'Was it in London?'

'Oh.' He shrugged and turned away. 'No. You wouldn't have heard of it, it was . . . Ugh, damn it, I've broken another pencil lead. Hang on a minute while I just . . .'

Once he was ready he settled on the rug, with an A3 sketch-book open on his knees.

'Thank goodness for the house,' he said unexpectedly. I didn't understand; I was still thinking about art schools.

'What house?'

Cory flicked the sketch-book open and ran his palms in

slow circles over the clean sheet. The page was yellow in the candlelight – smooth, pure and inviting. It was like fresh snow at sunrise, when you stand at the back door and look down the garden, loath to mark it with your footprints yet longing to do exactly that.

'The house,' Cory repeated, as if he'd only just registered my voice. He raised his head and waved one arm loosely in the air. 'Byrne Hall. We have to live off weddings, now there's nothing left to sell.'

I thought he was joking and laughed, but he didn't join in.

'You *sold* all the contents?' I said. 'Everything?'

'Almost everything.' He shrugged. 'It was mostly stuff from my father's side of the family.'

He seemed transfixed by the empty page, peering at it closely for minutes on end before turning to a new one, as if he'd spotted some flaw. I watched him trace an invisible line with his thumb and wondered what he was picturing. A half-moon, perhaps. The supple trunk of a sapling. The shape of a face, from chin to ear.

'I wish you could see it as it used to be, when I was little,' he said.

'Byrne Hall?'

Cory nodded. 'We still had money in those days. All my mother's friends were artists – or in the art world – and they used to stay here whenever my father was away. It was still crammed with treasures – Persian rugs and harpsichords, and God knows what – and everyone was always drinking, and playing music and working. They were probably off their heads half the time, in and out of each other's beds, but I don't remember any unhappiness – I just remember the laughter, and the stupid games and the indoor picnics.

They used to do impromptu exhibitions in the downstairs rooms, and there were parties that went on for weeks . . .'

He trailed off.

Whenever my father was away, I thought, although what I actually said was, 'I bet they made a pet of you?'

'I suppose. But my mother was the main event; she was the one they all adored.'

The idyll – the memory of it – played across his face in light and shadow.

'And then . . . ?' I ventured.

'The money ran out,' he said, matter-of-factly, 'and my mother got ill.'

'And . . . what about your father?'

Cory retreated into himself and shook his head. He was quiet for so long that I began to worry my question had annoyed him, but he was simply far away, his thumb swirling around the clean page, making hidden pictures.

'How would you like me to sit?' I spoke carefully, afraid of making him jump.

'Sit?' Cory resurfaced. 'Oh, sit however you like. You need to be comfortable, though.'

There was a double mattress in the darkest corner of the room; a shadowy tumble of pillows and duvet, which I'd noticed when I first came in and avoided looking at since. Cory turned to it now, chewing his lip.

'Why don't you lie down?' he said. 'You'll feel less constrained that way, and it doesn't matter to me if you doze off.'

I straightened the bedding and lay down awkwardly on my side. Cory placed a couple of tall candles near my head, and a whole cluster of tea lights on the floor. Every time he turned his back I adjusted my posture slightly, or scratched my nose, or fidgeted with some detail of my dress. He caught me at it, of course, and laughed.

'Here.' He raised my face by half an inch and slid my hand beneath it. He arranged the fingers of my other hand so that they were curled under my chin, and he stroked my fringe away from my forehead and laid a lock of hair across my shoulder. I was tense to start with, but he was patient and light of touch, and knew exactly what he wanted. I breathed into the jumble of sheets, silently coaxing my muscles into looseness as he worked his fingers round the crook of my left knee, bending it towards him.

By the time he was finished, I'd softened under his hands like a lump of wax, and my body felt warm and drowsy. This was precisely the position I would adopt if I were trying to go to sleep – one arm across my chest, the other cushioning my head, and my legs a little bent at hip and knee. The candlelight was heavy and still in that corner of the room, far from the draughty window, and I hoped it beautified me the way it beautified him: making his eyes gleam, and turning his skin the colour of set honey.

He sat close to the mattress with the sketch-book on his lap and began drawing with delicate caution. Every time he raised his head to look at me, his pencil hand would pause as if awaiting fresh instructions from his eyes.

I couldn't see what he was doing from where I lay, so I watched his face instead. After the first few strokes of the pencil his expression changed; he stopped evaluating me as if I were a problem, and his face lit up with a kind of grace. I kept expecting him to say something corny – tell me I was pretty or whatever – but he didn't speak, and the pressure to laugh slowly eased, like a weight lifting off my chest.

Stella throws my window wide open, despite the wind and rain, and I sit up in bed with a squeak of protest. She can't seem to do anything low-key tonight – not since Tom turned up on our doorstep around ten o'clock, ashen faced, with his wife's goodbye note in his hand. Everything Stella has done since, she's done with emphasis: hurling open the window, tossing her hair off her face, striding around my poky room as if it were a stage-set.

'The rain's coming in,' I say, and this is annoying because my English coursework notes are on the windowsill. I suppose it's petty to think about A-levels, though, in the context of Tom's ordeal.

'Who cares!' Stella flings her arms wide and lifts her chin, as if she is about to sing an aria, and if her nightie were longer she would make the perfect leading lady. Her nightie is black, with just the right amount of satin sheen and lace trim, and the thin straps leave her shoulders bare. I suppose her hands aren't exactly a heroine's – since she started her course at the college they've gone grey and powdery, and there is always clay beneath her fingernails – but they are barely visible in this light.

'I hope Tom will be all right,' I say, shivering in my penguin pyjamas. It was horrible, hearing him cry; worse than I could ever have imagined. I wonder what Dad has said to comfort him. I hope he hasn't talked too much. I hope he hasn't said, 'Things could be worse,' or 'Cheer up!' or 'At least you and Natalie hadn't got round to starting a family.'

The voices fall silent at last, and I hear Dad coming upstairs to bed. Stella and I made up the sofa bed earlier on, and Stella found a new toothbrush in the bathroom cupboard. I put a pile of books on the coffee table in case Tom couldn't sleep, but Stella said that was stupid – 'He's not going to feel like <u>reading</u>, you numpty!' – so I took them away again.

A rainy gust sends my coursework fluttering across the carpet. Stella slams the window shut with a 'Grrr!' as if I've moaned at her, although I haven't said a word.

'Look at us!' she says. 'Whispering and twittering in your bedroom like two little girls! Like children!'

'We've hardly talked at all,' I protest. 'It's just been you stomping about and acting weird.'

'I'm going downstairs,' she says.

I click my lamp on and swing my legs out of bed.

'Oh, no, no, no,' says Stella. 'You're staying here. There's no need for a delegation.'

I don't argue – you don't argue with Stella when she's in certain moods – and she pats me on the head. There are goose-pimples all over her arms and legs, and across the top of her breasts, but she shakes her head when I offer her my dressing gown.

When she's gone, I get out of bed to collect up my papers, and I keep popping on to the landing to listen. I can't hear anything. As I'm picking up the last sheet, Stella comes traipsing back upstairs to my room.

'That was quick,' I say. 'Is he all right? Is he asleep?'

She shrugs, pulling at her lower lip, and ambles over to the window. We can hear the rain blowing against the glass.

'It's cold,' says Stella, as if she's only just noticed.

She climbs into my bed without asking, and we sleep back to back for warmth. At first I assume she's here because *she wants to talk, but she doesn't say anything – not even goodnight.*

I feel cold, pressed up against the wall; we're too big to fit comfortably in a single bed. I'd planned to lie on my back with my hands behind my head and think about Tom on the sofa downstairs. Nothing sensational was going to happen in my going-to-sleep dream: I was just going to ask Tom if he would like a book, and he was going to thank me for my discernment and say that a book was exactly what he would *like, after which we'd have a conversation, ostensibly about reading, in which everything we said – and didn't say – shimmered with erotic subtext.*

A Tom-themed going-to-sleep fantasy is impossible with Stella in my bed, however, and it isn't just a question of physical space. Everything my sister sets her heart on becomes hers; she even has a monopoly on dreams.

Of course, she would protest that this is nonsense – that it's all in my head – but so what if it is? It comes to the same thing in the end.

7

Cory and I parted in the early hours and I sat alone in my room, at the foot of the four-poster bed. I picked up my phone and began a new message – *Hi Tom* – but there was too much to say, and I couldn't think it through in a text; it would be better to write in longhand. I found a biro at the bottom of my bag and tore some pages from one of my notebooks.

While I was thinking what to write, I rested my chin on my knees and looked out of the window. Sea and sky were still dark, but a silver fissure was beginning to grow along the line where they met. *What a picture of calm*, I thought, with the slightest of smiles. My body was weightless, as if the blood and bone had dissolved and been replaced with light and air. If I'd cut my finger just then I swear it wouldn't have bled; it would have oozed a pearly translucence to match the streak of dawn on the water.

Dear Tom,
I have to tell somebody, and you are the only person

No. I scribbled it out and started on a fresh page.

Dear Tom,
A proper letter seems funny, doesn't it? Actual paper and ink – well, biro! I was going to send you a text, but there's so much to say, and it feels more natural like this.

I keep thinking about the last time I saw you, and how difficult it was. I hate to think you're sad – and because of me, of all people! – when I am so suddenly and unexpectedly happy.

I also want to say how sorry I am for being moody and nightmarish – not so much then – although certainly then – but generally. You're a good friend to me and Dad, and we take you too much for granted. I don't know why you've put up with us for so long – but I'm glad you have!

I'd been waiting all my life – well, a long time anyway – for you to kiss me in the garden on a summer's night. So why – why, oh why – when the moment finally came, did it fall flat? I've been asking myself this question over and over again, and the answer has occurred to me tonight – which kind of explains why I'm writing this letter.

The fact is – and please don't take this the wrong way – the fact is that I was unresponsive because I was only half alive. I have been dying inside my old life – and by old life, I mean my life before yesterday; before I came to Byrne Hall – for years, and you are an elemental part of that old life. This sounds mean and insulting, but it's not supposed to. Nothing is your fault.

I paused and pressed my fingers to my forehead. I was too drunk to be writing letters; I wouldn't normally gabble like this. My eyelids drooped and I sat still, listening to the soft flicker of my own pulse.

Last night – or this night, whatever you want to call it – when Cory was sketching, I'd lain in a state of perpetual drowsiness, ringed by candles, never fully awake and never quite dropping off. They were some of the strangest hours I've ever lived, especially during the long ellipses when neither of us felt the need to speak. Time had seemed to stretch itself, or perhaps it shrank – at any rate, it dithered and lost its usual, purposeful, forward-marching beat. There had been spots of yellow light in front of my eyes, which sometimes looked like candles and sometimes looked like stars, and beyond them Cory's gigantic silhouette, and all the time I was conscious of the sweeping sound of pencil on paper, and the scritch of my hair on the pillow when I adjusted my head, and the rise and fall of our breathing.

'I remember you from one of the wedding parties,' he said at some point. 'You were in the garden, by the pond.'

He hadn't spoken in ages, but I wasn't startled. Cory's voice was like the darkness, intrinsic to the night, and I murmured a wordless reply.

'And then, later on, you went to sleep on the hall floor.'

I opened my eyes, but I was careful not to move. I knew he was drawing my neck because I could feel his gaze wandering round my throat and exploring the shadows under my chin. It was like having a butterfly walk over my skin.

'You looked like a mermaid in that long, green dress,' he said. 'You looked as if you'd been washed up by the sea and stranded on the tiles.'

I smiled. It didn't occur to me to apologise for trespassing; it was too late for all that. If there was anything to forgive, he had surely forgiven me by now.

'Before I fell asleep,' I said, 'I thought I saw your portrait of my sister.'

The pencil stopped moving across the page. I wanted to sit up and face him, but I didn't dare alter my posture.

'*Was* it her? She was on the back wall opposite the door – a girl with red hair – a kind of mosaic, with lots of ripped-up bits of paper all stuck together. When I woke up she'd disappeared, and I thought I must have dreamed her.'

The pencil began drifting over the paper again, making long, tender lines. The sound echoed on the surface of my skin, following the line of my jaw up to the base of my ear, and when I swallowed I knew he had noticed the dipping of my throat.

'It's possible,' Cory said. 'My mother's always moving pictures around, when she's well enough. Sometimes I think she's got nothing better to do.'

He drew a few strokes before closing the sketch-book with a sigh and stretching his arms above his head.

'I don't know about you, but I need to move. Come on.'

Cory retained my hand after helping me up, which was just as well because the landing was inky-black, and so was the staircase down to the hall. I thought he would switch a light on, but apparently he didn't need to see where he was going to move quickly and surely round the house.

I only knew we'd reached the entrance hall because I recognised the chill of the tiles under my bare feet, and the way the space made our voices ring, even though we were whispering. Cory led me forwards a few paces and reached upwards. An electric light stammered on-off-*on*: the same picture light that had died on me the other week. I suppose they'd replaced the bulb.

'Lady Caroline Augusta Fitzroy-Byrne,' said Cory. 'I take it she's not your sister's lookalike?'

I smiled slightly and shook my head.

'We had her valued a few years ago; thought she might turn out to be a Reynolds.'

'And?'

'Sadly for the bank balance – no.'

Lady Caroline's eighteenth-century gaze passed over our heads – pale, hooded and inscrutable. Presumably she'd had a coral-coloured mouth in the beginning to match her flowers, but the paint had faded over the years, leaving her with no lips and a couple of bleached roses clutched to her breast. The lap-dog looked several degrees livelier than its mistress: there was a slight sheen to its fur, and its eyes were like black cherries.

'She's supposed to have a look of my father,' said Cory. 'That's what people say. I can't remember and my mother doesn't keep any photos.'

I studied the painting again, searching for Cory himself, but there wasn't a trace in all that powdery pallor.

'Your father . . . ?' I ventured.

'Died when I was thirteen.'

'Oh!' I glanced at him. 'My mum died when I was five.'

Cory's grip tightened on my hand, but I wasn't sure if it was just a tic, or if he meant something by it.

'She had cancer,' I added with an awkward shrug, and he turned his face a fraction towards mine.

'My father drowned,' he said. 'He took his sailing boat out . . .'

I waited for him to finish the sentence, but he never did.

'Do you miss him?'

Cory hesitated and cleared his throat.

'No . . . I don't know. My father wasn't really a kind man, but I suppose I loved him, in some strange way. I expect your mother was a good person, wasn't she? I expect you miss her?'

'Yes. I don't remember her very well, but yes.'

We stood side by side, contemplating Lady Caroline, and

this time when he squeezed my hand I knew it was deliberate. It felt wrong – being so happy, I mean, in the wake of such a sad exchange – but I couldn't help it. I'd have squeezed his hand in reply if I could, but my fingers were trapped inside his, and I couldn't so much as wiggle my thumb.

'My world has shrunk so much since Stella died,' I said. It didn't quite follow from what we'd been talking about, but it seemed to make sense to Cory.

'Mine too,' he said, 'since I grew up, and my mother fell ill, and life stopped looking so . . .'

'. . . so promising.'

'Yes.'

The thing that made me happy – ludicrously happy – was the way we went into the garden without discussion, as if we had one mind between us. Cory didn't say, 'Would you think I was weird if I suggested going outside right now?' and I didn't say, 'Hang on, it's dark and wet out there and I'm not wearing any shoes.' We just went, strolling at first, then walking quickly, then running.

There was a moon, and the fiery-gold garden I remembered from the wedding had been reconstructed in silver and black. I didn't notice the gravel under my bare feet, but I did notice the sodden grass, and the soil between my toes, and my hand growing warm inside his.

We went to the marquee, where there were no tables or chairs anymore – only a carpet of muddled shadows, and a faint dripping sound, and canvas walls that glowed pearl-grey in the moonlight. We stopped in the middle of the floor, and I thought he was going to kiss me, but even though he put both hands on my waist and turned me to face him, and even though we drew so close that I couldn't see anything except the vaguest impression of his lips, he stopped short and smiled instead. *You're teasing me*, I thought – only this time it didn't worry me; it made me glad.

We lay down in the grass, regardless of the wet. He on his side, resting on one elbow; I on my back, with one hand behind my head – and he touched me so delicately that I could hardly tell if it was his hand gliding over my skin, or the breeze. I was an amateur in comparison, skidding and fumbling inside his clothes, but the sounds he made gave me courage. I half opened my eyes at one point, glancing down at the ditsy old sundress that had so embarrassed me earlier in the evening. It was getting grass-stained now, screwed up, soaked and twisted round my hips – but I was grateful to it and to myself for choosing it. It didn't seem too small, or at least not in the childish way I'd feared.

I kissed the old razor-blade wounds on his wrists, and wished that he would kiss me on the lips. For some reason I wanted him to do it – as he'd done everything else – without me having to ask; without me having to manoeuvre my mouth on to his.

'What are you thinking?' he said after a while. I swept my fingers over the dewy grass and brought them to his face, moistening his eyelids and the side of his nose. I thought of Stella: of how Cory had seen her but never known her; of how she was a sad, faded story for him, rather than a person. The limelight was mine. *Look at me*, I thought. *For once, Stella, look at me.*

'What are you thinking?'

I was thinking of Tom, the other night, and the longed-for kiss that went wrong. Whenever Tom looked at me or spoke to me – even when he kissed me – there was a weight attached, which spoiled everything: a weight of sadness and know-ledge, of Stella-loved and Stella-gone; a weight of history, and shame, and might-have-beens.

When I didn't answer straight away Cory darted at my thumb, catching it between his teeth, holding it to ransom.

'I'm happy,' I replied, laughing, and he released my thumb. His face was shining with rain. 'I'm happy because you don't know me.'

'You're not used to being happy,' he observed. After a moment's pause I nodded my head in agreement, and the grass filled my hair with delicious, cold rain.

'Neither are you,' I ventured, and just like me he waited for a second before nodding his head.

The thing is, Tom, I've hardly been away from home twenty-four hours, but I feel changed. It's like I'm looking down on myself from a hot-air balloon and understanding the lie of the land in a whole new way.

If you think I'm being overly dramatic then say so, but my life – and Dad's as well, for that matter – has been shaped by death – first Mum's, then Stella's – and guilt, and I've just realised, in a kind of flash, that this is wrong. Don't you think it's wrong? Before Stella died I had plans for my life – detailed plans about university and careers and travel and friends and marriage and kids – and I'm not saying those particular plans hold any appeal anymore – because they don't – but even they would be better than nothing; better than the life I left behind yesterday. What have I been doing for the last five years? Making up for what happened by acting like I'm dead too?

When Aunty May came over last Christmas I got upset
because she kept going on about how 'Freya is very young for
her age.' Do you remember me telling you at the time? She
got obsessed with it, and it was irritating – but she was
right, you know. I am too young for my age; it's like I
stopped growing when Stella died. I'm a teenager frozen
in time.

Since I came away to Byrne Hall – all of one day ago! –
and got this aerial view, I've become convinced that my life
has to change – soon, now, completely. I don't know how it's
going to happen – I've yet to work out the finer details – but
maybe – maybe! – I'll chuck in my job and have a crazy
love affair and become a poet – and if I do some, or all, of
these things then it's possible the world won't fall apart, and
I won't fall apart, and Dad won't fall apart

I'd been writing quickly, without much conscious thought, but my hand began to ache so I stopped and re-read the whole thing. I scribbled out 'and guilt' and replaced the words 'Making up for what happened' with 'Honouring Stella'. Those were the only changes I made before folding the letter into rough quarters and putting it in my pocket.

That big, bare room was chilly in the half-light and I couldn't stop shivering, even after I'd got into bed.

8

I HEARD THE CLUNK OF a car door in my sleep and it wove itself into my dream.

There was nothing to see – just the sound of two voices arguing – but I can still hear them now, if I close my eyes. The first voice was panicked; it kept yelling, *Come away! Quick! Come on!* The second, all coy and fluttery, said, *I'll leave just as soon as he's kissed me on the mouth. One kiss – just one – and then I promise I'll go.* Back and forth they squabbled, without making any headway, until the first one slammed her car door as a prelude to driving off – only the engine noise never materialised, and the dream began to fade.

Go, whispered the first voice.

You're only jealous, retorted the second voice, as I slid towards wakefulness. *You're jealous because I'm alive and you're not.*

'I am alive,' I said. In the bleary logic of my dream, the knowledge that I was alive had some connection with Cory Byrne, and it felt like joy – if joy is a molten heat that makes you sweat in your sleep, and stick to your bed-sheets.

I woke properly to the sound of men's voices below my windows. I lay still with my eyes closed, listening to their chatter and the rumble of laughter, and the crunch of shoes on gravel.

I got up before I was ready, all sleepy and crumpled, and hobbled to the window. The car – a dusty and dented Ford Fiesta – was unmistakably Tom's, and there was Tom himself with his back to me, zipping up a holdall in the boot. Cory Byrne was the one who had laughed – he did it again as I watched – and the person he was talking to was my father.

I sank to my knees, resting my arms on the windowsill and my chin on my arms, and swore softly. Dad and Tom had come to fetch me home – they must have driven through the night – and since they obviously needed me, I would have to go. Nothing about this scenario made any sense, and yet it seemed drearily inevitable. I closed my eyes and tried to will myself back to sleep.

Why? Why had they come? I must have missed something in all the excitement; must have overlooked some vital connection. I dug my phone out of my bag in case there was an explanation waiting in my inbox, and there was the text I'd written to Dad last night prefixed with a *Message Failed To Send* notice and a red exclamation mark.

Down on the driveway Cory clapped Dad's shoulder, and Dad didn't look remotely offended. I watched Cory point confidingly at my bedroom window, and just before I drew back I glimpsed Dad smiling and opening his mouth to reply. I was sure they were joking about me – about how I could still be flaked out at this hour of the morning, sleeping the sleep of the dead, or the just, or whatever the expression is. Dad would say, 'Oh yes, I can believe it. That sounds like my Freya.' In that moment I hated my father, because he was turning Cory into a normal person who could laugh and make small talk, and I detested Cory even more, because he was going along with it.

I sidled back into view and caught Tom's eye as he shut the boot. The others had their backs to the house now; they were admiring the view across the garden to the sea. It *was* late; late and hot. The sun was high in the sky and the sea looked flat and blue, and any glitter the garden had gained from yesterday's rainfall had already burned away. The magical night was over; had fizzled out before it had begun. Normal life was about to resume, with all its dullness and self-doubt.

Tom didn't tell the others he'd seen me. I couldn't manage a smile, but I moved my fingers in the ghost of a wave, and he replied in kind. 'Come down?' he mouthed. I nodded and looked round for my shoes.

I panicked in the corridor. It sounds stupid, but it was black as a pit after all that dazzling sunshine, and I was afraid of losing myself in a fairy-tale tangle of passages and winding steps.

I stood with one hand against the wall and let out a long, slow breath. It was a landing, not a labyrinth – all I had to do was turn right and walk until I reached the top of the stairs. There was no need to rush, as if there were ceilings coming down on me and trap-doors swinging open at my feet; as if I were feeling my way through a muddle of smoke and mirrors instead of an ordinary stretch of darkness.

I rushed all the same. My flip-flops had come to hand when I was hunting around for shoes, and I regretted them now because they slapped so loudly against my soles. I was no longer a stranded mermaid in flowing green, but a clumsy creature with webbed feet.

'*Wait!*'

I jerked to a halt. There. That was the kind of thing I'd been afraid of, and half expecting: the breathless voice of the house itself, addressing me out of the darkness.

Diana switched the light on and descended from the second floor, clinging tightly to the bannister. I was still blinking in the glare when she caught me by the wrist, her grasp so brittle that I couldn't resist, in case I hurt her.

'Wait,' she repeated, even though I *was* waiting – like it or not. Her touch was an icy wind blowing over my skin and bringing me out in goose-bumps, and I wondered how long she'd been loitering on the stairs when it was obvious she ought to be in bed. With none of the armoury – the strong shoes, the walking stick, the death-mask make-up – that had kept her together yesterday afternoon, she looked ancient and profoundly unwell. Her dusky-pink pyjamas might have suited a film-noir beauty from the 1940s. The silk jacket was made to accommodate a pillowy bosom but it hung loose over Diana's chest, and she'd had to make a bulky knot at the waist of the trousers just to keep them from falling down.

'You're staring,' she said, letting go of my wrist to pull the collar together. It was a defensive gesture but regal too, and I imagined her doing it in former times, when she was well – resting her fingers loosely on her throat and flashing costly jewellery at her party guests.

'You make me feel like a ghost,' she added, and if this was an attempt to make light of the situation, it didn't show in her face. I tried to smile, but I couldn't think of a single thing to say.

'We have to be quick.' She lowered her voice to a whisper and leaned forwards, till I could smell the mint imperial on her breath and the staleness beneath it. 'I need to talk to you about Stella.'

'*Stella?*'

Diana pressed a hushing finger to her mouth. She'd had pink lips yesterday, but today her mouth was just a thin, black line.

'Stella?' I whispered. 'My sister, Stella?'

Everything urged me to run outside at once; everything except a niggling need to hear it – *quickly, quickly* – whatever it was. It wouldn't be anything new. I'd read all the newspapers at the time, and the police report, and the coroner's report, and Cory had told me about his tenuous connection – that had to be enough. There was no breathing space left for mystery.

'Let me tell you what's going to happen,' she said, 'if you don't go away.'

'But I want to know what you mean about Stella—'

The front door opened down below and Cory's voice flooded the stairwell.

'I'll just grab a pair of shoes,' he called over his shoulder. 'I won't be a moment, and then I'll give you the guided tour of the gardens.'

His voice rang like a bell, echoing off the tiles and making the old woman wince. Our eyes locked as she began to retreat backwards up the stairs, one hand gripping the bannister, the other gesturing wildly. What would you call it, that gesture of hers? Waving? Scouring? Slashing? Not so much begging me to keep quiet as wiping the air clean of the possibility of sound.

The darkness absorbed her, step by silent step. I didn't dare call after her, or ask her to explain, but I followed her as far as the third or fourth stair and craned my neck to see where she went.

The girl, Freya, clatters down the stairs, eager for daylight and fresh air; eager for wholesome company.

Diana stops outside her bedroom door, listening to the receding footsteps, and is struck by a vision of what she was once, and what she is now. She – Diana – has become the whispering voice of the

93

house. No, more than that, she has become its mind and soul. This was not an eventuality she foresaw when she married Mr Byrne. She only ever meant to be the owner of an elegant estate.

The stairs have taken it out of her; it's hard to climb without Cory's arm to lean on. She drops into bed with a rustle of silk and bone, and her body makes next to no imprint on the sheets.

Diana used to run wildly downstairs, shaking the place with her energy. Over the years she slowed down and stopped, because Mr Byrne didn't like it. By the time he died it was too late: she'd lost the knack of carelessness.

When was the last time she ran inside the house? There was that summer evening a lifetime ago, when she was upstairs and pandemonium erupted in the garden. That might have been the last time. She'd heard it through the open window: her husband shouting violent things, impossible to make out, and Cory – little Cory with his three-year-old, tin-whistle voice – screaming 'Daddy!' and 'Stop!' and 'Please!'

Diana had run – no, she had flown – down the stairs, feet beating like wings in time with her heart, the house dissolving around her as she passed. It wouldn't be the first time he'd hurt Cory, but it might – by the sound of it – be the worst. The front door was wide open and as Diana descended the final flight she could see them on the other side of the lawn: her son upside down in the monster's arms, his little shirt rucked up around his armpits, his back bared, his hair dangling in the grass.

She tried to shout, but her voice had gone as weak as her knees. There was a vase on the hall table – a big, ugly, priceless thing – and she seized it on her way to the door.

'I'm a grizzly bear,' Mr Byrne roared, far away, 'and you're a slippery fish!'

Diana paused with the vase above her head and narrowed her eyes against the setting sun. Cory was sobbing – but sobbing with laughter. The vase grew heavy as she watched, and her arms began to tremble.

'I'm going to eat you up!'

'Daddy, no!'

Squeals of hilarity; gleeful growling.

She ought to have tiptoed away and left them to it. She ought to have been glad. Seconds passed. Diana glanced up at the vase – a hideous brown and green object, crawling with Chinese dragons.

'Tickle me again, Daddy!'

Diana leaned back and hurled the vase through the front door, exploding it against one of the serene white pillars that supported the porch.

Mr Byrne placed Cory on the grass and strode towards the house, picking up a couple of the larger shards of porcelain on his way, only to drop them again.

'Daddy?'

Diana retreated, but her husband caught up with her in the hall, yanking her by the hair and exposing her neck. He shoved her up against the wall so that her face was squashed against the cold plaster, and then he put his lips to her ear.

'Cory,' she murmured, before he had time to speak.

Mr Byrne turned and saw what she had seen – their son, watching from the doorway – and he let her go.

Diana presses her face into the pillow and tries to work out whether it's worse to remember those times, or to imagine Cory in the garden now, with the red-haired girl.

*She never did find out what her husband intended to say –
or do – about the vase. He left the same evening – a business trip
to New York – and by the time he came back a fortnight later
the bruises had faded from her cheek, and she'd filled the gap on
the hall table with a bowl of roses. He made no comment and
neither did she.*

9

THE SUNSHINE FELT HEAVY ON my head as I emerged from the front door. I'd braced myself for a scene but Dad was on the other side of the lawn, gazing up at a cedar tree and patting its trunk, as if it were a prize-winning horse. Cory had just re-joined him, having found his shoes.

Nothing altered in Cory's demeanour when he saw me. He didn't drop everything and run to me across the grass – he didn't even stop talking – he just waved a friendly wave as from one ordinary person to another. Presumably he alerted Dad to my presence, because *he* turned and waved too, before resuming his examination of the tree.

Something moved across one of the windows on the second floor and I looked up, but there was nobody there, only the sunlight dancing through the leaves and glancing off the glass. I turned my back on Byrne Hall and rubbed my arms against the non-existent cold. However closely I searched my skin from wrist to shoulder, last night's kisses had left no trace. I was strangely glad of the grass-stains on my dress, although I suppose they made me look a mess.

I couldn't go back inside and I couldn't face Cory – not now the rational, morning light had turned him into a rational, morning man – so I drifted over to the car instead. Tom was sitting sideways on the passenger seat with his feet on the gravel, wafting the front door back and forth like a hefty fan.

'Your Dad chain-smoked,' he explained, before we'd even said hello. 'I mean literally, all the way from London. My poor Fiesta will never smell the same.'

I dragged the fingers of both hands through my hair, pulling at the knots till my scalp hurt. Bits of grass and seed sprinkled my shoulders.

'Tom, I don't understand. What are you doing here?'

He stood up and shut the car door.

'Oh Freya, I'm sorry. I know what you must be thinking.'

'I just . . . I genuinely want to know why you and Dad are here.'

Tom dug a pocket of black earth in the gravel with the toe of his shoe.

'Your dad rang me up late last night, saying you'd disappeared and your phone had gone dead . . .'

'Oh no . . .'

'I did my best to calm him down, but I suppose you must have forgotten to text him after you arrived, and he got a call from the guest house saying you hadn't checked in . . .'

I shut my eyes and pressed against them with my fists.

'I told him you'd be OK, but you know what he's like. He was all for calling the police, but I said you'd be mortified, and anyway . . .'

'Anyway what?'

'Well, I had an idea where you might have gone.'

I loosened my fists and let them fall to my sides.

'He's fine now,' Tom insisted. 'Probably feeling daft. Your . . . what's-his-name . . . did all the hard work, charming him round. What is his name, anyway?'

'Cory Byrne. And he's not "mine". What did he say?'

I could feel Tom's eyes on my face.

'Something about you getting caught in the rain with your suitcase, and his mother inviting you to stay, and they couldn't run you down to town because they don't have a car anymore . . .'

I shielded my eyes from the sun and looked across the lawn. My father was shambling along at Cory's side, his hands behind his back and his hair fluffed up above his ears. He looked as if he'd been born doddery and mild-mannered.

'It turns out your friend's mother is some great luminary in the art world,' said Tom. 'Or used to be. Diane, is it? Or Diana? Anyway, your father recognised her name and went into raptures, and meanwhile your friend—'

'Cory.'

'Cory turns out to be the world's greatest admirer of your dad's reviews for the *London Globe*.'

'Oh, I see.'

We watched them weave their unhurried way around the rose beds, and I remembered last night like an improbable story I'd made up in my head. Cory was a stranger to me in broad daylight. The back of his head looked entirely unfamiliar as it disappeared through a leafy archway, and I couldn't believe my own self-assurance last night. How could I have lain on the wet grass with him, touching and being touched, drifting between sleep and bliss? Where did I get the confidence? Perhaps it had something to do with the darkness. Perhaps it was because the moonlight had broken him into manageable pieces – a row of knuckles here, a lock of hair there, a dusty foot, a glinting eye, a moistened lip.

'I don't know about you,' said Tom, 'but I could do with some breakfast.'

I turned to him and caught sight of my own reflection,

distorted by the curve of the car door: bulging forehead, squinting eyes, tapering legs.

'Breakfast,' I echoed. Tom checked his watch, and the pale flash of his wrist broke my trance. I looked at him – I mean, I really saw him – for the first time that day. His eyes were a scrawl of fine red lines, and his skin was ashen. I pictured him driving through the night at my father's behest – because Tom drove, and Dad no longer did, and that's what friends are for. Five hours at the wheel, fending off second-hand fag fumes and second-hand angst, and all the time, at the back of his mind, our conversation the other night, and the words of that awful review in yesterday's *London Globe*. What was it Dad had written? Something about clever-clever catalogue notes and waffle, and that phrase 'over-thought and over-wrought' in the closing paragraph.

'I'm buying breakfast,' I said, although it wasn't much of a gesture. 'I'll just fetch my purse, I'll be one minute—'

'No!'

I stopped dead.

'Sorry,' said Tom. 'But please don't go back into that house. It doesn't matter who pays.'

I rubbed the sleep from my eyes and frowned.

'If you go inside now, you'll never get away. I know what will happen. You'll run into your dad and what's-his-name . . .'

'Cory.'

'Yes. And we'll end up staying here for breakfast . . .'

'And?'

Tom reddened. 'It would be good to talk to you, on your own.'

Sounds ominous. I would have said it out loud in normal circumstances – in a light-hearted way – but not now.

I hung about while Tom scribbled a note for Dad and stuck it under the windscreen wiper. We set off down the drive towards Bligh, and I only looked over my shoulder a couple of times. The lawn was empty and, as far as I could tell, the house had all its eyes shut.

We plumped for the first café we saw. It was called Jeanette's and there was a tinkly bell above the door, which made everyone – the four customers and a waitress – look up when we entered. Tom sat with his back to the window, and I sat opposite with the sun in my eyes. The light was bouncing off the water in the harbour, so pure and sprightly that everything else seemed squalid by comparison. The air inside the café was thick with dust, and there were toast crumbs in the sugar pot and greasy little handprints on the window. The room was too small for the number of tables, and the whole place smelled of vegetable oil and frying.

'What are you having?' Tom sighed, rubbing his face, as I unstuck my elbows from the plastic tablecloth and reached for a menu. The cloth was decorated with pink ice-cream cones and cartoon seagulls with goofy eyes, and it seemed strange to me. Everything seemed strange and hyper-real. I kept blinking as if I'd just left the theatre; as if I'd emerged from a startling play and come back to earth with a bump.

'I don't know,' I said. 'You decide.'

The waitress came over and Tom ordered two bacon sandwiches and two coffees.

'It's a beautiful place,' he observed when she'd gone. 'Byrne Hall, that is.'

I nodded dully. I couldn't decide whether the flowers in the little white vase were real or fake; it was hard to tell just by looking. I touched the tips of the pink carnation and felt the prickle of plastic.

'And thingummy seems pleasant enough, Cory.'

Pleasant. I almost managed a smile. There was something funny about the way Tom said 'beautiful' and 'pleasant'. He didn't quite turn them into dirty words, but he made them sound suspect.

'What's his mother like?'

'Not very well. Confused, I think.'

Tom nodded and kept on looking at me.

'So? Have you seen the painting again?'

'What painting?'

There was a newspaper lying on our table; a copy of this morning's local rag. I turned the pages listlessly and read the upside-down headlines. They were all depressing. *Husband Led 'Double Life', Court Hears. Bereaved Couple Plead For Justice. Motorist's Tyres Slashed.*

'The painting.' Tom leaned forwards for emphasis. 'The painting of Stella. The whole reason you came back.'

I pushed the newspaper away and the radio came on with *Sunday Love Songs.*

'Oh, *that*,' I said. 'Sorry, I'd forgotten. There's nothing much to tell. Cory met Stella in passing, a few weeks before she died. She let him sketch her, and he turned the sketch into a painting, which is presumably what I saw at the wedding.'

Tom was full of questions: 'So Cory Byrne is an artist?' 'Did he and Stella only meet the once?' 'Did they talk?' 'What was her mood like?' 'Have you seen the painting again?' To which I replied: *Yes, Yes, Not much, I don't know* and *No*, in that order.

Every time I shifted slightly in my seat, I could hear the

unfinished letter rustling in my pocket. I couldn't remember exactly what I'd written to Tom in the early hours, but I remembered the general mood of it. I know I'd threatened to chuck in my job at K&G, and try my luck as a love-addled poet.

'Any sauces?' said the waitress who brought our order to the table, but I didn't hear the question till she'd gone. Tom asked for ketchup. I wasn't hungry anyway – the bacon sandwiches were all crust and grease and bulge. I cut mine in half and laid the knife down. The bread was pallid and floury, and it put me in mind of Lady Caroline Augusta Fitzroy-Byrne.

'What's up?'

'Nothing.'

'I'm sorry about showing up like this, Freya. I don't want you to think . . .'

'I don't think anything.'

'We can still . . . We are still mates, aren't we, you and me?'

'Yes.'

I managed a smile, because it was the least he deserved. One of the corners of the letter was poking out of my pocket, and I pressed it lightly, as if testing the point of a blade.

'In fact, I wrote to you last night.' Despite my gravity I had to laugh a little, because it sounded silly. 'A proper, old-fashioned letter. Well, kind of. I never actually finished it.'

I took the letter out of my pocket and laid it on the table-cloth between us.

Tom raised his eyebrows and smiled.

'Can I read it?'

'I suppose.'

He wiped his hands clean and drew the page from under my fingertips. I resisted at the last moment, before letting it go. Tom's manner was oddly reverent and careful, as if the paper might turn out to be something valuable – one of his beloved Raphael sketches in the original, perhaps, or a diagram by Leonardo da Vinci. I chewed my lip while he unfolded it and spread it out beside his plate.

'Dear Tom . . .'

'Not out loud!' I covered the letter with both hands.

'Sorry.'

He continued to read in silence and I tried not to watch. I sipped my coffee and scalded my tongue. I squeezed a blob of ketchup on to the rim of my plate, contemplated a group of pensioners walking past the window, scalded my mouth a second time and finally scraped my chair back.

'I'm going to the loo,' I whispered. 'Have my sandwich if you're still hungry.'

There were two cubicles in the Ladies, and one was already occupied. I locked myself in and stood with my back against the dividing wall, covering my nose against the bleach fumes. The other person flushed and ran the tap and held her hands under the dryer. I didn't move. My eyes roved over the graffiti on the door, some of it scratched with a blade, most of it in marker pen. There were names, obscenities, doodles – the usual stuff – and the words *fly away home* in a loose, looping hand, on top of all the rest.

Both plates were empty by the time I returned, and Tom was refolding the letter. Someone had switched the radio off, and the three remaining customers were eating quietly, at separate tables. He gave me a small – puzzled? Critical? Sad? – smile.

'Did you read it?'

'I did.'

Our voices sounded naked without any background hum, and we drew together across the table.

'You're right about one thing,' he said.

Only one! 'What's that?'

It was funny, seeing Tom's face at such close quarters; it felt intimate and unfamiliar at the same time. He had a tiny, brown freckle on his left eyelid, which only flashed into view when he blinked, and red dents on his nose where his reading glasses normally sat.

'When you write about wanting to start again,' he said. 'Putting the past behind you, handing in your notice at work, writing poetry . . . whatever. I think you should go for it; I think you've got every right.'

I narrowed my eyes.

'There's a "but" coming, isn't there?'

Tom didn't answer immediately. He swirled the remains of his coffee round and watched it slop up the sides of his mug.

'I just think you'd be better off doing it on your own terms,' he said. 'Going home, mulling it over, deciding for yourself what happens next. Somehow I don't . . .'

He hesitated and tipped his coffee round the mug again.

'What?'

'I think it's a mistake to assume Byrne Hall holds any of the answers.'

I was all set to protest – 'I don't know what you're talking about!' – but I thought, *Why bother?*

'It's just as well it doesn't,' I said, 'since I'm being fetched home.'

I leaned back in my chair until the freckle on Tom's eyelid was too small to make out; he remained hunched forwards with his elbows on the table. I don't know how long we sat like that, strangely sad and stuck for anything to say. The waitress gave us a funny look when she came to collect the dirty plates from the adjacent table.

'I'm sorry,' Tom said, and I was too depressed to say, *Don't be*. I was annoyed with Dad more than him, and myself more than Dad. The radio came on again, louder than before, and we flinched. The waitress carried her loaded tray away, and as she nudged the kitchen door open we heard the slosh and clatter of washing-up, and a man humming.

'There's no need to rush back,' Tom said. 'Let's just enjoy the walk.'

I slowed down to match his pace. Every so often we would stop to stare at one of the flashier yachts, or watch the seabirds, or inhale the fishy stink of the working boats. He was right, of course. There was no reason to hurry.

I kept glancing across the swing-bridge into the wooded hills, but Byrne Hall wasn't visible from the quayside. I wondered if you could glimpse it in winter, when the leaves thinned out. If a fire were lit in one of the grates, might you see a twist of blue smoke rising above the trees?

'Anyhow,' said Tom. 'It's good that you've cleared up the mystery of the painting.'

I need to talk to you about Stella. I shrugged the memory away, but Diana's voice had got stuck in my head and I kept seeing her on the stairs, in her silk pyjamas. *Let me tell you what's going to happen, if you don't go away.*

I had already decided not to mention that part of my visit to Tom; he might conclude there was still some riddle to be solved when there wasn't. There was just a crazy old lady with a half-memory of Stella's story in the local paper. Perhaps my red-headed resemblance to my dead sister scared her; perhaps she just didn't like the look of me. Maybe she preferred having her house – and her son – to herself.

'What are you thinking?' Tom whispered, as we passed the stone ravens and started up the drive. The contrast after the sunny harbour was startling; it was like entering a church with green walls. If you tipped your head right back, the boughs could be vaults in a lofty ceiling, and the smaller branches curls of Gothic tracery. Cory had asked me what I was thinking just a few hours ago, and I'd said, 'I'm happy.'

I've got to go home. That's what I was thinking now. *I've got to go home and invent a new life for myself, just like I said I would in that letter.* I tried to imagine the revolution, but my mind snagged on a thousand and one details: the sun-bleached wallpaper that Mum had hung in the hall a few months before she died; the teddy bears lining the end of Stella's bed; the penguin alarm clock that woke me every weekday morning at six. I'd never changed a single one of those things; wouldn't be able to; couldn't ask it of Dad.

'What am I thinking?' I echoed, playing for time.

I was thinking I had lost my inspiration, having only just found it. I was thinking I would like to cry until I felt hollowed out and cleansed – but there was no point telling him that if the tears weren't going to come. Crying has to speak for itself.

'I was just wishing I'd put some better shoes on.'

I made him stop, and he held my arm as I took the flip-flops off and brushed grit from the soles of my feet.

*

The garden was empty as far as we could see – no sign of Dad or Cory anywhere – but Tom's note had gone from underneath the windscreen wiper, and the front door was wide open. I avoided looking up at the second-floor windows.

'I'd better go and grab my things,' I said. 'I'll be quick.'

'OK.'

I made myself look up at the house. There was only one room with its blinds open, and I was pretty sure it was mine. The rest were blank and white, and they reminded me of my grandmother's eyes when her cataracts got bad. Occasionally one of the blinds would sway slightly, as if someone inside were touching it.

'If we're going, we should go,' I said, but I lingered. I wished I'd grabbed my bags this morning and brought them to the car, instead of dashing downstairs empty-handed. I could have waited here with Tom until the other two showed up, and run through the civilities with Cory, and it would have been over quite quickly and painlessly. *Thank you so much*, I'd have said, and *goodbye*, and *all the very best with your paintings*, and *I hope your mother feels better soon*. I might have shaken his hand; he might have kissed me on the cheek. And the three of us would have left, because it's a five-hour drive back to London.

'Do you want me to come with you?' asked Tom.

'It's all right. You wait here, in case Dad shows up. I'll be two minutes.'

He didn't argue or try to follow. I stopped at the door and looked back.

'Tom?'

'Mm?'

'I really loved your Raphael exhibition the other week.'

'Yeah, well.' He scuffed the gravel with his shoe. 'What

with one thing and another, I can't say it was the best night of my life.'

Everything I said, when I was talking to Tom, seemed to come out mean or obtuse. I started trying to explain myself, but he cut me off. He said, 'It's fine, Freya, it's fine,' and got into the car, and closed the door.

10

At the top of the stairs I stopped and listened for Cory's voice – or Dad's – but there wasn't a sound; even the breezy trees and the distant sea had gone quiet. We didn't get silences like this back home. It was a silence with character and colour; it was the wakeful mind of Byrne Hall, brimful of history and intent. I wanted to run away, but I set the suitcase down instead, as if I'd been told to wait.

If the silence had a focal point it was up on the second floor, with Diana. I wrapped my fingers round the bannister and climbed the first three stairs – and nobody stopped me. There wasn't even a squeak of protest from the old wooden floorboards. I moistened my dry lips and carried on, and the closer I got to Diana, the more the house seemed to breathe down my neck.

There was one window above the bend in the stairs, but it was clogged with ivy, which made the daylight meagre and green. All I could hear was the drum beat inside my head. The others must still be outside; perhaps they'd gone down to the sea.

I walked halfway along the landing and stopped. Stella had never been here; the empty outlines that haunted this house had never held the shape of my fleeting, flighty sister. I told myself that if she had stayed at Byrne Hall, I would know about it. One way or another she'd have left me a sign. A scent. A whisper. A message scrawled in dust. I would *know*. Diana had nothing new to tell me.

The first door opened on to a narrow, twisting staircase. An inconstant draught came whistling down from the attics, and I remembered those fallen tiles lying broken in the long grass at the back of the house. I climbed a couple of steps and drew back straight away, peeling cobwebs off my lips. There would be nothing to see up there except grey shadows and films of dust.

I twisted a different door handle and found myself on the threshold of a bedroom. It had to be Diana's – I knew it before I saw her – because it was the only lived-in room I'd come across, apart from Cory's studio.

An electric heater burned against the wall, thickening the air of the sick room and making it glow. A row of scented candles was alight on the dressing table, but even the combined efforts of jasmine and sandalwood could not mask the stench of disinfectant and sickness. I recognised the stiff red shoes under the bed, and the hump of the body underneath the sheets, and the curled hand across the pillow.

When I stepped on to the rickety floor, the hand tightened involuntarily. I froze, but she didn't stir again, and when I took another step – purposefully pressing down on the board this time, willing her to wake and see me – there was no response. I loitered at the foot of the bed, peering round, searching the room for clues, as if there might be some trace of what she'd said – what she'd *almost* said – about Stella, hanging from the walls, or lurking among the furniture.

Diana's room was smaller than mine or Cory's, and most of the space was taken up by a bed, a dressing table and a huge mahogany wardrobe. It didn't feel like summer up here; it felt like autumn – and late autumn at that – what with the light so dim through the trees and the electric heater on full blast.

It was untidy, like Cory's studio, but the effect was

oppressive rather than magical. The walls were covered in sun-bleached papers: a child's drawings, a child's handprints, a child's handwriting exercises. School photos. College photos. Exam certificates. Music awards. I moved in closer, looking for something without knowing what. I touched the corner of one of the papers, pressing it on to the Blu-Tack so it made a fragile, crackling sound.

My Mama, it said, in faded felt-tip. *My Mama is nise. My mamma is kind. She bys me things. My ~~mmam mem~~ mama loves me best. Cory Byrne. Class 2b.* Underneath the writing there was a picture of a stick woman with a huge head and a red smile.

There was a more sophisticated drawing above that, in grey pencil, showing a woman in evening gown and long gloves. *'Mother' by Cory Byrne. August 12th, 1999.* Her hair was thick and glossy, piled high on her head and studded with jewels. She had an indulgent and secretive smile, and I'd never have guessed she was Diana if it weren't for the inscription.

Aside from the candles, the dressing table was a clutter of lipsticks, hairbrushes, bottles of pills and fusty jars of old-fashioned sweets. There were tiny vases of flowers, some of them quite fresh, but some – the skeletal lavender stalks and hard, brown rosebuds – that ought to have been discarded months back. The rest of the surface was covered in a jumble of papers: letters from twenty years ago or more addressed to 'Darling Di' – *thank you for a fabulous weekend!* – invitations on yellowing sheets of card, and old photographs of dinner-jacketed men and ball-gowned women. Only one of the pictures had been put in a frame, and it was propped up against the mirror. I could hardly make it out in the poor light. It showed a child and it was oddly lit, in that the boy's tilted face was in shadow, while his hair shone out like a pale flame.

The floorboard creaked, although I hadn't moved, and something touched my arm. I spun round.

Cory wasn't such a big man that he could fill an entire doorway, but he seemed to do so all the same. He smiled, and his eyes flitted past me to his mother's bed.

'I wasn't snooping,' I said hastily. 'Dia— Your mum – your mother – wanted to talk to me, so I came to find her, but she's asleep.'

Cory crossed to the bed. How did he do that – how did he carry so much light and freshness with him? The air felt brighter and cleaner as he strode across the floor, as if a window had been thrown open.

'Where's my dad?' I asked.

'Outside, enjoying the garden. He's fine. What did she want to talk about?'

He had his back to me, so I couldn't read his expression, and he kept his voice low as he stood over her pillow – to avoid waking her, I suppose. I devoured him with my eyes and tried to discover the merest hint of last night in the way he looked and spoke. My skin was cold now where he'd touched me; there was no trace left, except in my mind. I would be embarrassed to mention it – even obliquely – unless he did so first.

'I think . . .' I faltered, picturing Diana on the stairs, slashing at the air with her hands, begging me not to give her away. 'Well, she said it was something to do with Stella . . .'

I blushed, conscious of blundering without being sure which of the two I was offending most, or how, or why. If only Cory would turn round so I could see his expression.

He placed two fingers on Diana's sleeping forehead. It was the strangest gesture – almost priestly – as if he were about to anoint her or mark her with ashes. He whispered something

113

and shook his head slowly from side to side. I couldn't tell what he said.

A child's plastic potty was poking out from under the bed. Diana must have used it when she was sick, and it hadn't been properly rinsed because there was a ring of pinkish grime near the base. I closed my eyes, but in closing them I lost my balance and had to sit on the edge of the mattress. I don't know how Cory came to be sitting beside me, but as I swayed I bumped against him, and he put his arm round me, and he was offering me a glass of water from the bedside table. I took a sip and let my head fall against his chest. Close up he had a soapy smell, which struck me as familiar and bittersweet, like a memory from years ago. Perhaps Mum used to wash our clothes with the same laundry powder when Stella and I were small.

'I went into town first thing, before your dad appeared,' he said, placing a brown paper bag on my knees. 'Bought you a present.'

I opened the bag and drew out a notebook. My throat tightened, and I thought I was going to cry.

'I can't write in this!' I said, turning the pages. 'It's way too beautiful.' It was one of those faux-leather hardbacks, with gold swirls up the spine and pages like vellum.

Cory kept his arm round me, stroking me from shoulder to elbow, and we sat without speaking for minutes on end. It's funny, because I never got round to crying, and he never spoke, but somehow we emerged from that stillness into intimacy, the way you might after a tearful heart to heart.

Diana sighed and twisted on to her other side. I raised my head and Cory sat up straight, and we both started speaking at the same time.

'Dad will be wondering where I've got to.'

'You will stay, won't you? Just a few days?'

Diana gripped the pillowslip. I couldn't tell if she was awake or not, because Cory was blocking my view of her face. After a while her hand relaxed again.

'You're not going to leave just yet?' he said. I looked for the joke – or the suggestion of a joke – lurking in his words, but he looked frightened. 'I thought, after last night . . .'

There were reasons why I had to leave. There was Dad, for a start, and my drab desk at K&G Financial Services, and my membership at the lido: the weary pull of routine. And it would be so presumptuous to stay on; I wasn't the kind of person to show up at a stranger's house with my suitcase and make myself at home. I wasn't, was I? I wasn't the kind of person who falls in love over the course of a single, reckless night.

I looked past Cory, to the window and the straggly shadows of the woods. Tom would be wondering where I'd got to; he might even come inside and start searching. I listened for the distant creak of doors, and the hesitant footsteps, and the calling of my name, but the house was silent. This is how it would sound if Tom were to give up and drive away.

'I'd better go,' I said, but I was only testing the words to see if they rang true. I got to my feet and Diana whispered in her sleep.

'You can't,' said Cory, springing up beside me. 'You can't go back to all that.'

All what? I wondered about his talk with my dad, and the things he must have gleaned, and for a moment I was offended. My life wasn't that bad, was it? In the next breath I loved him for seeing, and saying, the truth.

I looked at his outstretched hand, although I didn't take it yet. The house seemed to be holding its breath and listening

115

for my reply. Even the huddled trees looked as though they were eavesdropping at the window. Diana lay still with her eyes closed and her fingers in a tight fist.

Cory waited too, and when I didn't answer he kissed me on the lips.

It was four years and ten months since my last kiss. His name had been Dan and he'd had brown hair, and I couldn't remember anything else about him, except that we'd met in freshers' week, and he was going to read English, like me. We'd kissed for the first and last time the day before Stella's body was found; a few hours before the phone call came and I left university. It hadn't been a successful kiss – we were both rather gauche, and our teeth had clashed – but I'd thought, at the time, that it marked the start of everything.

Cory's kiss felt like the start of everything too, but unlike last time – unlike poor Dan – this was good and real. Our teeth did not clash. Cory's kiss was all that a kiss should be; it was all that a beginning should be.

'Will you stay? Just for a little while.' Cory's whisper ran over my face, passing softly across my eyes and lips, tickling my ear and stirring my hair. *'Please* stay.'

Sometimes, even now, I dream about that kiss. Cory and I are always in a dark bedroom, and the air is quivering with electrical heat, and I can't fill my lungs properly. Nothing is certain. I never know whether the trees are inside the window or out; whether I'm being propped up or pushed down; whether I'm suffocating or coming to life.

In every version I kiss him right back, and it's almost like the last scene in the movie – except that there's an old woman curled up on the bed, and her fingers are twitching restlessly on top of the sheets.

PART TWO

PART TWO

Stella

October 2009

THE TWO HALVES OF THE painting lie on the floor next to the old iron bedstead and Stella sits with her back against the wall, staring at them. It feels as if she's been sitting like this for ever. The first, fast-breathing minutes have become glassy-eyed hours; the hours have become days. She dozes and wakes, and even when she wakes during the night the painting is strangely visible. Its palest parts – the face and hands – seem to glow in the dark.

It's drizzling and the window is open a couple of inches – as wide as it will go – teasing her with the leafy scent and patter of water she cannot reach. Byrne Hall is like that. It's a cruel house. Even these neglected attic rooms are cruel. She used to wonder vaguely about the servants who slept here a hundred years ago and more – whether they resented the low ceilings and tiny windows; whether they craved more light and air – but she's too scared for herself now to spare a thought for them. It's nearly a whole day since she last had a drink. Her tongue feels big and furry, as if her mouth's been stuffed with flannel, and it hurts to listen to the swish of the sea below the garden.

Now that darkness is falling, Stella can no longer hear the ravens in the tall trees at the front of the house. Actually, she's not sure they're ravens – they might be rooks or crows. At any rate, they're black, hunched, witchy birds that caw and clatter.

She tends to assume that's what they are because 'Byrne' is a Gaelic word for 'Raven' – that's the first thing she learnt when she arrived in the summer, all blithe and wide-eyed. 'Oh, I love that it means Raven!' she'd cried. 'Wow! Raven Hall! I love that! That is so Gothic!'

Stella reaches out with one foot and moves the two halves of the picture together, so that she can see the whole face. The question is whether she should mend it or tear it to shreds? It is *The* Question. It's one of those life-and-death choices you're only supposed to get in fairy tales – a riddle, a judgement, a fingerpost – and the sensible answer may not be correct. The act of rash insanity may not be wrong.

It is – was – a big portrait, and it has split neatly down the middle, so that each side contains one eye, half a nose, half a mouth, half a chin and so on. It wouldn't be a difficult repair. If she were careful, the join would hardly show at all.

When she tilts her head to the right, the portrait resembles an angry version of her sister, Freya. The more Stella tilts her head, the more Freya-like and lowering it becomes – which is odd, because her little sister does not usually have an angry face. She moves the painting with her foot and it stops resembling Freya. It looks like the portrait of a mannequin: dead-eyed yet oddly sexual. *It looks like me*, she thinks. A couple of days ago she thought it a bad portrait, but she can't tell anymore. It's seeped too far into her soul – or her soul has seeped into it.

Stella smacks her head back against the wall. The house is unyielding and she'll have a lumpen bruise on the back of her head by morning – if morning ever comes. She has a hunch that it won't, though. Not this time. Not for her.

Stella slides the two halves of paper across the floor and lays them on her lap. She doesn't normally cry. When she's sad she goes quiet; when she's angry she shouts; it's only when she's frightened that she weeps. Her fingertips nibble away at the picture, and tears drip off her chin, and the girl floats apart from herself in tiny bits: an earlobe here, an eyebrow there, a cuff, a dimple, a shadow, a lip, a freckle, a lock of red hair.

'What are you *doing*?' she whispers to herself. 'What the hell are you doing?' But she never slows down or stops. One painting is hardly enough; she could tear the whole collection to bits and never be bored. She's even forgotten that she's cold and parched; shaman-like, she has risen above hardship and begun existing for the here and now. Collar-bones split between her fingers and fibrous eyeballs fall apart, and she experiences a bliss that she hasn't known in months.

The trouble with me, Stella tells herself, brushing bits off her knees, *the trouble with me is that I can't control my feelings. I never could and I never will.* She can't understand what came over her this summer. It is as if she's spent the last few months pretending to be her little sister – eager-to-please, goody-two-shoes, wouldn't-say-boo-to-a-goose Freya – and that was never going to work, was it?

Poor Freya.

Rain clouds are scudding across the sky, but every so often there's a scrap of moon to see by. Stella pauses to study the painted hands – they are all she has left now – and her buoyant mood slips. It was a mistake to start thinking about her sister; that's what's broken her rhythm. All at once the floorboards feel hard on her bum and she notices her back is aching. Her own eyes well up and she swipes at them, briskly, with her sleeve.

Stella fumbles in her pocket for a biro and turns the painted hands over, so that she can use the back of the paper. Not that she knows what to write, or who she's addressing – only that she doesn't want to die, and words are the grappling hooks with which she attaches herself to the world.

Rain hurls itself against the little window and the sound makes her even sadder; she keeps having to sniff and mop her eyes so that she doesn't drip all over her writing.

Stella Maria Lyell, she writes.

Stella Maria Lyell.

There must be something more intelligent to say, but she can't think what it is.

It rained like this when she ran away from home for the first time, at fourteen. It was the rain that drove her sheepishly back again, after a night on the streets. She hadn't planned sufficiently; she'd had nothing to sustain her but a hazy, dwindling resentment and £3.60 in small change. How ironic, now, to think she'd been defeated by a few spots of water. She would give anything to be out in it now – to lift up her face, open-mouthed, and feel it dribbling down her throat.

A new noise begins beneath the downpour; she feels it through her legs like a distant drum beat. It's the sound of feet on the stairs.

'Here we go,' she whispers, as her fingers fail and the pen rolls across the floor. 'Here it is.'

While the key is still turning in the lock, Stella manages to drop the paper inside the empty wash-jug. If it stays there unread till doomsday – so be it. It is hers; it exists; she has signed it with her name, and there's a funny kind of comfort in that.

Freya

September–October 2014

1

CORY'S ARM WAS HEAVY ACROSS my neck, and it was difficult to slide out of bed without disturbing him. Every tiny movement made the mattress roll and sag, and he'd already hauled me back twice, just when I thought I was free – knotting me up inside his sleepy embrace. I managed it the third time and dressed quietly in the dawn twilight.

The sun rose on the other side of the house from Cory's room, and the blinds were down, but I could still sense what we had in store: another day of honeyed light and long shadows, with the garden smelling of fruit and roses. Autumn was in the air, but only in as far as the daylight was richer and the colours warmer. It was still hot. I slipped jeans and a T-shirt over my swimming costume and didn't bother with a jumper.

Cory was sleeping on his front, with his hands either side of his head and his face twisted towards me, his lips slack and slightly open. There were pink ridges on his back, where the crumpled linen had left imprints, and I stooped to cover his shoulders with the duvet in case he got cold while I was out.

He always seemed so still when he was asleep – so calm and touching – and I wanted to kiss him, but I didn't dare. He

123

needed to rest. God knows how long he'd been awake last night, working away at his paintings while I dozed and slept.

The room had changed a great deal since the night of our picnic. I hadn't witnessed the beginning of the spring clean – Cory hadn't asked for any help – but the next time I'd gone in I'd been hit by the smell of linseed oil, and my voice had echoed when I spoke, which wasn't the case before. All the dusty frames and canvases that had been standing round the room with their faces to the walls were gone, leaving an airy emptiness behind.

Together, we had set up an easel in the middle of the floor, cleaned the brushes, sorted through the paints, sharpened the pencils, and unearthed stacks of paper and rolls of canvas. We'd brought a large, wobbly table from one of the downstairs rooms and set it up in the window, so that I could work there on my poems. I liked to sit with my back to the view and my notebook open, watching Cory prime his canvases. I hadn't written much yet – fourteen words, to be precise – but I wasn't worried. So many thoughts flowed through my mind as I sat at that table, in my Byrne Hall idyll, and I never doubted that they were gathering and settling, ready to be ordered into sentences. Someday soon – when this holiday was over, in that vaguely conceived future I'd have to create for myself in London – I would set them down on paper.

Cory's approach to work was more energetic than mine, and over the next few days his first attempts began to appear on the walls. The effect was discreet to begin with – a few small drawings tacked above the fireplace – but he added to them every morning as his style became quicker and bolder, and they began to spread across the room. He didn't ask what I made of them, and I was glad of that, because I wasn't sure how I'd answer. Perhaps I'd say that I admired his diligence, because the more he worked, the more precisely he'd learn to observe me.

I swung my towel over my shoulder and crouched beside the mattress, wishing I had any talent at all for drawing. Cory was beautiful – no question. The scars on his arms troubled me, because he wouldn't say why he had cut himself, only that it had been a long, long time ago. When we were lying together I liked to stroke the insides of his arms to show that I understood, even though I didn't. Last night I'd told him it was my final couple of days at Byrne Hall; that I had to go back to work after the weekend or lose my job. It was no surprise that my voice had wobbled, but his response had been equally emotional – in all its hair-tugging, nail-chewing, miserable silence – and it was because of those scars on his arms that I'd been frightened, as well as flattered.

I watched his stillness for several minutes and came as close to touching him as I dared, without disturbing him – which is to say I gathered my hair out of the way and kissed the empty air half an inch above his swollen eyelids.

It was a Saturday, and the gardens had been hired for an early autumn wedding party. There'd been workmen in last week, mowing the grass and tidying the flower-beds, but the marquee still needed sprucing up, and even at this early hour there were people milling about on the lawns with their arms full of cleaning equipment and folded tables. A car was parked on the driveway with its doors wide open, stuffed from top to bottom with ferns, gypsum and yellow roses.

I paused on the steps, where there was a mobile signal, and checked my phone. There was nothing from Tom – again – but why should there be? He didn't owe me a message. My boss had left a crisp recording on voicemail, expressing her hope that I'd be in 'for definite' on Monday, and asking me to phone her. I typed something quick and dull for Dad – *Having such a lovely time, Cory is looking after me really well, I hope you're fine and eating properly* – wondering, as I did so, whether my daily updates were beginning to grate on him as much as they were beginning to grate on me.

I pocketed my phone with a sigh and let my shoulders drop. Perhaps I should give Dad a ring later on and talk to him properly? Then again, I'd be seeing him tomorrow, so there wasn't much point. I kept forgetting that I had to go home. I was waiting for something to happen which would force me to stay a little longer. A rail strike would do, or a casualty-free inferno at the office.

'Lovely morning!'

The woman flashed me a smile as she reached into the car for a crate of flowers. *Mother of the bride*, I thought, and murmured my agreement. I spotted satin dresses in plastic coverings hanging over the back seat, and a bulging hatbox that wouldn't shut properly.

'You've got a beautiful place here,' she added deferentially, adjusting her hold on the florist's box so that it rested on her hip.

I was about to put her straight – honestly, I was – but the sun crept through the trees while I was considering what to say, and all at once the bouquets glowed in her arms, as if each bud had a light inside it. The grass glittered, the sea gleamed, and even the pond with the broken fountain seemed to shine like a flattened pearl. The sky was wider and higher than I'd ever seen it before.

'Yes,' I said. 'Yes, we do. Thank you.'

I blushed to think how Diana would react if she overheard me. We'd had no conversation since the day I trespassed into her room, but I caught glimpses of her all the time. I'd see her gaunt figure seated on a bench in the rose garden, or hear her making her painful way along the landing, or smell the trace of her perfume in an empty room. On the few occasions we'd come face to face, Cory had been with me, and she'd made scant acknowledgement of my shy hello.

The woman with the swim-cap was there as usual, swimming back and forth across the cove, alternating between front- and back-crawl. She was always there before me, no matter how early I arrived. On the first morning we'd smiled at one another in passing, and after that we'd got into the habit of saying hi, and yesterday she'd emerged, dripping, as I was about to leave, and called out – as if we knew one another well – 'See you!' People never did that back home, at the lido. I would miss her when I was gone. I'd miss my early morning scramble down the cliff path. I'd miss the space, and the quiet, and the cool, clean smell of stones and salty water.

I reached the foot of the cliff and undressed next to my usual rock. I wouldn't have wanted to swim from the main beach in Bligh, watched over by all those Victorian hotels and flats, but I liked this little bay beneath the gardens of Byrne Hall. It was completely hidden from view of the town, and I'd have thought it secret if it weren't for the woman in the swim-cap. She was taller and darker than Stella but sometimes, as I was scrambling down the cliff path, I narrowed my eyes and imagined that I'd surprised my sister swimming in the bay. All I had to do was brave the cold water to reach her and bring her back to shore.

I winced my way across the shingle and waded up to my knees. The waves were like icy tongues licking at my thighs and I half decided – as usual – that I wouldn't swim after all; I'd just paddle about and get out. I thought of Stella and our childhood holidays in Cromer, when we'd yelp and splash and go right under, holding our noses, on the count of three.

The woman powered past, her mouth twisting out of the water to catch at the air. She was a proper swimmer, as sleek as a seal in her black costume. I bet she timed herself, and kept a tally of lengths, and mildly despised me, with my goose-bumps and my green polka-dot costume and my dithering.

One . . . That was Stella's voice, whispering in my ear.

Two . . . *three* . . . I hesitated, even after the three, but I plunged forwards, pushing my feet off the sand and taking flight. The first split-second was painful, before the water loosed its icy grip and I was off. It was always the same. Once I was in, I couldn't get enough of it: I had to dunk my head under and fill my fists with sand from the floor, and roll on to my back, and try not to laugh within earshot of the woman.

It was the space that thrilled me the most. I swam away from the beach, until my toes could only just touch the bottom if I stood *en pointe* like a ballet dancer, and stretched my arms as wide as they'd go. The surface of the sea was mild and flat, all the way to the horizon, although the currents round my legs were sinewy and cold.

I dived and swam through the darkness for as long as I could hold my breath, and when I came up I found myself facing the other way. I wiped my streaming hair from my eyes and floated, looking back towards the shore. I could see everything from here: Byrne Hall at its best, like a summer palace, with its swooping tumble of lawns; the woods, still heavily green, but tinged here and there with autumnal yellows; the sea-cliffs that started off gentle but grew steeper and higher as they got further from the house, until they looked like fortress walls rising up from the sea, with tiny dots of birds perched on their craggy shelves.

Those were Stella's cliffs. Cory and I had gone for a walk along the tops last week, although he'd taken some persuading. 'Down there is where she died,' I'd said aloud – to myself? To him? To the elements themselves? – when we stopped at the highest point, but Cory had closed his eyes and murmured, 'Don't.' He held tightly to my hand as I peered down at the spume-washed rocks, where her body had been spotted by a dog-walker and retrieved by the coastguard boat.

Funny how I was drawn, rather than repelled, by those cliffs. I had studied them every morning during my swim, with a nagging sense that they could unlock secrets if only I paid proper attention. I balanced upright, my arms moving in languid circles as the water lapped the back of my neck, and pictured her standing at the top. She'd have made a stark silhouette if she'd arrived at this time of day, with the sky brightening behind her and the cliff face in shadow below.

I wondered what the light had been like in her last few moments, and whether she'd hung about for a while, and whether she'd looked down, and what had been going through her head. Did she not see the gulls balanced on the air like spinning plates, and did they not make her want to live? I wondered what it was like to fall so far, knowing you couldn't change your mind halfway down. Was it a semi-conscious rush, or a protracted round of somersaults, with time to think, and taste the spray from the uprushing rocks?

Whenever I was happy – as I was just then – I imagined my sister gliding rather than falling, with her arms outstretched like wings. I imagined her feeling free, the way I feel free when I'm drifting in the sea, only a thousand times more so.

The water churned. An arm swung on to my shoulder mid-backstroke, flashing like a blade, and our skulls smacked together. A gasp – was there even a scream? – and we were both splashing about and coughing and apologising and asking, with genuine concern and nervous laughter, 'Are you OK? Are you sure?'

'I'm fine,' I said, and the woman with the swim-cap said much the same.

'Sorry. I wasn't looking where I was going.'

I gestured at the expanse of ocean and sky. 'You'd think there'd be just about enough room for two people, wouldn't you?'

'You'd think so,' she agreed, and we both seemed to find this funnier than it was.

We trod water, side by side, while she caught her breath.

'I don't stop often enough to take in the view,' she puffed, pushing the goggles on to her forehead, and somehow that added to our amusement, although I think she meant it seriously.

We floated together for a while as our laughter subsided, gazing towards the shore, suspended in the beauty and oddness of the moment. We were facing Byrne Hall, and I was waiting for her to tell me how lovely it looked. I wanted her to know that those gardens and buildings were mine, in some small sense – I wanted her to know that I was with the man who owned it – but I couldn't just come out with it and expect to be believed.

'I've never liked that place,' said the woman. 'I always think it looks like an evil face.'

I stared, stupidly. The woman laughed and said something else – something friendly and light and unrelated – to which I made no reply.

'Well, anyway,' she said. 'I'd better get on. See you!'

I rocked gently in her wake as she swam away, and I looked again at Byrne Hall.

2

'CORY?'

He was always, always sleeping like a baby when I returned from my swim, so it felt strange to come back and find the bed empty.

I suppose it's silly to talk about 'always, always' when I'd only been at Byrne Hall for a few weeks, but the days had fallen into a fixed pattern and I'd come to know the difference between normal and awry. Of course, he might have slipped to the bathroom, and if so it was no great surprise to find the bedding in a muddle – only why was it such a violent muddle, with the duvet tangled round the legs of the easel, and the pillows scattered to all four corners of the room? And why was the bottom sheet cold to the touch? And why – although I waited five, ten, twenty minutes – didn't he come back?

I picked up one of the pillows and wandered to the window. The wedding preparations were in full swing now. The tables had been crammed into the marquee and dressed with silver cutlery and glasses and flowers. There were people on step-ladders testing the fairy lights, and men lifting speakers from a van, and the mother of the bride was in animated debate with someone over the phone. Perhaps Cory was out there too, having a quiet word with the organisers, letting them know that 'the family' were home today and would appreciate some privacy? There was something flattering about that idea. One of the workers – a girl crossing the lawn with a crate of wine-glasses – glanced up at my window. I moved out of view and sat down at the writing table.

All day I walk from room to room, just to hear my footsteps echo.

I re-read the line I'd been carrying around in my head for days and had written down on the first page of my notebook. I thought it would generate more lines once I'd fixed it on the page.

'All day I walk from room to room . . .'

I must have read those words a hundred times: whispering them out loud; closing my eyes against them; staring them out; altering the emphases and waiting, waiting for inspiration – but I couldn't get anything else to come. The phrase no longer breathed. All I'd done was to lay it out, neat as a corpse, on the faint blue line at the top of page one. I tapped my pen against my teeth, and wondered about ditching poetry and trying my hand at fiction.

At the beginning of my stay I'd lain awake at night, trying to make up poems about Cory, but it was hopeless and I'd given up. If I tried to describe his physicality, I just sounded trite – he has hair as brown as [insert simile] and his voice is low and gentle like [insert simile] and he has sad eyes. On the other hand, if I left out all mention of his body, with the intention of cutting straight to his soul – like the rain at night, like the wind over the sea, like . . . – the words stopped meaning anything at all. I thought – or I *had* thought – that there was more scope in writing about the house. Perhaps if I switched to prose it might still be true.

'Oh Cory, where *are* you?'

I threw my pen down and got up. It would be easier to

concentrate if I knew where he'd gone. I poked my head round the bathroom door, but there was no water on the floor and no steam on the window. The bristles of his toothbrush were dry. I wondered about taking my usual shower – my skin felt tacky under my clothes and my hair was stiff with sea-water – but it seemed important to find him first. I shrank from the thought of being alone and naked inside Byrne Hall.

'Cory?'

It took a certain courage to send my voice ringing through that house. Every time I did it I felt as if someone – or something – were pricking up their ears. Perhaps it was an effect of the darkness, perhaps of the silence; certainly it had something to do with Diana's presence in that stuffy upstairs room. I was glad of the wedding bustle outside, and whenever my search took me to the front of the house I made a point of pausing to watch their comings and goings.

I began on the ground floor, but every time I crossed the hall I felt Lady Caroline's eyes following me. It began to drive me mad; I had to switch the picture light on to assure myself of her lifelessness. I was glad she bore no resemblance to Cory. Her mouth was curved in the beginnings of a joyless smile, and her fingers were tighter than they ought to have been round the spaniel's collar. Neither of these details had struck me before. For the first time it occurred to me that it would be good to be in London again; to have some distance from this place. I might be able to make some sense of it from there, and turn it into writing.

Many of the downstairs doors were locked, and I couldn't see through the keyholes because they were clogged with dust. It was the same upstairs. The rooms I did manage to enter were as godforsaken as Sleeping Beauty's castle – that's if the castle had been burgled during its hundred-year trance, and stripped of everything except a few dreary oddments. A clothes horse, a baize card table, a mouldy roll of carpet, a heap of dirty magazines from the eighties, a tray crammed with sticky, dusty, half-finished liqueurs.

Every now and then I risked calling his name, but by the time I reached the foot of the stairs to the second floor, my voice had sunk to an urgent whisper. I found myself gritting my teeth as I set foot on the first step.

Cory was sitting on the stairs, and he stared at me vacantly when I rounded the corner.

'You're here!' I cried. 'I couldn't understand where you'd got to, and I wanted to find you and talk to you, and I was calling and calling . . .'

I gabbled on, but Cory's mind was elsewhere. When I knelt on the stair below him and peered into his face, I smelled alcohol on his breath.

'Something terrible has happened,' he said.

'What? What's happened?'

He hiccupped softly.

'I'm going to miss you, when you go back,' he said, slipping sideways past my question. 'I'm going to miss you so much; I think it's going to drive me to drink.' And he laughed strangely.

'Cory . . .' I hadn't seen him in this mood before; I wished he'd look me in the eye. 'What did you mean when you said something terrible has happened?'

'I'm going to miss you so much.'

I stroked his back, and shushed him, and wondered what I'd done to make myself indispensable. His head felt heavy on my shoulder, as if he had the stem-like neck of a newborn, incapable of supporting its own weight.

I kept whispering and hushing in his ear, and he raised his head and held my face in his hands. Perhaps I'd been wrong, and he wasn't drunk after all. He didn't look it or sound it anymore; not when he stroked my face and said, 'I love you.'

Neither of us had ever said that before. It's a tricky phrase to say with conviction – it has a habit of sounding over-weighted, or trite, or simpering – but Cory's effort was a triumph.

When it came to sex, Cory had always erred on the side of stealth – conscious, I suppose, of his mother's presence in the house – but we scattered our clothes all over the landing and stairs that morning, and it didn't seem to bother him at all. I tried to whisper warnings, but I only got as far as 'Wait . . .' or 'What about . . .' before he filled my mouth with more kisses. When we reached the shower, I was the one who kept glancing over his slippery shoulder at the open bathroom door; he never even looked round.

I didn't properly relax until we were on the mattress, with the door firmly shut; only in the melting darkness beneath the covers could I find my focus – and find him. In the privacy of our bed, my skin meshed with his skin in an equal warmth, my arms and legs slid easily around his arms and legs, and I finally fell into step.

We stayed in bed for the rest of the day. So much for phoning my boss and packing my bags for tomorrow. I slept through the afternoon and woke in the early evening, when the wedding party had begun to get raucous and the speakers were booming.

*

Cory was standing at the window with his arms folded and his forehead on the glass. I propped myself up on my elbow.

'I can see you watching me,' he said, and I realised he wasn't looking outwards at the garden, but inwards at my reflection.

I smiled.

'What are you thinking?' he said.

It was difficult to gauge his tone when he had his back turned and his face was a blurry reflection in the glass. An argument was brewing on the lawn: I heard a woman's slurred shrieks and a man's voice shouting over her, and the music went up several notches in volume as if to drown them out. I thought Cory would mind, but he didn't seem to notice.

'I don't know,' I said. 'I suppose I was thinking about having to go home tomorrow.'

When he shook his head, I got out of bed and looped my arms around him. I laid my face against his back and laced my fingers over his chest.

'I don't want you to go,' he said. 'It feels like the end of the world.'

I tried not to smile too much. With my face resting on his shoulder-blade, he was bound to feel the muscles move in my cheeks.

'It won't be the end of the world.' I was sure of myself, for once, as I let myself drift on the rise and fall of his breathing. 'It'll be the beginning. Why don't you come to London tomorrow? Stay with me and Dad for a while?'

I knew exactly what it would be like. He'd meet me every evening after work, and we'd stroll through parks under autumnal trees, and hold hands across the table in candlelit bars, and cook proper dinners for Dad, and visit galleries, and linger outside jewellery shops, and never stop talking and laughing. I'd buy myself some better clothes, and we'd look like a couple in an advert. It sounds banal when I spell it out like that, but in my mind it was beautiful.

Silence followed my invitation and I thought he was with me, peering down the same kaleidoscope as one scene shifted and tumbled to the next. I closed my eyes and pressed against his back, but the rhythm of his breathing had altered. The rise and fall had become jagged and choppy.

'Cory?'

He didn't resist when I turned him round and held him at arm's length, nor when my fingers probed the gleaming patches on his face, as if I were in any doubt they were tears. My hand fell away and I didn't know what to say. I felt as hot and weepy as an overwhelmed child. Whatever this situation was – good or bad – it was Too Much.

'Don't *cry*!' I said, half laughing. 'Why are you *crying*?'

'Something happened this morning.'

I shook my head slightly.

'You don't understand,' he said.

Was that the hint of an accusation? I began to protest – but stopped. Let him have his say.

'What happened this morning?'

'My mother . . .' He turned back to the window. I put my arms around him as before, but cautiously, in case he snarled or snapped. I laid my cheek lightly against his back, without leaning in, and rode the swell of movement as he wiped his arms across his face.

'She collapsed. I had to phone for an ambulance, and they came, and they were here for ages. Then they took her off to the hospital, but I didn't go with her because I was waiting for you—'

His voice failed, and I tightened my hold around his chest. *You might have mentioned this before*, I thought uncharitably, although I didn't say it. I wasn't up for a fight; that wasn't how our story went.

'I can't go back with you to London,' he said angrily. 'I can't go anywhere.'

I held still as the fairy lights came on in the trees – not the pale, starry ones I remembered from my cousin's wedding, but gaudy ones that flashed on and off, at hectic speed, in all the colours of the rainbow. Their reflections turned the pond into a cauldron that fizzed with reds and greens and blues.

Cory began throwing on his clothes. A bunch of keys fell out of his trouser pocket, and he snatched it up in his fist as if it mustn't be seen; as if it were the clue to some profane secret. The air was so thick with things unsaid that I found it an effort to breathe. I wanted to know what was going on inside his head, but I couldn't have coveted him so vehemently if I'd understood him the way I understood – say – Tom. My feeling for Cory was piercing and pure; it hadn't been muddied by friendship and long familiarity.

I reached for my jeans and put them on cautiously, in case he was provoked by the whisper of denim and the jingle of a belt. He turned as I was fastening the buckle and let out a shuddering sigh.

'Freya, forgive me. I'm sorry.'

'What for?'

'For being such a . . .' He spread his arms wide in a helpless shrug. 'None of this is your fault. I know you have to leave me now—'

'I won't. I won't leave you. I'll stay.'

139

He stared. After a moment he cupped his hands and held them out, like a child expecting a gift. Warily, I placed my own hands inside them, doubtful of making the correct gesture. He didn't throw them away, but he didn't grasp them either; he just kept staring, as if I were the one acting all opaque.

'But you'll lose your job.'

I shrugged – and if I also quaked slightly, it was with triumph as well as fear. I was at the wheel of a car, driving too hard and too fast down a winding road.

'So what? I don't care. It's nothing. It's just a dead-end, pedestrian job – sending emails and answering the phone for other people.'

All those unblinking screens and trilling phones, and the strip lighting, and the polystyrene cups, and the brilliant white walls with no windows.

Cory closed his hands slowly around mine.

'Never mind me,' I said. The decision was made and I was impatient of further discussion. 'What about Diana? When will you know more from the hospital? We could phone for a taxi and go to her now.'

'Wait . . .' Cory's tone of voice was effortful – as it had been before – but this time it wasn't anger he was struggling to suppress. 'I need to get this straight in my head. You're going to give up your job, so that you can stay here with me?'

'Yes.'

'Freya, are you *sure*?'

I nodded.

'Yes, yes. I'm sure.'

He pulled me forwards, releasing my hands only to wrap

me tightly in his arms. A minute ago it had bothered me that he was fully clothed while I was only half dressed, but it stopped mattering as soon as we were bound together.

'Thank you.'

He disappeared again in the early hours. I reached for him in my sleep, but the duvet was turned back at the corner and the mattress was cold. I sat up with a lurch and hoisted the covers up to my chin.

I wasn't afraid. The house was ours now. The worst of its mysteries had fallen away like veils, one by one, and there was nothing left to trouble us. Nobody to listen out for, or hide from, or suspect. Lady Caroline's faded eyes were not alive. Diana was in good hands somewhere else. Stella had never set foot inside the door. Cory Byrne needed me.

Cory needed me. I lay down and sure enough he came back, soft-footed as a thief. I didn't let him know I was awake; I just watched him wandering round the studio, peering at the drawings on the walls and pausing at the easel. The wedding party had broken up and the gardens were quiet, but the fairy lights were still on and our bedroom shadows were speckled with colour.

I think he stopped in front of every single drawing. He had a crayon or a charcoal stick tucked behind his ear, and occasionally he'd lean in to add an extra line or a patch of shade. Sometimes he made no adjustments but just touched the drawings with his fingertips, caressing them as if they were made of warm skin instead of paper.

I breathed sleepily and only my eyes moved under their half-closed lids, following his fingers over all those static faces and bodies. In the daylight their fleshy lips and shoulders put me on edge, but it was easy to like them in the semi-darkness. It was easy to think of them as me.

October 2005

'I'm sure we'll find her in Cromer,' I say, yet again.

'I'm not.' Dad grinds the gears on the rental car, as if he'd rather fight it than drive it.

I am sitting on the edge of the passenger seat with a map across my knees. It's not as if we don't know the way – we've driven to the Norfolk coast every summer since I was born – but because it's October, and because our motives are anxious, it feels like new terrain.

I am confident that we will find Stella here. I had a few moments of doubt about two hours into the drive, but after a while Dad noticed I was crying and I felt his eyes flitting between the road and my turned-away face. It's not that he said or did anything irritable, but I know he was thinking, <u>Please, I don't need another drama queen</u>, and actually that helped me to get over it. I'm fine now.

'She's talked about Cromer a lot, the last week or two,' I say as we enter the town. I scan the pavements, left and right, and everybody seems to be Stella from the back – old, young, fat, thin, man, woman – there's something of Stella in all of them, until I glimpse their faces. 'She feels happy here.'

But it's Dad who spots her first.

'There!' he says. 'She's there!'

She looks slighter than she did two evenings ago. Her hair is imperfectly tucked inside a woolly hat and she walks with her hands in her pockets, her arms tight against her sides. She glances into a shop window, pauses a second and walks on.

'For goodness' sake, Freya – shut the door! The car's still moving!'

Stella hears me call her name and turns.

'I said, shut the door!'

Dad's patience is wearing thin, and who can blame him? All the same, I wish he'd let his relief show. The first time Stella ran away, he hugged her hard when she came back, and I deceived myself into thinking it was a Happily Ever After.

Dad takes his time parking up and paying at the meter. When he does finally join us, he merely glances at Stella before announcing that he's off to the pub.

'I'm sorry,' he says – meaning he's not – 'but frankly I need a drink. Freya? You must be pretty knackered too?'

I shake my head and he walks away in the direction of the Red Lion without looking back. I take Stella's arm and we head into the easterly wind, past the entrance to the pier and down the steps to the beach. Last time we were here, seven weeks ago, we had our swimming costumes on under our clothes.

'He'll come round,' I say, as if she doesn't know the old routine as well as I do. 'He's just tired and upset.'

Stella hmms and shivers. She never takes enough clothes for these escapades. She never takes enough of anything. We're walking on wet sand, and her canvas shoes are beginning to squelch, but she doesn't seem to notice.

'I don't know why I do it,' she says flatly, pre-empting the question I wasn't going to ask. 'I don't know what's wrong with me.'

I hold tight to her arm and press my cheek against her bony shoulder as we walk. It's stupid to envy someone who is lonely and disturbed, but I do envy Stella. I would like to be enigmatic too. I'd like to think there were people out there – by 'people' I suppose I mean Dad and Tom – lying awake at night, pondering the mysteries of my soul.

'I'm so cold,' Stella says, and I cling more tightly to her arm. Usually she is hard and aloof for several days after she gets back, and I feel sick when I wonder who she's been with, and what she's been doing. This time she is not hard at all; she is a lost little girl and I feel older than my fourteen years as I spout platitudes about how much she's loved, and how great she is. We stop at the edge of the water and she watches the wavelets splash over her shoes. I don't think she's listening.

When I've finished speaking she says, 'Do you ever feel like you want something so badly you'll die if you don't get it? But at the same time, you don't exactly know what it is? Whether it's a feeling, or a place, or a person . . . ?'

'I'm not sure,' I say. 'Maybe . . .'

Stella nods, and I wish I could say something amazing and wise and helpful which would bring her back for ever. At least we are here now, with our arms intertwined; I will have to make do with that. She laughs slightly as a wave breaks over our ankles, and I glance at her and laugh too.

3

THE BAY BELOW THE GARDEN was deserted next time I went. I hadn't noticed the cloud cover as I left the house; it was only when I stopped halfway down the cliff path and took in the vista that I saw how grey and choppy the sea was. It wasn't weather for swimming.

It was disappointing; I'd been missing my old routine. Missing the sunrise over the water, and Stella's cryptic cliffs, and calling out 'Hi' to the woman in the swim-cap. I hadn't come for ages, because I didn't like to think of Cory waking up and finding me gone, but he never did wake till eleven at the earliest, and today I'd decided to risk it.

No. 'Risk' is too strong a word. If I'd grown wary of hurting Cory's feelings over the last few days, it wasn't because of anything he'd said or done. I suppose it was because his mother was ill, and because of the alcohol I'd smelled on his breath that strange morning, and because he seemed to get sad so easily and to love me so much.

I trudged back towards the house, pausing a couple of times to look round. I don't know what I was hoping to see. The sudden appearance of a lemon-yellow sea, I suppose, and long ripples fanning out in the wake of my friend's front crawl.

The gardens were wet and chilly under that low sky and the house had all its blinds down. I stopped to catch my breath, burdened by the prospect of four solitary hours before Cory woke up. I didn't want to mooch about the lawns, getting my feet soaked. I didn't want to sit on my own in the echoey kitchen, sipping tea.

The best thing would be to crawl under the covers and watch the shadows lighten on the ceiling while I waited for Cory's day to begin. After all, why not? There was something sweet about the idea, which fitted all my fantasies of happiness, but at the same time it made me twitch my toes and shoulder my bag impatiently.

The driver saw me before I saw him. I hadn't even realised I was standing at a bus stop – I'd only paused beside the harbour to shove my swimming towel inside my bag – but he must have thought I was waiting to flag him down. As the bus slowed I had time to read the words 'via Hospital' slide along the screen at the front, and then the doors were hissing open and the driver was leaning forwards expectantly.

'Hospital?' I said, as much to myself as to him. Cory hadn't mentioned his mother lately, and I hadn't dared ask. It would only make him go quiet.

'Are you getting on or not?' The driver was brisk, and before I knew it the machine was spitting out a return ticket, and I was fumbling in my purse for change.

Cory wouldn't mind me visiting his mother, would he? The answer came back straight away, as the bus pulled in at the front entrance: of course he wouldn't. Going to see someone in hospital was a nice and normal thing to do. I joined the other arrivals in the large revolving door – the heavily pregnant woman, the old man with the Zimmer frame, the middle-aged couple with the child – and followed them across the squeaky floor of the foyer.

The bouquets in the foyer shop looked sad – the flowers, such as they were, hidden inside layers of plastic packaging – but I bought one anyway. It didn't matter; it would give me something to talk about if Diana was awake. I could draw a rueful contrast with the gardens at Byrne Hall and offer to cut some roses for her next time I came. My palms began sweating when I thought about what she might say in return, and my fingers made smeary prints on the cellophane.

'Can I help?'

'Oh . . .'

The receptionist and I stared at one another, teetering on the brink of recognition. The name on her staff badge was Maggie Bailey. I was the first to twig.

'It's you!' I said. 'You're not swimming this morning, then?'

Her features relaxed into a comprehending smile.

'No. Maybe when my shift is over?' She rubbed her arms as if she were cold, although the foyer seemed stuffy to me. 'Then again, maybe not. I think summer's over, isn't it?'

The man behind me shifted and sighed, and Maggie drew herself up hastily.

'Anyway. How can I help?'

'Oh, yes.' The bouquet crackled under my fingers. 'I suppose I'm early for visiting, but I came on the off-chance . . . I can just leave these flowers if it's not—'

'What's the name, please?' Maggie turned to her screen.

'My name?'

'The patient's name.'

'Oh. Diana Byrne. I don't know which ward—'

'Diana . . . ?'

'Byrne. B-Y-R-N-E.'

'B . . . Y . . . R . . . N . . . E . . .' Maggie mouthed the letters

147

as she typed, her eyes darting over the computer screen. She frowned, tried again, shook her head. I leaned forwards, squashing the flowers against the desk, and the man behind me cleared his throat.

'I'm sorry,' said Maggie. 'I can't find that name on the system.'

She tapped her lips and stared at the screen, as if there were a chance it might solve the conundrum on its own, without further prompting. The man sighed again, and her shoulders dropped.

'Would you mind waiting for just one moment, while I help this gentleman?'

I wanted to say, *Listen, no, it's fine, forget I ever asked*, but I was too slow and the man had already taken my place. I shuffled to one side, and as I did so the queue grew by two, and then three.

It was warm in the foyer, and the scent of flowers was edged with decay. The rise and fall of voices in that bright, light space grew strange in my ears, as if everyone had stopped speaking words and begun to buzz instead, like angry bees. I tried to remember when I'd last eaten, but I could only remember Cory opening a bottle of wine last night, when he'd already been painting for a couple of hours and I was half asleep.

I bought a cup of hot chocolate in the hospital café and sat at a corner table. I'd leave just as soon as I felt better. I didn't want to talk to Maggie Bailey again. I wanted to be back at Byrne Hall with Cory, pretending that this had never happened.

'Phew!' Maggie sighed as she slumped into the chair opposite mine. I swallowed too quickly and scalded the back of my mouth.

'Another shift over,' she said. 'Sorry to make you wait like that, but the guy behind you was looking like thunder.'

She swigged an energy drink, and I dabbed at my chocolatey lips.

'Oh no, it's fine,' I said. 'Honestly, this whole thing – it's just a case of me being stupid. Mrs Byrne must have gone to another hospital. I should have listened properly; I should have checked before I came.'

Maggie glanced at me sceptically, as if she knew me better than I knew myself.

'What other hospital?'

'I don't know . . .' I blushed. 'A private one, maybe.'

It annoyed me, that sceptical look; it implied she had the right to probe, and opine, and expect straight answers. I didn't even know the woman and she didn't know me. I lifted my bag on to my lap and pretended to make sure my phone was still there, and my purse, and my bus ticket.

'She's not a close relative, then?' Maggie took another gulp from her bottle, but her eyes never left my face.

'No, she's . . .' I hesitated. 'Well, she's the mother of my . . . We're not close or anything; she's not expecting to see me. She fell ill the other day, while I was out and – well. I obviously got the wrong end of the stick.'

Maggie tilted her head.

'Byrne,' she said meditatively. 'Is that anything to do with Byrne Hall?'

'That's where I'm staying at the moment, with her son.'

'Oh! And there was I the other morning, being rude about it.'

'Oh, yes.' I narrowed my eyes and repressed a smile. 'You think the house looks like an *evil face*.'

'Sorry.' Maggie took another swig of her drink and started

laughing. 'Please, just ignore me – what do I know? I'll tell you what it is: I've been prejudiced against it for years, ever since I got shouted at.'

I sat forwards. 'How do you mean?'

'Oh gosh, it was so long ago. I mean, like two decades or something. Me and my mates, we were in our teens, and we were messing about on the beach with a campfire and a few drinks. Anyway, this man comes charging down the cliff path with a little boy in tow, and he's unbuckling his belt and yelling about how it's private property and how he's going to flay us alive.'

'Wow.'

'I've been swimming there ever since, on principle. Actually, that isn't as brave as it sounds because the owner – I assume he was the owner – is supposed to have died or moved away quite soon after.'

Cory's father, then? Cory's father with a little boy.

'What did they look like?'

'Like two peas in a pod. Smug, tanned, sporty, gorgeous types.'

So, not Cory? Surely none of those adjectives ever applied to him? Not in the way she meant, anyway.

I dropped the teaspoon into the empty mug and zipped up my bag.

'It was nice talking to you,' I said, 'but I'd better go.'

I swung my bag over my shoulder and scraped my chair back. The bouquet slid under the table, but I didn't bother to retrieve it.

'OK, but listen, you take care of yourself.' Maggie looked at me uneasily. 'And I hope you find Diana Byrne.'

I didn't know how to answer that.

'Maybe I'll see you at the beach again, one of these mornings?' she said.

'Maybe.' That sounded grudging, so I added a smile and said, 'I hope so.'

Dad had messaged me first thing. I glanced over his text as the bus jolted off the main road and over a series of speed bumps. It was a long one, for him. I skimmed it for any reference to Tom and my eye snagged on the word *prerogative*. Only Dad would use a word like *prerogative* in a text message. I wasn't sure I had enough patience to read it all just now.

I turned to the window, but my eyes lost their focus, and the greens and greys of the suburban morning passed by in a blur. I could see Dad hunched over the screen, his lower lip jutting as he typed with his forefinger. He always punched the keys too hard, as if he were using a typewriter, and then he got cross when the touch screen did something untoward. It must have taken him ages to type such a long message, given his slowness and his idiosyncratic vocabulary.

I sighed and took the phone out of my bag again.

My dear Freya,

I'm sorry I wasn't communicative last night. Rest assured that I'm not angry in the least – you are a grown-up woman, and you know best how to live your life. Neither have I any axe to grind with Cory Byrne; it's not his fault he lives in a place with sad associations for our family.

Anxiety is, however, a parent's prerogative. I suppose, of my two children, I always characterised – caricatured? – you as the steady, thoughtful one, and your sister as the

151

rash, startling one. It may not be fair, but it goes some way towards explaining why I feel apprehensive now.

I'm not writing to ask anything of you – except that you stay safe, well and happy. I want to apologise for having been a difficult man to live with, and to tell you that I love you, very dearly.

Dad. X

The woman across the aisle darted me a look, so I turned to the window and hid my teary face against the glass.

Here, at last, was Bligh with its wheeling gulls and swaying masts, and the sea coming into view like a blank, grey wall thrown up across the end of the road.

4

LATER THE SAME DAY I floundered downstairs, rubbing my eyes. I didn't know what time it was, but it felt like mid-afternoon. The dull skies had darkened, and the sunlight that reached through the open front door was cool and thin.

'Here she is!' Cory cried. 'Sleeping Beauty awakes!'

He crossed the hall and swept me off my feet as if we were on a film set, about to go into a dance. I yelped and grabbed on to his shoulders, trying to take it in good part.

'You've been asleep *for ever*,' he said, spinning me round and round the chequer-board floor. *Black, white, black, white, black* . . . I closed my eyes, but that only made things worse, so I clung to whatever I could – the collar of his shirt, his neck, his hair – and willed him to stop. There was no point struggling; I was afraid, if I did, that I might fall.

He had no idea, then, that I'd been up and about already, jolting across town to the hospital where his mother wasn't – apparently – a patient? Certainly, he'd appeared to be deeply asleep when I got back, and he hadn't stirred all the time I was undressing and sliding back into bed. I'd lain for a long time staring stiffly at his back without daring to touch it, waiting for a wide-awake voice to ask where I'd been. The warmth of the duvet and the rhythm of his breathing must have got to me. I don't remember giving in to sleep; I hadn't intended to. I'd intended to think.

I shrieked as he flipped me up and caught me – easy-peasy – with one arm under my knees and the other supporting my back. I had to clutch him round the neck – there was nothing else for it – but although I laughed, I couldn't quite laugh the way he wanted me to.

'Oh, come on, Freya Lyell! Don't be grumpy!'

Cory hitched me higher until our faces were almost touching, and kissed the tip of my nose.

'What's up?'

I smiled without meeting his eye.

'Nothing,' I said. 'I'm just sleepy.'

He let me slither to my feet and I staggered as the hall floor spun. Lady Caroline and her pop-eyed dog were watching from the back wall, as if they liked me a little less each time they saw me.

'Freya . . . ?'

When he picked up my hand I thought he was going to lead me to the kitchen and a mug of tea – but no. We were heading for one of the big rooms at the front of the house. I dragged my feet, but Cory couldn't seem to walk like any normal human being. If he wasn't pacing backwards he was bounding like a puppy, or twirling me into a waltz.

'I've had the most amazing idea,' he said. 'I've been thinking about it all morning, while you were asleep.'

'Oh yes?'

I couldn't take in what he said; I was too distracted by the pulse in my head. *B-Y-R-N-E*, it went, on and on, round and round. Maggie's voice seemed to echo between my ears, one letter for every beat, and I saw her frowning at the screen. *Byrne. B-Y-R-N-E. I can't find that name on the system.*

'Freya?'

'Sorry, sorry. You've been thinking . . .'

'What's the first thing you notice about this room?'

Cory kept hold of my hand and twisted elegantly away, holding me at arm's length as if we were performers awaiting applause.

I looked around helplessly. The front room was empty, except for a plastic garden chair on its side. The wallpaper must have been a heavy, Victorian affair when it was first hung, but it was fragile and faded now. The dust was so thick on the wooden floor that our feet left prints, and with every step a blizzard of motes whirled up round our legs.

'You've raised the blinds?'

'Mm-hm. And?'

'It's . . . big?'

'Yes!' Cory squeezed my hand, as if I'd said something clever. 'So . . . ? What does that put you in mind of?'

He grabbed both my hands again and began turning me in a circle, ring-a-ring-o'-roses fashion.

'Um . . .' My nose was starting to itch.

'In relation to me . . . ?' he prompted. 'And you, for that matter.'

I pulled free and smothered a sneeze against my sleeve.

'I'm not sure.'

There was an edge of impatience to his smile as he put his hands on his hips.

'What do I spend all my time doing?' he said.

'Um . . . drawing? Drawing and painting.'

'Drawing and painting *you*. Yes.' He seemed to stop and study me – not critically, exactly, but thoughtfully, as if puzzling something out in his head. A second later his eyes

155

lightened, and he reached round the back of my head to undo the clip, so that my hair tumbled over my shoulders.

He smiled and pocketed the clip. 'So . . . ?'

'So . . . you could make this into your new studio?' I frowned as I fingered my loosened hair. 'It's bigger than your room upstairs. And lighter. Possibly.'

Cory growled in mock exasperation.

'Not a studio, Dumbo. A *gallery*! And not just this room but the whole of the downstairs.'

He was off again, sliding in his bare feet across the hall, dancing me into another room. The blinds were up, and it was in much the same state, except that the pink wallpaper was actually coming unstuck, and there were strips hanging off the plaster like giant, curling tongues. Cory began ripping them off and dropping them by the armful at my feet. This was the room with the sofa, where I'd helped Diana the day I arrived.

'Can't you just see it?' he said, as I fought another sneeze. 'The floors all polished up and glossy, and the walls painted? I was thinking white at first, but perhaps something dark would be classier, to make the portraits stand out. And we'd have to sort out the lighting and the frames, and we'd have to think about how to present the show: maybe starting with that sketch I did the first day we met, and working through chronologically? It could be a kind of story that people follow round. Or we could put all the drawings in one room, and all the paintings in the other? I'm not sure – what do you think? We could call it "Portraits of Freya", or maybe . . .' he drew a curve in the air, as if to reveal my name in lights '. . . maybe just "Freya". And for the opening we'd have Byrne Hall decked out in all its glory, with the chandeliers working, and flowers, and music, and a champagne fountain . . .'

I broke away and wandered on my own round the room, running my fingers over the fraying wallpaper as if its condition interested me in the least. Some small and furtive creature – a mouse? – scuttled behind the skirting board, and I comforted myself with the thought that Cory's scheme would come to nothing. The house was too tired. Nobody would be interested.

'I caught a bus this morning, while you were still asleep,' I said. 'I didn't plan to. I walked into town and just . . . got on.'

Cory stood still at last.

'A bus?'

'To the hospital. I thought your mum might appreciate a visit. I bought her a bunch of flowers in the foyer shop.'

I turned to look at him and his eyes dropped to the ribbon of wallpaper in his hands. He frowned.

'If you mean the main hospital on the edge of town,' he said, 'she isn't there.'

'I know that now.'

'The place where she is . . . it's more like a hospice . . .'

'Oh.'

I felt awful when he said that, and my suspicions seemed silly. I couldn't even articulate them in my own head.

'I'm sorry,' I said. 'I didn't mean to be interfering. It was a spur of the moment thing; I just thought she might enjoy having a visitor . . . Maybe we could go together some time?'

It was intended as an olive branch, but Cory snapped.

'She doesn't want *visitors*. For God's sake . . .'

I held my hands up. 'I'm *sorry*.'

Cory made a vicious rip in the wallpaper and I didn't know what to do. I approached him cautiously and put my arms

157

around his waist. We stood nose to nose, for minutes on end, while I searched his eyes for some way in.

'Talk to me about this exhibition,' I ventured. 'I love to see you all happy.'

It took him a while to soften, but I think it was the right thing to say.

The pasta shells had gone past their 'use by' date, but they looked and smelled all right, so I clattered a few handfuls into the pan and covered them with boiling water. There wasn't anything that would do for a sauce, except a tin of tomatoes at the back of a cupboard, and the date on that was illegible.

'We ought to go shopping.' I glanced round to see if Cory was listening, but he was absorbed by his laptop.

'What are you reading?'

I left the cupboard door ajar and leaned over the back of his chair. His hair tickled my nose and I breathed in its musky scent.

'I'm researching gallery walls,' he said. 'A lot of them are dark red, aren't they? Look . . .' He clicked through several tabs. 'These are rooms in the Louvre . . . the National Gallery . . . the Fitzwilliam . . .'

I snorted.

'What?' His fingers froze over the keyboard.

'Nothing!' I burrowed into his hair. 'I'm just admiring your ambition. National Gallery . . . Louvre . . . Byrne Hall . . . Why not?'

The pan boiled over, extinguishing the gas flame, so I kissed the crown of his head and returned to the hob. I stirred the pasta with a fork and opened the tin of tomatoes, aware of having created a silence. I told myself he was entitled to be touchy, because of his mother.

'Come to think of it,' I said, 'the walls in the main room of the Wingate Gallery are a kind of dark, velvety red. They used to be, anyway. I think they still are.' I was trying so hard to sound serious that I came across – to my own ears, at least – as ironic.

'The *Wingate*.' Cory's voice had a cold and peculiar emphasis. The pasta wasn't ready, but I drained it anyway and stirred in the tomatoes.

'How will you . . .' I didn't have a question at the ready, but I felt an urgent need to move the conversation along, one way or another. 'I mean . . . Who were you thinking you'd invite to the opening?'

'Oh, that won't be a problem.' He gave my 'interested' face a hard stare as I brought the bowls to the table. 'All I need is my mother's address book. It might be a few years out of date, but it'll be full of contacts: dealers and collectors and so on. She used to be quite a mover and shaker on the London art scene. I've told you that before, haven't I?'

I nodded sheepishly at the mention of Diana and ground too much salt over my pasta. 'And . . . so . . . what kind of timescale are you thinking? Opening night in the spring? Summer?'

He laughed frankly, rocking back on his chair, and the kitchen echoed like a cave. I shivered. This room was too big for two people. The whole house was too big for two people, come to that, but I always felt it most in the kitchen. It was a relic of olden times, when Byrne Hall was a bustle of servants. It was meant to be an engine room, bright with fire, foggy with steam, and filled from floor to ceiling with the clatter of feet, and the barking of orders, and the smells of roasting meat.

'Oh, Freya, I love you,' said Cory. 'You're so cautious and . . . I don't know. What's the word? *Quaint.*'

I prodded the pasta glumly with my spoon. It was chewy.

'I don't think I'm cautious,' I retorted. 'I wasn't cautious when I chucked in my job to be with you.' I wasn't going to argue with 'quaint'; I didn't want to hear what he meant by that.

'Don't be like that! I didn't mean it in a bad way!' At least he was elated again. 'I was thinking in terms of a few weeks. November? The end of October, even.'

I looked up.

'Oh, right! Wow!'

We both waited in case I was going to come up with anything more adequate, but I didn't, so we bent our heads and ate. The silence was immense and the spoons resonated against our bowls like a chime of little bells.

The wind had got up. A herring gull hovered over the trees with its wings outstretched, struggling to steer a course. *I think summer's over, isn't it?* Maggie had said at the hospital – and she was right. Darkness permeated the air like a corrosive chemical, bleaching away colour and warmth. Cory was still downstairs, wading through his pasta, and I wondered how long it would be before he came to find me. He'd say, *What are you doing here? I thought you were just going to the loo?* And I wouldn't know how to justify myself.

We had to have our first argument at some point, I accepted that, but it ought to have been a proper fight, with lots of noise and tears and sparks flying. It ought to have ended in peace.

Whereas . . . what *was* this, exactly? What should I call it? Hardly a fight. More a slippage, or a misalignment. I didn't know if it was over, or if it mattered at all, or if it was something I'd be wise to refer to again. I rubbed my goose-pimpled arms and lingered at the window.

Stella had run away from home for the first time on a day like this. There'd been precisely the same wind-raked, emptied-out kind of sky, and there'd been birds – starlings rather than gulls – wheeling over the rooftops. When the police had finished talking to me I'd gone up to my bedroom and shivered in the semi-darkness, and whenever my eye had fallen on the ordinary things around my room – the candlewick bedspread, the teddies, the crumpled heap of school uniform on the floor – I felt she'd be fine, but whenever I looked out at that sky I felt sure they'd find her dead. I was eleven. She turned up again the next morning and said sorry for scaring us, and we got over it, and life went back to nearly normal.

'Are you all right?'

Cory's voice made me jump, and I tensed when he placed his hands on my arms. He massaged my rigid shoulders, and I wanted to respond by loosening up but I couldn't will myself to do it. All the little locks that ought to have clicked under his touch were jammed.

'What are you doing up here?' he said.

I closed my eyes so I didn't have to look at my own frowning face in the window. Various answers tempted me. *I was about to phone my friend Tom for a heart to heart. I was about to rip all the pages out of the notebook you gave me. I was packing my bags.*

Gently, his fingers came to rest on my neck.

'There's something I want you to have,' he said. 'Can I show you now? And then let's finish eating and I'd better get back to work.'

My mind was still on Tom and I nodded without thinking. Cory kissed the back of my neck and said my name.

'Here, Freya, look.'

He fumbled in his pocket and various bits fell out – a pencil end, a receipt, a champagne cork – until he found whatever it was and held it out. My first view was a reflection in the darkening glass, but I couldn't believe what I was seeing, so I turned and stared at the real thing.

'Take it,' he said, but my arms hung heavy at my sides, as if I were carrying weights.

'It's a ring,' I said, like an idiot.

My reluctance to hold it – even to touch it – was not so much a state of mind as a physical impediment. It was an ache in my brain and in my fingers; a shiver in the vicinity of my heart. Cory opened my hand and laid it on my palm, and I peered at it through the half-light. It was a silvery, complicated thing: an elaborate whirl of curlicues and Celtic knots. It was the sort of ring Stella would have liked. Perhaps I liked it too.

'Aren't you going to put it on?'

Cory tried it on all my fingers in turn, but the only one it almost fitted was the fourth finger of my left hand. I looked swiftly into his face, but he seemed unaware of the significance.

'Does this mean we're engaged?'

It was, I felt, a question I ought to know the answer to without having to ask outright.

'Would you like it to mean that?'

'I don't know.'

162

I twisted the ring round, exploring its points and ridges with the pad of my thumb. It was tight, but just about moveable.

'Yes,' I corrected myself belatedly. I looked into his face and said it again. 'Yes!'

I stroked his fist, but it was like trying to soften a stone, so I raised it to my lips and kissed it. There was no response. I kissed it again.

'I didn't mean to equivocate. I was surprised, that's all. I'm sorry. The answer is yes.'

Nothing.

Over and over again, knuckle by knuckle, I kissed his hand.

'I won't stop doing this,' I warned, turning it over and starting on the other side, 'until you stop being cross.'

Slowly, he unclenched his fist and we both began to laugh.

Diana can't tell where she is. Sometimes she seems to sense the outlines of her own bedroom, but if this is Byrne Hall then why has everything gone quiet? She and the house have kept up a lively dialogue for years and, as far as she's concerned, there are still things to say. In her most anguished moments Diana imagines she's been removed to some sinister institution: a hospital, perhaps, or a 'home'.

She hasn't known this depth of quiet for a long time. It resembles the quiet that fell on Byrne Hall thirteen years ago, after her husband died.

What a strange quiet that was. Diana thought the house would sing for joy when that man died and it surprised her – surprises her still – that it didn't.

'I'm opening a bottle of champagne,' she'd announced, as the sun melted into the sea. Nine hours had passed since her husband

was discovered, washed up on the beach like a length of driftwood. 'We could go and drink it in the garden, just you and me?' She'd already made her way through half a bottle of brandy over the course of the afternoon. People kept recommending it for shock.

'I'm thirteen.' Cory glared at the floor. 'I'm not supposed to drink alcohol.'

'Well, I won't tell if you won't . . .' She nudged him gently with her elbow, but he twisted away as if she'd wounded him.

'I'm going to bed.'

Diana stood alone in the kitchen, listening to the trudge of his feet on the stairs and the slam of his bedroom door. After a few minutes she popped the cork and took a thoughtful swig, straight from the bottle. She kicked her shoes off and went outside, making silent toasts – to the sea, to the house, to her sleeping son, to herself – as she wandered bare-foot among the roses.

It grew cold when night fell, and Diana came indoors. Champagne bottle in hand – there were still a couple of mouthfuls left – she went up to the bedroom and threw open the wardrobe doors.

Top-quality, well-ironed shirts had been important to Mr Byrne and he'd amassed quite a collection over the years. Every time he unfolded a fresh one he would inspect it closely, and if there were creases or signs of wear he'd have something to say.

Diana tossed them over her shoulder one by one, forming a silky, crumpled, champagne-stained carpet on the floor. She walked across them with her soil-caked feet, and sat on the chair by the window.

The house – like her son – was studiously silent. Diana thought about her pale, tongue-tied boy with the bruise under his eye.

What had the bruise been for? Failure in some school exam? Well, there'd be no more of that. Let's call it a parting shot, *she thought with a thin smile,* and watch how quickly it fades.

The moon was white and bloated like her husband's face, when he lay on the beach with his mouth and eyes agape.

'You leave my son alone.' *She pushed the window wide open and spoke into the night.* 'Now that you're gone, stay gone. Byrne Hall has enough ghosts without you.'

The moon stared back at her, speechless. Diana staggered to her feet, drained the last of the champagne and made for the bed. A man's torso was lying on top of the quilt: headless, handless, sprawling and obscene, his arms thrown wide and wild. A whole minute passed before she dared to hook a finger under the well-starched collar and drop the shirt on to the floor.

5

'YOU'RE BRAVE!' I CALLED AS I reached the sand, and Maggie came wading towards me out of the surf. It was a cloudless sunrise but cold, and I'd brought my towel and costume out of habit rather than intent. I was wearing Cory's sweater over my T-shirt; he'd given it to me the other day when I was complaining I'd only packed for summer.

'It's all right once you're in,' she said, breathing hard and rubbing her hair with a towel. I sat on my usual rock, hugging my knees and looking away while she dried herself and dressed. She took a thermos flask from her bag, poured a cup of milky coffee and handed it to me, shaking her head dismissively when I thanked her.

'I'm glad you came,' she said. 'I wanted to ask about your friend's mother. Have you found out what's going on?'

'Oh, there's nothing "going on". Cory told me—'

'Cory?'

'My friend.' I decided to stick to 'friend', even if it was rather demure. 'Fiancé' didn't come naturally yet. 'Mrs Byrne's son.'

'Oh.'

'He just said she's in a hospice – or something a bit like a hospice – and she's not ready for visitors.'

'But surely *he* visits?'

'I suppose . . . I don't know . . .'

'But he must do. Where is it, this place that's "a bit like a hospice"?'

'I don't know,' I repeated. 'Look, Cory doesn't want to talk about it, and I don't like to press him . . . Quite honestly, it's none of my business.'

Dad loathed it when I used the phrase *Quite honestly*, or *To be honest with you*; he said my honesty ought to go without saying. I took a sip and tried not to wonder what Maggie was thinking.

When I passed her the cup she grasped it in both hands, as if she'd get more heat out if she squeezed hard. A breeze passed over the surface of the sea, sending ruffles in odd directions, and we both shivered.

'You ought to ask him,' said Maggie definitely. 'You ought to know what's going on.'

I picked at the limpets that freckled our rock.

'It isn't the kind of thing that needs to be secret,' she insisted. 'If you're too scared to ask him a simple question, he can't be much of a friend.'

'I'm not *scared* of asking,' I said with a noise that resembled a laugh. 'It's not like that.'

'OK . . .' She sounded sceptical as she balanced the cup between her knees and slid a hair-bobble off her wrist. I could tell she was watching me from the corner of her eye.

My mouth – not my eyes – formed a dull smile as Maggie gathered her damp hair into a bunch at the back of her head.

'You remind me of my sister,' I said. 'So full of your own . . .'

I petered out. Why did I always do this? Why did I always add Stella to the mix? I'd been irritated with Maggie in a perfectly straightforward way, but now I'd gone and complicated things.

'Is that so?' said Maggie. 'Well, what does *she* have to say about all this?'

All this. There wasn't an 'all this'. There wasn't an 'all' any-thing. God, I wished I'd never got on that hospital bus. I took the coffee back and sipped without tasting.

'My sister? She doesn't have anything to say about anything. She's dead.'

Maggie froze with her hands behind her head, her fingers mid-twist inside the bobble.

'Oh no . . .'

I kicked my heels against the rock and looked away, but in the end I told her.

I told her and she listened, although the bones of the story were bare. My sister Stella went 'travelling' in the summer of 2009, when she was twenty-one years old – apparently with a friend, although we never found out for sure – and after sev-eral months away from home her body was discovered at the bottom of a cliff, near the town of Bligh. That was it. I call it a 'story' but it wasn't even that. It had a beginning and an end, but it didn't have a middle.

How did we know she jumped? That was the first thing Maggie asked, and I couldn't reply for a while, because there were too many answers to choose from, and no answers at all. Because it's what the coroner concluded. Because it's the sort of thing Stella would go and do. Because of those other times, with the vodka and the pills, and the shouting, and the crying, and the running away from home. Because when we were little and discussing what we'd do if we were granted one wish, my ideas would chop and change every time, but my sister would always wish she were a bird.

We emptied the flask and started on other topics. Maggie told me about growing up in Bligh with her five siblings, and how she'd moved away in her twenties and come back a couple of years ago, and about her job at the hospital. I told her about my mum, and her death, and how my dad had coped. I tried to tell her about Cory and our bohemian idyll – an artist and a writer in love with one another, and in possession of a creaky old house – but I can't have chosen the right words, because even to my ears it sounded implausible and fey. I decided to play it down. I said Cory was a professional artist, and that I was going to start job-hunting soon.

Something moved on the edge of my vision. I turned and saw Cory coming down the cliff path. Maggie carried on talking, but her voice seemed to recede, until it had no more form and meaning for me than the swashing of the sea.

'Oh my word . . .' Maggie broke off. 'It's *him*, from when I was a kid. Except it can't be.'

I should have said, *Who? Who are you talking about?* And left some room for doubt, but I knew who she meant and said without thinking, 'Obviously it's not *him*. It's his son.'

I stood up and waved. At first I thought Cory had seen us, then I was unsure because he didn't wave back. It was impossible to read his expression from this distance, and anyway he was busy watching his footing on the narrow path.

'So I take it that's your "friend", then? That's Cory Byrne?'

Maggie stayed seated with her legs crossed at the knee.

'Don't hold it against him,' I urged. 'He's nothing like his dad, judging by the little I know. I swear you'll love him.'

The prospect of their imminent meeting excited me. I would get to see Cory through new eyes and Maggie would understand me – she would understand everything – differently. I liked them both, so it seemed inevitable that they would like each other.

'Cory!'

I gave a broad wave and a broader smile as he reached the sand, but he still made no response. Maggie was busy fitting the flask together, but she shot him another look.

Cory picked his way across the shingle, wincing on bare feet. Every now and then he stooped to gather up a shell, or a pebble, or a ribbon of seaweed. By the time he reached us he'd collected quite a handful, but when he finally caught my eye he let them slide to the ground and stuffed his hands in his pockets.

'Here you are.'

'Here I am!' I echoed. 'You weren't worried, were you? I just thought, since you were still asleep . . . And then I got talking to Maggie. This is Maggie, by the way.'

Maggie's mouth made the shape of a 'hi' and Cory moved his head in the semblance of a nod. They were equally aloof – but after they'd sketched their greeting Cory went back to watching me, whereas Maggie continued to watch Cory.

'I was worried,' he said, with his hand against the small of my back. 'You came out without your engagement ring.'

Cory opened his hand and presented it with a flourish. Maggie angled her head, as if she'd like to take a polite look, but I hid it inside my fist and Cory pulled me sideways for a kiss. I tripped on the edge of my flip-flop, grazing the side of my toe.

Cory wanted to make the kiss linger, as if we were alone, but I glowered and turned my face away. My toe was hurting.

Maggie cleared her throat and rolled her swimming costume up inside her towel. 'I'll be off,' she said. 'Nice to see you, Freya. Glad to have met Cory.'

She shot me a quick glance which said something quite different and more complex.

*

'Who was *she*?'

The two of us scrambled up the path, Cory in the lead. I fumbled with the ring, trying to push it on to my finger without dropping my towel.

'My friend Maggie. I told you. Why were you so rude to her?'

Cory shrugged.

The ring bumped over my knuckle and into place.

'Why didn't you like her?' I persisted.

He shrugged again. 'I don't know. She's got cold eyes. Plus, she doesn't seem to realise this is a private beach.'

He glanced up towards the house and I saw his face in profile. His lower lip was sticking out further than his upper one, and his jaw had tensed.

'I woke up at eight, wanting to draw you,' he said. '*Needing* to. And you weren't there.'

I kept my eyes on the path, resisting the urge to look round. The tide was out, and Maggie was making her way home along the shoreline.

'She's my friend,' I repeated. 'You could have tried harder.'

'Oh, Freya.' Cory reached for my hand, and when he squeezed my fingers the ring dug into my flesh. 'You take these things too much to heart.'

'But "these things" matter,' I said, yanking my hand free.

'No, they don't; they don't matter at all. In what sense does this Maggie woman *matter*? She's not part of our world.'

We were in the garden now, heading towards the house. Towards our world. I turned, but I could no longer see Maggie because she was hidden by the lip of the cliff.

'Look,' I said, taking a deep, patient breath. 'I've got an idea: why don't we get away for a while? Let's take a break from Byrne Hall and stay with Dad for a few days. You give the painting a rest, and I'll forget about writing for a while . . . After all, now that your mum is being cared for—'

'Freya!' Cory stopped and faced me. I had to stop too, or I would have walked into him. His voice was harsh but his eyes were wide and scared. He placed heavy hands on my shoulders and scrutinised my face.

'What? What have I said that's so bad?'

He opened his arms wide and dropped them in another shrug.

'This life we're building together, this "idyll", as you call it – it's not some little craze of mine. It's not some fad. It's not a *hobby* . . .'

He stared at me, lost for words.

I took his hand and we walked to the pond, where Dad and I had loitered on the afternoon of my cousin's wedding. Mottled, yellow leaves were floating on the black surface of the water and sticking to the statue of the little boy.

'You're talking about your art, really, aren't you?' I said. 'About your exhibition?'

'I'm talking about everything.'

I rested one knee on the low wall and peered down at our reflections. Our bodies had no edges down there in the water. We rippled in and out of one another, a muddle of shadow and light, and it was impossible to say where I ended and he began.

'I wish you understood,' he said.

I turned to look at him. His face was all the more lovable – and all the more agonising – for being opaque.

'I swapped my entire life for this,' I said. 'Of course I understand. Don't say I don't understand.'

6

'ARE YOU OK TO KEEP going, or do you need a break?' Cory asked, never taking his eyes off the easel.

'I'm fine.'

An abstracted smile parted his lips as he filled his brush from the palette and swept it across the canvas. The way he moved had changed since that tentative sketch on the first night: he'd become looser, swifter, more certain. There was no anxious hunching over sketch-books anymore; he was always on his feet in front of the easel, his back and arms arched like a maestro's.

He didn't acknowledge my answer, except by carrying on with his work. I watched him steadily, but he seemed unaware. The wind was light but cold, and it kept singing long, sad notes inside the chimney.

'Are you painting the goose-pimples on my arms?'

A long pause as he bit his lower lip, dabbed the canvas with a rag, and stepped back to look.

'What?'

'Nothing.'

I'd already agreed to pose with bare arms, so it wasn't fair to carp about it after he'd started. I shifted my hand to a slightly different angle, which gave the ring more prominence and made it flash in the light of the Anglepoise lamp.

'Try not to move,' he said from behind the easel.

Northanger Abbey was open on my lap, because Cory wanted

a picture called *Freya Reading*, but I didn't try to turn the pages. The last time I'd moved, to scratch my nose, Cory had made a tiny hissing noise through his teeth. I didn't want to read, anyway. I'd already done *Northanger Abbey* to death for want of anything else – Cory had sold off the Byrne Hall library and he wasn't a reader himself – besides which, I wasn't in the mood for Gothic satire.

The only other reading material I had was the catalogue from Tom's Raphael exhibition, and I suppose I could have brought that out – but what was the point, if Cory was going to wince every time I moved my eyes across the page? Anyway, we'd had a minor argument about the Raphael catalogue yesterday afternoon, which made me reluctant to mention it again. 'Speaking of portraiture,' I'd said, drawing it out of my bag, 'this might interest you ...' Cory had given the cover a cursory glance without taking it out of my hands, and said, 'Hmm,' and it all kicked off from there. As I say, it wasn't a big row.

I glanced at my notebook, and the sharpened pencil lying on top.

'I ought to be writing,' I said, although I was glad of an excuse not to. The other day I'd deleted that line about footsteps echoing from room to room and started a Gothic novel set in Victorian times. It wasn't progressing, though. There was no plot. I decided to cross it out later on and start again.

'So, what's it going to be about?' Cory asked. 'This novel?'

'I don't know,' I said. 'Maybe it could be set in Byrne Hall.'

Cory leaned closer to the canvas and shook his head.

'Maybe I could write about you and your mother—'

'I don't think so.'

I didn't think so either. Not really. Every now and then I would deliberately mention Diana, just to make sure we both still acknowledged her existence. I used to do the same thing to Dad, with Stella's name.

Cory's phone pinged and he wiped his fingers on a turps-soaked rag. I stretched my arms and yawned.

'Oh, great,' he murmured, once he'd swiped the message open. 'The emulsion's arrived.'

'What emulsion? By the way, I've gone and lost my phone. I think I dropped it on the beach yesterday morning.'

'The emulsion for smartening up the downstairs rooms. *Galleries*, I should say.' He looked up, pleased. 'Your phone? Oh no! I'll pop down later on and see if I can spot it.'

'Thanks.'

It's easier to talk about pragmatic things – emulsion paints, missing phones – than interesting things – would-be novels, missing mothers. I made this observation – not because I wanted to but because I couldn't help it – and filed it at the back of my mind.

'Do you actually *need* your phone?' Cory said, squeezing a coil of flesh-coloured paint on to his palette.

'Yes, Cory. I need my phone.'

I watched the paint wind from its tube like a pale worm. *I need it as a mooring rope to secure me to the real world. I need it in case Tom has texted, even though I know, in my gut, he hasn't.*

'I need it to keep in touch with Dad,' I said, which was also true.

Cory disappeared behind the easel, so that all I could see were trouser legs and bare feet.

'You worry about him too much. I'm sure he's fine.'

'I'm sure he is.'

'After all, he's a grown man. No doubt he can remember to brush his own teeth without regular reminders from you.'

I spread my hands in indignation. The giant canvas jiggled as Cory jabbed at it with the brush.

'I wish you'd come out from there,' I said, 'and make your snide comments to my face.'

Cory carried on working as if he hadn't heard, and the sight of his naked feet and the rolled-up ends of his trousers was unbearable. I scraped my chair back and went to stand at the window, watching the view come and go through the steamy circle of my breath: a blanched lawn; a forest of falling leaves; a colourless sea reflecting a colourless sky. I had to clasp my hands together to stop them from shaking, and even then they weren't properly still. I folded my arms and gripped my elbows instead.

'You wouldn't think like that,' I said, once I could trust my voice, 'if you knew the first thing about Stella.'

During the silence that followed, I resisted the temptation to turn round. With the mention of Stella's name the brush stopped dabbing and scraping over the canvas. After a while his footsteps came softly over the wooden floor, and I sensed him standing at my shoulder.

'I'm sure that's true,' he said, after a long pause. 'I'm sorry.'

It was a victory of sorts. I felt as if I'd won a single round in a long and complicated game.

'I wish you'd tell me about Stella,' he went on. 'What was she like?'

I tightened the grip on my elbows. This wasn't the first time Cory had asked questions about my sister, but I'd never given much of an answer before. That unaccustomed feeling of triumph made my voice harsh. It made *me* harsh.

'What was she like? I don't know; where do I begin? Arsey. Diva-ish. Destructive. Self-absorbed.' I was about to add 'reproachful' but it was only since her death that she'd become accusatory, and I didn't want to talk about that.

I set my jaw and dared him to be shocked. At the same time my eyes prickled, and the subdued colours of the trees seemed to waver and mix like dilute paint. Something landed lightly on my shoulder and I glimpsed his stained fingers through the corner of my eye.

'Oh, look.' I rubbed my cheeks and shook my head. 'I don't mean that. Or rather, I do mean it, but it's only a fragment. I could have said she was lovable and funny and full of life.'

He hesitated. 'But that wouldn't be true?'

'Yes! Yes, it would!'

I pressed the heels of my hands into my eyes and held them there until, by conscious effort, I'd managed to turn my impatience away from him and towards myself instead. I always made a mess of expressing things; it was no wonder he'd failed to grasp my meaning.

'It would be true,' I repeated, all the force gone from my voice. 'All of those nice things would be equally true.'

'But when I asked you what Stella was like, all her bad points came pouring out first. That must mean something, mustn't it? Don't be annoyed, I'm just curious . . .'

I kept my hands over my eyes as he drew me back into the room. When I uncovered them I saw, behind him, the painting of the girl who was meant to be me. I moved closer to his face until the girl passed out of view, and then I stood on tiptoes and kissed him on the forehead.

'Stella seems less dead when I talk about her bad points,' I explained. 'People don't speak ill of the dead, do they?'

He laughed uncertainly, as if I'd cracked a joke that he didn't quite get.

'Seriously,' I said. 'If I told you that Stella could light up the room with her smile, it's not that I'd be lying. It's just that it sounds so elegiac; it's the sort of thing people said at her funeral. If I told you she had an unforgiving streak – which is also true – then it doesn't feel quite so . . . morbid.' Our noses were touching, and I was too close to read his expression. 'Does that make any sense whatsoever?'

I touched Cory's face. He hadn't had much of a beard when we first met, but he'd let it grow over the last few weeks. I think it suited him, but it also increased his inscrutability – entirely concealing his upper lip whilst emphasising the lower one, and making something new and strange of his mouth. These days I found his lips almost as enigmatic as his eyes.

'Tell me more about her,' he said. 'I want to understand everything you've been through.'

I wondered whether he would shave the beard off if I asked. I'd never demanded a favour like that before, and I didn't like the idea of testing him – or being tested in return. *If you loved me, you'd shave . . . Well, if you loved me, you wouldn't ask.*

'Freya? Tell me something else about Stella.'

'Something else . . . I don't know. I can't think.'

There were so many stories I'd pondered over the years, but none that I'd told out loud. I sifted them cautiously, picking them up one at a time and blowing off the dust.

'You have to promise to tell me one of your memories too,' I said. 'Your childhood . . . Your father . . .'

'Yes, all right, but you go first.'

Cory's voice was soft in my ear, and I liked feeling that his focus was on my words rather than my body. I liked having the attention of the human being rather than the artist.

'OK, let me think . . . I suppose there was the fifteenth-birthday incident.'

'Yes?'

I laughed uncertainly. Was this a funny anecdote? I suppose it might be. Unless, of course, it was tragic.

'Well, Stella decided to make this amazing dinner for my fifteenth birthday. And, I mean, when Stella decided to do something, she didn't hold back. She must have spent weeks planning it out and sourcing all these obscure ingredients online. I remember she even turned down an invitation for the night before, because she was too busy prepping some complicated chicken dish she'd dug out from Mum's old recipe book. She was so lovely and excited about it, and if I told her she didn't have to, she'd say, "You're only fifteen once, Freya Lyell!" '

I paused and Cory kissed the rim of my ear.

'So, anyway, my birthday arrived, and we sat down for dinner – me and her and Dad – and we ate blini with smoked salmon, and asparagus soup, and raspberry sorbets in little shot glasses, and it was all going swimmingly until the main course – the complicated chicken thing. It looked fabulous, but the meat was still bloody when we cut into it.'

'Ugh.' Cory's lips twisted against my neck.

'With anybody else I'd have set my knife and fork down straight away, but this was Stella's long-awaited feast, her birth-day extravaganza, and I was . . . I was *scared*. I do know how ridiculous that sounds, but it's true: I had a kind of hot flush, from head to foot, and I remember thinking, *Maybe I should just eat it and say nothing; maybe it'll be fine; maybe it's better to be sick later on than to upset her now.*'

Cory drew back slightly so that he could look me in the face. 'You *ate* it? You ate the raw chicken?'

'No, because Dad's a whole lot more straightforward than me, thank goodness. He said, "Lovely idea, Stella, but completely inedible," and that was that.'

'How did she react?'

I rested my chin on his shoulder and rolled my eyes.

'Well, that's the really stupid part because – against all the odds – she was going to be fine about it. I know she was. I know by the way she looked at me across the table. She was about to say something self-deprecating, and we were going to bin the chicken and eat the dessert and laugh the whole thing off, but then Dad – I don't think he even glanced at her, I don't think he even *thought* about it – he just said, "Now, Stella, it's not the end of the world, so don't start sulking." And before you know it, we're in the middle of this ludicrous row, with Dad saying, "I knew it! I knew you'd get in a strop!" And me saying, "Dad! She's fine! Just leave her be!" And Stella, all teary and shrill, going, "I'm not in a strop! Why are you telling me I'm in a strop?" '

I thought for a moment I was going to cry, but I started laughing instead.

'It all blew over though?' Cory sounded serious. 'I mean, presumably . . . ?'

I sighed and wiped my eyes. 'It did in a sense, but she never, ever cooked again.'

'What . . . literally never?'

'Literally never, for the remaining three years of her life. I presume Dad was meant to notice, although I'm not sure he ever did – it's not like she cooked much anyway – but I did. I noticed. I mean, there was nothing casual about it: she wouldn't

180

even pick up a saucepan, wouldn't switch the oven on. If I said, "Can you give that pan a stir, Stella?" she'd go deaf, or wander off, or "forget". There was something principled about it; something utterly implacable . . .'

'Utterly *weird*.' I stiffened when he said that. 'Sorry, Freya, but she does sound quite weird.' I smiled lamely, and told myself he was only voicing what I'd already implied. He didn't mean to be dismissive.

'She was generous too,' I said guiltily, but Cory didn't respond. I got the impression he wasn't interested in that aspect of the story.

'Anyway, it's your turn now,' I said. 'Tell me about your dad.'

'Later.'

He kissed me unexpectedly, a lip-bruising kiss that bent my head backwards and made my neck hurt. It was a couple of seconds before I'd recovered enough to meet him half-way, and although I did so with vigour – trying my best to make it a wings-of-passion, soul-meets-soul kind of a kiss – I couldn't do it. We missed each other's mark, somehow: perhaps he was fractionally distracted; perhaps I was trying too hard. After a while we gave up and moved apart. Cory sniffed and scratched his neck. I drew invisible circles on the floor with my big toe.

'I'm glad you're not like that,' he said. My mind had frag-mented; I couldn't think what he meant.

'Like what?'

'Like your sister.'

Pairs of painted eyes accused me – not just from the easel, but all around the room. They were supposed to be my eyes but they could just as well have been Stella's, since we had the same colouring. I looked at my feet and thought of the adjectives I'd used against her. *Arsey. Diva-ish. Destructive. Self-absorbed.* I shivered when I remembered what I'd done to her.

'You're lovely,' Cory said, picking his sweater off the end of the mattress and placing it round my shoulders like a cloak.

If only you knew, I thought as I pulled the sweater tight.

'You're my muse.'

I laughed a little at that.

'Oh Cory, I don't think that's how you're supposed to compliment a woman in the twenty-first century.'

But he was back at work already and didn't hear me.

New Year's Eve, 2008

We have never had to call on an emergency plumber before. We have never – as far as I can remember – hosted a New Year's Eve party at our house before.

'What are the odds of both happening at once?' I ask – rhetorically – as I top up Aunty May's Bucks Fizz.

She answers under her breath, 'At least two to one, I should think, with Stella around.'

Well . . . it <u>is</u> Stella's fault that the upstairs has flooded. I don't know exactly what happened, but she's been making her sculptures in the bathroom ever since Dad banned them from the kitchen, and something went badly wrong this afternoon when she clogged the U-bend of the basin with clay and then tried to unclog it with a screwdriver. Credit where credit's due, though: just as stress levels ought to be rocketing – what with our sitting room full of guests, and water dripping through the ceiling on to the carpet, and the

182

cheapest plumber in the phone book charging £150 an hour – it's thanks to Stella that the atmosphere lifts.

'Freya!' she cries, bursting into the sitting room with a bucket for the drip in one hand and a box of deluxe Christmas crackers in the other. 'Look what I've found! We forgot to pull the crackers on Christmas Day!'

Before we know it, we're all donning paper crowns, Aunty May is telling fortunes with a cellophane fish, and John from three doors down is failing to get his head round a joke. 'Question: What cheese is made backwards? Answer: Edam.' Stella turns ABBA up to cover the noise of the drip, and then she climbs on to the sofa, glass in hand, and bounces from foot to foot as she sings along to 'Fernando'.

Stella is astonishing in her cheap, shimmery dress. She is like a fire: everyone's instinct is to draw near and stare. Even the plumber pauses in the doorway, on his way upstairs to the bathroom. Even <u>Dad</u> – who has more reason than anyone to feel annoyed – seems to soften when he looks at her. As for Tom – I don't wish to downplay the suffering he's gone through with his broken marriage, but I can't help suspecting there's a guilty corner of his mind that's glad to be free.

I call it a New Year's Eve party, but it's pretty low key. Apart from the three of us, there are only six guests: a couple of neighbours, one of my school friends, Zoë from Dad's office, Aunty May and – of course – Tom. Stella hasn't invited any of her own friends, although she's been checking her phone all evening, and smirking every time it pings.

I bought a dress too, in the post-Christmas sales, but I didn't try it on in the shop and it's not a great fit. I ought to stop tugging at the skirt and wriggling my shoulders, but I do it without thinking. Poppy – my school friend – joins

183

Stella on the sofa-cum-trampoline, and so does Zoë, and then 'Dancing Queen' comes on, and even Aunty May starts singing and tapping her knee in a dry kind of way. Dad rolls his eyes at me and Tom comes over with a plate of mince pies.

'Are you all right?' he says.

I take a mince pie and tell him I'm fine.

'How are you?' I ask in turn. After all, it is only a month since Natalie left.

'Oh, you know. Not bad.'

Stella turns the music up full blast while Tom is still talking.

'What?' I push my hair aside so that he can speak into my ear.

'Thank you for asking,' he yells. I smile and shrug, and he smiles back.

Dad pauses the CD when the plumber reappears, and they go into the hallway to talk. Stella jumps off the sofa, breathless, and starts refilling everyone's glass to the brim, deaf to protests.

When she reaches me, she looks me up and down, puts the bottle on the table and adjusts my dress – first around the neckline, then around the hips. She picks up a length of my hair and lets it fall again, before taking a step back and shaking her head.

'Must you wear your hair down?'

'You're wearing yours down.'

'Yes, but I . . . oh, never mind. It doesn't matter. I will always love you.'

I open my mouth to retort, then close it. There's no point calling her out on it – not here, anyway, not now. She'll just say, 'What? What's wrong with saying I love you, you paranoid freak?'

Anyway, the moment is gone. The music is loud again, and Stella is prancing with Zoë on the rug – all smiles and laughter and 'Gimme, gimme, gimme!' at the top of her voice.

7

CORY AND I SKIDDED DOWN the cliff path, clutching one another's hands in the dusk. We had left it too late, really, to start searching for my phone.

'Hang on.' Cory tapped his own screen. 'Let's try calling it again.'

'But if it fell out of my pocket when I was talking to Maggie, the tide—'

'Shh!'

We stopped and listened. Nothing. Nothing but the faint *brrr* from Cory's phone and the hush of the waves. I scanned the beach for a pinprick of light, but all I could see was greying sand, and black seaweed, and sweeping arcs of shingle.

Cory tried again at the bottom of the path.

'It's still ringing,' he said, 'which implies it's not been washed away—'

'Shh!'

We froze, hand in hand, until it went to voicemail.

'Nope,' I said sadly, as Cory switched off his phone and put his arm round me. 'Nothing.'

A mist was moving in from the sea, turning everything a soft, cold grey. I glanced at the clifftops. A figure was standing on the very lip of the drop, her shoulders hunched up to her ears. She – if it was a she – stared down at the water without moving.

'Cory, look!'

'What?' His voice rang out too loudly, bouncing off the walls of rock.

'Shh! Up there!'

Cory turned his head, and I knew he'd spotted her by the way he went still.

'She's very close to the edge.' The panic was rising in my voice. 'She shouldn't be that close; she'll fall.'

He didn't answer, but I felt his grip tighten round my shoulder.

'What shall we do?' I whispered.

Cory's arm slackened and dropped to his side. He didn't exactly laugh, but his voice took on a relieved lightness.

'It's gorse,' he said. 'It's a gorse bush.'

I looked again – looked hard – and the figure changed. He was right. I'd noticed it before, in the sane light of day. The hunched shoulders didn't resemble shoulders once you knew they weren't; the twist of neck and arms was nothing but a twist of branches.

We ought at least to have smiled and I wondered, even at the time, why we didn't. I expected Cory to tease me, but he hugged me tenderly and kissed my hair.

'It's a lonely spot,' he remarked. 'I don't like to think of you coming here alone.'

'But it doesn't feel like this in the daytime.'

'That doesn't mean it's safe.'

I felt a pang of longing for home. At the least, I wanted to be indoors, in a small-ish room with closed curtains and a TV.

'I can always come with you,' Cory said, 'when you feel like leaving the house? It would do me good to get more fresh air.'

'Oh, but that's just silly . . .'

I don't think I said it with enough conviction.

'It's not silly at all.'

Cory sounded sure.

I tried not to shiver as we stood and watched the mist creeping in, like long white fingers from the sea.

'I ought to ring Dad,' I said, once we were back in the studio. Cory had already uncorked a bottle of red and returned to his canvas.

'Of course,' he said. 'Go ahead.'

'So can I borrow your mobile?'

He passed me a tumbler of wine and gestured with his foot at a rotary-dial phone, which sat on the floor in a nest of tangled wires. I'd noticed it before, but taken it for bric-a-brac.

'Use that,' he said. 'It should still work.'

I picked up the receiver. It was crackly, but had a dialling tone.

Cory stooped over his palette and twisted the lid off a tube of paint. 'You don't mind if I carry on, do you?' he said. 'I'll be very quiet.' He didn't appear to notice that I made no reply. Once he'd mixed the paint, he dipped his brush and began making dribbly yellow slashes to the left of my – her – head.

I turned to face the wall when my father picked up.

'Dad? It's me.'

'Hello? Who's there?'

'It's *me*.'

'Freya! Hello, love!'

Dad took a bite of something crisp, which he chewed and swallowed at the same time as saying, 'How are things?' A voice murmured in the background, and I heard the careful closing of a door.

'Is this a good time?' I wasn't anxious for a lengthy

conversation, as long as I knew he was all right. 'Have you got someone round?'

'Not at all, don't worry. Lovely to hear you.'

'You too.'

We fell silent and I heard a gush as he filled the kettle. There *was* somebody else there, because that was way too much water for a single mug of tea, and Dad was economical about things like that. It was probably Tom, in which case I wished Dad would just say so. All he needed to do was reassure me that he was fine, and that Tom sent his love. Or whatever.

'So, what have you been up to?' we asked simultaneously.

'Nothing much.' I darted a glance over my shoulder. Cory was still absorbed with his yellow slashes, although he had obviously decided against letting them dribble, because he was tidying them up with a bottle of white spirit and a rag. 'Cory's been doing lots of painting.'

'And what about you? Still going for your daily swim?'

'It's getting a bit chilly for that now.'

I twisted the cord round my finger until the engagement ring was entirely concealed. No, not quite concealed; I could still make out a hard-edged glitter through the gaps. At the other end of the line, Dad prised the lid off the tea-caddy and spooned loose leaves into the pot. Cups chinked and the cutlery drawer chimed.

'Are you still there, Freya?'

'I'm here!' I drew myself up.

'I was just saying, what shall I do with your post? There are a few letters here, bank statements and so on – should I be forwarding them on to Byrne Hall?'

'I don't know. Yes, I suppose so, if you don't mind.'

I told him about losing my phone, and mentioned my writing.

'How's the novel?'

'Oh . . . it wasn't really working. I'm thinking I might try short stories instead.'

I asked what he'd eaten for dinner, and how things were at work, and whether he was sleeping well. All his answers were brief and breezy. 'Fine! Absolutely fine! Sleeping like a baby!'

'And how is everyone?' I asked.

'Everyone?' He sounded oddly guarded.

'Well . . .'

'Let me see,' he said. 'Mrs Adeyemi next door has had her baby. Aunty May's had to have her cat put down – the tabby one. Um . . .' He stopped to think.

Tom? I pleaded inwardly. *What about Tom?*

'Oh yes, and Tom's on the move. He's got a new job lined up.'

'Where?'

'Somewhere in the north-east. Newcastle, I think. He's not leaving till January. But the two of you are in touch, aren't you? I expect he's told you about it?'

The fridge door clunked as he fetched the milk.

'No, not really,' I said. 'What with my phone . . .'

'Speaking of work,' he went on, 'what about you? I'm still not entirely clear what you've got in mind. Are you job-hunting down there, or . . . ?'

I closed my eyes.

'I'm not entirely clear myself yet, Dad. It's early days.'

The cord slipped off my finger and I started to wind it round more tightly, leaving fewer spaces. I wondered to myself when early days would stop being early days. I couldn't think of anything else to say; I couldn't even think of a question. Tom was moving to Newcastle.

'Freya?'

'Yes?'

'You're not angry with me, are you?'

'No!'

'Because I keep reassuring you that *I'm* not cross, but I get the feeling you don't believe me. I'm delighted that you're happy! And I don't want you thinking I dislike Cory, either, because I don't. From the little I know, I'd say he suits you down to a T.'

'Thanks, Dad.'

I pressed the receiver more tightly to my ear.

'Freya?'

'Yes, Dad, I'm still here, but what do you mean exactly?'

'About what?'

'About . . .' I couldn't look over my shoulder again – it would come across as shifty. I lowered my voice. 'About *suiting me down to a T.*'

I didn't disagree with him; I just wanted to hear about it from a fresh perspective.

'Sorry, love, I can't hear you well. The line's quite crackly.'

'Oh, look, it doesn't matter.'

Cory's paintbrush tapped and scraped across the canvas. I tried to think of something else to say.

'I told you I'd lost my phone, didn't I? So I'll keep ringing you on this landline until it turns up, but I can't very well text unless I borrow Cory's phone, so you must remember not to worry.'

'I will remember not to worry!' he said. I could hear a smile in his voice, as if he thought me daft but endearing.

'OK.'

'Well . . .'

It was obvious he wanted to go. I heard the kitchen door creaking open, and Dad muffling the receiver – imperfectly – as he whispered, 'Can you manage the tray?'

'Who've you got with you?'

'No-one.' Dad sounded embarrassed. 'A friend from work.'

We said goodbye shortly afterwards. I told him I'd better get on, and he had the grace not to ask, *With what?*

Cory had broken off to refill his glass and study the progress of his painting. When I put the phone down he looked round and smiled – or at least, I think he did. It was difficult to tell what he was doing under that beard. His eyes met mine briefly and slid away.

'Everything OK with your dad?'

I knew by his subdued tone of voice that I'd blundered. What, though? What had I said that was wrong? I raked over the phone conversation, but it was all so stilted and unexceptional. Food . . . Phone . . . Sleep . . . Work . . . Perhaps it was something I'd *failed* to say? The engagement ring . . . ?

'You never mentioned the exhibition.' Cory dabbed at a blob of paint with his forefinger, gave a self-deprecating laugh, shrugged and drank, leaving a smear of yellow ochre down the side of the glass.

Sometimes Cory's sadness seemed to plumb greater depths than I could bear to imagine. It was ingrained in him; it made him look – beard and all – like a lost little boy. I bet his mother's heart used to bleed for him when he was a child. I bet he was hard to say goodbye to at the school gates.

'I didn't know you wanted me to,' I said defensively. 'I didn't know it was public knowledge.'

'It's fine,' he said. 'I'm not blaming you. But your father isn't "the public", is he? He's the Arts Editor of the *London Globe*. He's my V.I.P. reviewer. Obviously we can't set a date for the opening without consulting him.'

I actually laughed at that. I said, 'Oh Cory, you're not serious. You don't want *him* to write you a review!'

'Why not?'

I laughed again, but now it was just a way of buying time. I almost said, *because he's so bloody brutal*, but that would be tactless. *Because he's incurably honest* would be worse. I pictured Dad in front of one of Cory's painted girls – his face screwed up, his eyes concealed behind his spectacles – and I felt a plunging sensation, as if I were falling through ice.

'Cory?' I was speaking from underneath the ice now, my mind in slow-motion. 'Do you mean it? You want Dad to write a review for the *Globe*? The actual *London Globe*?'

'Why not?'

I hesitated.

'I don't think you understand what you're asking.'

'Oh, come on, Freya, it's only one evening of his life! It's not such a big ask, is it, given that you're his only daughter? I'll offer to pay his train fare if you want, and he can stay the night here.'

'It's not a question of the train fare.'

'Anyway, he likes me; we got on extremely well that day he came. You didn't see us together.'

'It's not a question of that, either.'

I tried and failed to smile, and Cory softened. He wiped his hands on the rag and crossed the room.

'Don't worry,' he said, stroking the hair from my face. 'I'm not annoyed or anything, but will you please remember to mention it next time you speak? Once we've fixed a date with him, we can start sending out all the other invitations.'

He planted a quick kiss on my forehead and returned to the easel. I stayed in the corner of the room, tugging at a loose thread on my jumper, watching him at work.

Diana sleeps and wakes, dreams and thinks. Memory ought to be the comfort of the dying – isn't that the common wisdom? So why do all the happy times elude her? For example, she's been trying to remember those high-octane bashes she used to throw before she was married, with youth on her side, and money to burn, and a glut of friends on the London art scene. Instead she keeps thinking about the parties she hosted at Byrne Hall after her widowhood, which turned out to be nothing like parties at all.

'Di?'

She remembers her guests coming downstairs in a posse while she was setting out drinks and nibbles, and grouping themselves in the doorway. They looked like a chorus from a Greek tragedy, with their sad, closed faces and their sudden knack for speaking with one voice. Oh God, they were going to say something about Cory. Diana smiled – a casual, nonplussed, questioning smile that only trembled slightly.

She emptied a packet of cashews into a bowl. Well, they could say what they liked. They had no idea, these people, these 'friends'. None of them had children. They were know-nothing, arty-farty urbanites, the lot of them.

'Di, we were wondering . . .'

'We just wanted to ask . . .'

'Is everything all right with Cory?'

She gave a little shrug and ate a nut.

'He's fine,' she said, tossing the empty packet on the fire and watching it shrivel to nothing.

Cory had become the dark star Diana circled, day by day, as a matter of course. In some horrific sense – hitherto unvoiced – she was used to it. Her guests had experienced it for the first time last night when they arrived from the railway station, full of gush and chatter. All he did was stare and say nothing and retreat to his room – it could have been so much worse – but nonetheless they'd been dragged into his orbit.

'Honestly, he's fine.' Diana arranged the gin bottles in order of height. 'He's a teenager, isn't he? Say no more!'

Nobody smiled back.

'Losing his father like that,' someone ventured, 'at the age of thirteen. I mean, can you imagine? It must be tearing him up inside.'

Diana bit down hard on another cashew.

'He's fine.'

8

My arm was starting to ache now, and I was losing my grip. I set the roller down on the paint tray and flexed my fingers.

'What date is it today?' I wondered, straying to the window and massaging my wrist.

'I can't remember.'

'Or what day of the week, even?'

Cory shook his head and carried on painting. The roller made a sticky, sucking noise as he swept it back and forth across the gallery wall.

'You know why we've lost track?' I said. 'It's because we haven't left the house for so long.'

The greens and greys of the garden were like balm on my eyes, and I fell into a trance. The emulsion we were working with – the shade Cory had chosen for his gallery walls – was called 'Pamplona Red'.

'We'll go for a walk later,' he said. 'Let's just get this first coat done.'

I suppose it was the way the drive was angled, but from my vantage point the trees and shrubberies appeared to encircle the house entirely, like a fairy-tale forest, and it looked as if there was no way through. Recently I'd begun to suspect – as I used to suspect when I was little – that the world didn't exist beyond what I could see of it.

I hadn't spoken to Dad in ages. I was scared of what would happen if I mentioned the invitation to the opening, and scared of what would happen if I didn't. I tried to call Tom a few evenings ago, on a whim, but Cory came back from the bathroom as I was starting to dial, having forgotten his towel. I jumped when I saw him standing in the doorway, and nearly dropped the phone.

'Oh!'

We stared at one another. He must have climbed into the bath before realising about the towel, because he was naked and dripping, and the thin scars were shining on his damp arms.

'Sorry, Freya. Were you phoning your dad?'

'Yes.' I lied without hesitation as I put the receiver back. 'He didn't pick up, though. He must have gone out.'

Cory returned to the bathroom, and while he was there I concocted a tall tale about my father going away on holiday and leaving his mobile behind, and a family friend calling me up to pass the message on. It took twenty-four hours of internal practice before I could recite it with conviction, but I did it.

'So you see, I can't talk to him about the exhibition until he gets back, and I'm not sure when that will be . . .'

Cory didn't take it well, but I'm almost sure he believed me.

'Are you all right there, Freya?' Cory was refilling his roller and starting on a new section of wall. 'Not tired already?'

I broke away from the view and picked up my tray. The sooner we finished in here, the longer we'd have to rest and eat before Cory started on a new canvas. After all, there was no getting out of it; I could hardly refuse to help. I couldn't even claim to be busy with my writing – not credibly. Cory had mentioned it this morning – 'Would you mind helping me paint the gallery walls, or are you too busy? I wouldn't want to interrupt your flow.' But he was either being polite or sarcastic, and I couldn't decide which was worse. We both knew that my efforts to write short stories were going nowhere. Our bohemian studio – the rich, colourful, messy muddle of it – belonged to Cory. My notebook was still lying empty, except for a few half-hearted notes and crossings-out.

Half an hour elapsed as the blood-red rollers squelched up and down. I sneezed a couple of times. Cory moved the stepladder to different parts of the room.

'Are you happy with Pamplona Red?' I asked, switching the roller to my left hand. I thought it was a good idea to speak, every now and then. If we left it for too long then the silence grew monstrous and our voices – when we did use them – sounded loud and strange. They did to me, anyway; I don't think Cory noticed.

'Yes! Why?'

'No reason. Just wondering.'

The other day, when Cory told me that his order for Pamplona Red had arrived in a DIY store across town, I got excited. I thought we would have to go and collect it, in a taxi or a borrowed car, and I looked forward to seeing Bligh again. But the paint was delivered to the house by a taciturn bloke in a van.

We'd taken to having everything delivered over the last few weeks, even our groceries – such as they were. I told Cory I wouldn't mind popping down to town, but he said, 'We save time this way.'

My left arm wasn't as wieldy as my right. I'd finished the lower section of wall to the right of the fireplace, but now I was having to reach up. Every couple of strokes I stopped to roll my shoulder and let my arm drop. Cory had his eye on me.

'It's freezing in here,' I said. 'I'm going upstairs for a jumper.'

He nodded vaguely and carried on painting.

My clothes were jumbled up with Cory's on a chair in the corner of the studio. I call them 'my clothes' but I'd borrowed the warmer ones from him and – as much as I hated it – Diana. I kept meaning to go on a shopping expedition to Bligh but, one way or another, it hadn't happened yet.

A bunch of keys fell out of Cory's trouser pocket as I rummaged through the pile and I stooped to pick them up. There were half a dozen or so on a loop of string, mostly old-fashioned mortise keys – the kind a Victorian housekeeper might have carried on her belt.

There was a knock at the front door, and the noise roused me from my daze. I shoved the keys back in Cory's pocket, fished a woollen cardigan from the pile and put it on. It didn't feel right wearing Diana's clothes – all those quality yarns, and expertly darned elbows, and pearl buttons – but being cold was marginally worse.

The knock sounded again, swift and smart. I heard Cory cross the hall to open the door, and then I heard a woman scream.

She screamed again as I came charging down the stairs three at a time, and when I reached the hall she shoved Cory aside and ran forwards with her hands over her face. I didn't understand what was happening. The woman was Maggie, and she kept shouting at me, 'Oh my God! Freya! What's happened? What did he do to you?'

We met at the bottom of the stairs and she made as if to grab me, but something stopped her. She looked me up and down instead and touched me gingerly on my arms, my elbows and my paint-stained hands. She peered into my puzzled face and let out a long, shaky breath.

'Oh no!' She dropped my hands and pressed her fingertips to her mouth. Her eyes welled up as she started to laugh. 'It's paint, isn't it? It's red paint.'

Maggie looked from me to Cory and back again, her features anxious even while her shoulders shook with laughter. I suppose she was hoping we'd laugh too and make it all right. I smiled quickly so that she'd know I wasn't offended, but Cory turned away.

'I'm so sorry,' she spluttered, as he made his way back across the hall. She tried to pat him on the arm as he went past but she couldn't quite reach, and he took no notice of her gesture. I couldn't laugh – not a proper belly laugh like hers – but she was right; he did make a grisly spectacle. He'd got his hands covered whilst pouring the paint into the roller tray, and then got the worst off by wiping it on to his T-shirt and down the sides of his jeans.

'We're painting the downstairs rooms for Cory's exhibition,' I explained, as we followed him into the half-painted room.

'Bloody hell.' I wasn't sure if she was swearing or describing, but either way I knew what she meant. Last week, when Cory had prised the lid off the first tub, I'd swallowed a similar reaction. 'Very *art gallery*,' I'd enthused, as he wiped his fingers across the inside of the lid and dabbed them on the wall. 'Very *Louvre*.' If there was a trace of irony in my tone, he didn't seem to notice.

'Have a seat,' I urged Maggie, righting the room's single item of furniture – the plastic garden chair, which was lying on its side on the floor. She ignored me. She was too busy turning slowly on the spot, while Cory topped up the roller tray and towelled his hands on the front of his T-shirt. I wished he'd say something, even if it was something boring. They were mistaken about one another, and it was up to me to explain away the mistake, but I couldn't work out where to begin.

'The red . . .' I paused to clear my throat. 'I suppose it's quite intense, isn't it, on its own?'

I followed Maggie's gaze from wall to wall and picked at my lips. 'It'll look fine though, once it's covered with pictures. It'll look good.'

Maggie removed her coat and lowered herself into the chair, still staring round at the walls.

'Could I bother you for a drink?' she said eventually. 'It's quite a trek up that driveway.'

I gave Cory a couple of seconds to answer, but he remained silent. He was halfway up the step-ladder now, reaching for the cornice.

'Of course,' I said. 'I'll make a pot of tea. Do you want one, Cory?'

He peered down vaguely, as if he'd caught the sound of his name from a long way away. Maggie got up, slinging her coat over her arm.

'I'll come with you,' she said, without waiting for him to reply. 'We can have a catch-up while the kettle boils.'

'I wanted to make sure you were all right,' she said, locating a clutch of mugs in a cupboard and removing two. 'It's been ages since I saw you out and about.'

'That was kind of you.'

It *was* kind of her – I didn't mean to come over all crisp and thin-lipped – but why wouldn't I be all right? I flicked the kettle on and stood over it, my hands flat on the counter, as if it needed watching. I was tensed for an inquisition, so her next question almost made me laugh.

'Sorry, Freya, but where's the toilet?'

'The nearest functioning one . . .' I steered her back into the hallway '. . . is at the top of the stairs, first door on the left.'

'Thanks.'

She took hold of my wrist and fingered the pearl button on my cuff with a critical air.

'*Are* you all right?' she whispered. 'Really?'

'Yes, of course! I don't know why you think—'

'And his mother. Have you found out yet—'

'Shh! No!'

I took her by the shoulders, turned her round and shoved her gently towards the stairs.

Cory came in as the kettle was rolling to a boil and washed his hands at the sink. I slipped an extra mug from the cupboard while his back was turned.

'Where is she?'

I barely caught the question; the tap was gushing noisily over his hands and spattering the draining-board with dilute paint.

'She went to the loo.'

'Yeah, right. She could be anywhere. She could be nosing about upstairs.'

'I'm sure she's not.'

He snorted and shut the tap.

'Oh, come on, Cory! What was I meant to say? *No, sorry, Maggie. You'll just have to cross your legs?*'

Cory wiped his gory hands on a tea-towel and flung it on the floor. He stood at the window with his arms folded across his chest, although there was nothing to see beyond a shock of brambles and nettles.

'Why couldn't we have laughed,' I wondered aloud, 'when Maggie thought the paint was blood?'

Cory drummed his fingers on his chin, rolled his eyes at the ceiling, made a big show of racking his brains. 'Um . . . I don't know. Let me see. Maybe because it wasn't funny?'

'It was quite funny.'

We both narrowed our eyes, but he was the first to look away. Perhaps this was the kind of conversation he'd been hoping to ward off when he told me, *I'm glad you're not like your sister.*

'What the hell is she *doing* up there?' He kicked the tea-towel across the floor and I stooped to pick it up. It trembled in my hands like something half alive.

'What does it matter?' I said, draping it over the back of a chair. 'Even if she is nosing about, what's the worst thing she's going to find? A dead bluebottle?'

He folded his arms tightly, stuffing his fists under his armpits.

'Or are you worried she's going to steal one of your paintings?' I raised my eyebrows and attempted a smile. 'Do you think she might try and smuggle one out under her coat and flog it on eBay?'

'Don't try to be funny, Freya. It doesn't suit you.'

I sat down at the table. The surface was messy with crumbs and blobs of jam and rings of wine. Cory began pacing, picking things up from the counter and putting them down again – milky cereal bowls, a saucepan, a used wine glass, a bread-knife. Everything he touched got smeared with red paint.

Upstairs the loo flushed – it was a Victorian monstrosity with a gurgling roar – and Cory stopped dead with the bread-knife in his hand.

'There,' I said in a small voice. His hand tightened briefly on the handle of the knife before he put it down.

Maggie came rushing on tiptoes down the stairs, hissing, 'Freya! *Freya!*' I knotted my fingers under the table and fixed my eyes on the door.

'Freya!' She burst into the kitchen, her voice high-pitched and out of breath – and stopped short when she saw Cory. He pulled out a chair and gestured for her to sit.

'Goodness,' he said. 'You seem excited. What happened up there? Are you all right?'

Maggie hauled up a different chair – the one next to me – and sat on it.

'Nothing happened. I'm fine, thank you.' She tidied her hair and placed her hands on the table, loosely clasped, as if she were about to conduct an interview.

'What's going on?' Cory persisted, stirring the teapot. 'Did you see a ghost?'

'No! Why? Is Byrne Hall haunted?' She laughed lightly. 'Tea! Wonderful, thanks. I'm parched.'

Cory's eyes flitted from her face to mine as he poured. Maggie rested her chin on her hands and looked about the room, the picture of ease. Cory wouldn't have been able to tell, from where he stood, that she was perched on the edge of her seat, or that her toes were fidgeting inside her shoes.

He passed the mugs round and sat himself down. Maggie found my foot and trod on it hard – but what could I say? *Cory, don't let us keep you from your work.*

'If something happened upstairs; if you've something to say . . .' Cory wasn't going to let it go.

'I've nothing to say.' Maggie smiled cordially. 'I don't know what you mean.'

We sat in silence, the steam unfurling from our mugs like genies from their magic lamps. I wondered what I'd ask for, if I were granted a wish right now. I'd probably mess the whole thing up, the way foolish people always do in fairy stories. I'd word my desire ambivalently and end up with something I hadn't intended.

Maggie leaned towards Cory with a confidential air.

'I hope I'm not keeping you from your work?'

'Not at all.'

She smiled tightly and shifted in her seat.

Cory won, of course. Maggie was permitted to sip tea and attempt conversation for as long as she could bear it, but then he showed her out, and got in the way when she tried to hug me, and slammed the front door shut when she was barely clear. The hall seemed intensely dark when she'd gone, like the darkness that succeeds the blowing out of a candle.

'I don't get it,' I said.

'What?'

'I don't get why you dislike her so much.'

'I don't get why you *like* her.' He gestured with his outstretched arms at the dark hallway. 'This is our world, Freya! Yours and mine! Why would you want to dilute it?'

He waited for me to agree, but I just looked at him.

'You used to think the same way,' he said. 'Only a few weeks ago, you used to think like me. You've changed.'

He turned on his heel and went back to the gallery. The

first coat was nearly done: there were just a few patches of bare plaster left beneath the cornices, and one above the door. Now that the sun was going down the emulsion was losing its dazzle, and until he switched the light on it looked more black than red.

'Maybe I have changed,' I called after him. 'What happens then?'

After a minute or two I followed him into the gallery, and began working my roller over the tacky tray and slamming it against the wall. It was his turn to speak; I wasn't going to break the silence again.

9

THE EARLY MORNING MIST TURNED the garden into a strange place. It muffled the sounds of the sea and invented weird shapes which slipped in and out between the trees.

I never doubted Maggie would come, after what had happened yesterday, but I did worry we might miss one another. It's not as if we'd ever arranged a meeting time in the past; we'd just got into the habit of arriving on the beach around sunrise. But there was no sunrise today. There was no sun. There were only pale shadows and dark shadows, and an autumnal smell of rotting fruit.

When I got to the end of the garden I could hear the tide lapping on the shingle at the foot of the cliffs, which meant that the beach would be largely submerged and the rock, where we'd sat and shared her flask of coffee, out of reach. Oh, this was stupid; I might as well go back to bed. I paced up and down on the lip of the cliff, chafing my arms for warmth. *Two minutes*, I told myself, and began counting to one hundred and twenty, but when she still didn't come I began counting again.

I kept glimpsing something white on the edge of my vision, and it made me jump, although it was just the wedding marquee. The guy ropes had gone slack and the canvas sides were clammy and sunken, like an old, ill face. I turned my back on it and wondered what time it was. I must have come too late. No, I'd come too early; it was still the middle of the night.

'Freya!'

Maggie was coming up the cliff path and growing clearer through the mist. Pebbles rattled from under her feet as she half ran, half clambered towards me. She was only whispering, but there was something loud and definite about her presence, which made me glance over my shoulder at the ever-vigilant house.

'Oh Freya, I'm so glad you came!' She held on to me for support as she halted and caught her breath. 'I was worried you wouldn't be able to.'

She was hunched against the cold in a big, padded coat with a hood. I was still wearing Diana's cardigan, and the wool was already saturated with dew. I was going to have a cold later on; I could feel it in my throat when I swallowed.

'I was worried . . .' she repeated. 'Anyway, let's not stop here. We can talk back at my place, once you've had some sleep and something to eat.'

'No, no, no.' I stepped out of her grasp, pulling the cardigan tight and shaking my head. 'You've got it all wrong,' I said. 'You've got *him* all wrong. I can't just . . .' I laughed. 'I can't just *leave*.'

'You *can*.' She approached carefully, making her voice soft and slow, as if she were talking to a nervous dog. 'You can. Nobody can force you to stay here against your will.'

'It's not *against my will*!' I laughed again and shoved my hair out of my eyes. 'Look, this isn't why I came to meet you; I just want to know what happened yesterday. You came rushing downstairs to tell me something.'

Maggie weighed me up as the mist weaved around us. A foghorn boomed further down the coast, its echo drifting along the cliffs.

'Let's sit for a minute,' she said.

The grass was soaking, so we made our way to the pond with the broken fountain and perched on the edge of the low wall.

'He won't be able to see us from the house,' Maggie whispered, reading my mind. 'Not in this light, and with the mist and everything. Hey, you look cold; take my coat.'

Maggie pushed back the hood and shrugged it off. I shook my head, but she shuffled closer and spread it like a cape over both our backs.

'You look awful, Freya.'

'Thanks.'

'No, but seriously. I've only known you for – what? A few weeks?'

'You don't really know me though, do you? I don't really know you. We've only had a couple of conversations.'

Maggie folded her arms.

'OK, but what I'm trying to say is that you've altered. Even I can see it. Your face has gone all bony – *you've* gone all bony – and your hair has lost its shine.'

She picked a tangled strand off my shoulder and ran it critically through her fingers. I scraped my hair into a fist and dropped it over the other shoulder, out of her reach.

'You always used to wear it up, in a clip.'

I replied without thinking – 'Cory prefers it down' – and she made me feel the pause that followed; transformed the silence into a picture frame and put it round my words, so that they looked more significant than they were.

'And your eyes are raw,' she went on, 'like you've been crying.'

'I haven't been crying.'

'Does he hurt you?'

'*No!* Why would you think that?'

'It's just . . .' She sighed. 'I don't know, there's just something about him. He gives me the creeps.'

Maggie fumbled in her pocket and drew out a tube of mints. I shook my head, but she kept holding them out until I changed my mind and took one. I thought I disliked peppermints, but it turned out they tasted of childhood, and long car journeys, and home.

'It's not as if you've nowhere to go,' she argued. 'Your dad would welcome you back with open arms, wouldn't he? From what you've told me?'

'I can't go back. I can't. It would be so . . .' I cast about for the right word. 'Just so *humiliating.*'

'Why? What do you mean?'

I buried my face in the fluffy lining of the hood and closed my eyes. The flavour of peppermint was so sad. What did I mean? Only that I'd staked everything on Byrne Hall, and I couldn't bear to lose.

'Cory and I, we've only been together a couple of months,' I said. 'We need time.'

'Listen, Freya . . .'

Wearily, I slumped against her shoulder while she argued and pointed out and persuaded and suggested things that no doubt made sense. *You are free . . . you can choose . . . you are not alone . . .* She was one of those people who gesture a lot with their hands as they talk, so my head kept jolting about and bumping from side to side.

'Freya? Please help me to understand. Why are you letting this happen to you?'

I was playing with the engagement ring; it had become my habit to twist it round and run my thumbnail over the knotty bits of metal. I didn't notice she'd stopped speaking until she repeated the question.

'Letting *what* happen?' I said. 'Nothing is happening.'

Maggie kept her eyes on my fidgety fingers.

'Listen to me,' she said. 'Don't wait around. Don't go imagining there'll be some magical moment; some sign . . .'

It hadn't occurred to me that I was waiting for a sign, but perhaps I was. Or, if not a sign exactly, then a flash of clarity. A word from Cory – a single gesture – which proved his worth, for good or ill.

Maggie stood up and wandered to the steps, leaving me the coat. I watched her pace the carpet of slimy leaves in her cotton dress, while the mist turned to drizzle around her. She kicked the wall and sighed unhappily. I bunched the fleece-lined coat to my chin and let my shoulders curl forwards.

'Freya, listen! This whole thing about his mother being ill and in hospital . . . has it ever occurred to you that she might not have gone anywhere? That she might still be at Byrne Hall?'

I frowned.

Maggie went on. 'Yesterday, when I was in the bathroom, I thought I heard a noise from upstairs.'

'What kind of noise?'

'I can't even say.' She splayed her fingers helplessly. 'It was so quick and quiet, it could have been anything: a voice or a footstep, or even a trapped bird. I don't know, but I'm sure I didn't imagine it. I decided to run up to the second floor while you and Cory were talking in the kitchen. I thought I might hear it more clearly from there – whatever it was.'

'And did you?'

'No, I never got as far as the second floor, because when I came round the bend in the stairs, I nearly walked into a tray.'

She paused, as if I might need time to react.

I shrugged and buried my chin in the coat again.

'On the tray,' she said, unfurling a finger for each item, 'there was a glass of water with red lipstick prints on the rim; a half-eaten bowl of broth; a china vase with a rose in it; and a packet of tablets with a prescription label made out to *Mrs Diana Byrne*.'

I did look up at her then.

I pounded up the stairs, and for the first time in weeks I didn't care how loud my footsteps were. I wanted Cory to emerge sleepy-eyed on to the landing, so that I could shove him out of the way while my courage was up.

'At least take my phone number,' Maggie had said, when she'd failed to persuade me to leave with her. She told me the number, which I immediately forgot, and her address – 16 Christie Street, Bligh – which seemed to have stuck. I don't remember anything else we said – I don't even remember saying goodbye – because my mind was full of lipstick stains. With mental effort, I might explain away the other items on the tray, but there was something unanswerably vivid about the lipstick on the glass of water.

I twisted the handle on Diana's bedroom door and pushed. It was locked. I tried a couple of the doors on either side, but they opened smoothly on to a bathroom and an empty box-room. I went back to Diana's door and knocked lightly, in case she was able to open it from the inside, but as I did so I recalled those old-fashioned keys in Cory's pocket. *Like a Victorian housekeeper*, I'd thought yesterday, in my innocence. *Like a jailer*, I thought now.

'Diana?' I stooped to peer through the keyhole. The corner of the window was visible, and part of a bed-post. 'Diana? Are you there?'

There was no sound. However still I held myself, nothing beyond the door was louder than my own heartbeat. I sank on to my knees and leaned my head against the door. God, I felt ill. My skin was prickly with heat, and at the same time I felt chilled through and through. If I'd been granted that one elusive wish – right there, right then – I'd have been in my narrow bed at home, with the covers over my head, and Byrne Hall would be a feverish dream I'd left behind in my sleep. I'd describe it to Stella when she popped in to check my temperature and she'd say, 'You weirdo. Why don't you dream of something nice?'

I tried the door handle one more useless time. 'I'll come back, I promise,' I said with my lips to the keyhole. 'Don't . . .' I faltered. *Don't what? Don't go anywhere?*

'Don't be afraid,' I said, but I was starting to shiver, and it made the words sound feeble.

'Cory!'

I stood over the bed, trying not to sway on my feet, trying to think above the buzz in my ears. He had fallen into bed fully clothed, dead to the world, and didn't stir at the sound of his name. I looked around for the keys, but of course they were in his pocket, safe beneath the weight of his body. I gave his shoulder an experimental jab, and he muttered but didn't move.

I took my damp clothes off and got into bed. I couldn't think with my skin so clammy and my feet like ice; I might manage better if I were warm. Cory was giving off a drowsy heat and usually I would have wrapped myself round his back, but now I stuck to my side of the mattress, lying right on the edge, as far away from him as possible.

Perhaps Maggie got it wrong. I kept seeing the tray – with the rose, and the tablets, and the lipstick-stained glass – which proved Cory a liar. *I just have to work out how she got it wrong.*

After a while I turned to face him. He was definitely asleep. There was nothing fake about that slackened mouth, or the strand of saliva crusting on the pillow. Even from my side of the bed I could smell stale wine on his breath.

I lay flat on my back again and tried not to make the mattress shake. At least there weren't any paintings up there, but I wished the ceiling would stop moving. Every time my eyes began to close it seemed to jolt a little closer, like a trap that had been set to crush me in my sleep.

Somebody is at her side in this incurable darkness. It's him. Diana hears her son's voice and feels his dry hand on her forehead. Does he sound sad? She thinks he does, even though he's only murmuring about the weather; about how cool and autumnal it's become. She tries to beg him to stay, but while she was sleeping her mouth forgot how to shape words. The memory hasn't disappeared for good – she can feel it unfurling in her brain – but it's so slow, and he's gone before it's ready.

'Cory!' she croaks, at last, into the void. 'Stay!'

Diana had won him back with a birthday present. It's almost funny to recall how anxiously she hovered outside his bedroom with the parcel in her hands, working up the courage to knock. What if he gave her that hating look? Or stood there with open cuts on his arms? Or resented the idea of turning fourteen?

214

What if he didn't open the door at all?

It was only mid-morning, and a Saturday, so perhaps she should leave him to sleep. Diana lowered her knuckles, but Cory opened the door anyway; he must have heard her loitering. In those days – in the first year of her widowhood – her son's body seemed to have become smaller and skinnier, while his facial expressions had become entirely adult. There was no denying – try as she might – that he had a look of his father.

'I didn't know what to buy,' she said shyly, holding out the present. 'You always used to like art, so I thought . . .'

Cory took it into his room and sat on the floor to unwrap it. A dozen drawing pencils, needle-sharp, in a tin; also a sketch-book, an eraser, and two books called How to Draw People *and* How to Draw Animals. *There was a time she might have caught his eye with a wink and whispered, 'Don't tell your dad,' but that sort of quip seemed riskier than ever now Mr Byrne was dead.*

Mr Byrne thought art was wet, especially for a boy. He would have bought his fourteen-year-old a rugby kit, or a macho watch, or a manual on how to be a start-up millionaire.

Cory hadn't slammed the door in her face, which was practically – wasn't it? – an invitation to come in. Diana took a deep breath before entering, but she needn't have worried: her son's room was ordinary to the point of expressionless. A bag of school books on the floor; a few clothes over the back of a chair; a couple of dirty mugs. An exam timetable taped to the wall.

'You used to draw me,' she ventured. 'Do you remember? You had a real gift for it.'

Cory nodded absently. He was levering the pencils out of their tin one by one, and testing their relative softness on the cover of the sketch-book.

'Perhaps you'll get into it again?'

Diana was hardly talking nineteen to the dozen but he, with his silence, made her feel as if she were. She noticed – not for the first time – how his eyes had changed over the course of the year. They used to look outwards at the world, whereas now they looked inwards at his own secret thoughts.

'Thank you,' he said, unexpectedly.

She sat by the window and leaned on the sill with her chin in her hand. He didn't tell her to go away. After a while she heard the irregular sweep of pencil on paper and knew he was sketching her, but she resisted the impulse to look. A cloud passed over the sun and her bare arms felt cold. She watched a sparrow hopping about on the grass and tried not to notice the pins and needles in her feet.

'Dad would not *approve of this,' Cory said. There was a smile in his voice; a slight, conspiratorial smile.*

Diana gripped her chin and stared at the sparrow, as if her son's observation hadn't changed everything; as if nothing much had happened.

'He would hate it,' she agreed, as soon as she could say anything. 'But that's not a reason to stop, is it? You've got a real talent for art – I mean a real *talent – it would be a shame not to use it.'*

The pencil kept scritch-scratching across the paper.

'Mum? The more you yatter, the harder it is for me to draw your mouth.'

She didn't say another word, but it was hard to keep her lips still when they kept wanting to quiver into a smile.

Diana lies in bed, half dreaming, half awake. She has her home, and her boy, and her moments of peace. As long as she keeps picturing that day of his fourteenth birthday – as long as she refuses to recall what came next – the darkness and the dying don't seem to matter much.

10

CORY WAS PAINTING WHEN I woke. It was only a small water-colour sketch, and rather than standing at the easel he was sitting cross-legged near my pillow with the board across his knees. He'd sat like that to draw me on our first evening, before I'd kissed him; before I knew I was going to stay.

'What are you going to call it when it's finished?' I croaked. '*Freya with a Snotty Cold*?'

He put the board to one side and got to his feet.

'I thought of calling it *The Convalescent*,' he said. 'They don't all have to have "Freya" in the title.'

I had an upside-down view of his drawing as it lay on the floor. The girl in the bed was colourless and fragile; she could have been drawn by one of those Victorian artists with an avowed interest in angelic females, and a sublimated interest in sex and death. You wouldn't know that my upper lip was raw and my nostrils dripping.

I pulled the covers over my chin. Cory picked my clothes up and began folding them – pulling the cardigan sleeves outside in, shaking the jeans straight, stroking the creases out of my shirt.

'Why are they all damp?' he wanted to know. 'Have you been outside this morning?'

'Only into the garden.'

I blew my nose, hiding my face in the rough paper towel

that I was using for a tissue. Cory kept reams of the stuff for blotting paint.

'I thought we'd agreed . . .'

'What?'

He shrugged.

'What did we agree? That I'm not allowed out on my own?'

He shrugged again and turned away.

'Well, frankly it was quite stupid,' he said without any tenderness, and the rain pattered against the window as if to back him up. 'No wonder you feel rough.'

I think that watercolour – *The Convalescent* – was the only portrait Cory ever failed to complete. He was usually a stickler for finishing what he'd started.

He spent the rest of the morning downstairs – painting his galleries Pamplona Red, I suppose – and in the afternoon he began bringing empty picture frames to the studio and dusting them with yellow cloths. I watched from under my eyelids, and if he ever glanced my way I pretended to be asleep. Sometimes I actually slept. There was a mist at the windows, and time never seemed to move between one doze and the next.

'Freya!'

Tom's voice was whispery in my dream, and when I opened my eyes the room was a dim mingling of night and candlelight. It was Cory, not Tom, but I smiled in an effort to prolong the dream, and after a while he smiled back. I propped myself on my elbow and he wrapped my fingers round a mug.

'Drink this,' he said. 'Brandy and hot water.'

I sat up, shivering, and while I sipped he placed a dressing gown round my shoulders. I suppose it was Diana's – it smelled of her musky perfume – but I didn't have to think about that. The drink was fiery, and there was plenty of it. It was the first thing I'd tasted in twenty-four hours, unless you count cold water sucked from the bathroom tap.

Tom – or was it Cory? – touched my hair, and my eyes swam and spilt, as if I'd never known kindness like it.

The next time I woke it was dark and Cory was asleep beside me, his breathing regular and deep. I whispered his name but he didn't stir, so I peeled the sheets off my body and let cool air into the bed. I'd spent all day with the shivers but now I felt sticky and hot, and my head was throbbing.

Cory had put a lighted candle on the windowsill. It was burning low – there was barely an inch of white wax left in the neck of the bottle – and the flame was wavering. The rain kept blowing in gusts against the window, and the candlelight made it look as though a dripping, golden web had been strung across the glass.

I put my hand over my eyes and tried to remember. I'd been standing on a stage, taking a deep breath before I began – began what? – and all the people in the audience had been sitting forward in their seats, rustling with anticipation . . . I uncovered my eyes and Cory's paintings and drawings seemed to crowd in from the walls, all those identical girls with their empty eyes and pouty lips, craning and jostling to see what I intended to do.

My legs were shaky at first, but I felt better once I'd tied the belt on my dressing gown and made it to the windowsill to pick up the candle. I didn't relish the idea of exploring Byrne Hall by candlelight, but it was safer than flinging electric lights on all over the place.

Perhaps my cold had made me deaf, but the floor seemed strangely silent under my feet as I made my way to the door. Cory had disappeared in a huddle of shadows and bed-linen, and if I hadn't known better I'd have doubted he was still there. The idea that he might be up and about made me halt, dry-mouthed – but that was silly. There: that pale line was the edge of his ear, and that slope followed the curve of his shoulder, and hadn't the duvet just shifted, ever so slightly, with the rise and fall of his breathing? His clothes were in a muddle at the foot of the bed, and all I had to do was slide my fingers into the correct pocket and take a tight hold of the keys, so that they wouldn't jangle as I lifted them away.

I'd forgotten there was a window on the landing, and my reflection made me jump when I reached the top of the stairs. It wasn't my own face that bothered me so much as the idea of another face appearing behind it. I put a protective hand on my neck, and as I did so the briefest flutter of movement seemed to sound in the depths of the house. Instinctively I turned round, but of course I couldn't see anything. The stair-well was a black pit.

I was tempted to blow the candle out, so that I could blend in with the darkness. A draught from the attic door almost did the job for me, but I cupped my hand around the wilting flame and saved it after all. I tried a couple of keys before I found the one that fitted, and as soon as the door opened I recognised Diana's room by its smell. It was the smell of the clothes I'd been wearing all week; of the dressing gown I was wearing now.

I stepped inside and held the candle high, sweeping it round in an arc. A face flashed at me out of the shadowy clutter; a death's head, resting on a pillow. I hugged the wine bottle against my chest, and one of my hairs fizzled in its flame.

I heard her breathe – a long, dwindling exhalation – and looked again.

'Diana?'

I put the candle on the bedside table among the pills and knick-knacks, and knelt beside her head.

I really thought she was dead at first; that I'd just witnessed her final breath. With its pools of deep shadow and ridges of parchment-yellow bone, her head seemed even more skull-like than it had in that first, nightmarish flash. Her hair was so thin she was almost bald; her skin fell away from her teeth in such a way that she seemed lipless; her eyebrows and eyelashes had dwindled to nothing. It was as if someone had taken an eraser to the face I'd seen in August and tried to rub it out.

Diana's hands were clumped on top of the coverlet like pale, dry twigs, good for nothing but kindling. Her open eyes glittered in their black sockets. She let out another long breath, and there was a jaggedness about it this time – an agitation – which made me think she was aware of my presence. Against every instinct I touched her, resting my hands stiffly on top of hers.

'It's all right,' I whispered, without conviction. I was reluctant to look at her face – every time I did so I thought of Cory's canvases, stretched and stapled to their plywood boards – but what else could I do? The candle's unsteady reflection was like a raging fire inside her eyes.

I didn't know what to say. She was too weak to address my haul of questions. She was too weak to answer anything; too weak to talk at all.

'I'll go and get help,' I faltered. 'The ambulance people will come and take you to the hospital, and everything will be all right.'

The head on the pillow moved slightly from side to side, and the mouth tried to say, 'No.'

Her voice was husky and small, as if she were on the verge of tears. She moved her hand from underneath mine and touched my face, but frailty had stripped her gestures and expressions to such a bare minimum that I didn't know what to make of it.

'My beautiful boy.'

Her voice creaked up and down a crazy arpeggio, and I couldn't make sense of that either. I dragged my hair to the other side of my neck, so that she could see my face.

'It's me,' I whispered. 'Freya Lyell. Do you remember . . . ?'

'My beautiful boy,' she repeated, resting the tips of her nails against my face. Now I felt sure it was emotion that had roughened her voice, because there were tears sliding down her face and trailing under her jaw.

'Cory's fine,' I soothed. It wasn't Diana's fault her son was a liar – or if it was, this wasn't the time for heaping blame. I wanted to comfort her, but it was difficult to know how, when she and her unhappiness were such mysteries to me.

'I'm going to get help.' I stroked her hand and stood up. 'You shouldn't be abandoned here like this; I'm sure there are things they could do to help you . . .'

The candle flame shrank to an orange dot with a blue halo. The last thing I saw, before it went out, was the wet and watchful glint of an eye.

'Everything will be fine,' I whispered, although it sounded absurd in the total darkness of that room.

PART THREE

Stella

October 2009

WHEN CORY'S HANDS MEET AROUND her neck, Stella finds she can't contemplate death anymore. It's come too close; her mind sheers away and fixes on other things.

She wonders what that noise is. That whispering, rustling, pattering? It isn't just the rain. Clouds flit over the moon and she glimpses ghosts from the corner of her eye. The attics at Byrne Hall must be full of them – flocks of consumptive housemaids and tragic governesses from the olden days. One of the maids is wearing her hair in a braid, like Freya used to wear hers for school.

'I loved that painting.' Cory is so grief-stricken he can hardly get the words out. 'It was the best one I'd ever done. It captured your soul.'

The painting in question is a drift of stained snowflakes at their feet.

'Why did you tear it up?' Cory presses his thumbs into her throat. 'Why, Stella? Why, why, why?'

He is startled into silence as the door opens.

His mother?

But Diana is meant to be away; she's not due back until tomorrow.

Stella knows it really is Cory's mother, and not another ghost, when the light comes on with a rickety click and the

225

bare bulb gives off a smell of singed dust. A few seconds pass before anyone moves or speaks.

'What is all this?' Diana says at last. 'What's happening?'

She removes her smart gloves, folds them, places them in her handbag. Cory's hands fall to his sides and he retreats to the corner of the room, where he turns his face to the wall. Diana helps Stella sit on the edge of the bed and drops a handkerchief – ironed and scented – on to her lap. Stella is in a daze. She blows her nose and bursts into tears.

'I'm so thirsty I could die.'

A bottle of sparkling mineral water materialises from Diana's bag and Stella glugs it down.

Mrs Byrne has been in London for ever, but she's come back in the nick of time, and now she's poised in the centre of the room, surveying the chaos. Stella's explanations are incoherent for the time being, and Cory can't seem to say anything at all – but Diana doesn't press. That's not her way. She begins to circle the room – picking up scraps of paper, shutting the window, covering the chamber pot, gesturing towards a restoration of order.

Stella waits in the attic while Cory is 'put to bed' – his mother's words – and after a while Diana returns with a bottle and two glasses on a tray. All Stella can think to say is, *How is he?* but there's no way she's going to, not even to fill an awkward gap.

Diana clears a careful space amid the shredded papers and sets the tray on the floor. The bottle is shaped like a violin and painted with garlands of white flowers. Diana uncorks it and pours clear liquid into the two tumblers – a large one for Stella and a small one for herself. Her hand trembles as she pours and Stella wonders if she's had a few already.

'It's an Austrian schnapps.' Diana is frowning at the label. 'At least, I think it is. You buy these things on holiday, don't you, and then they sit about the house ever after. It'll warm you up, anyway, and that's the main thing.'

Stella sips and grimaces. The schnapps tastes of resin and bitter herbs, and it burns a trail from her mouth to her stomach. *A mug of tea would have done*, she thinks. *I wish I was at home.*

Diana is on edge. She keeps her coat on and paces the room, stopping every now and then to glance at her reflection in the window. Stella thinks she is a magnificent human being although that might, in part, be a side effect of fame. Marginal fame. Years and years ago – when she was still unmarried and wealthy and given to patronising famous artists – Diana was interviewed and photographed by the *Sunday Times* magazine. Stella has seen the copy that Cory keeps flat inside a folder.

'How was London?' Stella asks, as if this is a suitable occasion for small talk.

'I spent every single second longing for Byrne Hall.'

Stella remembers that the trip involved an appointment at a private medical clinic, and bites back her instinctive, slightly facile reply – 'Just as well for me!' – in case Diana is seriously ill.

Diana gulps the last of her schnapps, tops up both their glasses and returns to the window. Stella watches her face in reflection. The older woman's eyes are hidden inside shadows and the tumbler obscures her mouth, and Stella can't help thinking that this would be an interesting set-up for a portrait; better than any of Cory's humdrum ideas. *Shoulders straight, Stella . . . Keep your hands folded on your lap, Stella . . . Pull the dressing gown open, Stella . . . Don't wriggle . . . Don't smirk . . . Stop staring at me like that, you smug bitch.*

227

'Cory thinks he's God's gift to art,' observes Stella. 'He thinks he's really something, doesn't he?'

It may be unwise to let rip in front of his mother, but having started it's difficult to stop. Anyway, one of them needs to mention what's happened, and Diana shows no sign of wanting to talk.

'He goes on about capturing my soul like he's some kind of satanic priest,' Stella continues, 'and then you look at what he's done, and it's flat and dead and mediocre. It's not even *bad*. It's not even strong enough to be *bad*.'

Stella pauses for breath; Diana's reflection sips and stares. There's one similarity between Diana and Cory: both of them can do powerful things to silences. They make you feel as if your own thoughts are cavorting naked in the street, while theirs are safely hidden behind a veil.

'I'm sorry. I know he's your son and everything.' Stella stops, annoyed with herself for saying sorry – how very British; how very Freya-like, in the circumstances – and takes a defiant swig of schnapps. She's almost enjoying the taste now; it hardly makes her squint at all.

'Don't apologise,' Diana says. 'You're wasting your breath. You forget that I know him better than anyone.'

'Of course you do. Sorry.' She means the apology this time; she feels faintly ashamed. Who knows what horrors Diana has had to put up with from her son, over the years?

Stella knocks the schnapps back in one gulp. It's really tasty, she's decided; better than a cup of tea. There's a fire blazing in her belly now, spreading its flames to the tips of her fingers and toes, and she pours herself another inch, just to keep it stoked. She offers Diana a top-up, but Diana shakes her head and covers the glass with her hand.

Stella hiccups.

'Between you and me,' she confides, 'I've given up on men. I mean, when I think about it, Cory's a monster in human form and Tom . . . well, the less said about Tom the better. But you don't know him, do you? Tom Gardiner.'

Just as Stella is starting to laugh, her face falls. She sways and catches at the bed-frame.

'I'm sorry I never knew you better,' she whispers solemnly. 'It's a pity Cory kept us at arm's length; I got it into my head you were standoffish. I suppose we've missed our chance now?'

'I suppose so.'

Diana changes her mind about the schnapps and pours herself another measure.

'The thing is,' Stella clarifies, 'as much as I would like to get to know you, I can't stay at Byrne Hall. I need to go home.'

Diana replies with a smile which makes her look tired and sad. Stella wonders what time it is; it must be the middle of the night.

A door slams down below. Those are Cory's footsteps, traipsing along the landing to the bathroom: he's not asleep, then. Stella shivers and drains the last of the schnapps in one choking gulp.

'You're right.' Diana winds her loosened scarf round her neck and fastens the buttons on her coat. 'You're absolutely right.'

Stella looks up with a question in her eyes.

'It's time you left,' Diana explains, helping the girl to her feet.

Freya

October–November 2014

1

I FELT MY WAY ALONG the corridor to the top of the stairs after shutting Diana's door behind me, and considered the feasibility of escaping from Byrne Hall now – immediately – in dressing gown and bare feet. I didn't want to go back to Cory's room, but I wouldn't get far – or fast – along the driveway without shoes, and I'd probably be arrested if I were found wandering through Bligh in the early hours dressed like this. Clothes would be a definite plus, as would my purse.

I felt for the bannister with one hand and the opposite wall with the other, and made my way downstairs.

My clothes were still damp from yesterday and I worried he'd feel my shivers through the floorboards. There was a horrible moment when the belt jangled on my jeans, and another as I zipped my bag, and one more – the worst – when I jostled the easel as I was feeling around for my pumps. Each time I froze, waiting for a drowsy voice to demand what was going on, but he didn't stir.

I didn't have time or inclination to scribble a note, but before I left I removed the ring from my finger and placed it on the mantelpiece.

*

The sky was a pre-dawn grey when I left the house, but it was night beneath the trees, as though the sun had had second thoughts about rising. A couple of times I lost the path and stumbled into a wilderness of roots and knee-high ferns. The silence was immense, but it was also imperfect, and every snap, rustle and chirrup made me jump.

Once I saw a flash of white light arcing through the drizzle ahead of me. I thought it was a torch but then it disappeared, and it seemed more likely to have been the headlights of a car moving along the harbour road, or even a fishing boat on its way out to sea. I must be nearly there; nearly at the end of the drive. I quickened my pace, sloshing unevenly through puddles and bruising my ankle on a fallen branch.

The gates. *Finally.* I breathed out and rested my forehead against the wrought-iron bars.

My eyes flicked open and I lifted my head.

What gates?

Slowly, meditatively, I wrapped my fingers round the rusty bars. *What gates?* I thought back to the day I'd arrived, and all I could remember was a gap between two stone pillars.

I stepped away, picking shards of flaky paint off my hands with deliberate carefulness. It didn't matter. It didn't mean anything. Perhaps this was a different entrance; perhaps the driveway had diverged at some point. It's not like I'd have noticed in the dark. But the sky was turning pale ahead of me, and the two stone ravens were in silhouette on top of their posts – one headless, both chipped by old age and weather. I recognised them, and I recognised the mossy posts themselves, and the road I'd trudged in August, and the back of the dilapidated sign that read – if I remembered rightly – BYRNE

HALL. NO TRESPASSING. Either side of the gate-posts was a solid muddle of ivy-covered brick wall, and shrubs, and rusty barbed wire.

So the gates had been open in August and now they were closed. What of it? I gave the bars a gentle shake. They yielded an inch, jarred and bounced back. I pushed again, more roughly, and the same thing happened. I ran my hand along the join and found a keyhole without a key, and a chain, and a rust-free padlock.

I moistened my lips and brushed my hands down my jeans. It was silly to panic when I could see the public road; could reach through the bars and touch the wet tarmac if I wanted. For heaven's sake, I could see the masts in the harbour, and lights in some of the guest houses. Day was breaking, and someone – a dog-walker, a boat owner, a postman – was bound to come by at any minute. I was not trapped. I could not be trapped.

I rattled the gates, swore at them, tugged at the padlock. I wasn't going to cry; the whole thing was too stupid for crying. If I could climb over? Or if one of the bars turned out to be loose? I gave each one a vicious, two-handed throttle, and ended with my hands around the padlock.

This wouldn't have happened to Stella. Stella would have melted the metal bars with her eyes; she'd have toppled the stone gate-posts with her bare hands. I couldn't do anything properly – *anything* – not even running away.

'Open,' I muttered, yanking at the metal loop. '*Open* . . .'

When it didn't budge, I roared. I'd never made a noise like that before; I didn't know I could. Even five years ago, when Stella died, the roaring had stayed inside my head.

'Freya!'

I spun round, crashing my back against the gate and

bruising my shoulders. Cory shone the torch in my face, forcing my eyes shut. I kept trying to open them, but whichever way I turned and twisted, he was there.

'Where are you going?'

His voice sounded so sad and simple, I believed I'd be able to reason with him. I opened my mouth to speak – I was going to explain that I wanted to leave, and tell him that his mother needed help, and ask him to unlock the gates – at the same moment as his fingers found my neck. With his other hand he squeezed my jaw, distorting my lips and cheeks so that I couldn't bite, or spit, or talk. The torch spun off into the undergrowth, but there was just enough daylight for me to see his face. I couldn't make any sense of it; it wasn't beautiful anymore. It was too close-up and twisted.

For one second – no more than two – he crushed my neck and face with all his strength, then he let go. It was over in a flash.

'I'm sorry,' he whispered, his hands trembling over his own mouth. The places where he'd pressed felt hot and sore – not just on the surface of my skin but deep in the tissue – as though I'd been branded. Later on I studied myself carefully in the bathroom mirror, but there wasn't a great deal to see, and I felt oddly disappointed as well as relieved. I'd expected red, indented fingerprints and deep bruises. I'd *wanted* them, as evidence against my own self-doubt.

Cory backed away, full of whispered apologies. If only somebody would choose that moment to walk by – but the chances were low and anyway, with the gate still locked, I wouldn't be mad enough to yell for help. More likely I'd stand still, holding my breath, while the dog-walker glanced our way and carried on.

'Freya?'

Cory began to draw close again, and I listened for some sound other than our rapid breathing. It didn't have to be another human being; any old noise would do. Jackdaws cawing. Waves lapping. Trees creaking . . . I suppose the silence was because of the mist – the rain had softened and thickened at some point since I left the house – but it felt like an effect of Cory's approach, as if the closer he got the more fragmented and faraway everything else became.

'Freya?'

He was frightened to touch me, even with his gaze.

'Please don't leave me, Freya.'

I tried to kick him, but he went down on his knees and pressed himself against my legs, trapping my wrists with one smooth movement of his hand. My mouth felt dry. He looked up at me, his face a raised blur in the dusk, as if it were his fate that was in my hands and not the other way round.

'Everything is for you,' he said. 'You are my inspiration. I love you. I need you.'

Blah, blah, blah, I thought. *The great artist and his muse.*

I wonder what he saw when he looked at me like that. A soft-focus dream, as kitsch as anything I'd ever indulged in. A glittering spread of royal-red rooms; pictures in golden frames; hordes of admirers ooh-ing and ah-ing over his genius. The two of us flitting from guest to guest: *You must be so proud of him . . . You must be so grateful to her . . .* and the whole house in high spirits, although there's concern that the champagne is running low and we can barely make ourselves heard above the chatter. My father clapping him on the back and scribbling eager notes on a paper napkin. *Your fortune is made this day, my boy.*

Cory leaned into my knees. He began kissing my thighs and

stomach, and with every nudge of his lips I remembered those days and nights at the end of the summer. I looked away, but the pot-holed drive was cold and dark, unilluminated by fantasy.

'Stay with me,' he whispered. 'Let's be like we were before. I didn't mean to hurt you; it was a split-second, a moment of madness.'

I think he was trying to hypnotise me – he said these things so many times and between so many kisses. If my hands had been free I could have stroked his forehead and fondled his rain-frizzled hair and forgiven his 'moment of madness'. Or I could have dug my thumbs into his eyes.

'You're such a liar,' I said.

Cory didn't deny it, or ask what I meant, he just made excuses – 'I only ever wanted what was best for everyone. I would never hurt my mother, I would never intentionally hurt *you*' – to which I paid no attention. Lying was the offence I accused him of, but it was hardly my biggest concern; it had stopped being my biggest concern when he seized me by the throat. *Don't wait for a sign*, Maggie had warned me – but I had waited, and here I was with bruising on my neck.

'You will stay, won't you? We can put all this behind us, can't we? We can go back to where we were; it can be like it was in September?'

'*September?*'

I looked into his face.

I think he must have heard the yearning in my voice and taken it for a yes; at any rate he loosened his grip on my wrists. I placed my hands on his hair and closed my eyes.

'All right,' I said. 'All right, you win, I'll stay.'

I'll wait till you're asleep, I thought. *I'll go to the beach when the tide is out, and walk round the foot of the cliffs to Bligh.*

2

CORY PRODUCED A BUNCH OF keys from his pocket, like a cheap conjuring trick. It was surely the same bunch I'd stolen from him earlier in the night and left in Diana's bedroom door.

'You were following me,' I said, as he stooped over the padlock. 'All the time. All those little noises in the house . . .'

He shot me a look from under his eyelids – apology mixed with mirth – and my heart gave the lurch it had been conditioned to give from the day we met.

'No,' I said.

'Huh?' Cory glanced up as the padlock clicked open.

'Nothing. I was talking to myself.'

Cory Byrne was a fraud, I told myself, and everything he did was suspect. The little glances, the shy touches, the humour, the gallantry – none of these things was real. He pushed the rusty gates open and stood aside to let me pass, but I folded my arms and said, 'After you.' He didn't quibble.

'Why did you lock them in the first place?' I wanted to know, when we were standing in the road.

'What? The gates?' He sounded surprised. 'We often lock them at night. I know they're not exactly cutting-edge, security-wise, but they're better than nothing.'

It wasn't a bad answer, but Cory was bound to be full of not-bad answers.

'Where are you taking me now?'

'I'm not *taking* you anywhere; I thought we could go for a stroll. We can talk as we go along, and I'll explain everything.'

'Everything?'

'Everything. I promise.'

I gauged my chances of making a run for it there and then, and decided against. Cory had firm hold of my hand, and even if I managed to pull free he could catch me without breaking a sweat. Tantalising lights glimmered across the harbour in increasing number: fishing boats, windows, a bicycle, a couple of cars, a delivery van – but they were too far away to help.

Cory led the way uphill, away from town, on a road that skirted the walls of the Byrne Hall estate and took us into the woods again. It obviously wasn't a popular thoroughfare: the tarmac was cracked and slippery with moss, and a line of grass grew up the middle, dividing the track in two. Our feet pressed a fresh, green, squelching fragrance from the surface with every step, and I felt my head clearing as we got higher and the trees began to thin. *A moment of madness*, I kept thinking. What did that mean? Was an act – any act at all – the more forgivable for being momentary and mad?

'It's nice to get out of the house,' said Cory, swinging my hand. 'I think it was starting to drive us out of our minds. It does that.'

I let the remark pass because it felt true, but then I stopped.

'Wait,' I said. 'I'm not *out of my mind*. I didn't run away because I was *out of my mind*. I ran away because I discovered your dying mother locked in a poky upstairs room, when you'd told me she was being cared for in a hospice.'

'I know, I know.' He squeezed my hand. 'I know how it looks, but it will make sense once I've explained.'

'Well, go on then. Explain.'

Cory looked away, as if he hoped to find inspiration among the dwindling trees.

'Let's walk a bit further,' he said at last, tugging on my arm. 'We'll find somewhere we can sit and talk properly.'

Eventually the road emerged on to a hillside, springy with sheep droppings and cropped grass, and we stopped to catch our breath. Byrne Hall was visible beneath us – or at least the tall chimneys were, and the dilapidated roof with its many gaps and bird droppings and strutting jackdaws.

'How strange,' I said. It *was* strange, seeing the house from up here. The pristine frontage wasn't visible at all; you'd think the whole place was derelict.

Cory didn't ask what I meant; he probably thought I was talking to myself again. Perhaps I was.

Sheep dotted the hills; the sound of their baa-ing was faint and distant. I traced the road with my eyes as it meandered down to the edge of Stella's cliffs, and wondered how often anyone came here. The rising sun was hidden by low cloud, and the sea looked leaden. Further down the coast a light-house flashed and faded.

'Cory?' I began. 'This whole thing we've got going—'

'What thing? You mean *us*? You and me?'

'Well, yes,' I said, 'except there's more to it than just *you and me*. There always has been.'

I didn't want to use the word 'idyll'. I'd used it in the beginning – when we set up our shared studio – and attached no irony to it at all. Now, looking back, I was embarrassed by my own earnestness. What had I been thinking? That we could live our entire lives like characters in a romantic opera?

Perpetually in love, and making money from dashed-off novels and paintings?

'It's not working for me,' I said. 'I'm not doing anything; I'm just hanging about, being your so-called muse. For goodness' sake, I don't know how to be a poet or a storyteller. I mean, who was I kidding? I want to go home. I don't like it here anymore.'

It was my intention to hurt him. I was tempted to add that I didn't like him either, but that was a step too far; a self-fulfilling prophecy I wasn't quite ready to fulfil. Also, I was conscious of being alone with him on a deserted hillside, and I was nervous for my neck.

'I'm not sure I ever really wanted to write,' I said. 'I don't know. Maybe I just wanted to be A Writer?'

I could feel him looking at me. 'Isn't that the same thing?'

'No, it's not.'

It wasn't the whole truth, either, because I had wanted to write. I was being hard on myself in order to be hard on him; on 'us'; on the whole stupid set-up.

Cory faced the road and held his hand out, implying he'd rather we talked as we walked, but I sat on the grass and drew my knees up to my chin. He hesitated before sitting down beside me. We watched the sky grow paler, turning the leaden sea to silver. A trawler emerged into view, carving a long, clean ripple in its wake.

'You *can* write.' Cory made as if to stroke my hair, but held off when I winced. 'You'd find it easier, though, if you stopped over-thinking everything.'

I narrowed my eyes. 'Meaning what?'

He was ready with a fully fledged answer; clearly he'd been turning this over in his mind for a while.

'You always try to be too deep and elaborate,' he said. 'You ought to just write what you know; what you see; what's *there*, in front of you.'

'That's your method, is it?' I said. 'When you paint me, you just put down what's there?'

'I suppose.' Cory shrugged and plucked at the grass. 'Anyway, what does it matter if you can or can't write?'

I tore my eyes from the fishing boat. 'It matters a lot! It matters to me! Being a writer, a real writer, that was part of the whole . . . thing . . .' *The whole idyll.*

'All I mean is – I'll still love you, if you never write another word.'

I ground my teeth and returned to the view.

'What? Freya? How is that irritating?'

'I don't know.'

Truly, I didn't know. Wasn't that what I wanted: to be loved for myself? Wasn't that what everyone wanted?

The lighthouse flared one last time and went out. The morning felt more ordinary without it.

'It's lovely up here.' Cory spoke in a forced way, as if anxious to fill the silence.

'It's not,' I said. 'It's depressing.'

I wanted him to refute this; to persuade me that the world at our feet – the huge, rickety house among the trees, the empty hills, the sea – was authentically lovely, but he didn't even try. I hugged my legs more tightly, hid my face against my knees, and tried to work out what was going on in my own head. It was either that I hated him, or that I couldn't bear to hate him, or a poisonous combination of the two.

'Talking of your paintings . . .' I said, desperate now to hurt him.

'Were we? What about them?'

'They never change, do they? The ones you're working on now look much the same as the ones you did in September.'

'I don't want them to change.' He sounded perplexed rather than hurt. 'It's like I said: you are what you are. I paint you as I see you.'

The trawler was leaving the coastline behind, and I could just make out the fishermen on deck. The water was choppy on the open sea and it was a wonder they could stand upright, let alone move with such purpose. It must be good to be on a boat, I thought, with the air salting your skin and something definite to do.

Cory stood up. 'Let's go.'

'We haven't talked properly yet. You haven't told me about your mother.'

'I will, but I think we should start heading back.'

'Back the way we came?'

'No, we'll carry on and do a circle. If we cross this field we'll meet the clifftop path, and that'll take us into the gardens.'

I stood up slowly, brushing sheep droppings off the seat of my jeans.

'Those are Stella's cliffs,' I said.

Cory seemed to ponder this before shaking his head impatiently.

'They're just cliffs.'

The grass was so steep and slippery that we had either to tiptoe or break into a downhill run. We tried both, falling over and getting grass-stains on our backsides, and I have to admit it was hard to stay serious. Cory laughed without inhibition; a couple of times my mouth trembled on the brink of a smile.

We were out of breath by the time we reached the clifftops, though Cory was in a worse state than me because he'd been laughing so hard. A middle-aged woman came round the corner with a spaniel on a lead and raised her eyebrows at the sight of our flushed faces. The three of us nodded briskly and said, 'Morning!' or 'Hello!' and I watched her disappear round the bend in the road.

'So . . . ?' I prompted, once we'd found the footpath and begun pushing through the gorse.

'My mother,' Cory said. 'You want to know . . .'

He seemed loath to complete the sentence.

'Cory, I want to know why you lied to me. I want to know why she's not being properly cared for. I want—'

'She *is* being properly cared for.' He hadn't spoken so sharply since the incident at the gate; he recovered himself quickly and softened his tone. 'I know it looks bad, but whatever else you blame me for, you have to understand that she's there of her own accord. Yes, she's bedridden, but it's the illness that's holding her prisoner, not me.'

The footpath met a stile, which took us away from the sea and into the woods again. Through the trees I spied the fading greens of the garden and the blank walls of the house. *Back again*, I thought. A few moments beyond the boundaries – a stolen glimpse of the outside world – and back again to Byrne Hall.

'Home!' There was real – if tentative – pleasure in Cory's voice, as he picked up my hand and kissed it. He said, 'My mother would rather die at Byrne Hall than eke out her last days in some institution.'

'Which is all well and good,' I retorted, 'but why not tell me that in the first place? Why lie?'

I looked at his familiar hand, with its broad knuckles, and fine hairs, and paint-clogged nails. I almost kissed it in return from sheer habit, but I resisted the temptation. I wanted my explanation first.

'It's cold.' Cory sighed. 'Let's go inside and talk there.'

The cold inside the house was still and stony, instead of fresh and outdoorsy. We wandered the empty galleries for a while, but Cory must have moved the sofa and chair when he polished the floors yesterday and there was nowhere to sit.

We ended up side by side on the dark stairs.

'So . . . ?'

'I've always been protective of her,' Cory began.

'Of your mother? Because your father . . . ?'

He nodded and looked away. 'You've probably gathered that he wasn't the best of husbands. It was a pretty one-sided bargain from the start, actually: she was beautiful, popular, wealthy, clever, and the rest; he was none of those things. OK, I suppose he was fairly good-looking, but basically I reckon he was just a posh man with a big house, in need of funds.'

'And what was he like as a dad?'

'I don't know how to answer that. He wasn't exactly nice, by any stretch of the imagination, but he was my dad and . . .'

He stopped again, and I stroked his hand grudgingly. I'd have needed a heart of stone to make no gesture at all.

'Well.' Cory's voice took on a shaky lightness. 'I was going to say *he loved me in his own way*, but I'm not even sure what that means.'

'Why? What did he do to you?' I asked the question too quickly, making it sound like raw curiosity – which, in part, it was. *Fair enough*, I thought, when Cory shook his head and pressed his lips shut. I let it go and waited for him to carry on.

'I've told you about my mother's parties, haven't I, and all the friends she kept up with? She was an extrovert, a minor celebrity, an art collector, a party animal, used to throwing her money around. I know it's hard to believe when you see her now. My father hated parties and extravagance, but he was away a lot so . . .'

'While the cat was away?'

'Exactly.'

Cory shifted his position and the joists creaked under his weight. The noise was almost human, like the groan of a tired man, and I glanced over my shoulder to make sure we were alone.

'After his death, my mother changed; she became withdrawn and afraid. You'd think she'd have been wild with relief, but it didn't work out like that, somehow. Friends still came to visit – or they did to begin with – but she didn't enjoy their company anymore. She would come across as reserved, or distracted, or else she'd take offence at the tiniest thing.'

'Like what?'

Cory thought.

'Like, for example, when one of her friends patted me on the back and said, "Your father would be proud." It wasn't for anything important – I think I'd been selected for the school cricket team – but my mother told him to apologise or leave.'

'And which did he do?'

'He left.'

I considered the story.

'Did you play?'

244

'What, for the cricket team? I can't remember. No, I don't think so. I was off school a lot that summer with illness.'

I was going to ask what kind of illness, but he'd already carried on.

'My mother . . . she just became *odd*. She started talking to herself a lot. There were arguments with my dead father, conversations with the house, murmurings I couldn't quite catch. She moved out of her big bedroom at the front of the house and into the dark little room you've seen. I was scared, but I didn't know what to do. Gradually people stopped coming to Byrne Hall – or perhaps she stopped inviting them, I'm not sure which way round it happened.'

My fingers played along the inside of his arm, skimming the razor scars. He stiffened momentarily, but didn't shake me off.

'There was no-one to talk to; she couldn't seem to tolerate anyone other than me. That's how I started drawing portraits, actually; it was something to do while I kept her company. She didn't want to do anything herself, or go anywhere, or see anyone, but she was happy to sit still for hours on end.'

'So she never even left the house?'

'Rarely. She came to visit me a couple of times when I went to art college, but I could tell it made her uneasy. The trouble was, people were so *interested* in her – people in the art world, anyway. If she turned up at an exhibition, say, there'd be sidelong looks and whispers, and she just couldn't cope with that.' He sighed. 'Well. I chucked in my course anyway after a few months, and came home.'

'Would she not get any help?'

'She wouldn't admit there was anything wrong until she got ill – physically ill, I mean. At least after she was diagnosed she'd accept *some* help.'

'When was that?'

'About five years ago. I've looked after her ever since, and I have to say, she's not been a demanding patient. Not exactly. All she wants is to be at home with me, and for everyone else to stay away.'

'Everyone else . . .' I said. 'Cory, that's an awful lot to ask of you. I wish you'd told me all this in the beginning.'

'I know, I'm sorry. It was . . . it seemed easier.'

Now that he was calm, I thought, it was just possible he might understand my reasons for wanting to leave. I opened my mouth to explain, but he got in first.

'Freya?'

'What is it?'

'I think we should go and see her now.'

'Together? But—'

'I want her to see you. I want her to know that you're here, and that you're different.'

'Different from . . . ?'

He hesitated.

'Just . . . different from other people.'

While Cory tidied trays and counted out pills, I loitered by the bed. Diana's face was small and grey in the daylight, like an old photograph that's fading to nothing, and I told myself I wasn't frightened of her anymore.

I opened the window, even though the air was dank and chilly. A match rasped as Cory lit the scented candles and moved them to the bedside table. It seemed intrusive to turn and stare, so I fiddled with the latch and pretended to look at the trees.

Cory was humming under his breath – a lilting tune that

might have been a lullaby, although I didn't recognise it. Occasionally he stopped humming and spoke. I couldn't catch what he said, but his tone was indescribably gentle, like a mother talking to her baby in the middle of the night when she's trying not to wake the rest of the house.

I heaved the window up another inch. This room needed air. The candles had started spreading their sickly scent, and the atmosphere was as heavily floral as a funeral.

'It's all right,' he half whispered, half sang. 'It's only us. It's only me and Freya.'

I glanced round. Cory had swung his legs on to the bed, and he was sitting propped up on the pillows, holding his mother in his arms. I wondered if she was really asleep; somehow I preferred to think she was.

September 2008

The Wingate Gallery are calling this their autumn exhibition, but Stella and I discussed it on the way here and we agree it's still summer. Stella's shoulders are pink with residual sunburn, after all, and I've got Norfolk sand in the seams of my sandals.

Stella has begun her course at art college, I've started my last year at school, and we're happy tonight. We chat nonstop. We agree that the goat's cheese thingummies are fabulous; that Stella's shoes are too squeaky for these wooden floors; that we adore the drawings of Augustus John. Stella sits down and slips her shoes off, while I keep a lookout for gallery attendants. Are there any rules against bare feet at exhibition openings? We're not sure.

I only glimpse the woman briefly, from the back, while I'm waiting. It's probably the red hair that catches my eye, although hers is a shade darker than ours and slickly pulled back into an elaborate 'do'. She walks like a ballet dancer, lithe and erect, and as she crosses the gallery floor groups of people part to let her through. After she's gone they follow her with their eyes, and only gradually resume their conversations. Despite the warmth of the evening the woman is wearing a fur shrug over her black dress, and I bet you it's real fur.

'I recognise her,' says Stella, as we resume our stroll. 'I'm sure I saw her in college a couple of weeks ago . . . Yes, I did. She was at the freshers' welcome party.'

'She doesn't look much like a fresher,' I say. 'Or a tutor, for that matter.'

'No.' Stella has remembered now. 'No, she was dropping off her son – he's in my year – and the principal invited her to stay, so she did, but she wouldn't stay for long and she wouldn't have a drink.'

I turn to look at the empty doorway, but the woman has gone. I can't help wishing I'd seen her face.

Idly, we circle the room. Dad is standing with his hands behind his back, gazing at 'Dorelia in a hat, circa 1907'. Tom and Natalie, his new wife – his wife! – are in a chummy huddle with the Wingate's director and a couple of other curators. Tom slips us a smile as we pass.

'So, what's her son like?' I ask.

'OK, I think.' Stella ponders the question. 'Quiet. Flaky, maybe.'

I consider joking, 'Takes one to know one,' because given the mood she's in, she would probably laugh – but it's high risk, and I decide against it.

'He got a C-grade in week one,' Stella tells me. 'I forget what it was for. Lino-printing, I think. Anyway, he took it badly and walked out, and then for a couple of days there were rumours—'

'What kind of rumours?'

'Oh, it's probably nonsense . . .' Stella shrugs. 'As I say, he came back after a day or two and he's been fine ever since. People like a melodrama.'

'Yes, but what exactly—'

We are distracted by a waiter with canapés, and Stella swipes a handful of the moreish goat's cheese ones. Tom and Natalie appear, and I pause to speak but Stella steers me away. Our lazy stroll becomes a brisk walk, the pictures mere background to Stella's thoughts.

'Yes, that's what I want to be,' she announces suddenly. 'I want to be _her_.'

'Who? Natalie?' I am suitably astonished, but Stella's 'No!' is frosty all the same. We don't discuss Tom's wife very much, but we know we don't like her.

'No! Of course not _Natalie_! I mean _her_. That woman.'

'Oh, OK.'

Stella doesn't elaborate, but I think about the woman's classy walk, and the fur shrug, and the way people stared – and I do know what she's getting at.

3

It was a dream.

I woke in a sweat, clutching the pillow in two tight fists, Stella's voice ringing in my ears.

But it wasn't a dream. Or it wasn't *only* a dream, because it had also happened, in real life. Augustus John at the Wingate Gallery. The woman in the fur shrug – forever with her back to me; forever disappearing into a different room. The son Stella had known from college. *He's OK*, she'd said. *Quiet. Flaky.*

Cory's arms and legs were wrapped around mine and he was breathing through my hair. It was a chilly night, but under the duvet we were stewing in one another's sweat. I couldn't stay put any longer, even though the darkness was heavy and morning felt a long way off. Carefully, I lifted one of his dead-weight legs from my thigh, and slid my head out from under the crook of his arm. I needed to think, and I couldn't do that when I was knotted up inside someone else's limbs. Perhaps I should run a bath. I pictured lying in the soapy, steamy water with my eyes closed, and the threads of my dreams and memories untangling smoothly, all by themselves.

It didn't turn out quite like that: apart from anything else the water was tepid, because I'd forgotten that the boiler went off overnight. I lay shivering under the bare bulb, staring at the bowl of pot-pourri on the bathroom windowsill, preferring to focus on those sad, dust-caked flowers than on my own altered body. Every time I bent my legs, my knees turned so poky and yellow that I seemed to be looking straight through the skin to the bone, and no matter how hard I soaped myself, my body smelled rotten. I'd tried not to notice these things before.

I thought about the woman at the Wingate Gallery. Russet hair, black dress, fur shrug: that was all I had, apart from the few things Stella had said about her and her son. It was like holding a couple of jigsaw pieces in my palm, knowing there was a whole picture to be made, if I could only find the rest. That New Year's Eve party, when Stella kept smirking over her phone – was she messaging Cory? What about the fact that he'd never told me which college he'd attended, only that he – like my sister – had dropped out after a few months? And the 'friend' we thought she'd run away with? And the location of her fall?

I dried myself and dressed, looking to the window for some softening of the darkness, but finding none. I considered going back to the studio and asking him outright: *Tell me honestly, Cory, did you and Stella know each other?* It was the most obvious solution – or it would have been once. My fingers wandered to my neck and found the tenderness – the something-not-quite-right – deep down beneath the skin. I remembered Diana and how she'd stopped me on the stairs, right back at the beginning.

We have to be quick, she'd said. *I need to talk to you about Stella.*

But then Cory had come through the front door, and I'd allowed her to fall silent and retreat upstairs for good.

The electric light was dull in Diana's room, but better than a candle in a bottle. I stood over her pillow and said her name but, true to form, she kept her eyes closed. Even when I spoke in her ear and jiggled her shoulder, she made no response. I was disappointed. All the way up the stairs I'd imagined something happening between us at last – some long-awaited communication; some last-minute understanding.

'Diana?'

I touched her hand, but there was no answering pressure.

'Wake up,' I pleaded. 'I want to know about Stella. Cory can't overhear us; it's just me, just Freya.'

There was nothing in her face I was competent to read; nothing but a muscled tension that meant she was still alive. The dead wouldn't hold their lips so taut.

I stood up straight and looked round the room: at the clutter of candles and pills and half-dead roses, and the dozens of papers she'd stuck to the walls. *Handprints! C. Byrne, Class 1b*, and to the left of that *A portrait of my mother in charcoal, Dec. 2006*, and above that *Mum, 12.05.03*. In and among the drawings there were certificates – *This is to certify that Cory Byrne was examined in Grade 4 guitar and passed with merit. Summer term, 2001* – and photos – a grinning, gap-toothed little Cory sitting astride a branch of the cedar tree; an unsmiling teenager in school blazer and tie. Cory as a baby, Cory as a toddler, Cory, Cory, Cory . . .

I lifted the edge of a pencil sketch to look at the photograph half hidden beneath, and for a second I didn't move. I felt nothing. Then I ripped the sketch off its Blu-Tack dots and let it fall.

'There,' I said triumphantly, although I was really afraid.

I hadn't seen that photo in years – it had disappeared from the mantelpiece when Stella died – but I recognised the horse-chestnut tree, and the big glass building in the background, and the tiers of matriculating students.

Gainsborough Art College, 2008. Same tree, same building, same year, same people, with Cory Byrne smack in the middle of the front row and my sister Stella behind him.

'What do I do now?'

Run away was the most obvious answer – that's why I'd grabbed my bag from the studio and made it halfway to the front door. Cory was definitely still in bed, definitely still asleep, and this time I knew my way out. Yet here I was, sitting on the stairs, tearing at my hair and whispering, 'What do I do?'

Was I asking myself? Or was I asking Byrne Hall? Cory said his mother talked to the house, and he'd meant it as a mark of her madness, but it was starting to make sense to me. Byrne Hall had a listening, whispering air. It was never bored, or distracted, or unconscious.

I rummaged inside my bag for my purse, and my hands closed on Tom's exhibition catalogue. I pulled it out and laid it on my lap. If I could have talked to anyone in the world at that moment, I'd have chosen Tom.

I wasn't in the mood for reading, but I opened the book and leafed through it slowly, saint by saint, angel by angel. Maybe I thought I'd find some comfort in their sad and faraway eyes, but they didn't have anything to tell me just then. I tried reading the text.

Raphael's reputation was almost inevitably going to suffer in an artistic climate that valued 'Sturm und Drang' over quiet grace and calm.

Tom wrote that. I knew it was part of his essay even before I'd spotted his photo at the foot of the page, because it came to life in his voice. One moment the printed letters were lying flat on the page, the next they were up and about, and Tom was saying them inside my head.

I read the sentence again, but the effect wasn't as strong a second time. I tried over and over, but the more eagerly I reached for him the faster he seemed to fragment and fade. There was nothing left in the end – just my own internal voice, echoing round my head. I wasn't sure what *Sturm und Drang* meant.

'Tom?'

I said his name aloud in an effort to summon him back, and the house sighed. I closed my eyes and dropped my face against the glossy pages of the book. I suppose it only smelled of newness and ink, but it hit me like the scent of a lovely and unreachable world.

Cory was still asleep, the night was still dark, and the house had more to tell me, if only I knew how to listen. It seemed impossible – unthinkable – that Stella could have been here and left no trace at all.

I wandered the rooms – upstairs and down – but I knew what I'd find because I'd seen it all before. The cobwebs, the debris, the oppressive emptiness.

The only part of the house I'd never visited was the attic. I'd poked my head up the stairwell once, a long time ago, and concluded there was nothing to see. Cory had dissuaded me from going up. 'It's just a load of empty rooms,' he'd said, 'and I'm not a hundred per cent sure the floorboards are safe.'

I turned the lights off in the downstairs rooms and stopped in front of Lady Caroline's portrait.

The attic, then?

Lady Caroline looked into my eyes and her mouth curled at the corner.

'Freya?' Cory's voice came sleepily over the bannister. 'What are you doing?'

I hesitated, but only for a moment. 'I couldn't sleep. I came downstairs to make some tea.'

He yawned noisily. 'Can you make me one too?'

'Sure.'

Later, I told Lady Caroline and, judging by her sly smile, I'd say she understood.

We spent most of the day putting the portraits into frames. Some of the pictures had gone to a professional framer, but the rest fitted into frames that Cory had used previously and stashed in a box-room. A couple of nights ago, while I was asleep, he'd brought them into the studio and propped them up around the walls. All of them were empty, but you could tell they'd been used before because the backing pins were askew.

It was a time-consuming and dusty job – working out which frame could be matched with which painting, cleaning it up, backing it and stringing it with cord. I didn't mind. If I was pasting brown paper on to a board, or twisting a screw into a hanger, then I wasn't expected to talk, or return kisses, or exchange little smiles with Cory.

I went downstairs mid-afternoon to make coffee, and when I came back there was a frame sitting on the easel, facing the door. He must have fetched it while I was gone. It was grander and more decorative than any of the others, with its golden apples and moulded leaves. It was unmissable, unforgettable – redolent of an August evening when I was hot and befuddled in a long, green dress, and the sun had set the sea on fire, and

I thought I'd glimpsed my sister's face in a mosaic of glue and torn-up paper.

Cory looked round nonchalantly as I stood in the doorway with a mug in each hand. Was he watching for a reaction? I don't think I gave him much, if so. Anyone would pause, wouldn't they, faced with a flashy showpiece like that? I only looked at it. I didn't raise my eyebrows, or gasp, or comment. I handed him his coffee, and retrieved my pencil and ruler from the table.

'It's a nice frame.' Cory stopped in front of it, his arms folded across his chest. 'Don't you think so?'

'Hmm.'

'Shame none of the portraits quite fit,' he said.

I could only see the back of it now, from where I was kneeling. There were crooked pins all along the inside edges, sticking out at wonky angles where the previous picture had been dislodged. He can't have removed it carefully; he must have clawed and bashed until it tumbled on to the floor.

'Shame,' I agreed, returning to my work. I'd already measured the strip of backing paper, but there was no harm in measuring it again. It gave me an excuse to lower my eyes.

'There.' Cory turned the easel round, as if it mattered that I could see it properly. 'Perhaps we could adjust one of the Freyas to fit? If we backed one of the smaller paintings on to a larger board ... It seems a pity not to use it, don't you think?'

Wearily, I raised my head. There was a rumbling noise on the driveway – quiet and faraway, but growing.

'What's that?' we said at the same time.

We listened and waited. Tyres crackled across the gravel, brakes squeaked, metal doors clanged. Cory and I stared at one another in equal alarm; it was so long since anyone had come.

'A van?' I kept my voice small, as if we were both in hiding. Cory went to the window.

'Oh, bother,' he said. 'I'd forgotten about them.'

'Who?'

'The marquee people; they always come around now to take it down for the winter. I suppose I'd better go and have a word.'

I laid the ruler across the pencilled line and sliced briskly with the point of the craft knife. I needed to change the blade; it was getting blunt.

'Go on, then,' I said. 'Don't worry about me; I'll just carry on here.'

But he sighed and lingered.

'What's bothering you, Cory?' I unscrewed the handle and slotted in a fresh blade. 'Are you worried I'll run away again? That I'll make an *unsupervised* phone call?'

'No, of course not. Don't be like that.'

The marquee men were talking loudly amongst them-selves, and one of them banged on the front door.

'I'll be as quick as I can.' He touched his hand to his lips as he passed and mussed my hair with a kiss.

The attic comprised a long central corridor with doors to either side and daylight seeping through the broken roof. The first few doors opened on to mouldering floorboards and cobwebbed windows. One room housed a wardrobe; one a broken packing case and a pile of dust-sheets; most contained nothing at all. I'd grown used to living in bare rooms since I'd come to Byrne Hall, but the attics were bare in a different way from the downstairs – not so much faded grandeur as inbred desolation.

The furthest room was a bleak little hovel, much like the rest – a servant's room, I suppose, with an iron bedstead, a chipped wash-basin on the floor, and a matching jug on the windowsill. The ceiling was low and there were long, sad drips down the walls, where the rain had come in. A bird must have fallen down the chimney once and got trapped, because there were droppings all over the floor, and tiny bones and feathers in the grate.

I don't know why I went in; none of the other rooms had lured me. Perhaps I wanted to look more closely at the bird's skeleton; perhaps I was drawn by the footprints in the dust. I can't remember. I went slowly – wary of the weak floorboards – and there she was, to the right of the fireplace, leaning with her back against the wall and staring straight through me.

She'd lost her frame, of course, but I recognised her at once: the deadpan eyes; the paper mosaic and the web of shiny glue; the gap where her hands had been ripped off at the wrists. I hadn't realised until then that she was naked. It wasn't immediately obvious because of the way her red hair hung, like a veil, to her waist. I wondered why Cory had chosen to rip her up like that, only to stick her back together again. And why no hands? The glinting web of glue had an oddly powerful effect on her presence, as if something wild – a churn of heat and light – were about to burst through the surface of the picture from the other side.

At first I thought she was on her own. It was only as I turned to go that I saw the others: a whole chaotic pyramid of boards, papers and canvases; a bonfire waiting to be lit. Some of the pictures were torn, some bent; a few were still framed, most were not; all depicted red-headed girls, gathering dust. For one befuddled moment I thought they must be portraits of me, but then I crossed the room to take a better look and it became obvious that they were not Freyas; they were Stellas.

Cory had never posed me like this; had never studied me with such a raw appetite. If there was too much flesh in his paintings of me, and not enough soul, then at least he tried to disguise the fact by showing me reading, or sitting at a window looking vague and otherworldly. I was always clothed and my eyes were usually averted.

Lucky for me, I thought.

I took pictures from the heap, one after another, and studied them for as long as I could bear to. Stella – I mean Cory's version of Stella – tended to be naked, and her smile was pointed and cold. Even when she had clothes on – as in this one, where she was wearing a long red dress – she seemed strangely denuded, as if he had stripped her of her personality layer by layer, and reduced her to a piece of animate meat. I held up one of the smaller oil paintings, which showed her on a bed with her head thrown back and her arms above it. The colours were horrible – lurid pinks and purples – and the focus was not her face or even her breasts, but her exposed neck.

Lucky for you, said Stella's voice in my head, but it did nothing to lessen the ache I felt in the pit of my belly.

I tossed the picture away. It was supposed to land face down but it didn't, so she lay naked at my feet, thrusting her salmon-pink neck at me. I trod on it – on her – as I crossed to the window.

The hinge was caked in rust and wouldn't open far, but I pressed my nose and mouth to the gap and sucked in the cool air. I felt ill. I could hear the sea at the foot of the cliffs, as well as the tap of mallets and the ring of men's voices. Imagine if he came up here and found me standing among his secrets. What would he say? What would I say? I swung round to face the door, and my elbow caught the china wash-jug, sending it flying off the sill.

'Shit!'

The jug broke into large shards, and a scrap of paper fell out. I stared at it for a second before stooping to pick it up.

It was yet another of Cory's paintings: a pair of watercoloured hands folded loosely inside one another. I glanced across at mosaic-Stella, with the missing section on her lap, and I didn't need to cross the room to double-check. It was obvious from here that my find was a perfect fit.

I studied the hands more closely. Cory was a pretty good observer of superficial detail – I'd always given him that. He had captured the willowy outline of Stella's fingers, and the square shape of her nails, with ease. It was her self he failed to touch on. Even in his depiction of a pair of folded hands he had managed to leave out what mattered: the high tension that had strung my sister together; her nail-bitten impatience; the way her fingers used to dance. Cory had drawn passive hands, and however well he thought he knew her, he was wrong to do that.

I turned it over.

Stella Maria Lyell, she'd written on the back. *Stella Maria Lyell, Stella Maria Lyell, Stella Maria Lyell* . . . like a poem down the centre of the sheet.

The sight of my sister's handwriting made my throat feel fat and full. She'd written hastily in biro, the letters more gaunt and flyaway than usual, but still familiar to me. I traced the loops of her signatures with the tip of my little finger and read each one in turn, word by word, line by line.

When I eventually looked up it was the lurid oil painting that caught my eye, and the grubby footprint I'd made.
In sympathy, or out of habit, I touched my own throbbing
neck.

I folded the torn paper and put it in my pocket. In all this
dross – this horror – I glimpsed a tiny grain of gold.

Stella hadn't killed herself, after all; therefore I hadn't killed
her, either.

*Cory wouldn't hurt a fly – or so his mother used to think. She
would have vouched for him with her life, once upon a time,
when he was still her golden boy. Before he grew up and went
away. Before Stella.*

Diana visualises her life in terms of four eras.

1. *Before Mr Byrne.*
2. *After Mr Byrne.*
3. *Before Stella.*
4. *After Stella.*

*Diana lies back on her pillow and follows the cracks in the
ceiling, with all their twists and divides, trying not to remember
but unable to stop.*

*Cory only attended that two-a-penny art college to bolster the
little heaven that he – they – had managed to make for themselves at Byrne Hall. Oh, the irony! It would make her laugh if
she weren't already crying.*

*'Mum, we can't keep selling off the contents of the house,'
he'd said. 'It isn't sustainable. Whereas if I were a real artist,
with a professional qualification . . .'*

Yes, oh yes, she'd followed his reasoning; seen what he saw;

thrilled at his excitement. If Cory were an acclaimed artist then Byrne Hall could live its glory days at last. There would be exhibitions and heady, happy parties, and wonderful new friends, and features in the press, and a vast income.

'All well and good,' she said, as they clutched each other's hands, 'but why bother with college? Qualifications are overrated; talent is the thing, and with my connections . . .'

'I think I would prefer,' he said, 'to do it this way.'

'But—'

'You can come and visit me, and I'll be home for the holidays.'

'But—'

'Mum! Let me go.'

So she let him go.

Diana closes her eyes. She fidgets with the edge of her bed-sheet, making as if to tear it into little bits, but the brushed cotton is thick and her fingers have wasted away.

4

THE EXHIBITION WAS ALL BUT ready. Most of the framed paintings were downstairs, stacked against the hall walls; there were just a couple of 'late Freyas' – as he called them – left in the studio. Cory had decided to display the pictures in chronological order, from the first sketch on the greasy bakery bag to the unfinished *Convalescent*. Earlier in the week he'd toyed with the idea of titling the whole thing 'Freya: A Love Story' – 'because that's all it is, in a way' – but happily he'd changed his mind. 'Let's go minimalist. Let's just call it "Freya".'

Two days had passed since my discovery of the attic, and Cory didn't know I knew. I'd spied him from the window when I got downstairs, standing by the van and chatting to the marquee men. Tonight he was writing catalogue notes on his laptop, while I numbered the paintings and matched them with titles.

'Where are you off to?'

I froze in the doorway, with one foot on the landing.

'The bathroom,' I said.

'You must have been half a dozen times this evening.'

'Well, I want to have a wash and get ready for bed. I'm tired.'

I felt for Stella's paper inside my jeans pocket. I'd folded it over so many times in the last two days that it was bullet-sized and bullet-hard, and I could swallow it in one gulp if I had to. I filled my mouth with saliva, in case it came to that.

Cory's eyes strayed back to the computer screen. He tapped a pencil against his teeth and scribbled a note. Was that all right then? Permission granted? I backed out, and he didn't look up again.

Walls had ears at Byrne Hall; the closest I ever came to feeling alone was in the bathroom. I perched on the edge of the tub, took the paper from my pocket and unfolded it for the hundredth time. It had grown soft and silent with much handling.

I still took a deep breath every time I turned the drawing over.

Stella Maria Lyell
Stella Maria Lyell
Stella Maria Lyell

My scalp prickled, and I was scared to raise my eyes in case I found her standing in front of me. It was an impossible piece of paper with an impossible message. Supernatural, I'd have said, if I'd dared to believe in ghosts.

'Everything all right in there?'

The door handle rattled and I leapt to my feet, knocking a cake of soap into the bath.

'Coming!'

I flushed the toilet, ran the taps, folded the piece of paper and bundled it back in my pocket. I couldn't go on like this – just reading her name over and over again – it was time I made something happen.

'Won't be a second!'

Cory didn't answer, but he used the silence to let me know he was waiting.

*

At first I thought the word 'revenge' was too heavy for some-one like me; that I'd never be able to carry it off; that it had too many connotations of Shakespeare, and mobsters, and histrionic hand-wringing. But it's funny how quickly words lose their mystique when you turn them over often enough in your mind. It's a bit like chewing gum: after the initial zing you're left with a flavourless lump and you hardly notice it anymore, but you keep chewing all the same. Only a few hours after the discovery of Stella's note, I could lie in the bath whispering vows of vengeance under my breath without feeling actorly at all.

At some point during the night Cory's pillow slipped to the floor, and he slept with his head thrown back and his chin in the air. I lay on my side for hours, staring at the white mound of his throat and the taut tendons of his neck, and thinking of the paintings in the attic. At one point I got up to fetch the craft knife and brought it back to bed with me. It cut so beau-tifully, now that I'd changed the blade. You didn't have to press on it at all; you just touched the paper – or whatever you hap-pened to be cutting – and an incision appeared as if by magic.

I raised myself on my elbows and tested the blade on the mattress. It slid right in without a sound, and came out with a tiny feather attached to its tip. I picked the feather off and blew it across the bed, towards Cory. This revenge business would be a lot easier if his neck were stuffed with little brown goose feathers.

It was difficult to know how much the blood itself would bother me; perhaps it was impossible to know until I saw and smelled it. There were other aspects that definitely did bother me, though. I would mind being cast as a killer for evermore, and I would mind the expressions on the policemen's faces when they came to arrest me, and I would mind what Dad and Tom thought of me. I worried about how my conscience would cope in the long run.

Cory moaned as he rolled on to his front, and I couldn't see his throat anymore. His face was so pale that it seemed to shine in the half-light before dawn; he was like a marble sculpture gleaming in a deserted museum.

I twisted on to my side, so as to watch from a more comfortable angle. He had the right features for a sculpture – a Greek Apollo, perhaps, or a Roman general. Occasionally his lips twitched, as if at a private joke, and it prompted me to try out a smile on my own face. Even without a mirror I could tell I was getting it wrong. Somewhere along the way, I'd lost the knack. I could do a wan turn-up of the mouth, and I could do a sarcastic grimace, but an actual smile – all glitter and light, like his – was beyond me.

I relaxed my grip on the knife – God, my knuckles were aching! – and pushed it underneath the mattress for safekeeping. I knew now what I wanted for Cory, and it wasn't death. I could see the look he'd give me as the blood splashed up my arms, and we'd both know the joke was on me.

'What are you doing?'

Cory sat up in bed, croaky-voiced and squinting. I swung round with the phone in my hand and a guilty 'Oh!', implying surprise. Apparently I was still unable to smile – I tried, and came up with something that was far from nice – but I don't suppose he could tell from there. It was barely light and the blinds were down.

'I was lying awake, thinking about the exhibition,' I said, 'and it occurred to me that we still haven't invited Dad to the opening. He'll want notice if he's going to do a review for the *Globe*.'

Cory rubbed his eyes. 'But I thought . . .'

'What?'

'I thought you didn't want to ask him?'

'Of course I want to ask him! It's just that he's been away, and I couldn't get hold of him. I think he'll be home by now.'

Forget blades and blood: humiliation was the thing. That was the way to hurt Cory Byrne.

Once I'd grasped that – sometime during the early hours of the morning – I'd begun finding pleasure in the prospect of revenge. Like a seasoned sadist I lay awake, relishing every detail of my nascent plan: my father, the great critic, giving nothing away as he meandered round the 'Freya' exhibition; Cory watching him in fatuous hope. Dad going home and picking up his pen; words blooming over his scruffy notebook and crystallising in newsprint. The *London Globe* rolling off the press – copy after copy, like rapid-firing bullets – and finding its mark on half a million doormats, one Saturday morning in November.

I'd tossed and turned, and tried to imagine the moment when the newspaper fell into Cory's hands. How would it happen? Would we go into a shop, or would he arrange to have it delivered? What did I risk by being present? Oh, but I had to be present, even if it was the end of me. It was my father's review, but it was *my* revenge.

Cory's face would glow pink as he began searching the paper, and he'd say, 'Freya, come and help me, my fingers are shaking too much to turn the pages.' So I'd turn the pages for him with a slight tremor of my own, until we came to the Arts section with the featured review by Robert Lyell, and the headline . . . What would the headline be? I'd drifted off to sleep trying to think of something snappy. Whatever I came up with, Dad's idea would be better. Dad knew how to fashion words into knives. He could twist them into thumbscrews and red-hot pokers.

I dialled the first few numbers and Cory sat up, wide-eyed. He looked like a little boy on Christmas morning as he bounced forward on to his knees and waded through the duvet to the end of the mattress. If he came any closer he might see my non-smile for what it was, so I turned to face the wall while I finished dialling.

'What date are we going for, then?' I said, as it began to ring. 'The fifteenth?'

'Saturday the fifteenth of November. But listen, listen – we can alter it to suit him. Whatever's best for him, Freya, I don't mind—'

'OK.' I held up my hand for silence. 'Let's see what he says.'

Cory hauled me back to bed as soon as I put the phone down. I turned my head aside on the pillow and closed my eyes – because closed eyes might imply pleasure, mightn't they? – and his wet lips planted thank yous in my ear. I should have anticipated this; should have picked my moment more wisely.

Respond to me. His kneading hands demanded it; as did the rough suck of his kisses; as did the sheer weight of him, thumping the breath from my chest. Pretending to be the same old Freya had been easy until now, because all we'd done in bed for the last few nights was sleep. My duties had been limited to helpfulness, and telling him how great his pictures were.

Respond, I told myself – but how do you make believe you're warm when you're bristling with cold?

I braced my chin against his shoulder and bit down on the bed-sheet until it was over. Even then he stayed on top, as heavy as a corpse, and my breath came in stutters as if I were crying. I wasn't crying. Up and down ran Cory's hands, lazy and quiet, and wherever he touched me, my skin broke out in goose-bumps.

One and a half weeks to go.

'November the fifteenth?' Dad had said doubtfully. 'I suppose I could make it . . .'

I'd given Cory a quick 'thumbs up', and he'd flopped on to his back with his arms outstretched.

'. . . if only to catch up with my long-lost daughter. But a piece in the *Globe*?'

'Please, Dad. *Please*. A great big review with photos and everything.'

'It's a heck of a lot to ask for a little, local exhibition.'

'I know it is.'

'And I can't . . .' He lowered his voice. 'Well, you know how it works. *No* favours.'

'I know, and that's not what I'm asking.'

My father was silent for a moment. The house – my old home – was silent at the other end of the line.

'Freya . . . ?'

I tensed – what was coming? What had he sensed? – but all he said was, 'Would you mind if I brought someone with me?'

I gave a little shrug. 'No, of course not. Who?'

'Would you mind . . . if . . .'

His discomfort was so overt it was funny. Even I sensed it.

'If what, Dad?'

'If I brought Zoë?'

'Zoë.' My mind was a blank. 'Zoë as in Zoë Stefanidis? From your office?'

'Mm.'

'No, I don't mind, but why . . . ?'

'Just . . .'

'You mean, you and she . . . ?'

'Sort of. Yes.'

I hadn't met Zoë Stefanidis often – a couple of times when I'd popped into Dad's office; once when she came to our New Year's Eve party – but that was years ago. I remembered her as mildly hippie-ish, with huge earrings and a happy laugh. Was she with Dad, filling the heavy-hearted spaces and silences of our house? And was that a good thing or a bad thing? I wasn't sure. Good, I suppose, if it made him happy.

'Freya? Say something. Have I upset you?'

'No, not at all.'

I began to understand how far I was from my old life; how little it belonged to me now. A couple of months ago this news would have been astounding, for better or worse. Now it was merely distracting.

'I'm glad,' I said.

'Thank you. Going back to this exhibition of Cory's . . .'

'Yes.'

'You genuinely rate him, then? You're not just being partial?'

I glanced round. Cory was lying with his hands over his face – he might have been miles away, or he might have been hanging on our every murmured word.

'Freya?'

270

'Just come,' I whispered. 'Bring Zoë – bring whoever you like – but please, Dad, do this for me.'

We began writing invitations the same afternoon. It felt last-minute – one and a half weeks' notice? *Really?* – but Cory was confident of pulling in a good crowd. 'We can name-drop your father now, as well as my mother; of course they'll come. They'll come in their droves.'

Cory wanted the invitations to be handwritten, and – on the basis that Aunty May had given me a calligraphy kit for my birthday several years ago, which had resulted in a brief enthusiasm for ornate lettering – the job fell to me. We went to Diana's room, because that's where her address book was kept, and he sat me down at the dressing table with a pile of cream cards, a pot of black ink and a fat-nibbed pen.

> *Byrne Hall,*
> *Bligh,*
> *Devon.*

> *Dear* _____
>
> *Mrs Diana Byrne is pleased to invite you to the launch of an exhibition of paintings by her son, Cory.*
>
> *The exhibition, entitled 'Freya', will open at 6 p.m. on Saturday 15th November, at the family home.*
>
> *Award-winning critic and journalist Robert Lyell will be in attendance as Guest of Honour.*
>
> *Canapés and champagne will be served.*
>
> *Dress code: black tie.*
>
> *RSVP*

'Do you think the wording is OK?'

I suppressed a shrug. 'Sounds all right to me.'

I'd already written four cards and I was waiting for Cory to provide me with some names, so I could fill in the blanks after *Dear*.

I looked into the mirror, beyond my own face. Diana was restless today. Sometimes she whimpered in her sleep; more than once I caught the glint of an open eye. Cory sat alongside her with his feet on the bed, leafing through the thick address book.

'The Bayley-Manninghams,' he read. 'I remember them; they always used to come and stay with us round Easter time ... Jack and Loretta Cunningham – you've crossed Loretta out though, Mother, so does that mean she died? Or – no, she divorced him, didn't she? ... Archie Lamott ... Olivia something-or-other, can't read your writing ... Charles Pemberton. I remember him. He was supposed to have had a Picasso in his downstairs loo.'

The bed-sheets rustled as Cory crossed his ankles, and a makeshift peace descended on the room. All day long he'd been finding excuses to touch me: little kisses on my neck, pinches on my earlobes, fingers down my spine. 'I'm only being affectionate,' he would say defensively when I froze. 'I only love you, Freya.' If he was testing my reflexes, he wasn't going to admit it, and neither was I. 'Ditto,' I kept saying, smiling my frigid smile.

Now he was engrossed in the old address book, and my attention was allowed to wander over the faded pictures and photos on the wall. The Gainsborough College photo was irresistible, but I only dared a flicker of a glance, and even that made my cheeks burn. I took a fresh card from the pile, dipped the pen and began to write. The 'D' of 'Dear' wobbled badly, and I had to scrap the card and start over. I could feel Cory's eyes on my neck, and I clogged the nib with too much ink, which meant I wrecked another.

'Maybe you should do the lettering in pencil first?' he suggested, getting up from the bed. 'Go over it in black afterwards?'

He leaned over my shoulder and rested his cheek against mine. Obediently, I reached for a pencil and sharpened it, and the clean smell of the shavings made me think of home, and Tom, and my exercise books with their old, useless poems.

The ghosts cluster in dark places – behind the door, on top of the wardrobe, in undusted corners – and swell into bright focus when Diana's pain is at its most exquisite. As the spasm fades, so do the faces and voices of the dead.

Most of these old shadows leave Diana unfazed. After all, she's known them – half glimpsed and half heard them, anyway – for years. She could bear them all – even her bloated and fish-nibbled husband – if it weren't for the red-haired girl. Stella's ghost looks more real than the others, and she's always hanging around Cory, as if she has a claim on him. She seems more subdued than she used to be, but no less malevolent for that.

'I win,' she seems to tell them both constantly, although she never utters a word.

Cory tired of art college after a few months. He appeared on the doorstop one day looking lean and tanned and healthful, as if he'd walked all the way from London, although he said he'd come by train. Diana managed to refrain from chucking him under the chin and saying, 'I knew it wouldn't last!' – partly because it seemed impolitic; partly because he wasn't alone.

273

'Mum?' he said, in a voice that fluctuated between terror and joy. 'This is Stella Lyell.' There was no need for him to add that he thought he was in love.

'Two college drop-outs together!' the girl added, which was the closest she ever came to explaining herself. Even there, on the doorstep, in the first few seconds, the imbalance was obvious: Stella only had fleeting, friendly glances for Cory whereas he devoured her with his eyes.

Byrne Hall was the focus of her attention; she kept saying, 'Oh my God, this place is so cool!'

Stella Lyell brought mess and noise in her wake; the house had never known anything like it. She hadn't arrived with a lot of luggage, but somehow her screwed-up clothes littered every room; her music filled the house; her wild moods sucked up all the oxygen and made it difficult to breathe.

Diana had been mildly anxious about her forthcoming appointment at the Harley Street clinic – a recurring twinge is probably just a twinge, but still . . . Now she began looking forward to it, as a few days' break from her son's guest.

One afternoon Diana thought they'd gone down to the beach – Stella was a keen swimmer and where Stella led, Cory followed – so she sneaked into his room to take a look at the paintings. When the twinge came on she went to the window and stood still, holding her side, waiting for it to pass. The girl was in the garden, lying on the grass in short shorts and a bikini top, but there was no sign of Cory. Diana turned round and there he was, curled on top of the bed, looking back at her with raw eyes. His cheeks were pink and wet.

'Cory! Sweetheart . . .'

Diana knelt beside him and held his limp hand. When she stroked his hair he squeezed his eyes shut, but the tears leaked out anyway. She thought he was going to tell her something terrible – she didn't know what, only that it would be terrible – but when at last he managed to get the words out, all he said was, 'She's so mean!' He might have been fourteen again, and Diana almost smiled.

'Have you had a tiff?' she said. 'Everyone has tiffs. It'll blow over.'

The things Diana really wanted to say would not be well timed – 'She wasn't for you . . . We didn't really like her, did we? . . . Perhaps it's best if she goes home now' – so she saved them up for later.

Cory said, 'I love her so much.'

Diana's relief warped into fear. The way he said it – 'I love her so much' – made her feel sick. He sounded cold and strange and not childish at all.

She hesitated before patting his hand.

'So much,' Cory repeated. 'You have no idea.'

Diana remembers lying in bed that night and staring at the ceiling, much as she is doing now. It was only five years ago, but there weren't as many cracks in the plaster back then.

Cory was not in love, not even at the start. You only had to look at the febrile, un-tender paintings he made of the girl to know that they weren't inspired by love.

If only Diana still had her faculties – her mind, her voice – she would take pleasure in pointing this out to the red-haired ghost.

5

CORY OPENED THE DOUBLE DOORS of his mother's wardrobe and dived in with both arms. Metal hangers clanked along the rail and plastic covers – the sort you get from a dry cleaner's – swashed from side to side. Colours and patterns and fabrics flashed by: pinks and greens, zig-zags and stripes, silks and chiffons.

'I have considered selling them, in the past,' he said. 'It's not like she's ever going to wear them again, and most of them probably count as vintage nowadays. They might fetch quite a sum.'

'Shh.' I put my finger to my lips. Diana was asleep only a few feet away.

'Anyway,' he went on, oblivious, 'it's a good job I didn't. I can't *believe* we haven't thought about your outfit until now. Like, eight hours before the guests start arriving. How did we manage to overlook that?'

He puffed his cheeks out and shook his head. It was a gesture he'd made more than once this morning; he did it every time there was a glitch, or the faintest possibility of a glitch. I was tempted to be flippant – 'Actually, I thought I might just swan around naked?' – but he'd hate that, and if my betrayal was to have impact, he needed to trust me in the first place. Cory unhooked a dress from the rail and handed it over. As far as I could tell through the crinkled cover, it was a blue cocktail dress with big shoulders. Very 1980s.

'No,' he said, as I held it under my chin and turned to face the mirror.

'No,' I agreed.

Diana's meagre shape was visible in the bed behind me, her head sunk into the pillow. It's not as though she was watching us – she rarely seemed to wake anymore – but I wished we could do this somewhere else.

'Do you think any of them will fit?' I said doubtfully.

Cory glowered and rifled through the bagged-up dresses. He hadn't smiled all morning – not even to himself – and it was making me nervous. Neither of us had slept for several nights in a row, and there was an edginess – a faint hysteria – around, which felt like an infection of the atmosphere; like something noxious we were both breathing in. I could practically taste it on my tongue.

Whenever Cory was unable to sleep he got up and paced the floor, whereas I lay still with the duvet over my ears. Somehow his footsteps kept time with my pulse – or was it the other way round? Either way, his bare feet beat inside my brain all night, every night – up and down, back and forth, round and round. This morning, at first light, I saw him standing with his head held high and his hand on his heart, as if he were on a stage, accepting applause. I almost sat up and clapped, just to make him squirm.

'This one,' he said now with conviction, pulling the plastic cover away.

It was a white dress – high-necked, long-sleeved, lacy and beribboned – that had faded over the years to ivory. In anyone else's company I'd have risked a 'Wuthering Heights' joke and hummed a few lines of Kate Bush, but Cory was frowning and glancing at the clock.

'Very virginal,' I said drily, expecting him to laugh or contradict me, but he said nothing. He was miles away. I checked the mirror in case Diana was watching us, but there was no movement from the bed, so I undressed and slipped the dress over my head. Cory zipped it up at the back.

Well, the fit was all right. It was the colour – or lack of it – that looked all wrong. There was something terribly tired – tired to the point of sickness – about the yellow-white lace at the wrists, and the yellow-white collar, and the yellow-white pallor of my own face.

'You look beautiful,' said Cory breathlessly, like an actor speaking a predictable line in a predictable film.

'I look like a ghost.'

As it happens, I didn't have Stella in mind at that moment – or not consciously. She wasn't the reason I said it. I chose the word 'ghost' because it sounded marginally less facetious than 'corpse bride'.

Cory turned his back on me abruptly, and continued flicking through the dress collection.

'What are you talking about? What ghost?'

'Oh, I don't know,' I back-pedalled rapidly. 'Any old ghost. What about that one? The red one?'

Even in the depths of the wardrobe it seemed to shine, perhaps because of the tiny, glinting beads that covered and stiffened the bodice. Cory brought it out, but he made no move to help as I unwrapped it and slid it off its hanger.

'Red?' he said as I held it up. 'On you? No. You wouldn't suit red.'

I frowned. 'Why not?'

'It would clash with your hair.'

I was stumped for a moment, then: 'What about the walls? We painted the gallery walls Pamplona Red, and you never said anything about it clashing with my hair.'

'That's completely different; that works.'

I snorted.

'I don't understand,' he said. 'Why are you angry? Since when have you had a burning desire to wear red?'

Diana's scarlet satin flowed from my collar-bone to my toes, the precise shade of red that had run through my recent dreams. I wanted to run my hands down its liquid sheen, but I was afraid of leaving sweaty marks. Cory was right – dress and hair clashed, like musical notes in a crunchy chord.

'I just happen to like it. That's all.'

Cory didn't exactly laugh, but he stuck his bottom lip out and puffed.

'No,' he said finally. 'I'm sorry. Take it from me, it's not your colour. It makes you look—'

'Makes me look what?'

But he wouldn't say.

He wrestled the dress back into its cover and shunted it to the far end of the wardrobe. Briefly he fingered a pink floral number, and the blue one we'd already looked at.

'It's got to be the white one,' he said, as the wardrobe doors closed with a bang.

The red, I retorted inwardly.

I knew better than to argue out loud. It didn't matter. I'd get changed in secret later on and come downstairs to a hall full of guests, and Cory wouldn't be able to object for fear of making a scene. Dad would be there, milling about and taking notes. Tom would be pocketing his car keys and staring around. *Freya!* he'd say, when I tapped him on the shoulder. *It's been ages!*

At which point I'd be safe, no matter what colour I was wearing.

*

All the way downstairs, Cory talked about what shoes I ought to wear, if any; what jewellery; whether my hair should be pinned up or left loose. Walking through Byrne Hall with those long, white skirts clinging round my legs, I was taken back to the summer – a lifetime ago; three months ago – when the floors had been lovely and cool on my feet. I was chilled to the bone now. I shouldn't have left my jeans and jumper in Diana's room.

'We ought to have had the chimneys swept and then we could have lit fires in the downstairs rooms,' Cory fretted. 'Although I suppose the smoke wouldn't do the canvases much good. OK, so, next job: we need to dig out as many heaters as we can find and try to warm the place up.'

I hugged myself in an effort to suppress my shivers.

'Freya?'

'Mmm?'

'You're not wearing your engagement ring.'

'No.'

These days, I could hardly bear to look at Cory – all I could do was direct my eyes to his left ear and hope he wouldn't notice the difference. I think he did notice on this occasion though, because he stopped talking and stared at me expectantly. I shuddered from head to toe, as if someone were walking over my grave.

'I'll wear it this evening,' I said.

He took me by the shoulders and held me at arm's length.

'We are together, aren't we, me and you?' he said. 'You're on my side?'

Behind him, the landing seemed to go on and on: two rows of closed doors receding into infinity. It was too dark to see all the way to the end.

'Tonight . . .' he said. 'The exhibition . . . It's sacred to you, isn't it, the same way it's sacred to me? You know that? You feel it?'

I mumbled a reply along the right lines and told myself I'd be out of here by this time tomorrow. I'd be at home with Dad, getting back to normal. Cory's world – where people whispered in corridors, and wore ghost-like dresses, and turned words like 'sacred' and 'beautiful' inside out – would be gone for ever. It would not have altered me. I would not find that it had dyed me, through and through, a different, darker colour.

'You're not crying, are you?' he said, alarmed. 'Why would you be crying? This is what I mean: there's something about you today that I don't understand.'

'I'm not crying,' I insisted, flicking an ivory sleeve across my cheeks. The fabric smelled faintly of mould. 'I think we're both tired.'

A wintry draught stirred the still air, as if a door or window had been flung open. There were footsteps in the entrance hall, and a voice yelled up the stairs, 'Hello?'

My first thought was, *Diana*, which tells you something about my state of mind. It struck me as more likely that Diana had risen from her deathbed to stalk the house and shout at the top of her voice than that an outsider had burst in on us, uninvited.

'That woman!' Cory's whisper was testy.

'What woman?'

'Your woman. What's she called? Maggie.'

The voice came again, a powerful sing-song. *'Hello?'*

'I'll deal with her,' said Cory. 'You wait here.'

I let him get halfway down the stairs before I shook my head and followed.

*

This wasn't the first time Maggie had called, although Cory didn't know I knew. She'd come last week as well.

I'd gone to the bathroom to re-read Stella's note, and when I emerged – quietly, because I'd heard a knock at the front door and a murmur of voices in the hall – I tiptoed on to the gallery and leaned over the bannisters. Cory's voice was barely audible, which made Maggie's seem all the more strident.

'Is Freya around?' she asked. I could feel fresh air on my skin, and hear it in the echo of her voice – Cory must have managed to keep her outside on the doorstep.

'No. She's in London, visiting her dad.' It was hard for him to sound anything but shifty when his delivery was so quick and quiet.

'Hmm,' said Maggie.

I was dying to rush downstairs and prove her right. Perhaps I should have done; it would have been one way of turning the tables. But I knew, by then, the kind of revenge I wanted – knew it precisely, detail on detail – and it required me to be patient.

'In that case,' Maggie said, 'could you give me her mobile number? I did promise her I'd stay in touch.'

I waited for Cory to tell her I'd lost my phone, and to explain that I hadn't replaced it yet, but he said, 'Yes, of course. I'm sure she'd love to hear from you.'

Maggie rustled through her handbag – searching for her own phone, I suppose, or pen and paper.

'Ready?' And when she said yes, Cory reeled off my number.

'Sorry not to invite you in,' he said. 'I'm just . . .'

'Not at all.' Her tone was as sweet as his, with the same sour undertone.

Cory began to close the door.

'How's your mum?' She lobbed that one through the gap, just as he thought he was safe.

'My mother's well. Thank you for asking.'

The door shut with a clack.

'Ah,' Maggie said now, as I came downstairs. 'You're back from London, then?'

Cory turned to look at me, and I could swear he was frightened. His shoulders weren't as straight and square as usual.

'Hi Maggie.'

If I hadn't already seen my reflection in the mirror I'd have known, by the way she looked at me, what a spectacle I made. A few hours more and I'd be able to explain everything – *Oh Maggie, this isn't my dress, and this isn't me, and whoever you think I've become I haven't* – but I didn't dare breathe a word until my revenge was in the bag. I sidled up to Cory and took his hand.

'Yes,' I said, in answer to her question. 'I've been back a few days now.'

If I was going to be a liar, I might as well be whole-hearted about it. Cory was sharp, and if I tried to send her a private 'look' he would sense it. He returned the pressure on my hand.

'And you're definitely all right?' Maggie insisted, scrutinising our linked hands, my clothes, and finally my face.

'I couldn't be better. We're really excited, aren't we?' I turned to Cory. 'The exhibition opens this evening.'

'Did you get my texts?'

'Your texts? Oh Maggie, I'm sorry, I lost my phone.'

She nodded slowly.

'Right.'

Cory seemed to have frozen.

'I don't think we've any other news,' I said. 'How about you, Maggie? Are you well? Have you been swimming lately?'

'Swimming? . . . No.'

Cory lifted my fingers and touched them with his lips. Maggie wheeled round, as if she couldn't stand the sight of us any longer, and I can't say I blamed her. I would have let go of his hand at that point, but his grip was strong and I couldn't pull free without a tussle.

The hall was crammed with paraphernalia for the evening – floral pedestals, trestle-tables, white tablecloths, boxes of champagne flutes on loan from the off-licence – and it smelled brightly of polish and paint. Maggie lingered. I'd grown used to thinking of her as a spark of light in a place of shadows – the only person in this strange world who wanted me to speak, and breathe, and be free – and that's why I needed her to go away now. She was too nice for me and Cory; too straight-forward for Byrne Hall.

'OK.' She knotted her scarf. 'Well. So. I suppose I ought to get going?'

It was a question for me – my last chance – and all I could do was smile a flavourless smile and wave. My other hand seemed to have melded with Cory's.

'Good to see you, Maggie,' he piped up, finding his voice at last. 'Take care!'

Once she'd gone we unfolded the trestle-tables and covered them with the white cloths. I set the glasses out in rows, while Cory positioned the floral arrangements and tested the re-wired chandeliers for the hundredth time. His shoulders were squared and his swagger was back; he was brimming with a good feeling that he didn't know how to give voice to.

I set out the final glass, adjusted the lines until they were straight, and stood back to judge the effect.

'Brilliant,' Cory said. 'You've made a brilliant job of that.'

'Of what?' I tried to rid my smile of weariness. 'Of setting the glasses out? Or of giving Maggie the cold shoulder?'

He kept shooting little looks at me; shy glances that made my heart ache unexpectedly. I grieved for the Freya I'd been back in September, when I thought Cory was my route back to life.

'Wait there,' he said.

He removed the empty boxes to the kitchen and came back with my long-lost phone.

'Here.' He pressed it nervously into my hands. 'Your phone. You'll be pleased to know I found it . . .'

I stared, speechless.

'. . . and I thought it was about time you had it back.'

My eyes moved from his face to the phone.

'Cory . . .' His name wedged like a hard object in my throat. 'When . . . ?'

It was going to be the first of several questions, but he batted it aside.

'Does it matter?'

I kept on staring like the idiot I was – down at the phone, up at his face, down at the phone. Well, *did* it matter? When I considered what else Cory Byrne had done – when I considered Stella – did it matter if he'd stolen my mobile?

'Sorry,' he said softly. 'It's entirely my fault. I should have known I could trust you.'

I went upstairs alone, to change out of the white dress. It was barely two hours since I'd chucked my normal clothes on the floor of Diana's bedroom, but already they felt dank. I crouched behind the end of her bed before pulling the dress off and wriggling into my jeans and jumper. I didn't realise, until I'd finished, that the wardrobe mirror was reflected in the dressing-table mirror – and vice versa – which meant I wasn't hidden from her line of sight, after all.

I'm almost sure she was asleep. Her left cheek was resting on the pillow, facing the window, and her milky eyes were half closed. She'd been dying for a long time now, and I wondered how much longer she'd have to wait.

I turned my socks the right way out and took my time putting them on. I didn't want Cory's humiliation – however it played out – to touch his mother. None of this was her fault; she'd done her feeble best to warn me away. When I visualised the near future I saw Diana at peace in a sunlit room, with nurses moving calmly round her bed, and a smell of starch, and fresh-cut flowers on the windowsill.

In the long nights, when the windows are black, the pain takes Diana in its jaws and shakes her.

In calmer moments she is chilled by sudden certainties which never occurred to her before. 'Cory hates me' is one of them, and 'I'm too weak to look after him,' and 'The house has gone silent on me.'

Diana cannot exactly think anymore – thinking implies a degree of inner order – but memories come like violent flashes of light, occurring and recurring in the present tense.

'I saw the doctor,' she says, because a whole week has passed since her consultation in Harley Street and the subject needs to be broached. Cory is absorbed by a piece in the local newspaper and doesn't look up.

'Cory?'

He stares at the paper.

'Cory?'

His eyes creep to her face. Diana has always, always intended to break the news gently – her son's feelings being her first consideration – but his preoccupied air makes her brutal.

'I'm going to die,' she declares. 'They may be able to stave it off for a few years, but they can't cure me.'

'Stella's body,' he says. 'She . . . It . . . She's been found.'

Cory's hands are shaking and his face is hanging like a tragedy mask. He holds up the newspaper so his mother can see the headline, and the short accompanying article, and the photo of the little orange coastguard boat.

Cory is drinking wine at the kitchen table – lots of it – and Diana moves the bottle aside so she can lay the picture before him; the one that Stella ripped to shreds.

'Darling, I've mended it! Look! I know it's not the same as it was . . .'

She is grey with exhaustion and half blind, her fingers lumpy with glue. Does he notice? Is he aware that she's accomplished the all-but-impossible?

'Bloody hell.' Cory stares at her handiwork with a nascent smile. It's the kindest thing he's said in weeks.

But: 'Hang on, what about the hands?'

'There weren't any hands. I scoured the attic floor but . . .' She tries to shrug. 'There weren't any hands.'

Diana thinks she might cry if Cory insists upon the hands. He's about to – she can tell – but he glances at her sick face and thinks better of it.

287

6

WHEN EVENING CAME I LOITERED in the studio, eating sugared almonds from a jar and watching headlights weave through the trees to the front of the house. The almonds had been gathering dust on Diana's dressing table, and as soon as I'd spotted them I'd realised how desperately I needed to eat. They were pink and white and slightly stale, but I was too hungry to care, and I'd been picking at them all day. I was down to my last handful now and the first guests were beginning to arrive.

It was a filthy night for a party. The rain was marching in columns off the sea and drumming against the house, and the gravel couldn't drain quickly enough so puddles were starting to form between the parked cars. Earlier in the day, Cory had managed to unhook the white fairy lights from the tall trees at the end of the garden and hang them round the pillared porch, where they now swung wildly in the wind, failing to provide much light. I couldn't distinguish anybody's face from here, only wet glints on hurrying umbrellas and huddled raincoats. One woman sat in her car for ages after she'd parked, as if bracing herself to get out. Another stumbled on her high heels as she crossed to the house and the man who was with her said, 'Bollocks to this!' as he caught her by the arm. He must have said it pretty loudly, because I couldn't make out anyone else's voice, except Cory's.

'Welcome! Come on in!' he shouted every time he opened the door. We'd planned to prop it open until everyone had arrived, but that wasn't going to work when the weather was so blustery. 'Welcome! Let me take your coats!'

I ought to have hurried downstairs and joined him before he came up to fetch me. I'd already heard him apologise for me several times. 'Freya will be down in just a moment,' he'd said, and one of the guests must have queried this because he'd replied, 'No, no, not Diana. *Freya*. Freya is my ... I'm afraid my mother won't be here at all; she's not feeling well.'

The fairy lights blinked and dimmed. Yet another car emerged from the woods, just as I'd persuaded myself to leave, and I hung on in case it was Tom's Ford Fiesta. Not that I'd be able to tell. Even when it had parked up and the passengers were piling out, I couldn't see much from here. I reached for my phone.

Where are you?xxx

It was the first message I'd written in two months, and I sent it to Dad because Tom would be driving. Whether anyone had messaged *me* during those two months was a moot point: either they hadn't, or Cory had deleted everything from my inbox. That was the likeliest explanation, wasn't it? Somebody – *somebody* – must have tried to get in touch? I crunched the last few sugared almonds.

Maggie! I remembered gratefully, dusting crumbs from the front of my dress. Maggie had texted me – she'd said so this morning. I put the empty jar down, squared my shoulders and turned towards the door.

With every step I took the red dress swished, as if a pair of shears were slicing through the fabric. Quite what wild and wonderful creature I thought I'd become when I put it on, I no longer knew. A firebird? A dragon? A sorceress? It turned out I was still myself, the same old Freya Lyell, zipped inside a 1970s ball gown with massive sleeves, tight cuffs, and too many beads on the bodice.

I had to stop when I reached the landing because I thought my knees were going to buckle. This whole situation was impossible. I should have gone down ages ago; I should have been there from the start. Now I would have to sweep down the stairs in a flash of bloody-minded red that I wasn't feeling as much as I ought.

I nearly dropped my phone when it lit up and beeped.

Turning into the drive now! Dad x

Forty-odd guests seems a lot when you're writing the invitations by hand, but the high-ceilinged spaces swallowed them up. A few people noticed me racing down the stairs, but not many, and they didn't seem particularly intrigued. Half of them still had their coats on. The champagne was being handed round but I heard someone mention hot coffee, and I knew for a fact we were out of coffee.

'It said on the invitation that Robert Lyell would be here,' one man grumbled, and another replied with a doubtful, 'Hmm . . .'

I brushed past them and made my way to the front door, where Cory was waiting for guests. Perhaps it was too dark for him to notice the colour of my dress, or perhaps he was too nervous to care – either way he smiled and murmured 'Hi', and squeezed my hand so tightly that the engagement ring hurt my finger.

The noise of the storm ruled out conversation, so I simply

yelled, 'Dad's here,' and jabbed my thumb in the direction of the drive. We stood side by side beneath the pillared porch, hugging our separate selves against the wind and staring across the garden. Before long a couple of headlights did appear through the trees, but it was a red Mini, so it couldn't be Dad.

'They'll be here any second,' I insisted. 'He said—'

But Cory was making a dash for the Mini as it bumped over the gravel and parked in front of the garden steps. He opened the passenger door – doing his desperate 'Welcome, welcome!' act as the rain plastered his hair to his scalp – and my father emerged, squinting, with his collar turned up to his ears.

'Dad!'

I splashed down the steps, hitching my skirt round my knees so as not to trip. Dad being Dad, when I seized him and flung my arms around his neck he undermined the moment by muttering, 'Steady on now!' and 'Can't this wait until we're inside?' but his heart wasn't in it. His heart – for that brief, brief moment – was in agreement with mine, and he hugged me back in spite of the rain.

It couldn't last. 'Come in!' Cory kept shouting, and in the second it took for me to shut the car door, the entire Lyell party – Zoë? Tom? Anyone else? I hadn't had chance to notice – had been ushered inside, and another carful of arrivals had pulled up between us. By the time I got indoors, they'd disappeared into one or other of the galleries.

The wind burst with me into the house, making the paintings wobble on their hooks. I slammed the door shut and the hall went quiet, except that I could hear Cory's voice, exuberantly loud, in the gallery to my right. He had dumped everyone's wet coats and umbrellas in the corner of the hall any old how, and some of the guests were glancing unhappily at the heap as they sipped their champagne. We ought to have thought about what to do with coats. Perhaps I ought to think about it now.

Someone shoved a tray of half-filled glasses into my elbow and muttered, 'Drink?' The caterers had sent two waitresses along – school friends who smirked when they caught one another's eye. They were meant to be handing out canapés as well as drinks, and I should have checked if that was in hand, but the girls moved on before I remembered. I took a swig from my glass and turned away from the wet coats, so that I wouldn't have to worry about them.

Nobody was mingling. The people who'd come in pairs or groups remained in pairs or groups; those who'd arrived alone were looking down into their glasses, or up at the chandeliers, or checking their phones. There was a small gathering round the portrait of Lady Caroline Augusta Fitzroy-Byrne, and when one person remarked of her, 'Rather fine,' there was a grateful hum of agreement.

Most of the Freya pictures were in the rooms either side of the front door, but there were two in the entrance hall, including the one with the fancy gold frame. You couldn't exactly miss them, and yet everyone seemed anxious to do just that. I heard a few people speaking kindly about Cory himself – 'A relief to know the poor kid survived adolescence!' 'Isn't it just?' – but nobody mentioned his paintings, or not in my earshot.

I crossed the hall, swishing in my satin and smiling dumbly at anyone who would meet my eye. At some point, Cory was going to pinch my arm and demand to know what the hell was going wrong with his party. Perhaps I could suggest it had something to do with the lighting. Cory had dreamed of a candlelit glow, but the newly wired chandeliers were giving off a bluish glare which hadn't been apparent when he tested them this morning. It did something bad to the walls; took all the warmth from the Pamplona Red.

I held my hand against the electric radiator that Cory had brought from upstairs, but its effect was puny in the cavernous hall. There was a halogen heater near the stairs which gave off a cosier glow, but it kept making odd buzzing noises, as if it were about to die.

Music, I thought vaguely, and Cory must have had the same idea, because the CD player started up.

'Schubert!' someone declared.

'Lovely!'

There were nods and murmurs all round, as if the inarguable loveliness of the music was a relief to everyone.

Cory had been worrying about music all afternoon. 'Schubert quintet?' he kept asking. 'Or Miles Davis?' He had tapped his nails against his teeth and hung about in front of me, demanding an answer.

'Freya, seriously, what do you think? It's got to be something classy – but are we talking classy classical or classy jazz?'

I'd said Schubert just to shut him up, although as far as party spirit was concerned, the jazz would have been a better bet. There weren't enough speakers for all this space, and the music sounded small and faraway, as if a quintet of ghosts had struck up in the cellar. To make matters worse, the wind was picking up outside and the music couldn't compete; it could only add a thread of unease to the bigger, crazier sounds of the storm.

'Listen, Robert, I don't mind,' a happy and half-familiar

voice was saying in one of the front rooms. 'I'm just glad to get out of London for a while, and spend some time with you.'

I peered round the edge of the door, and Zoë Stefanidis spotted me straight away.

'Here she is!' she cried. 'Here's Freya!'

Zoë bounced towards me with her arms outstretched, and I didn't resent her warmth as much as I thought I would. I let her hug me and half hugged her in return, keeping my left hand behind my back so she wouldn't spot the engagement ring. She smiled and her earrings clanked as she kissed me not once, not twice, but three times on the cheeks.

Dad was lurking behind her, thin and hunched, like a question mark. I could tell, without looking directly, that his mood had darkened since he'd entered the house.

'I hope you don't mind me coming tonight,' Zoë said, and it was worry rather than pleasure that lit her features. 'I wasn't sure. You know what your dad's like, all vague and airy and *Oh, don't worry, Freya won't mind.*' She lowered her voice. 'Actually, between ourselves, I think he's embarrassed of me . . . No, no, I don't mean that –' as Dad muttered a protest – 'I don't mean embarrassed of *me*. Just worried what you'll think about us.'

It was one of those moments that might have been awkward in another life. Maybe next week, maybe even tomorrow, this whole Dad and Zoë thing would bother me, but I couldn't think about it now. One of the waitresses appeared with a tinfoil platter.

'Oh, fantastic!' said Zoë optimistically. There wasn't much to choose from: a pile of grissini, a khaki dip, and some brown olives on cocktail sticks. We all took something, but Zoë was the only one who actually ate. Judging by the pristine state of his glass I don't think Dad had touched his champagne, and his fingers kept twitching round his pocket, as if he could kill for a cigarette. He met my eye without smiling, and I got that hollow feeling in my knees again. Perhaps he was just upset – understandably – by Cory's paintings, but in that case why was he glaring at *me*, as if *I* had committed some offence?

'Where's Tom?' I wondered, glancing over Dad's shoulder. Whatever else was going on, that was still the crucial question.

'Tom?' The way Dad said it, you'd think there was some doubt as to which Tom, out of many, I was referring to. 'I don't know. I didn't realise he was invited.'

'Oh.' I stared at my father. 'But I just assumed . . . Did he not drive you down?'

'No, no, Zoë brought her car. Anyway, I barely see him these days – I suppose he's busy getting ready for his big move up north. We would have offered him a lift but, as I say, I didn't realise he was invited.'

'No,' I said. 'Well, no. I suppose he wasn't exactly, come to think of it.'

I remember staring at my cocktail stick with its glistening olive, and wondering what on earth it was and why I was holding it. It bothered me that Dad's hands were full – what with the un-sipped champagne and un-nibbled canapé – because that meant he couldn't take notes. He ought to be making notes for his review.

'Do you want to put those down somewhere?' I said.

'Pardon?'

'Cory printed off some catalogue notes, if you want to scribble on one of them? Or I'm sure I can rustle up some paper—'

'No, thank you.' Dad's voice was crisp, as if my suggestion

had been in poor taste. 'By the way, I meant to say: you're looking terribly grown-up this evening.'

The bitterness in his tone was unmistakable, and I was a child again – the great, big, twenty-three-year-old child I'd been before I left home for Byrne Hall. Was *that* Dad's problem? My appearance? I didn't think so, deep down. It sounded like a casual swipe; a symptom of some other mysterious displeasure.

'Dad? What's up?'

'Oh, I think it's a *fabulous* dress,' Zoë piped up before he could answer, and then there was a touch to my elbow and Cory was saying, 'Hello again, Mr Lyell! How wonderful to see you!'

Cory wore his behaviour like a handsome and well-fitting suit, and since I intended never to be alone with him again, this meant I would never know his thoughts about the red dress. Even if I seized him by the shoulders and peered into his eyes, he would smile for the sake of his guests and give nothing away.

I'll see Tom tomorrow, I thought. *Come hell or high water, I'll see Tom tomorrow.*

'Thank you for coming all this way,' Cory was saying. 'Freya tells me you've booked into a hotel in Bligh, but you'd be most welcome to stay here . . .' and so on and so on, his voice shimmering with kindness.

Dad asked after his mother, and introduced Zoë properly, and Zoë kissed his cheeks three times: *mwa . . . mwa . . . mwa*. I doubted anyone would notice if I sidled away. Dad started thanking Cory – again! – for inviting him to the opening, although he made no comment on the paintings themselves. Even when Cory stood back with his arms slightly spread, and surveyed the walls with an inviting, 'Well . . . !' Dad just turned his attention to the olive he'd been holding for the last ten minutes and said, 'This is an impressive spread! Did you make the food yourselves, or did you get people in?'

Zoë saw me backing away, but I shook my head ever so slightly, so that she'd understand not to make a fuss. She did understand, to her credit. I think she was worried, though, because when she told Cory, 'It's an absolutely stunning house you've got here!' she had one eye on me, and her tone of voice no longer matched her superlatives.

'Thanks!' Cory said, as I made it to the entrance hall.

'Oh, yes!' Dad remarked. 'You should see the gardens in summer!'

There were still a lot of champagne flutes standing in tidy formation. We had catered for too many as far as drink was concerned, and too few in terms of food. I drained a glass in one go and picked up another.

There were two women in the gallery to the left of the front door, conversing quietly with their backs to the pictures, and they didn't acknowledge my entrance. I strolled from painting to painting, drinking quickly and allowing myself to seethe. It was as if I'd only ever peeped sideways at Cory's work until the other week, when I found the Stellas in the attic. That had been my moment of revelation; the slap across the face that had shocked me into seeing straight. I'd made so many excuses for him over the months – *he needs time; he needs practice; he needs to know me better* – as if the problem with the way he painted was simply a question of skill.

I could admit it now, to myself; I could admit how much I hated Cory's pictures. I stared hard at all the Freyas, with their drugged eyelids and puffed-up breasts; their milky whites and jaundiced yellows; their dead faces, like masks with no-one behind them. *Freya Reading a Book . . . Freya Sleeping . . . Freya by the Window . . . Freya Sitting on the Stairs . . . Freya with her Chin in her Hand . . . Freya, Freya, Freya upon Freya,* looming from the dark-red walls.

The women were still murmuring as I left.

'That was my thinking precisely,' I overheard one of them say, 'but apparently she's ill.'

'Oh! So you mean she's not going to put in any appearance at all?'

'Apparently she's not well enough.'

The second woman tutted with annoyance and the first one said, 'I know.'

There were no pockets on the red dress but the sleeves were capacious, and I'd worked out a way of tucking my phone inside the cuff where no-one could see it. I went upstairs to the landing and leaned over the bannisters while I searched for Tom's number. Everyone was standing about vacantly down in the hall, like people on a railway platform whose train is still some minutes off. A few were gravitating towards Dad; a few were still drawn to Lady Caroline's lipless smile. I could only see the tops of their heads from here, and it struck me that nearly all Cory's guests were white-haired, or greying, or bald. They were Diana's generation – not his.

I turned my back on the party and carried on climbing. It wasn't that I wanted to return upstairs. Going upstairs had been on the long list of *Never agains* that I'd been ticking off all day – *Never again will I have to wake up on this mattress, Never again will I have to get dressed in front of Cory,* and, at long last, earlier this evening, *Never again will I have to climb these stairs.*

All the same, it was restful to leave the cold, glittery gathering behind, and push my way into the darkness.

I didn't risk pressing *Call* until I reached the second floor – Diana's floor – but even that felt too exposed, so I slipped up the attic staircase as it started to ring and felt my way to the top. The cold was different up here – more airy and mobile than below – and the rain was loud on the roof.

'Freya! It's you!'

'It's me!'

'It's so wonderful to hear your voice! Are you all right? How's it going?'

Tom's voice was huge and too happy. I walked the length of the corridor and ducked into the room where Cory had dumped his Stella portraits.

'It's awful,' I whispered. 'Oh Tom, it's awful. I wish you were here. I wish—'

I stubbed my toe on something sharp, and when I crouched to rub the pain away, the phone-glow caught on the intricate, gluey lines of the mosaic, torn from its golden frame and flung on the floor. I could just make out the fracture lines across my sister's cheek and nose.

'Why? What's happened?' asked Tom. 'You're all right, aren't you?'

The fear in his voice was thrilling to me; a thing of weight and value.

'Freya, say something.'

'I'm here, I'm fine, but—'

'What's going on? I thought it was the opening tonight? Is your dad not there with Zoë?'

'Yes, yes, they're here, but Dad's acting strange, like I've done something wrong, and Cory's paintings . . .'

'What about them? Freya, what is it?'

'They're horrible, Tom. I've wanted to tell someone this for so long—'

'Tell someone . . . ?'

'No, not someone. You. I've wanted to tell *you*. They're such horrible pictures, and I . . . I don't know . . . I feel so stupid.'

The bedsprings creaked wildly as I sat down. Tom was quiet, listening to my words and silences.

'It's good to hear your voice again,' he said, with less exuberance and more depth than before.

'It's good to hear yours, too.'

I smiled sadly down the phone, and pictured him smiling back in much the same way.

'Everything's gone wrong,' I said, knotting the blanket round my fingers.

'So come home.'

'But you're going away.'

He started to reply, but then he sighed and fell silent.

The other paintings were still in a heap against the wall: I could just make out the shapes of their various faces and bodies. I counted to ten in my head.

'I've been thinking about Stella a lot lately.'

'Oh yes?'

My shoulders relaxed. Talking to Tom was like discovering I had more space to move in than I realised; more fresh air to breathe than I knew.

'Do you remember when she went off to Gainsborough Art College and decided to become a sculptor?'

Tom didn't say, *That's a random question* or *Where's this going, then?* He just said, 'Yes, I remember. She kept getting wet clay all over everything and driving your dad round the bend. Didn't she block the bathroom sink?'

'That's right. We were having that New Year's Eve party. We had to get an emergency plumber.'

'I couldn't forget that.'

His laughter made me smile.

'She was really keen,' I said, 'but Dad put her off. Told her she'd never be any good.'

I think Tom sighed again; the line blurred.

'My dad's not always the most sensitive when it comes to things like that, is he?'

A brief hesitation and: 'No, he's not, but still . . . I don't think blaming him for what happened . . .'

'Oh, no!' I sat up straighter. 'I don't!'

Although I suppose I used to, just a little. I used to blame myself most of all, and then Stella herself, and then Dad – but that was before Cory absolved us all by turning out to be a monster. I picked one of the pictures off the pile and peered at it, but it was too dark to make much out.

'If anyone's to blame, it's me,' said Tom.

'You! Why would you say that?' I tossed the picture back on to the pile. 'What do you mean?'

The line crackled as he let out another sigh.

'Did . . . ?' he began. 'Did Stella ever tell you . . . ? No, I can't imagine she did.'

'What?'

'She asked me to go with her.'

'She . . . ?'

'A day or two before she left for the last time – a couple of months before she died – she came to see me one evening and asked me to run away with her. Just like that; straight out of the blue.'

'What did you say?'

'I said no. I told her not to be daft, and she got all huffy and said, "Plenty of people I know would give their eyeteeth to be propositioned by me." So then I went and laughed, didn't I? Which was completely the wrong thing to do, because she got upset and stormed off, and then . . . that was it. That was the last conversation we ever had.'

'I didn't know.'

I almost said, *So you mean you weren't in love with her?* but it felt like an unsubtle question in the context of our conversation – like an unfair accusation, or a demand for clarity where there was none to be had.

We were quiet again, and this time I couldn't picture Tom's expression. I thought of asking him to go to the nearest mirror and describe his face to me in minute detail – from the turn of his lips to the furrow between his eyebrows.

Before either of us could say anything, though, the phone flew out of my hand. It made a dull crack as it hit the floor, and the ceiling light came on.

Cory wrapped his arms around me from behind and buried his face against my neck. 'Hello,' he said. His breath was damp and I could feel the edges of his teeth on my skin. 'Hello' wasn't a weak non-word, the way it looks on the page, but jagged and full of intent.

I couldn't see where my phone had gone, but I knew the connection with Tom had been lost. I pictured him standing in his study, staring at his own blank screen and wondering why I'd left him so abruptly.

The rain was still hammering on the roof but there was a silence beyond it, peculiar to the little attic room, which meant that Cory and I were alone.

August 2009

Dad buys a Chinese takeaway to celebrate my A-level results, but he accidentally orders Stella's favourite – satay prawns – instead of mine – lemon chicken – and although I insist it's fine, somehow it isn't.

While we're eating, we try to talk about me – my exam results, my university place, my long-term plans – but the conversation always finds its way back to Stella. She's been gone for eight and a half weeks now.

'At least she occasionally phones,' I observe, chasing a prawn around the foil carton with my chopsticks. 'And we know she's staying with a friend this time. And after all, Dad, she is *an adult . . .'*

My father stops pretending to eat and puts his chopsticks down. He refrains from pointing out that it's ages since she last phoned, or that it's far from clear whether she really is with a 'friend', or that, yes, she may be twenty-one years old, but she is also Stella.

I give up too, and sit back with a sigh. Every so often I remember my A-level results with a guilty twinge of pleasure. It's getting late, and I can hear birdsong through the open window. Light is seeping from the lilac sky, and the houses at the other end of the garden are turning into silhouettes. I don't find it gloomy but Dad obviously does, because he reaches for the wall switch, and suddenly the

303

view is replaced by the kitchen light, reflected twice in the double-glazing.

'The whole thing's my fault, isn't it?' Dad takes his glasses off and wipes his weary eyes. 'You think it's my fault. I should have told her she was destined to be the finest sculptor the world has ever known.'

'No!' I protest, but I can't look at him. I start tidying spilt rice from the tabletop, grain by grain. 'You were just being yourself; you have to be able to speak your mind.'

I think of my exam results on purpose – just for the twinge of pleasure – but the more often I do it, the less I feel. It occurs to me that we'd be sitting here just the same if I'd failed – playing with our food and talking about Stella. The cat jumps on to my lap, sniffs the rice, and jumps down again. Dad pours more wine. I can't tell if he's reassured by what I've said or not.

The phone rings. 'I'll get it,' we say simultaneously, but it's Dad who picks up – and it's her. It's Stella. I straighten my shoulders and wipe my sticky hands on my napkin. She's remembered! I almost laugh out loud. Why did we doubt her? I hope Dad doesn't tell her what grades I got; I want to tell her myself.

Dad's mouth barely moves as he's talking and his eyes narrow. Oh no. I hate it when they ad lib; I wish I could script their conversations. If he would only say, 'I'm sorry I hurt your feelings,' and if she would only say, 'I love you, Dad,' then everything might be all right. But they're both as perverse as each other, and they won't.

'So, tell me,' Dad is saying. 'To what do we owe the pleasure?'

I get up and wrest the phone from his hands.

'Stella?'

'Oh, hi Freya.' She sounds distracted, and I wonder if her mysterious friend is there too. 'I thought it was about time I rang; I just wanted to let you know I'm OK.'

Dad opens the back door to let the cat out and follows it into the garden. I watch him walk down the path to the back fence, and maybe it's just the odd light but his body seems meagre and bent.

'I got straight As,' I say, but my tone is so dull that she fails to understand.

'You . . . what? Sorry, the line's not great.'

'My exams.'

'What? Speak up!'

'It doesn't matter.'

There's a heat rising inside me, and I know I must damp it down but I can't. This is what happens to Dad when he speaks to her; it's why he can't stick to my placatory script.

'So . . .' she says, as if it might be time to start winding up this non-conversation.

'So . . .' I echo, although I can hardly breathe. 'So where the fuck are you, Stella?'

She's surprised into silence for a second, and then she says, through a smirk, 'Freya! Language!'

Is there somebody with her, stifling laughter? She – they? – wait for me to amuse them again and, ever-obliging, I do.

'Do you know what I'd wish for if I could have anything in the world?' I say.

'Oh, not this again – you can never decide. A lifetime's supply of Maltesers?'

'No.'

305

More giggling at the other end of the phone. Stella is only half listening; she only ever half listens to me.

'Stella?'

'Sorry, Freya, what were you saying? If you could have one wish . . .'

'Shall I tell you what it would be?'

The receiver feels sticky in my right hand, so I switch it to my left. Before I speak, I check on Dad's whereabouts, but it's all right: he's at the far end of the garden, lighting a cigarette.

'I'd wish that you would go away, once and for all, and never, ever, ever come back, or phone, or write, or bother me and Dad in any way whatsoever. I'd wish for you to disappear into thin air and just, just . . . die.'

I make my voice calm and slow, because I know it will be more effective than shrieking.

At first I think she's going to yell at me, and then I think she's more likely to hang up, and then I hear her say, ever so quietly, 'Got it.'

I'm not to know it's the last thing my sister will ever say to me.

We trade silences for a good ten seconds before I end the call.

7

I MADE A DASH FOR the door but Cory got there first, and I wasn't about to wrestle him. I wasn't going to touch him, if I could help it. We stood poised and staring like cats, until I backed away and he slid into a sitting position against the door. He didn't seem to care that he was getting dust all over his suit – or perhaps he didn't notice. Under the bare bulb his face looked bony and white.

'How much did you hear?' I asked foolishly.

Cory drew the Stella mosaic on to his lap and scrutinised her face.

'Oh, Tom!' he piped in falsetto. 'I've been wanting to talk to you for so long! I've been wanting to tell you about all the horrible, nasty pictures . . .'

I retreated, step by backwards step, until I hit the wall. My phone had landed by Cory's foot, and we both saw Tom's name lighting the screen as it began to ring. I thought he would get mad and stamp on it, especially when it stopped and started up again, but he didn't get mad. He just waited until it stopped for good, which it did, of course. I couldn't expect Tom to keep trying for ever.

'What now?' I said. 'What are you going to do?'

Cory lifted his hands from the floor one by one, and studied his dusty palms. A cobweb hung from his fingers like a length of dirty lace, and he wiped it on to his trouser leg. I wanted to know what he was thinking, but I wasn't going to ask again.

Even while he was staring at me, he kept stroking Stella's portrait. His eyes were bleaker than the sea at its most wintry and grey, and I wondered if Stella had been in love with them at any point, and whether they were the last things she saw before she died.

'I sometimes used to think your sister was a horror,' he said, smoothing her ripped-up face. 'But at least she had class. You're something else entirely.'

'You think you can shock me,' I said. 'But I already know about you and Stella.'

He smiled faintly.

'Stella laughed when I talked about exhibiting these paintings,' he said. 'But at least she laughed to my face; at least she didn't pretend to be on board and whisper about me behind my back.'

'I know it was you who killed her,' I said.

His smile faded. 'You know nothing at all.'

My phone started up again, but the ringtone was different – it was the ragtime tune that signified 'Dad'. The screen lit up with his name.

'Answer it.' Cory pushed the phone towards me with his foot. When I hesitated he took the craft knife from his jacket pocket and turned it over in his hands.

Dad was already speaking as I brought the phone to my ear, although I could hardly hear him over the crackle of static.

'. . . Freya, it's your father. I don't know where you've got to, but frankly I'm not prepared to hang around in this godawful . . .' *crackle* . . . 'Zoë and I are leaving.'

I cast my eyes about the room – at the dusty light bulb, and the rain-jewelled window, and the many painted faces of my sister. I glanced at Cory's knife, with its bright triangular blade. 'Hang on. Dad . . .'

'No, I won't "hang on". You've put me in a most embarrassing position . . .' *crackle, crackle* '. . . most unlike you to be so . . .'

The line was terrible. They must be outside in the wind. Or perhaps they were already in the car, heading for a brandy and an early night in their plush hotel.

'Dad, please don't go.'

Cory had been leaning forwards, but he shot to his feet when I said 'don't go' and his face seemed to tighten, like a photograph coming into focus.

'He's not leaving,' he whispered, sliding the knife under my chin. 'Don't let him leave.'

But Dad had got the bit between his teeth. '. . . that I have a huge respect and liking for Cory, but he's no artist as you surely know . . . If you've got problems with your relationship, that's none of my business but . . .' *crackle* . . . 'how unkind of you, very disappointing, frankly . . .' *crackle, crackle* . . . 'to drag me into some kind of vindictive plot . . . As if humiliating your boyfriend in a national newspaper was some kind of . . .'

'But you're not going yet?' I shouted. Nothing but the static shouted back and I had to raise my voice another notch. 'Dad? We haven't even said goodbye.'

'I don't claim to understand what you're playing at, Freya . . .'

They must have been driving because the wipers were squeaking and I heard Zoë say 'Ooph' as they bumped over a pot-hole.

'. . . but I don't like it, whatever it is, and I'll have no part in it. You're on your own.'

'Dad!' Even with the point of a blade against my throat,

309

I could only inject so much desperation into a single syllable. Perhaps my father heard petulance, or perhaps he didn't hear me at all. Either way, with an angry fizzle of breath he'd gone, and although the attic was still thrumming with rain, Cory and I seemed to plumb new depths of stillness. A good minute went by before he lowered the knife.

I stared at the blank phone and wondered what was happening downstairs – whether the Schubert was still playing and the champagne still flowing, or whether everyone had begun to drift away. They *would* drift, now that Dad had left. They'd have to, if Cory didn't go down soon and give them a reason to stay. Nobody would come looking for us.

'What did he say?' Cory took the phone from my hand and studied the screen, although there was nothing to see except my fingerprints. 'Please tell me he hasn't left . . .'

'Could you not hear?'

'Just tell me.'

I felt blindly for the wall behind my back. I would have liked some time to think.

'He got an urgent call from work. There was nothing else for it: he had to go home.'

Cory was listening in all seriousness, pinching his lower lip. This was like tightrope-walking in the dark, each word another forwards step, nothing to go on but instinct.

'He won't have time to write your review . . .'

Cory's knuckles whitened, and the plastic knife-handle cracked.

'. . . but he still wants to publish one, so he's asked me to write it instead.'

'*You?*'

The knuckle-bones were still sliding and straining beneath

his skin. My mouth was dry, but I licked my lips and swallowed. The wall was too smooth beneath my palms – I needed something to hold on to or I would fall over. I moved my feet apart for better balance.

'Dad said I'm to write it tonight and bring it to him tomorrow, and he'll definitely get it into next Saturday's paper.'

The handle made another cracking noise as Cory's fingers relaxed a fraction.

'Definitely,' I repeated.

He thought for a moment. 'When you say "bring it to him" . . . ?'

'It's got to be hand-delivered. By me.'

Oh God, any idiot could tell I was making it up as I went along, and Cory was no idiot. My hand rose to cover my throat, but his expression didn't change.

'I don't understand,' he said. 'Why can't you just email it from here?'

My pulse fluttered against my fingers like a trapped butterfly.

'I don't know,' I said. 'The line was terrible. I think perhaps he's worried about me.'

The knife turned and twisted in Cory's grasp, and I never took my eyes off the shining blade.

Shit. That was all I could think. *Shit, shit, shit.*

Cory thought about what I'd said for a long time. Eventually he returned the knife to his pocket, along with my phone.

'All right,' he said dubiously. 'If that's how it is . . . I'll bring you some paper and a pen, and you can write while the party's winding up. If you need help –' our eyes met and parted – 'I'll come upstairs once everyone's left.'

I was backed up against the wall with no retreat. Cory's

thumb traced my jaw in the ghost of a tender gesture, but he was just as clammy and shaky as me, and I don't know who he thought he was fooling. He even tried to smile, as if his 'all right' had meaning; as if there were something left to us worth fixing.

'We'll catch the London train first thing,' he said, and kissed me on the forehead.

He brought me my beautiful notebook, along with a pen, a blanket, a cushion, a plate of leftovers and a mug of tea. We didn't speak to one another and he turned the key in the lock as he left. Once I was sure he'd gone I blew on the hot tea, took a careful sip and opened the book at a fresh page.

Cory Byrne is a very talented . . .

I crossed out 'very' in the name of self-respect.

Cory Byrne is a talented portrait artist whose debut exhibition opened last Saturday in Bligh . . .

Writing for my life was easy; the platitudes poured from my pen like water from a tap. After a while I stopped worrying about the occasional 'very'. Let him have as many superlatives as he could swallow – they meant nothing, and they upped the word count. My pen skimmed across the paper without a pause while my mind wandered. I listened for evidence of the party downstairs – the faintest echo of music or chatter – but I was too far away to catch it, or the rain was too loud, or they had all gone.

The tea was still warm by the time I glided to a halt on the third page – *A first-class act, Cory Byrne is most definitely one to watch!* – and threw my pen down. Job done. I pushed the pad away and rubbed my eyes.

I felt sick – perhaps it was just the champagne sloshing

about on an empty stomach. I tried to eat a bread-stick, but I caught Stella's glue-streaked eye as I took my first bite, and retched. Next thing I knew, my face was crumpling, and tea was arcing across the room, and the china mug was bouncing off the door. It didn't even have the good grace to shatter, so I picked it up and pounded it against the wall until the handle was the largest piece left and my fingers were studded with blood.

My notebook was spattered with tea now, and the biro didn't want to write on wet paper, but I made it write anyway – marking the page with gouges and rips where I couldn't mark it with ink. I scrawled all over my previous work, using every obscenity I could think of and some I made up, tossing his name into the mix without even trying to make sentences, and when I'd run out of space I started on a new page. My wrist was beginning to hurt, but I couldn't imagine losing momentum. I'd keep going with this for ever. After I'd used up the notepad, I'd use the walls and floor and ceiling, and once they were full I'd carry on writing across my own skin.

I stopped after a dozen pages, in order to cover my head with my arms and give myself up to crying.

I didn't notice how cold I was until I'd calmed down. The damp wind sneaked into the room wherever it could – in between the roof tiles, round the door, up through the floorboards – and I shivered, even after I'd wrapped the blanket round my shoulders and pulled it up to my chin. My face felt sticky and puffed up, and I wanted another mug of tea.

It was difficult to tell how much time had passed since I came upstairs to phone Tom. It might be nearly dawn by now; it might be as early as midnight. The window was still black, and the only source of light was the bulb on its frayed cord, which cast everything in stark light or shadow. I drew the notepad towards me and rested it on my knees, laying the pen on top.

A quarter of an hour went by. I slid the ring off my finger and rolled it back and forth to help me think. It made a juddering sound on the wooden floor, because of its silvery twists and knots. I drew a smooth breath and let the ring go, watching as it rolled away and dropped through a gap in the skirting board. I waited for a rattle or a ping, but it disappeared without any sound at all. In my mind's eye it fell and never stopped falling, as if there were an eternity of cobwebbed darkness beneath me, instead of just a house.

I uncapped the pen.

' "Freya",' I wrote at the top of a fresh page. 'An exhibition of portraits by Cory Byrne.' I rubbed my eyes and settled down, finally, to write.

Cory Byrne once gave me some advice. 'Write what you know,' he said. 'Write what you see; what's there, in front of you.'

It would have been good advice if it hadn't been offered so glibly; as if seeing – or knowing, or painting, or writing – is ever a simple thing . . .

It took me a while to shape my first ideas into sentences, but once they were on the page they gave rise to more. I forgot I was imprisoned in an attic, that I was freezing, and that Cory was going to kill me. There were a lot of crossings-out, but they weren't passionate scrawls or furious scribbles – they were just lines I drew through the words that didn't work.

I don't think any amount of nakedness or intimacy or
contortion can make a painting obscene. It's only when
humanity gets left out that things turn ugly. I don't
mean that the subject's soul ought to be hoisted up
a flag-pole and waved about for all the world to see, but
I do think it has to be referenced, subtly. Take Freya
Sleeping, *which manages to be obscene without any*
nudity at all . . .

I was like a diamond setter, dealing in words rather than
stones. I took my time over each one – turning it over, holding
it to the light, weighing its implications, comparing its
alternatives – and it might be allowed to stay, or it might be
scrapped, or it might just fill a space until a better one turned
up. How precisely to describe the way Cory painted a woman's
eyes? Were they 'tawdry' or 'lifeless', and what was the difference? Was 'interiority' a clumsier word than 'soul', or a more
nuanced one? I rattled the biro against my teeth and tried
them all; then I found others and tried them too. I wanted an
adjective that meant 'sexual but not sensual'. I needed an economical way of describing someone who can see another
person in minute detail whilst missing everything that matters. I ransacked my brain and hankered after a thesaurus. The
first draft filled fourteen pages; the fair copy barely made six.

It's always interesting to see the accidental themes that
emerge – and fail to emerge – in an exhibition like this. For
example, self-satisfaction runs like a dye through the 'Freya'
exhibition, although I'm sure Cory Byrne never meant it to.
Perceptiveness – which, as a portrait painter, he presumably
hoped to achieve – is notable by its absence . . .

My back ached by the time I'd finished, and I'd got cramp in my legs. I stood up and walked round the room while I re-read the piece, wincing as my toes revived. After a couple of tiny changes – 'insight' rather than 'perceptiveness', 'pornographic' rather than 'obscene' – I dated it – 16/11/14 – and signed it – *F. Lyell* – although I was too tired and elated to form the letters neatly.

If I'd been in my right mind I wouldn't have considered this little essay worth dying for; all I'd done was to articulate some thoughts about my ex-boyfriend's bad paintings. At the time, though, it felt like the great triumph of my life, and I couldn't bring myself to care what came next.

I tore the pages out of the notebook, folded them in two and slid them under the locked door – giving them a good shove to ensure they were out of my own reach.

I stayed on my feet for as long as I could, pacing up and down. Perhaps I was destined to be a ghost, stalking the attics of Byrne Hall for centuries to come in a 1970s ball gown. One day another young woman might come here and fall in love, and these footsteps of mine, echoing through time, would be her first intimation that something was wrong.

I had to stop, just for a moment, and close my eyes against the whir of my own thoughts. I swayed into the wall and slid into a crouch, and I was out like a light before my head hit the floor.

It wasn't a good sleep, because I knew I ought to be awake. Time and again I dreamed that Cory came into the room and knelt at my side, stroking my throat – except that the sensation was more delicate than the touch of a hand; it was more like a length of red silk trailing across my skin.

Cory keeps hanging his Stella paintings up and Diana keeps taking them down again.

– Diana moans into her pillow and wonders if this ever actually happened. It has the character of an exhausting nightmare.

The game goes on for years after Stella's disappearance, although they never talk about it. They never talk, anymore, about what is foremost in their minds. Some vast, lurid nude will appear in one of the downstairs rooms, and Diana will unhook it and put it in Cory's studio, facing the wall. She is more dogged than he; gradually she gains the upper hand.

– It did. It did happen.

'Just get rid of them,' she pleads in her braver moments, but he won't do that. She wonders why, but tries not to wonder too hard.

The mended picture is her one concession; she allows it to hang in the hall, opposite the front door. It has a kind of moral heft, she decides, given how the three of them created it together: Cory with his genius, Stella with her ill-will, Diana with her love.

Diana opens her eyes in the darkness. The room smells of roses and urine, and she's not sure which is more distressing. Where is Cory? He was here, and now he's gone.

A voice calls out his name; Diana suspects it of being her own. Not that it matters whose voice it is, because nobody answers.

One hot evening – was it last year? This year? August? – Diana finds Cory in his studio. She needs a walking stick now, to negotiate the house, and yet she can't rest; the pain drives her on from room to room.

Cory has brought the mended Stella painting upstairs, from its place in the hall. He is breathing too quickly as he hugs it to his chest, and his eyes are wild.

'Goodness!' Diana exclaims, in fear rather than jest. 'You look as if you've seen a ghost!'

There's a noisy wedding in the garden. People are laughing and talking, and there's a jazz band playing 'Dream a Little Dream of Me' under the fairy lights. There are bridesmaids in pale green dresses – mere tots – running amok in the rose garden.

Cory usually scoffs at any mention of ghosts, but this time he just breathes hard, and stares, and trembles.

8

A COOL DRAUGHT ON MY face: that couldn't be right. Even in my nightmares I knew I was shut inside the little attic room.

Cory must have come when you were asleep and left the door open, said the voice in my dream, and when I opened my eyes I discovered it was true – at least, the part about the door was true. There was no sign of Cory. I touched my throat and my finger came away with a speck of blood. I stared at it for a long time. Was I awake, then, or asleep? Alive or dead?

Dust drifted from my hair as I got stiffly to my feet. I had become like a ghost, lacking colour and definition. I touched my throat again, and the little red droplet reassured me. It seemed safe to assume that ghosts didn't sting, or bleed, or ache.

The notebook was gone, as was my review. I stepped through the unlocked door and walked the full length of the landing to make sure it hadn't drifted into some dark corner, but it was nowhere to be seen.

The rain had stopped. The only sound was a fast and constant *tick-tick-tick-tick*, like a clock gone mad, and it took me ages to realise it was just a drip from a broken gutter. A breeze came up the stairs, smelling sweetly of wet leaves and grass, and I concluded that the front door must be open. I pictured a swift and simple escape, down the stairs and into the open air, and it made the blood pound in my ears – but I didn't move. The silence was as complete as ever, and as brimful of meaning. I forced my feet to the top of the stairs, and started down.

'Cory?' I whispered, and the two syllables dropped like pebbles into the deep, dark well of the house.

I found a rose petal on the second-floor landing and picked it up. Something was wrong – even more wrong than usual – yet everything looked the same. I hovered outside Diana's bedroom for a long moment without going in. It was the same on the first-floor landing, when I stopped outside the closed studio in a quandary of attraction and repulsion, unable to open the door and unable to turn my back on it. The scent of the garden drew me downstairs, in the end.

There was carnage in the galleries. A bloodless massacre. I stopped and stared, holding tight to the bannister. For a moment I thought there'd been an explosion – that the walls and ceilings had caved in – but as I moved closer I realised Cory's paintings were the only casualties. All his beloved Freyas. My legs seemed to disappear from beneath me as I looked from frame to butchered frame, until I sat with a bump on the bottom step.

I picked a jagged ribbon of canvas off the floor, ran it through my fingers and let it fall. The sheer energy of the slashing spree turned my stomach. I made myself get up and walk about the galleries, pausing for a second in front of each frame. Shreds of paper and canvas still clung to the backing-boards here and there, but most were scattered across the floor: the whites and the auburns, the pale greens and yellows, the pinkish shades he'd used to depict my skin. All the glass-fronted frames had been shattered, so I had to be careful where I trod with my bare feet.

Last night's plates and glasses were tidied away and the pile of damp coats had vanished. I had to search hard for evidence that the party had happened at all – for the odd grubby print of a high-heeled shoe, for pastry crumbs on the floor, for a flimsy polka-dot umbrella forgotten in the porch. Cory must have been alone when he took his knife to the paintings. The guests must have said their goodbyes, and the waitresses cleared up and left, before he began. I wondered whether anyone had sensed his unease. Were the girls whispery and afraid as they washed the last of the champagne flutes and hurried them into their crates?

The front door was wide open. I glanced at the garden as I meandered round the hall and thought how innocent it looked, washed and purified by last night's rain. The mist had lifted, and the trees made clean lines against the white November sky. Beyond the end of the lawn the sea rose up, meeting the clouds in a neatly ruled horizon.

The violence of Cory's rage – that's what I couldn't take in. I toured the galleries for a second time, ending up in the hall, and my fingers kept returning to the stinging cut on my throat. Only Lady Caroline remained intact in the shadows, complacently observing the wreckage, and me.

Heavy footsteps crunched over the gravel towards the house and I retreated upstairs. I ought to have gone to the kitchen and forced a window, or grabbed a knife of my own, but Cory had reached the front door and it was too late for second thoughts.

He came inside without a word and stopped. I heard him take a few more cautious steps and stop again. What was he doing? Listening? Sniffing me out? I backed into the bathroom because at least it had a lock – but I failed to notice how wet the floor was. I slipped and floundered, making a noisy grab at the door to stop myself from falling over.

So much for stealth. The footsteps came quickly across the hall and ran up the stairs. My fear was real, and yet I found myself distracted by the state of the bathroom floor. It wasn't just soaking wet – it was red. It wasn't usually red, was it? I thought of all the times I'd perched on the edge of the tub with Stella's note in my hand, staring fixedly at the worn linoleum. No, it wasn't usually red.

My feet had gone red too, and there were red splashes up my ankles. Cory had reached the landing, and I was half aware that I must either shut the door or turn to face him, but I stayed put, staring at my feet. I didn't look at the bath. All I could think was that somehow the dye had leaked from my dress and flooded the floor, although it puzzled me how this could have happened when the material was bone-dry.

It wasn't Cory who came up behind me; it was Tom. I knew because he spoke my name as he reached the top of the stairs. He stopped in the bathroom doorway and something else came from his mouth – not my name, not even a word, but a startled sound – and I had to look up to see what he had seen.

I saw pieces of the picture, but I couldn't fit them together in my mind. I saw the bathtub overflowing with a thin, red soup. I saw a white arm hanging over the side of the tub, and a craft knife covered in pink droplets. I saw fleshy gleams under the water, and Cory's head beside the taps. I saw his chin resting on his chest, and the ends of his hair floating, and scrunched-up papers drifting like water lilies on the surface, and the writing on them – my handwriting – blurring and running, and trailing inky tendrils under the surface of the water. I kept waiting for Cory to raise his eyes, and braced myself for the look I'd get, but he never stirred.

Tom was saying things, doing things, dialling numbers into his phone, and I jumped when he touched my arm. He asked a halting question or two and apparently I answered quite sensibly, although I don't know how, when I couldn't hear a thing above the roaring in my head.

There were a lot of questions that day, although not many more from Tom, because he was too kind to persist. He even tried to answer some of the questions on my behalf, but the police didn't like that. They wanted my account.

Your name? Your address? Your age? Your next of kin? Your relation to Cory Byrne? To Diana Byrne? When did you last see Mr Byrne? Talk to him? What was his mood? And what about all the paintings? And can you talk us through events, starting with last night? Starting with yesterday morning? Starting as far back as you like . . .

They couldn't decide how to label me, that was the problem. Witness? Victim? Collaborator? Perpetrator? It was difficult to be much help when I wasn't sure myself. Also, I felt very tired. I kept expecting them to confront me about the papers in the bath.

'Did Mr Byrne ever hurt you?'

'He hurt my sister.' It was the most definite thing I'd said all morning. 'He murdered her, and made us think it was suicide.'

There was a moment's pause, and the questions began afresh.

Your sister's name? And the date of her death? And the circumstances . . . ?

I touched my forehead where it ached, and someone said, 'She's dead on her feet.' I thought for a moment he meant Stella, and I almost contradicted him because of course Stella didn't die on her feet; she died in flight.

'Those bits of paper in the bath . . .' I said.

'Go and sit in the fresh air,' the voice went on kindly. 'Your friend can go with you, and we'll bring some tea over.'

Tom and I sat on the steps at the top of the garden. My teeth were chattering, so Tom gave me his coat and we drank our sugary teas.

'Is he definitely dead?'

Tom was slow to reply but at last he said, 'Yes.'

'Are you hesitating because you're not sure? Or because you're worried I can't bear it?'

Was that fear in Tom's expression? If so, I hoped it was because of what had happened – because of Cory in the bath – and not because he'd grown afraid of me.

'Freya, it's . . . He's definitely dead.'

I nodded, staring across the lawn to the patch of flattened grass where the wedding marquee used to stand. Thunder and lightning had been flaring when I came to the house in August; it ought to be flaring this morning as well. What a banal day for Cory Byrne to die, with the light so milky and flat. I rested my chin on the rim of the cup, and the steam warmed my face.

'You drove for hours, all the way from London,' I observed, 'just because our phones got disconnected.'

Tom shrugged.

'Something was obviously wrong,' he said. 'I couldn't abandon you.'

He said it lightly, but with the faintest emphasis on the word *you*. 'I couldn't abandon *you*.' I wanted to ask what, if anything, that meant, but I hesitated. Perhaps – surrounded by high drama, and with police cars slewed across the driveway, and the bath full of bright, red water – perhaps this wasn't the time or place to be questioning the nuances of a casual phrase. I picked through the gravel at the top of the steps, sorting the stones into whites and pale greys.

'Do you mean, you couldn't *abandon* me?' I said eventually, because – propriety be damned – I had to know. 'Or do you mean, you couldn't abandon . . . *me*?'

Tom added a white stone to the white pile, and a couple of greys to the grey pile.

'I mean,' he said, 'that I couldn't abandon . . . *you*.'

We carried on sorting the stones, as if we were doing something delicate and important, and sometimes our fingers touched. One of the policemen came down the steps muttering about phone reception, and we drew apart to let him pass. His shoes scattered the gravel piles, and we glanced at one another behind his back.

'Why are there two ambulances?' I said.

'One's for . . . you know. The other's for his mother. They're taking her to hospital.'

'Oh.'

We fell silent. There was a lot of brisk, quiet talk behind us, and footsteps went in and out of the house. Blue lights swirled and walkie-talkies crackled.

'Poor Diana,' I murmured.

I put my half-drunk tea on the step and got to my feet. One of the ambulances had its doors wide open, and it must have been Diana inside, although even when I came close I could hardly see her for people and tubes. One of the paramedics stood aside momentarily, and I glimpsed an oxygen mask where her face ought to be.

The man stood and watched; there was nothing else for

him to do. He was only a boy, younger than me, with haunted eyes and a shaving rash. He said, 'There were roses on the bed.'

I frowned.

'Roses?'

The man looked round at the house, and back at Diana. He wasn't telling me as such; he was just trying to get those roses out of his system.

'A bunch in her folded hands and petals all over the bed. They were completely rank, half of them. It was like something out of . . .'

A poem? I supplied silently. *A horror film?*

'. . . a weird dream.'

He shivered and climbed aboard.

Tom came up beside me, and we watched Diana's ambulance lumber down the pot-holed drive, the wet woods reflecting its flickering lights. The bustle of voices and footsteps carried on behind us; I heard someone running up the stairs and a phone ringing in the hall.

'Aren't flowers supposed to be dead by November?' I wondered out loud.

Tom followed my gaze across the lawn, towards the rose garden, but he didn't answer.

Perhaps they *were* all dead in the real world; perhaps it was just at Byrne Hall that roses bloomed out of season. The few that Cory had left on the bushes looked sad and exhausted, though. Even the best were tinged brown.

Stella

October 2009

STELLA KEEPS FORGETTING THE URGENCY of the situation. She stands with her arms outstretched, buffeted by wind and rain; drunk on schnapps and nostalgia.

Is 'nostalgia' the word she wants? This is better than nostalgia, isn't it? It's the bliss of coming home after an Odyssean absence; after an eternity of adventure and soul-searching and missing Dad and Freya – and Tom. Not that she's there yet – she keeps having to remind herself she's not quite there. She's still at Byrne Hall, waiting under the porch for Diana to bring the car round. She fills her lungs and wonders what this wet, leafy, woody smell has to do with homecoming; why it makes her feel so happy and restored. It's not as if their poky London terrace ever smells like this, even in the rain.

A car is starting up round the side of the house. Stella steps out from under the porch, tipping back her head and sticking her tongue out. The rain merely trickles down her throat and she yearns for great, choking mouthfuls of the stuff.

She hops from foot to foot and tries to stop glancing back at the house. *Hurry up, Diana.* None of the lights have come on in the front windows – not yet – but *he* is almost certainly awake and must have heard the car. The rain clouds have thickened over the moon and Stella can't see a thing, but that's not to say she's safe, because Cory can see in the dark. Really, he can.

She shudders and tries to remember what his eyes look like.

Come on, Stella, what colour are they? Grey? Green? She can't seem to shift the idea that they're yellow, with thin lines for pupils – but that can't be right. Even the undiscriminating Stella Lyell would not have fallen for a man with cat's eyes.

Oh God, those are his feet thundering down the stairs. Stella wraps her jacket tight across her chest and runs to meet the car. At least Diana's on the same wavelength – you can tell by the way she accelerates too fast round the corner and brakes too hard in front of the house. The passenger door springs open at the same time as Cory bursts on to the porch, and Stella is barely inside before the tyres are spitting gravel and they're off. Cory's bellow hardly even registers – she's too busy righting herself, and reaching to close the door, and working out what those tall, pale stripes are that keep flashing past the windscreen. Tree trunks? Are they into the woods already? Out of habit she fumbles for a seat belt – but she can't find it, and she can't care.

The car tosses her from side to side as it weaves down the drive. Stella kneels up on her seat and looks back, but the house is already out of sight. All she can see are the tree trunks flitting along the edge of the road, lit red against the deeper darkness of the woods.

Stella laughs out loud and hugs the back of her seat. Diana hasn't spoken yet. Her sharp face is green in the light of the dashboard, and her hands are tight on the steering wheel. Perhaps she is afraid of going home again and having to face Cory? Stella will think of something kind to say about that, just as soon as she can keep a straight face.

One minute she's whooping, the next she's feeling sick and struggling to open the window. They've left the drive behind

328

and the road is climbing, but Stella has no idea where they are. At one point she thinks she sees the lights in Bligh harbour, but she's not certain.

'That window doesn't work,' says Diana. 'I ought to get it fixed.'

Stella makes a little moan and Diana slows the car right down. A couple of minutes later they pull into a lay-by. Stella flings the door open and gulps the cold, wet air.

It's wilder up here, unprotected by the trees, and the car judders in the wind. Stella closes her eyes. There's a subterranean rumble which makes her think of underground trains, but there can't be any underground trains because they're not in London yet.

'It's the sound of the sea at the foot of the cliffs,' Diana explains, although Stella hasn't asked. She goes on: 'That's where Cory's father died – just down there.'

Stella's head is flung back against the seat, but she does her best to nod. She ought to say something appropriate, but the schnapps is churning and her breathing is getting shallower; she lurches out of her seat just in time to throw up on the verge.

It's freezing out here, she thinks, as she rests on her hands and knees, and hangs her head. The rain is falling through the blackness like a hail of arrows, piercing her hair and clothes.

Something catches her on the cheek. It's the hem of a woollen coat – Diana is standing beside her.

'Better?'

Stella nods, takes the proffered hand and clambers to her feet. Her teeth are chattering, but she does feel better, and eager to make up for her lapse.

'Cory's father,' she says, peering in what she thinks is the direction of the sea. 'It was a sailing accident, wasn't it?'

The silence stretches uneasily and Diana concludes it with a non-committal noise that makes no sense; a 'humph' that resembles a laugh.

Stella wipes her sleeve across her sticky mouth and wonders how to change the subject.

'Shall we get back in the car?'

But Diana has taken her by the arm and they're walking off in a different direction. Stella is too woozy to protest. When she looks back she sees that the car headlights are still on, and bright rods of rain are falling through the beams.

'People like that have it coming,' says Diana.

'People like . . . ?'

'People like him. People who think they're entitled to hurt my boy.'

They are wading through shrubby grasses and heathers and gorse, and Stella wishes her ankles weren't bare. The wind whips her hair across her face and makes her jacket fly out behind her. As they walk, the boom of the sea becomes louder and she tries to wriggle free, but Diana keeps tight hold of her arm.

They stop. Stones loosen under Stella's feet and tumble into the darkness.

'There,' says Diana. 'That's where they found him – down there.'

Stella shivers. Diana is gripping her arm with both hands and it's starting to hurt.

'You ripped Cory's picture to pieces,' she's saying loudly, over the wind. 'Hundreds of tiny little pieces.'

Stella wishes she understood where Diana is going with this. She doesn't like it. She wants to be back in the car.

'Who do you suppose is going to mend it?' Diana asks.

330

'I'm afraid it's beyond mending.' Stella tries for and fails at a humorous tone. Everything in front of her face is blacker than black and she's losing her bearings. She's locked in the attic again, but the walls are crumpling and the floorboards are giving way under her feet.

'I am,' Diana says. 'I am the one who will gather them together, bit by painstaking bit, and fit them back together.'

I wouldn't bother, Stella thinks. 'The car?' is what she says out loud, but Diana hasn't finished yet. Talk, talk, talk – who knew she was such a talker? She doesn't seem to realise that she's making no sense. The downpour hisses on the surface of the sea, muffling her voice, while the wind amplifies odd words and silences others.

'. . . while I've breath in my body . . .' Something about a 'fragile child'. Something about 'I'm dying'. There's more, but Stella is losing patience. She's hurt and ill, and she wants to go home.

A couple of hundred feet below, water collides with rock and explodes, and the thunder of it reverberates up, up and up – through the strata of the cliff, through the soles of Stella's feet, through every cell of her body – and there's a fury inside her that answers to the force of it. She is sick to death of being clutched at and clung to, of being kept down and hemmed in and trapped. With a sudden resolve she jerks free, and for a couple of seconds she is standing alone, swaying with the wind.

'Get off me!' Somehow Diana has got hold of her wrists and twisted them behind her back; she cannot bear this. 'Get *off*!'

Pebbles rattle into oblivion as Stella kicks the earth away from under her feet, and her pinioned body unfurls on a gust of wind. Diana has to let go and Stella knows she won't be caught again. She arches her back, spirals and somersaults, and her hair spreads into the wind like fire. In this free-falling darkness she becomes a blend of strange shapes and contortions: an upside-down and disintegrating miracle. A shooting star. A flying fish. A bird. None of the things that Cory Byrne appreciates in a girl.

She remembers her sister when they were both very small, sleepy on the sofa, taking her thumb out of her mouth to speak.

Stella? What would you wish for if you could have one wish?

Can't I have three wishes?

No, ONE. Just one.

If only Freya could see her now.

Freya

January 2015

I'D SET ASIDE A WHOLE day for packing, but I was done in a couple of hours. I sat on my bed and surveyed my emptied bedroom, with its bare furniture, and grubby walls, and general air of inconsequence. Apart from practical things like clothes, I would be taking two boxes of books, one box of oddments – alarm clock, DVDs, bedside lamp, calendar, etc. – and that was it. It was a good job I'd decided against hiring a van; this lot would fit easily in the boot, and along the back seat of the car.

'How nice!' Zoë had said earlier on, when she brought me a mug of tea. 'Oh, to be footloose and fancy free!' She didn't sound especially wistful; I think it was her way of saying, *You don't own much stuff, do you?*

There were a couple of posters on my wall – Pre-Raphaelite prints I'd loved when I was a teenager – but I'd torn them down as I was packing and thrown them away. I lingered on the spaces where they'd been, and the shadows they'd left on the wallpaper . . . but I didn't have time for thoughts like that. I rearranged my books so that I could fit the Open University prospectus on top without bending it, and I looked round for something else to do. There must be something else to do. There always had been – one way or another – over the last couple of months.

'Photos!' I said aloud, and ran downstairs to fetch them from the dresser drawer. The house felt considerably smaller whenever Zoë was here. It also felt warmer, because she liked to have the radiators on. She and Dad were in the kitchen at the moment, cooking my farewell meal; I could smell grated ginger and garlic, and frying onions.

Dad was chopping red peppers when I went in, but as soon as he saw I was holding the photos he stopped and wiped his hands on a tea-towel.

'What are you doing with those?'

It was the hushed voice he always reserved for Mum and Stella, and it put me on edge.

'Would you mind if I took one with me?'

I pushed aside the felt coverings. It was difficult – try as I might – to avoid echoing his reverent tone.

There were half a dozen photos to choose from. I'd meant to leaf through the pile so that Dad could say, 'Yes, take that one,' or 'No, leave that one for me,' but the frames were slippery and bulky, and I was afraid of dropping them, so I just stood there and held them out.

Zoë pushed gently between us and peered over her glasses. I shuffled aside to give her a better view. The first photo showed the four of us – Mum, Dad, Stella and me – on a log flume, and I could never decide if I remembered the thrill of the fall and the splash of cold water on my legs, or if I only seemed to remember because of this picture. Mum and Stella were shrieking with excitement and throwing their arms in the air, while Dad and I crouched behind, half hidden, our features tight and fearful.

Zoë picked it up and studied it closely. She laughed – genuinely laughed – as if she saw a funny snap from a theme park, instead of a picture that had been darkened beyond recognition by circumstance and time.

'Oh, that's lovely!' she said, propping it on top of the cereal boxes so that she could look at it while she stirred her pan of onions. 'It's very sweet! You ought to have that up somewhere, Robert.'

I tried to see it as she saw it; as it was meant to be seen when my parents bought it from the booth. Dad tried too. He said, 'Perhaps . . .'

I chose a different one – Mum and Stella making sand-castles in Cromer – and Dad said it was OK for me to have it.

I went out after we'd eaten and washed up. Dad and Zoë were settling down to watch the news, but I was too excited to join them, and definitely too excited to go to bed. There was a sting in the January air and the pavements rang crisply under my shoes. Since there was nowhere in particular that I wanted to be, I headed for the park. I walked quickly because it was cold and I hadn't brought a hat and scarf, and because the faster I went, the more I could fill my head with the sounds of my own footsteps.

My thoughts wandered, circled, slowed – hovered over Byrne Hall like a sea-bird readying itself to dive. I quickened my pace till I was almost running, and I remembered I had a phone call to make. I slowed down and fished in my pocket for my mobile. Maggie had rung this afternoon when I was queuing at the bank, and I'd promised to call her back.

'Freya!'

'Hi Maggie! Is this a good time?'

We talked for a while about obvious things: her work, and my new job – 'I wanted to wish you luck for your big move tomorrow,' she said. 'I meant to send you a card . . .' – and about Dad and Zoë, and her forthcoming holiday, and her sister's wedding in Scotland. We'd talked about all these things before.

'Well,' I said, when we were running out of topics. I was nearing the park now; I could just make out the sharp tips of the railings and the indistinct masses of the trees. 'I suppose I ought to go . . .'

'I popped in to see Diana today,' Maggie said.

'Oh, right.'

'It's amazing, the way she clings to life, although I don't think she has much longer now. The nurse I spoke to reckoned a couple of days.'

I stopped inside the entrance.

'I see.'

The sweat started cooling on my skin and I shivered.

'Maggie? Will you do something for me?'

'Sure . . .'

'Will you let me know when she does die? I'd like to know.'

'Sure, I can do that.' Maggie sounded faintly surprised. 'No problem.'

'Thanks.'

I was glad. It had been on my mind since November; it was the reason I kept buying copies of *The Times* and checking the obituary pages. Until I knew Diana was dead, she risked living on in my mind, fading forever whilst never quite fading to nothing.

'I wonder what will become of Byrne Hall?' Maggie mused, but I wouldn't be drawn on that.

I pushed the park gate open and walked between the empty flower-beds, from one pool of lamplight to the next. My breath

336

formed clouds in front of my face, so that I seemed to be walking through a mist that waxed and waned.

After a while I sat down on a bench beside the pond. Even in the lamplight, the water looked ugly and brown, and there were crisp packets and takeaway cartons floating in the reeds.

I glanced at my phone, and noticed I'd missed a call from Tom while I was talking to Maggie. In a moment I would ring him back. I held the prospect like a bright jewel in my hand, and closed my eyes.

Please understand: the nostalgia I gave in to that evening wasn't for the autumn that had passed. I didn't want to go back; I didn't miss Cory; I never remembered his kisses and thought, *Perhaps, despite everything* . . .

It was just that sometimes my heart would snag on an old idea of Byrne Hall. I'd catch an imaginary whiff of salt air, or a glint of sun-dappled green, or a flash of white stone and I would ache – not for the actual place, or the time, or the man – but for the elusive dream I'd gone there with, and the poems I'd meant to write, and the person I'd imagined becoming.

I drew a jagged breath and stood up. A scent of snow was in the air, mixed with pondweed and stale chips. In a moment I would speak to Tom, and we would carry on making plans. Evening would turn to night as I made my way home, night would turn to day as I slept, the world – the real world – would move forward as it should, and I would be a part of it.

I pulled my jumper over my chin for warmth, and stuck my hands in my pockets. As I began to walk I felt that the earth was good and solid beneath my feet.

Acknowledgements

My heartfelt thanks to the following people, without whose help *The Whispering House* would never have seen the light of day: my agent, Joanna Swainson, for her unfailing help and enthusiasm; the wonderful team at Transworld, especially Suzanne Bridson, Jane Lawson, Kate Samano and Claire Gatzen; Masie Cochran of Tin House, for her invaluable input from across the pond. Many thanks to Katherine Reed for her sympathetic and straight-talking advice, which has meant so much to me over the years, and to Linda Harding for being an encouraging early reader.

A big hurrah, as always, for Manx Litfest!

Finally, lots of love and thanks to my family and friends, in particular Chris, Isabelle, Stephen, Mum and Dad.

Elizabeth Brooks grew up in Chester and read Classics at Cambridge. She lives on the Isle of Man with her husband and two children.

Please look her up on:

Instagram @e.f.brooks

Facebook @elizabethbrooks1979

Twitter @ManxWriter

CALL OF THE CURLEW

Elizabeth Brooks

Virginia Wrathmell has always known she will meet her death on the marsh.

One snowy winter's night, when she is eighty-six, a sign arrives that the time has finally come.

New Year's Eve, 1939. Virginia is ten, an orphan arriving to meet her new parents at their mysterious house, Salt Winds. Her new home sits on the edge of a vast marsh, a beautiful but dangerous place. War feels far away out here amongst the birds and shifting sands – until the day a German plane crashes into the marsh.

What happens next is something Virginia will regret for the next seventy-five years, and that will change the whole course of her life.

'Bewitching and haunting' Eowyn Ivey

'Atmospheric, beautifully paced . . . I didn't want to let go' Claire Fuller

'Like Daphne du Maurier . . . a place, a time, and a story that are unforgettable' Rosamund Lupton

Also by Elizabeth Brooks

CALL OF THE CURLEW

and published by Black Swan

Praise for *Call of the Curlew*

'Like Daphne du Maurier ... powerfully conjures
up a place, a time, and a story that are unforgettable.'
ROSAMUND LUPTON

'An atmospheric, beautifully paced novel about
sacrifice, the urge to belong and revenge. It's full of
well-drawn characters I loved to hate, and those that
I didn't want to let go, even after I closed the last page.'
CLAIRE FULLER

'A beautifully written, atmospheric novel – reminiscent
of *Jane Eyre* ... bewitching and haunting.'
EOWYN IVEY

'Melodic and beautiful.'
Prima

'Really special.'
Good Housekeeping

'A twisty, atmospheric treat.'
Woman & Home